Praise for *WRATH*

"In the fourth installment of her Seven Deadly Sins series . . . Murray delivers another intense morality tale. . . . Offer Murray's novel to readers who are looking for gritty Christian romantic suspense about love gone wrong."

—*Booklist*

Praise for *ENVY*

"[*Envy*] captures the drama of *The Real Housewives of Beverly Hills* while also bringing this well-developed work of urban fiction to a satisfyingly redemptive conclusion."

—Kristina Giovanni, *Booklist*

Praise for *LUST*

"Murray has penned hot, steamy scenes in which her protagonist's imagination runs wild, followed by the consequences of her realizing her dangerous dreams. A jarring twist at the end has the reader wondering who the good guys really are."

—*Booklist* (starred review)

"Murray mixes quite a bit of passion, a touch of treachery, and some good old-fashioned revenge."

—*Library Journal*

"Keeps you at the edge of your seat until the last page."

—*Urban Reviews Online*

"A topsy-turvy tale of passion on steroids."

—*Essence*

"Priceless trash talk marks this story about betrayal, greed, and stepping on anyone in your way. A great choice for folks who spend Sunday mornings in the front pew."

—*Library Journal*

Praise for *NEVER SAY NEVER*

"Readers, be on the lookout for Victoria Christopher Murray's *Never Say Never*. You'll definitely need to have a buddy-reader in place for the lengthy discussion that is bound to occur."

—*USA Today*

Praise for *THE EX FILES*

"The engrossing transitions the women go through make compelling reading. . . . Murray's vivid portrait of how faith can move mountains and heal relationships should inspire."

—*Publishers Weekly*

"Reminds you of things that women will do if their hearts are broken. . . . Once you pick this book up, you will not put it down."

—*Urban Reviews Online*

Praise for *DESTINY'S DIVAS*

"With *Destiny's Divas*, author Victoria Christopher Murray triumphs again. The depth and storytelling mastery in her latest novel demonstrate why she is the grande dame of urban Christian fiction."

—FreshFiction.com

Praise for *SINNERS & SAINTS*

"Murray and Billingsley keep things lively and fun."

—*Juicy* magazine

"An excellent entry in the Jasmine Larson Bush Christian Lit saga; perhaps the best so far. . . . Fans will appreciate this fine tale . . . a well-written intense drama."

—*Midwest Book Review*

Praise for *A SIN AND A SHAME*

"Riveting, emotionally charged, and spiritually deep. . . . What is admirable is the author's ability to hold the reader in suspense until the very last paragraph of the novel! *A Sin and a Shame* is a must-read. . . . Truly a story to be enjoyed and pondered upon!"

—RomanceinColor.com

"*A Sin and a Shame* is Victoria Christopher Murray at her best. . . . A page-turner that I couldn't put down as I was too eager to see what scandalous thing Jasmine would do next. And to watch Jasmine's spiritual growth was a testament to Victoria's talents. An engrossing tale of how God's grace covers us all. I absolutely loved this book!"

—ReShonda Tate Billingsley, *Essence* bestselling author of *I Know I've Been Changed*

Also by Victoria Christopher Murray

Wrath

Greed

Envy

Desire

Stand Your Ground

Forever an Ex

Fortune & Fame (with ReShonda Tate Billingsley)

Never Say Never

Friends & Foes (with ReShonda Tate Billingsley)

Destiny's Divas

Sinners & Saints (with ReShonda Tate Billingsley)

The Deal, the Dance, and the Devil

Sins of the Mother

Lady Jasmine

Too Little, Too Late

The Ex Files

A Sin and a Shame

Grown Folks Business

Truth Be Told

Blessed Assurance (contributor)

Joy

Temptation

PRIDE

A Seven Deadly Sins Novel

VICTORIA CHRISTOPHER MURRAY

G

GALLERY BOOKS

New York   London   Toronto   Sydney   New Delhi

Gallery Books
An Imprint of Simon & Schuster, Inc.
1230 Avenue of the Americas
New York, NY 10020

First Gallery Books trade paperback edition April 2023

GALLERY BOOKS and colophon are registered trademarks of Simon & Schuster, Inc.

For information about special discounts for bulk purchases, please contact Simon & Schuster Special Sales at 1-866-506-1949 or business@simonandschuster.com.

The Simon & Schuster Speakers Bureau can bring authors to your live event. For more information or to book an event, contact the Simon & Schuster Speakers Bureau at 1-866-248-3049 or visit our website at www.simonspeakers.com.

Manufactured in the United States of America

10 9 8 7 6 5 4 3 2 1

Library of Congress Cataloging-in-Publication Data

Names: Murray, Victoria Christopher, author.
Title: Pride / Victoria Christopher Murray.
Description: First Gallery Books trade paperback edition. | New York : Gallery Books, 2023. | Series: A seven deadly sins novel ; [5]
Identifiers: LCCN 2022054314 (print) | LCCN 2022054315 (ebook) | ISBN 9781668012901 (trade paperback) | ISBN 9781668012918 (ebook)
Subjects: LCGFT: Novels.
Classification: LCC PS3563.U795 P75 2023 (print) | LCC PS3563.U795 (ebook) | DDC 813/.54—dc23/eng/20221116
LC record available at https://lccn.loc.gov/2022054314
LC ebook record available at https://lccn.loc.gov/2022054315

ISBN 978-1-6680-1290-1
ISBN 978-1-6680-1291-8 (ebook)

PRIDE

PRIDE

He's the one who got away!

I stood at the threshold of Ethan's office in the prestigious Williams Towers, where he sat behind his mahogany desk with only the dim light of the desk lamp illuminating the space.

It was a wonder he didn't hear me enter; he should certainly be more aware of his surroundings at this time of night. Although I guessed with a thirty-second-floor office in this zip code, there were no concerns about safety. And I knew how Ethan was when he focused. Without even a glimpse of his brown eyes, I imagined his expression—thoughtful—as he studied the papers on his desk. A legal brief, perhaps?

For a moment longer, I stood staring at the man I once loved. And then something stirred inside me. Once loved? Everything I felt for Ethan Thomas was supposed to be long gone, severed by the last words he'd spoken to me before he walked out of my door.

But now old emotions collided with common sense and exploded into confusion. I wasn't sure what to feel. There was a time when something would have stirred inside Ethan, just having me in such close proximity. But now . . . I guessed not.

I tapped on the door. Ethan raised his head, and his shoulders straightened.

"I'm sorry," I said when he didn't speak. Stepping inside, I added more to my apology: "I didn't mean to startle you."

His eyes followed me as I sauntered toward him, but still, he said nothing, and I tried to discern what I saw in his eyes. If his complexion were lighter, I believe I would've seen the heat rising beneath his skin. Or maybe just the opposite; maybe I would have watched the blood drain from him, since the way his eyes widened and his brows shot up, he looked like he'd seen a ghost.

Finally, his lips moved. "Journee . . ." He still said my name like it was the opening notes of a love song. "What . . . what are you doing here?"

Slipping my shawl from my shoulders, I tossed it onto one of the high-back vintage chairs facing his desk. But I remained standing. "It's good to see you, too, Ethan," I said, as if he'd expected this visit.

He shook his head before he stood, then buttoned his suit jacket, always needing to look composed. He said, "I'm surprised."

"I can understand that."

"Security didn't . . . um . . . call to tell me you were coming up."

"That's because I didn't stop at security." With a shrug and a half smile, I said, "You know how I do."

I didn't give him a chance to reply as I moved to the massive windows behind his desk. The floor-to-ceiling glass exposed the still-somewhat-heavy traffic on the 610 freeway—even if it was already well after eight. Life in Houston, especially on the Thursday night before Labor Day. My eyes made their way to the gushing fountains below. That tourist attraction was a more beautiful sight in the night's light.

"What an amazing view." Glancing back, I took in the expansive corner office with its wall-to-wall windows. The mahogany furniture alone—the desk, chairs, credenza—could be a down payment on a home. "I like your new office. You've done well." I wanted to add a question to my compliment. Ask if he had any regrets that here, in his own law firm, was where he'd ended up instead of pursuing his political dreams.

He nodded, then gestured toward the chairs. "So, when are we going to talk about why you're here?"

"Now is good." I took my time rounding his desk, my hips swaying, knowing his eyes were on me. I'd dressed for this occasion. He was seeing me for the first time in almost fifteen hundred days, so I'd chosen this purple (his favorite color) Chanel (his favorite designer) wrap dress. When I sat down and crossed my legs, I watched him watch the hemline of my skirt rise. He cleared his throat before he sat down but didn't make a move to add more light to his office. Just left us sitting there, staring at each other in the glow of the lamp on his desk. It felt almost . . . sensual. It seemed almost . . . purposeful.

He said, "So, I know you weren't just in the neighborhood."

"Actually, I was. I just finished a business dinner at Roka Akor." His head tilted at the mention of that four-star restaurant, but I didn't elaborate. There was no need for Ethan to know this was at least the twelfth dinner I'd had over the past three months as I pursued a multimillion-dollar city contract—the WestPark revitalization project—for my firm.

When I stayed silent, Ethan asked, "And so, you decided to drop by on your way home?"

"Not heading home. Not yet. I have to stop at my office, and that's not too far from here."

"Your office is in River Oaks, not the Galleria."

That made me sit back a bit. "I know why I knew where you worked, but I didn't send out announcements, the way you did, when I opened J. Alexander and Associates." I paused. "You've been keeping tabs on me?" There was joviality in my tone, but I was more serious than not. It pleased me that I was still on his mind.

He shook his head, a bit too quickly for me to believe him when he said, "No, I just know someone in your building and saw your name on the directory. But I know you didn't come here to discuss that." He pressed the tips of his fingers together, and I recognized that stance. "So, Journee, this isn't a social visit."

I nodded. "It's not." I took a deep breath before I said, "I need your help."

His eyebrows rose. "*You* need *my* help?"

Now the chuckle was in *his* tone, which annoyed me, and I half expected Ethan to launch into a lecture about how surprised he was to hear those words come from me.

I was grateful when he didn't add anything else, and I pulled my cell from my purse, scrolled through my texts, then held the cell so Ethan could read the screen.

**You're going to spend the next twenty years in prison.
Vengeance is mine.**

Ethan's eyes stayed on my phone as if he was reading the message a few times. Finally, he sat back and gestured for me to speak.

I said, "I've been getting messages like these for a few weeks. It's weird. I'll get a message like that, and then another one, like this." Once again, I held up my cell.

This time, when Ethan leaned forward, he read the text aloud: "'The prudent see danger and take refuge, but the simple keep going and pay the penalty. Vengeance is mine.'" He paused, raised his glance toward the ceiling as if he was thinking. "The first part is Proverbs 27:12."

Impressive. But Ethan being a man of God was just one of the thousands of reasons I had for once loving him. *Once?*

"But the 'vengeance is mine' . . . that's New Testament. Romans 12:19." He steadied his glance on me.

"Every text ends with that scripture."

He said, "So someone is sending you scriptures."

"Scriptures and threats," I told him.

"Who could be sending these to you?"

I half shrugged. "The first time, I called the number, and all I heard was white noise, like the number was out of service. Since then, every text comes from a different number."

Ethan nodded. "A texting app. So, why would someone be sending these to you?"

Again I shrugged, but this time rather than meeting his eyes, I glanced at the view over his shoulder. "I don't know . . . I'm not sure."

"Journee," he said. This time, my name didn't sound like music at all. Sounded more like Ethan was losing patience with me.

I connected my eyes with his. "Did you hear about Simon's arrest?"

He stared at me, and I waited for him to say something like, *I told you so.* But all Ethan said about the man who'd been my mentor, the man who'd taught me everything I knew about being a real estate broker, the man who'd made it so that I had the kind of lifestyle I could never have imagined when my mama had my sister and me wandering around the streets of Houston homeless, was "Yeah, I heard. A multimillion-dollar fraud investigation of one of the city's most notable residents is hard to miss in these streets. Not to mention how his arrest was a ratings draw for the media." His eyes narrowed. "But what does Simon's arrest have to do with those texts?"

I wondered just how much I should say at this point. "I got

the first text the day Simon was arrested. I think it's all connected; someone is trying to link me to Simon and all his troubles."

His gaze was steadfast. "Are you linkable?"

I squinted. Was that an accusation in his tone? "No," I said. "I left Simon"—my voice lowered—"and all his schemes behind. I left him not too long after you left me."

I half expected Ethan to say, *You finally listened*, but instead he said, "I'm glad to hear that." Then he cocked his head. "So then, why are you here? Because from what you've said so far, you *certainly* don't need me."

A thousand memories of the millions of times I'd spoken those words to Ethan cascaded through my mind. But rushing in right behind the memories of the few times we fought were all the moments we loved.

Dang! I was thinking about our love again. I sighed; it was amazing that all it took was this man's presence, and my heart was racing back to the past. Now all I could think about was that Ethan Thomas was the first man I loved—actually, the only man besides my daddy.

And Ethan had loved me, until he didn't anymore. Or at least until he told me that he loved himself and his career more.

The heaviness of what we once were hung in the air, but finally, I responded, "I do need you."

Ethan was stone-still, as if those four words shocked him. Four words he'd waited years for me to say. He finally said, "How do you think I can help?"

"I need to find out who's sending these texts. I need to know what they may know so I can figure out if I'm in any true jeopardy when it comes to Simon."

His eyes thinned. "If you left Simon, what would someone know?"

"I did . . . I mean . . . I just wonder . . ." I stuttered, then took a deep breath. "I'm sure this has something to do with my past business dealings. Not with how I conduct myself today."

He nodded. "Well, if you want to find out who's sending those texts, you need a private investigator." He leaned forward as if he wanted his next words to make a point. "But . . . you don't need me."

Inside, I flinched. He'd been waiting a long time to punish me with words I'd always said to him. Had my words in the past slashed him with the same sharpness I just felt?

"I know what I need," I said through my hurt. "And I know *who* I need. I need an attorney, a criminal defense attorney, the best criminal defense attorney in Texas." I held up my hands to proclaim my innocence. "Just in case. You know I'm always prepared." I paused. "And I came to you because you just handled Sara Nelson's case."

Sara Nelson had been a well-respected broker who'd been indicted along with two coconspirators for a false-appraisal real estate scam that could have landed her in prison for almost ten years.

"You kept her out of prison."

He nodded. "I did, but I don't understand what you're talking about here. You said you're not connected to Simon but, in a way, you think you are?"

"That explains it perfectly, and I want to make sure I'm not in a vulnerable position because of my early days with Simon. And if I need legal representation, then I'll have you."

He squinted, shook his head, sat back. "If you want my help, you need to tell me everything: what you *really* did with Simon, not just the things you told me about before. And then how you think these texts may be connected. I need to know anything and everything. And then I can decide if I want to help you."

"Decide?" I asked, shocked that Ethan had to consider this.

Why wouldn't he just agree to help? Wasn't I the first woman he ever loved?

"Decide whether I want to or even if I can help."

I nodded, averted my eyes again. Studied the beautiful view once more. "Okay," I said, finally facing him. "What do you want to know?"

Instead of answering my question, Ethan leaned back and chuckled. "Things have certainly changed. I can't count the number of times you made it perfectly clear to me that there was nothing I could ever do to help you."

"It wasn't like that." When he raised his eyebrows, I said, "Okay. Yes. I always thought I could handle everything myself. But not this." And then, because I thought it would help, I added, "I really do need you."

"What if I told you that saying those words now—it's too late?"

That blow came so quickly, it was shocking. Made me almost stand up, spin around, and march out of there. I didn't need this . . . I didn't need him . . . I didn't need anyone.

But all of that was a lie. It was hard for me to say, but I needed Ethan in so many ways, so I swallowed that pride. And even though it tasted like poison, I sat there ready to take more of his shots. I said, "I'm hoping you won't tell me it's too late."

"It is," he said. I sucked in air, but then he added, "At least, it's too late tonight." He glanced at his watch. "I have . . . another engagement."

Another engagement? This late? Was he just saying this to blow me off?

He said, "Let me think about this, Journee."

I reached for my shawl and wrapped it over my shoulders, hoping that would hide the way his words made me tremble. It was hard for me to digest what had happened in these past minutes. Ethan Thomas was really thinking about leaving me out there to handle this alone. I gathered myself and pulled out my trump card. "You once told me you loved me." I paused. Those words would move him for sure. But he said nothing. "And I'm hoping some of that love is still there," I said, pushing harder. Another beat passed; still nothing but silence. "I hope with everything in me you'll help me."

He peered at me, tapped the tips of his fingers together— still remained silent.

I continued with words that were so hard for me to say: "Please, Ethan."

Now, his silence was an insult. So I nodded, blinked back tears, then stood and spun toward the door. But before I took a step, Ethan spoke up. "I'll text you tomorrow. One way or the other. If you still have the same number."

A gasp pushed through my lips, but I didn't face him. I nodded, then kept moving out the door, out of the building, and into the night air. I'd walked into this building with such confidence about what my ex would do. But Ethan had shaken me, and now I had no idea how this was going to play out.

rolled to my left, folding my pillow under my head. Stayed there for about ten seconds, then flipped onto my back and stared at the ceiling until it began to close in on me. Tossing aside my duvet, I grabbed my cell phone from the nightstand: 6:16. Ugh! It was against my religion to get out of bed before eight.

I tapped my messages icon, then scrolled through my texts. One from Tasha, my assistant, reminding me to check my emails for the letter she'd drafted to thank Mr. Yung for the dinner last night. That was a good idea; even though Mr. Yung all but told me that I'd won the bid when he said I was the most impressive broker he'd met over these past few months, I wanted to stay on top of his mind.

Next text: UPS informing me of a delivery—something I couldn't remember ordering, as usual . . . and then:

The prayers of the righteous may availeth much, but no amount of prayer will save you now. Vengeance is mine.

"Argh!" I slammed the cell onto the duvet. Another text from my stalker but nothing from Ethan.

Wrapping myself inside my robe, I glanced at my phone's screen. That text had been sent just a little after three in the morning. *Who would stay up that late to do this to me?*

I staggered into my living room, a grand loft-style space that combined my living room, dining room, and kitchen and continued the color scheme from my bedroom—everything in my apartment was heavenly white, but right now, I didn't feel the heavenly peace that I always felt when I was home.

My legs were unsteady as I made my way to my espresso machine. Fumbling, I got what I needed onto the counter and tamped the coffee grinds; then, as the coffee brewed, I prayed that one night my eyes would stay shut for more than an hour.

A minute later, that first sip of espresso shocked and then calmed me; now I breathed, and for the first time, I appreciated the new day. The morning sun gleamed through my two walls of living room windows, shining as if it hung in the sky as my personal morning glory. I opened the balcony door, and the sounds of the early day—birds chirping, cars honking, a plane ascending—greeted me. Normalcy. What I craved.

But my life was far from normal, and I needed Ethan to help me get that normalcy back. I took another sip, leaned against the railing, and closed my eyes. "I need you, Ethan." I spoke those words as if somehow they would travel through the ether and ensconce themselves inside Ethan's heart.

It was surprising how easy it was to say those words now. In the past, it had been difficult to be vulnerable enough to need anyone. I knew it was all about my "mommy issues." I was thirty-four and still carried the scars of my mother's abandonment. Once I'd lived through that, I'd never put myself in jeopardy by needing another soul. But my pride didn't matter when the stakes were high and my freedom was on the line.

"Ethan," I whispered, "please reach out to me."

I was calling out to him, as if he would hear me, or at least feel me the way he used to. The way he did from the moment we met, with the most unusual introduction I'd ever had to a man:

"Journee!" Mrs. Thomas sang my name when she opened the door to her Third Ward house. "Welcome to my new home." She danced away, leaving me standing at the threshold.

I laughed as I stepped inside and watched the svelte fiftysomething swirl in the middle of the living room as if she were giving a performance. "Oh, Journee, I cannot believe this house is mine."

"You better believe it." I chuckled. "Because that mortgage payment is going to begin in about sixty days."

She stopped spinning, pouted, and glared at me, although her eyes smiled. "Is that what you came over here to tell me?"

"No." I laughed. "I come bearing gifts." I held up a bottle of wine and a gold gift box that was filled with some of my favorite essential oils.

Her smile was as bright as a thousand lights. "Thank you. My real estate agent didn't even do this. You're something special." She clapped. Taking the gifts, she said, "I'd offer you a seat, but . . ." We both looked around the empty room and laughed.

"When are the movers coming?" I asked, following her into the kitchen, where she rested the wine and box on the counter.

"Oh, Journee, you don't put new wine into old wineskins," she said, quoting one of the parables I remembered from Sunday school. "The new furniture will be delivered on Monday. So I'll be staying in a hotel for a few days. But I'll be here every day, just dancing, just because."

Once again, the woman who'd performed with Alvin Ailey leaped across the room, then ended in an arabesque, a term she'd taught me. "Forgive me," she finally said. "This always happens when I have so much open space. It's a tic I have."

"I thought I'd helped you with financing the perfect home. Who knew this would be a dance studio as well?"

"Only until I get the furniture; then I'll be normal again." Her smile faded a bit. "Thank you." She took my hands into hers. "I'm so grateful." Before I could respond, she snatched her hands away. "You know what? I've just thought of the most brilliant way to say thank you."

I shook my head. "You don't have to do anything."

As if she didn't hear me or didn't care what I said, she continued, "I'm going to set you up with my son."

"Oh, no." When she turned to me with a glare, I added, "That's so nice of you, but . . ."

"Why not?" She studied my camel-colored pantsuit with shoes that I'd had professionally dyed to match the gabardine fabric. "You got a man?"

"Actually, I'm in between relationships, but——"

"Then this is the perfect time for me to introduce you to Ethan."

"——I'm focusing on my career."

"Well, you can certainly go out to dinner, can't you? I'm not asking you to marry him . . . yet." She shrugged as if all of this should make as much sense to me as it did for her.

"Mrs. Thomas"——I shook my head——"I don't do blind dates, and I'm sure your son doesn't either."

"My son does whatever I ask him to do," she said as she grabbed her telephone.

I groaned. Mrs. Thomas was very attractive, with her shoulder-length, honey-brown hair, eyebrows so perfect she had to be plucking and shaping daily, and lips so full, so flawless, that if she hadn't been a dancer, she could have made millions modeling some giant cosmetic company's lipstick. But her son had to look like Shrek if this was how he rolled.

"Look at this face and then tell me no again." She held up her phone. "Check him out."

I steeled myself, preparing to do all I could not to laugh, but then I froze when I took in the photo of Mrs. Thomas standing next to a man who could have made his own millions as a mega movie star. "Whoa," I said, before I could stop myself.

She chuckled. "See what I'm saying? I know a piece of art when I create it."

Well, yeah, he was fine, but still, his mother was kinda acting like his pimp. There had to be something wrong with him.

"So are you saying it's okay to set the two of you up?"

In the three months I'd worked with Mrs. Thomas to find her the right loan for her dream home, I'd learned she was a professional dancer, she was a perfectionist, she was honest, and she was relentless—she didn't stop until she got what she wanted. Not only that, Mrs. Thomas would be giving me a ton of referrals from her Links and sorority sisters. So I said, "Yeah, okay," already formulating my plan. I'd take his number, then later, I'd find some excuse to explain why I never called him.

I watched Mrs. Thomas scroll through her phone, then frowned when she put the phone to her ear. "Hey, Ethan," she said. My eyes widened. "Guess where I'm at?"

No, she is not talking to her son. No, no, no!

"I can't wait for you to see this new place, but first"—she glanced up at me—"I have someone I want you to talk to."

I waved my hands like I was one of those aircraft marshalers at Hobby Airport. No, I mouthed.

"Remember, I told you about Journee, my mortgage broker? Well, all I told you was that she helped me finance this home. What I didn't mention was that she's brilliant and beautiful. And I only put brilliant first because I know that would be most important to you. So here, say hi." She thrust the phone in my face.

I whispered, "Mrs. Thomas—"

"Just say hello," she hissed back.

Since I couldn't click my heels together and disappear, I took the phone, closed my eyes, and said, "Hello, I'm sorry," just as Ethan was saying the exact same words. My eyes popped open. Then I laughed and he laughed. Ten seconds in each other's space and we were operating in such synchronicity.

FROM THAT PHONE call, Ethan and I had enjoyed three years of almost perfection. Except for the times when Ethan questioned my morals and my professional ethics. The sound of my doorbell echoed through my apartment, and I jumped up. Ethan! was my first thought as I sprinted inside. But then I backed up and slowed down. Even if Ethan were into surprises—which he was not—he wouldn't have made it past *my* concierge.

So there was only one person ringing my doorbell. It was—

"Hey, Sissy," Windsor said as she swept into my space. With her wild natural curls, carved wooden earrings, and wooden bangles up her arm, my sister was an Afrocentric fireball.

"Do you know what time it is?" I asked.

"Why does time matter if you're up?" she said with the vigor of one who'd been awake for hours. This was how Windsor rolled—from the moment her feet hit the floor in the morning, she was marathon ready.

She said, "It's going to be a beautiful day. I just finished sunrise yoga, and when I leave here, I'm going to take a Zumba class before I go in for my afternoon shift."

I needed another shot of espresso.

"So"—she bounced onto my sofa—"I do have a reason for being here. We need to march right into your closet so that you can pick out the most fabulous outfit for me."

I gave her a long side-eye. "Uh, didn't we just go shopping last week?"

"We did, but I had no idea I was going to have a second interview." Slowly, I turned to her; she grinned. "Yup," she said. "The Odom Group called me back. All because of you!"

"Oh, Windsor." I pulled her into a hug. "That's terrific. But it wasn't because of me. I just hooked you up with one of my clients."

"Your client who just happened to be the CEO of one of *Texas Monthly*'s 'Black Businesses on the Rise.' And because of that hookup, I need you to hook me up with something fabulous to wear." She jumped up, grabbed my hand, and then dragged me into my bedroom and master closet like she paid the mortgage on this place. "Now, I'm going to need everything, except shoes, 'cause your feet are too little." She giggled as we entered my closet. But then she paused. "Gosh, I love this place." Windsor sighed the way she always did when she raided my closet.

I do, too, I thought as I sat down at my vanity at the other end. My closet was the size of a bedroom . . . because, literally, it was. I'd bought this two-bedroom condo, and also the studio unit next door, just so I could have this closet.

Windsor combed through the rows of dresses before she pulled out one of my favorites—a fuchsia sheath. She studied it, then hung it to the side before she turned to my blouses and pants and suits. I sat back and beamed just because my sister was so happy.

Even though she'd come over here way too early and in the middle of my crisis, the person I loved spending time with more than anyone (even Ethan) was Windsor. No matter what was going on, and even with all the pressures she had, Windsor made life seem like a day at the beach.

Just watching her now, slipping from one outfit to another, made me remember how blessed I was that we'd found each other, or rather, that she'd found me. Windsor and I had spent only the first year of her life together before our mother gave me away.

But when we were reunited about ten years ago, it was as if those seventeen years of being apart faded away. I loved her as much now as I did the day my mom brought her to me as I sat in a chair in the corner of her room at Ben Taub Hospital. When I laid eyes on the baby, my love was instant, even if she was no bigger than the puppy I begged my mom to get from the pet store in the mall. My mom had always told me no to the puppy, but then she gave me something better.

"You know what, Journee? I want you to name the baby."

"I can give her a name like my baby doll?"

"Yes." Mama laughed. "Just like your baby doll. But this baby is going to be with us forever, so her name has to be very special."

I closed my eyes tight, something I always did when I was trying to concentrate real hard. Think! Think! I was just six years old, but I knew how important this was going to be.

I sat there thinking until . . . "I want her name to be Windsor," I said.

"Windsor?" My mother frowned.

"You don't like it, Mama?" I asked, thinking she was looking at me the same way she did when I wouldn't eat those nasty lima beans.

"Oh, no," Mama said. "It's nice. It's just that I never heard that name before."

"Yesterday at school, the librarian gave me a new book about a castle and the name of the castle was Windsor. I liked that name."

Mama was quiet, and then all the wrinkles faded from her forehead. "You're so smart, baby. That name is perfect. Yes, her name is Windsor because she's a little princess, just like you. And one day, all princesses grow up to be queens."

"I LOVE THE fuchsia one, but what about this?"

My sister's voice brought me back to my four-hundred-square-foot closet. Windsor stood in front of me in a royal blue designer wrap dress that looked great on her, even though her size 8 hips didn't fill the dress out the way my size 12 frame did. But she more than made up for it with her cleavage. I grinned. "You better work it! You look sophisticated. Just like a new advertising account exec."

"So . . ." Windsor posed to the left, then to the right.

"You know, that's a Terez original," I said, referring to my designer.

"Oh." Her voice was low. "I didn't know. Well . . ." She untied the sash.

But before she slipped it from her shoulders, I said, "Take that dress . . . and keep it!"

Her eyes were wide when she whispered, "Are you kidding me?"

"I'm not." I grinned. "I have an appointment with Terez next week for my winter wardrobe, and I'll have her make me another one."

The words were hardly out of my mouth before she wrapped her arms around my neck. "You are the best! I love you, Sissy." She held on to me. "And Mama loves you, too."

I pulled away from her embrace and turned to my four-drawer jewelry chest. "Do you need any accessories?"

"Journee."

I didn't turn around, just kept my eyes on the top drawer filled with my silver necklaces and bracelets.

Windsor's voice floated over my shoulder. "I know you don't want to hear it, but I was just thinking, look at our lives right now: everything is going so well. You were just featured in the *Houston Business Journal* as a Woman on the Move, and your career . . . My God, I don't think you could be doing any better.

"And now look at what's going on with me. I'm going to get this job, and soon, I'll be making as much money as you. Well . . . maybe not as much, but you won't have to pay for my coffee at Starbucks anymore."

I was so glad I wasn't facing Windsor, so I could have a moment to reset my expression. While I wanted to be mad that, once again, she was acting as our family counselor, I was in a battle to keep my lips from curving into a smile.

Windsor continued, "This would be the perfect weekend to come together, Sissy. Especially since you paid for it." She paused as if she expected me to chuckle with her. "You don't have anything planned, do you?"

I blew out a long breath, almost wishing I hadn't arranged

for this getaway. It was more for Windsor than my mother, and it was only to San Antonio, where they'd spend a couple of nights at a hotel on the River Walk. But now Windsor wanted to change that short vacay into a therapy session with a woman I hadn't seen in twenty-seven years.

"The more I think about it," she continued, "the more I know it's a good idea. You need to come with me and Mama."

Finally, I faced her. "You can bring this up every single day, and my response will always be the same. I'm not going to San Antonio with you because I don't want to be around Norma. I have the relationship I want with her. And she should be happy with it, too, since I haven't turned my back on her the way she turned her back on me."

"She didn't do that!" Windsor objected.

I ignored my sister and continued with what I always told her: "I've made sure that Norma is comfortable in a very nice home and—"

"And Mama would give you back that house and return to living in that ratty-ass apartment in Greenspoint just for a relationship with you."

"She *has* a relationship with me. I'm her ATM."

"That's not fair." Her tone sounded as though next she'd stomp her foot. "Mama's never asked you for anything."

"You're right," I said, keeping my tone even; it was easy to do because I fought to never give my mother a single moment of my emotions. "I gave her that house, I pay her bills, I send you two on vacations," I reminded my sister. "I don't need to or want to see her or speak to her."

Windsor's shoulders slumped. "Come on, Journee."

I shut the drawer to the jewelry case. "I guess you don't need any accessories, and now I need to get ready for work."

"I feel like I'm being dismissed."

"You are, because I'm sure you still have some packing to do. When are you and Norma leaving?"

"Really early tomorrow morning. We'll be in San Antonio by nine, so we'll have the whole day. I didn't want to deal with that traffic tonight." She sighed. "All right, I guess I'll get going." There was so much frustration in her tone, but she knew she couldn't pull me to her side. Whatever gene made her stubborn had been passed down to me, too. "I tried," she added.

"You always do."

I followed her out of my closet. But inside my bedroom, she spun around. "You know I'll never stop trying, right? Because I don't want you, my dear sissy, to one day wake up with regrets."

Inside, I flinched, but I kissed her cheek in reply. "I'm going to get in the shower. Let yourself out and make sure the emergency lock is on the door."

I sauntered into the bathroom and waited until I heard my front door close before I turned off the light and moved back to my bed. Windsor had been a blessing when she arrived; I needed her energy. But she'd dumped more burdens onto my shoulders. I didn't need to think about my mother. Now, though, because of Windsor, I couldn't stop thinking about Norma and how I had spent the early years of my life loving her. Then, from the time I was seven, how my heart had just longed for her. But when she returned to my life ten years ago by way of Windsor, from that day, my yearning had morphed into disdain and contempt; I spent few hours thinking about Norma Alexander.

But now, because my sister always made me remember, all I wanted to do was cry.

3

Too much time had been spent wallowing this morning, but I'd finally pulled myself together. It was almost noon, and I was going to do what I knew how to do—hustle. There were projects and contracts piled high on my desk. And then there was the greatest task before me—I had to get ready for the call from Mr. Yung, congratulating me for landing the city contract. In preparation, I needed to add new brokers—five or six, doubling my team. Then I had to plan our celebration to reward my current team for the long days and longer nights of effort that had been put in to win this bid. Three months of grueling work, but in a few days—the payoff.

Just as I moved toward my front door, my cell phone vibrated. I sighed with relief when I saw the text from Ethan:

If you have time now, I can meet you at the Starbucks next to your condo or I can drive over to a coffee shop near your office.

Thank God! I'm home, I texted. Come here.

Great, I'll meet you at Starbucks.

"No!" I shouted, and then typed the same thing. But I quickly deleted that and texted: Let's just meet at my apartment because—

Then I rolled back and deleted that as well. Leaning against the wall, I closed my eyes. I couldn't do anything to give Ethan room to change his mind. Knowing him, this could be a test.

Maybe Ethan was trying to determine if we could work together. Maybe he wanted to make sure I wasn't going to be difficult. Maybe he was trying to see if I would listen to him this time. So many maybes.

So I inhaled, then texted: **Okay, heading down now. See you soon.** I rushed into the hallway, and conflicting emotions stirred inside me: relief, but still some anxiety. It had taken so much for me to ask for Ethan's help. And if he denied me, there was no one else for me to turn to.

Inside the Starbucks, I sat at a table in the corner, facing the door, and a memory washed over me—this was where I'd sat the first time Ethan and I met in person seven years ago. On that day, Ethan was the one waiting when I walked in; I said hello, he said hello, and within minutes, I knew this "quick get-together over coffee" was going to be so much more. It was the comfort I felt being in his space, and letting him into mine. Our conversation was easy; we talked about our careers with passion, and shared the same ambition for our futures. We laughed over the new Chris Rock movie, but minutes later became serious when we discussed the state of our country.

I'd been so impressed, especially when Ethan told me he had political aspirations and how he'd planned his whole life to make sure he could fulfill them one day. He'd been in awe when I said I wanted to be the most important player in real estate in Houston.

It was no surprise that we couldn't wait to see each other again. So we met the next night for dinner. And then the next. And the next. Within a few weeks, we were inseparable. Within a few months, he'd moved in.

I gave my heart to Ethan quickly, something that was surprising and perplexing. Although I'd dated, I'd never let anyone in—the remnants of my mother's abandonment, I'd supposed.

But Ethan had found the key to open me; we just fit together. It was the way he was there, every day, supporting me, encouraging me, and loving me unconditionally.

Until that day when I first came to realize that no matter what a man (or a woman, for that matter) said, all love came with some conditions:

"Baby," I said the moment Ethan came through the door, "look!"

He was already grinning, even before I held the check up for him to see. He studied it, then turned to me with a slight frown. "Twenty-one thousand dollars." After a pause, he added, "That's nice," and handed the check back to me.

"No, you don't understand," I said, knowing Ethan was confused. We'd celebrated much bigger checks I received whenever I closed on a loan on the high-end homes that had become my specialty. "This isn't a commission check. This is my first bonus for working on a special project with Vivian and Simon."

Ethan was fine at the mention of my best friend's name, but the light in his eyes dimmed when I said "Simon." From the moment Ethan had met my boss and shaken his hand, he'd told me, "That guy is off." He said Simon was shady by the way he wouldn't look him directly in his eyes and didn't give him a firm handshake. He loosened his tie, then plopped onto the sofa.

"I know how you feel about him," I said, easing down next to Ethan. "But this isn't about Simon; this is about me. I could be getting checks like this every month. With bonuses alone, I could earn over two hundred thousand dollars this year."

He took the check from me once again, this time staring at the front before he turned it over and studied the other side. "Okay, I'll bite. What kind of project can bring in this much in bonuses?"

For the year we'd been together, I'd discussed every one of my real estate dealings with Ethan. But this one I had not, because of the way Ethan felt about Simon. I wanted to make sure this manifested first.

"Vivian came up with an idea, and Simon put together an amazing program that is close to my heart. I got this bonus by helping homeless people." The lines in his forehead deepened as I continued, "I recruit people who are down on their luck and introduce them to Simon. He interviews them, and then if they have all the information he needs, Simon gives them $1,000. In cash!"

Ethan shifted so his whole body faced me, and his cadence slowed when he asked, "He gives them $1,000 for what?"

"For their information," I said, still feeling as excited as I had this morning when Simon had given me this bonus for the seven homeless people I'd introduced him to over the past few months.

But Ethan wasn't sharing my enthusiasm. "And, Journee," he said, sounding as if he were talking to a child, "what is he doing with their information?"

"He's buying houses," I told him, surprised he hadn't figured out that part yet.

"He's buying houses in their names?"

There was so much incredulity in his tone that the excitement I'd felt began to wane. "Yes," I finally said. "Simon uses their information to buy homes in their names. But," I added quickly, "remember, he pays them."

Ethan sprang up from the sofa so fast, he gave me whiplash. "Journee, what in the hell are you doing?" he shouted.

"What?" I asked, feeling discombobulated. In all of our time together, Ethan had never raised his voice.

"I told you that guy was shady. This is illegal."

"Why?"

His eyes widened when he said, "You had to pass an exam to get your brokerage license, and I still have to break this down for you? Simon is buying homes in other people's names. That's fraud."

I shook my head, not understanding why Ethan was so upset about this. "If it is, it's a victimless crime. No one is getting hurt, so why would that matter?"

His stare was intense as he peered down at me. "You cannot be this naïve."

"I'm not naïve at all. I'm thinking about the people on the streets who are receiving more money than they've ever seen. That's what's most important. And then Simon is legitimately buying the homes and not hurting anyone."

"He's not legitimately buying anything. The applications are fraudulent," he said, not taking his volume down. "He's faking information, probably forging signatures—all of that is enough to put you behind bars for decades."

"I think you're making a big deal out of this because you don't like Simon."

"I'm making a big deal out of this because it's a crime."

"I can't really tell you everything Simon is doing with the paperwork because I haven't asked him. But what does it matter when this is a win-win situation? From what Simon has told me, he can't buy twenty homes under his name, but he can help twenty people who are living on the street. And then he wins by buying these homes in their names, flipping them, and making a profit. No one is getting hurt."

"And no matter how many times you say that, hurt or no hurt, it's still illegal!" Ethan raised his hands in exasperation. "Honestly, Journee, with what I know about Simon, I doubt he's really flipping the homes. I've seen this scam before. He's probably using their information to buy those homes, sets up fake bank accounts, and then takes the equity out before he ever makes a payment. Once he takes the money, he lets the property go into foreclosure. What does he care? None of the homes are in his name, and the bank will never find the person whose name was on the application."

"That's not what he's doing."

"How do you know?" he challenged me. "You said you don't know what he's doing with the paperwork."

I pressed my lips together, folded my arms, and glared at Ethan, shocked that in just a few minutes, he'd snatched all my joy away.

"This is the kind of stuff that will land you in prison for years. And you're in the middle of this mess."

"I'm not." Now I jumped up from the sofa and faced him. "All I do is recruit the people and I'm happy to do that because I once lived on those same streets, remember? And my mother would have given anything to receive that kind of money. Maybe if she'd had that kind of money, she wouldn't have given me away!"

He pushed the tips of his fingers against his temples, massaged them for a moment, then stepped closer to me. He took my hands into his. His voice was lowered when he said, "I know what happened to you is sometimes a trigger."

"It's not a trigger," I growled. "It was my life."

"I get that," he said, his voice softer and more even now. "And that's why I'm so upset: because Simon is using you."

"This was Vivian's idea."

"I don't care who thought of it. This is Simon's company, and he's playing on the fact that you and Vivian are young and because of your background, you will look past the crime. But no matter the lens, this is not positive. I'm not making this up because I don't like Simon. I'm an officer of the court. I know a crime when I see one. You have to stop this now." When I said nothing, he kept on: "I can't save Simon, but I can save you."

I snatched my hands from his. "How many times do I have to tell you, Ethan? I don't need you to be my savior. I've been saving myself since I was seven years old. I don't need you or anybody to step in now."

"Maybe my choice of words could have been better," he said, his *voice remaining low and steady. "But I'm just telling you what I know because I don't ever want to see you in the kind of trouble that will be waiting for you if you continue this. I know what I'm talking about."*

Ethan didn't know squat. He didn't know anything about being homeless, he didn't know anything about real estate, he didn't know anything about making big money. Yeah, he made about $90,000 a year, but last year I doubled that, and with this plan with Simon, along with my commissions, I could quadruple that.

Seemed to me that I was the expert, and he was the lowly DA. There was no kind of advice he could give me that could equate to what I already knew.

Gently, he touched my chin with his fingertips and nudged me to face him. "I love you, baby. I just want what's best for you."

His words were meant to soften me, and then, when he pulled me into his arms, I guessed I was supposed to acquiesce.

"We good?" he whispered in my ear.

I nodded because I didn't want to speak the lie out loud. We weren't good, but we would be. Because, from this point, I wouldn't share my business with Ethan. There was no need if this was how he was going to respond to me making major moves.

I BLEW OUT a long breath at that memory. I hadn't realized it then, but that was the beginning of our end.

It was interesting that I was thinking about that now. In the years since we'd broken up, I hadn't spent a single moment wishing to have Ethan back. Instead, I'd thrown myself into my work, wanting to prove to everyone that I didn't need Ethan; I didn't need anybody. The only partner I wanted was success.

But after seeing Ethan last night, after feeling those emotions again, I wondered, was there anything I could have done to save us? And the more important question . . . was there any-thing I could do now to put us back together?

I wondered . . . and I waited.

I WAITED FOR twenty-two minutes. I knew the exact time be-cause I'd checked my watch every two minutes, and in between, I searched my texts. But finally, twenty-two minutes after I asked myself if I wanted Ethan and me to be a couple again, he entered the coffee shop. As he strolled toward me, I held his gaze and answered the question I'd been asking since last night—I did want this opportunity to get back with Ethan. Perhaps this was God's way of giving us another chance.

"Hey, you."

Those two words brought a tsunami of new memories—of all the times I had walked into my condo and Ethan met me at the door with those words and a kiss.

"Hey. Thank you for coming." I took in his white golf shirt and khaki pants. It seemed Ethan's holiday weekend had begun.

He nodded as he slipped into the chair across from me. "I owe it to you to at least hear the whole story. So, do you want me to grab an espresso for you?"

First his greeting, and now I remembered how he'd brought me espresso in bed every morning. "Sure," I said. But then I glanced around at the packed café. "You know what?" I began. "I'm not sure we should do this here."

"Why not?"

"Well"—I leaned forward and lowered my voice—"the things we'll be talking about . . ."

I shrugged, and Ethan nodded. "Good point," he said.

"We can just go upstairs to my condo."

The ends of his lips dipped just a bit, and he hesitated. Why? Then all at once, I got it. Seeing Ethan had stirred all of these feelings inside me. Of course it had to be the same for him. And now he was uncertain about going upstairs because that condo held so many of our wonderful memories. A few minutes up there and who knew what would happen?

But then he said, "Okay," and stood. And my heart palpitated.

All kinds of hope rolled through my mind as I moved from the back of the coffee shop to the front door. As I'd waited for Ethan, I'd been thinking about the beginning of our end. But now here we were at what could be the start of a new beginning.

Ethan pushed open the door for me, but when I crossed the threshold and moved to the right, he went left. "This way," he said.

"My place is—"

"Let's talk in my car."

I stopped walking and crossed my arms. "Really, Ethan?" Having a meeting inside a car was beyond ridiculous when I had a perfectly comfortable condo upstairs.

He didn't even look back when he said, "Really, Journee!" He kept walking and his message was in his pace—either we'd do this in his car or there wouldn't be any discussion. With a grunt, I followed him, trotting to catch up. "I parked right over there."

When we rounded the corner, the scowl I wore gave way to my chuckle. Ethan's car was nice enough; it was a top-of-the-line BMW 5 Series. But I had talked him into buying this car a year before we broke up, which meant it was five years old now. At least he kept it so clean, it looked brand-new, but this said so much about Ethan . . . or maybe it said more about me, since I'd had two new vehicles since he'd purchased this one.

With his fob, he unlocked and then opened the door for me. My eyes followed him as he made his way to the driver's side. Was I on point about why Ethan didn't want to be alone in my condo? Was he afraid because he still loved me? I pressed my hand against my chest, thinking about his vulnerability. We wanted the same thing. We wanted us.

By the time Ethan opened the driver's door, I made up my mind. Yes, we needed to talk about my situation, but we needed to discuss our relationship now. Ethan had to know that I'd grown so much in the years we'd been apart. I wouldn't do anything to put him or his career at risk.

He slid into the driver's seat. "Excuse me for a moment." He tapped on his cell as if he was sending a text. I wanted to glance over, see who was important enough to interrupt this moment between us. But I kept my eyes forward.

"Okay." He glanced up with a smile that reminded me of old times. "I can't say I've had many meetings in my car."

"It's certainly unconventional."

"Agreed, but it will get the job done, because all I want to do right now is hear you out and talk this through." He shifted in his seat, and now his eyes were only on me. "So let's do this." His smile was gone, and his voice was filled with that business-only tone I'd heard him use through the years with clients. "Why do you think you're linked to Simon's case?" But before I could answer, he held up his hand. "And tell me everything, Journee." There was a warning in his tone. "If you want me to work with you, I need to know the complete picture, so be totally honest."

I understood his concern. After that first conversation Ethan and I had about my bonus check from Simon, I never told him the truth again—until I had to. And he'd caught me in more than a few lies. But this time, I would tell him everything—at least what he needed to know. "Okay, I guess I should begin with the specifics, at least the little that I know, of why Simon was indicted."

"I know all about that." Ethan waved his hand. "After we talked last night, I read up on everything. This indictment came after a two-year investigation. Apparently, they have proof that he falsified information on hundreds of applications, and then transferred millions of dollars in mortgage refinancing proceeds to his personal account." He paused. "So when exactly did you leave his company?"

"Right after you left me," I said, repeating what I had told him last night. When he raised his eyebrows, I continued, "That's no judgment; that's the truth. Right after we broke up, something happened . . ." I paused. Did I really want Ethan to know why I'd left Simon? I redirected my words. "When we broke up, I was forced to think about everything you said. I thought about what I was doing, and although I believed that helping the homeless was right, I asked myself, did I really want to build my business with questionable tactics? I wasn't falsifying records, but what I was doing was still wrong." I lowered my voice when I added, "Still illegal."

Not a beat passed before Ethan said, "Well, I'm glad you finally saw the error of your ways."

He'd been waiting a long time to say that, and I wanted to protest. Tell Ethan again that my focus the whole time was on helping homeless people. But we'd had that discussion ad nauseam, and right now, my goal wasn't to win a debate. I had only two objectives: to make sure there was no connection between me and Simon and to put Ethan and me back together again.

I said, "I finally agreed with you." Then I paused and added, "You were right," because I wanted Ethan to know that I'd been changed. "I'm sure Simon stopped that homeless scheme once I was gone. There was no way he was recruiting homeless people himself, although he could have trained another broker to work with him." I shook my head. "But I don't think that's what happened. After I left, I think he got into something else," I said, leaving off what I knew for sure. Simon had ended the homeless scheme well before I left his firm because he'd found something more lucrative for both of us.

He nodded. "Well, whatever he was doing, Simon is in real deep. He's facing twenty years for real estate, wire, and bank fraud."

"Wow!" I exclaimed. "Twenty years. That's exactly what was in the first text I received."

Ethan nodded as if he found that interesting, but while he said nothing, now I knew for sure that these texts and Simon's case were connected.

I asked, "Could he really be sentenced to that much time?"

"Oh, definitely," he said with what sounded like a bit of glee in his tone. "The feds would love to make an example of him. So, now, knowing you were gone before the investigation began, do you still think you could be connected to Simon?"

"Only because of our past. I mean, couldn't Simon try to make a deal with the feds? Could he say, *I'll give you the names of other people who worked with me*, so he could get less time or even get off?"

Ethan shook his head. "Simon Wallace isn't getting off no matter what he gives to the feds. He's going to prison, that I know for sure. I don't know how much time he'll serve, but he needs to get his life in order, because he'll be behind bars for more than a couple of years."

I groaned. "That's what worries me. I know Simon. He will not go down without a fight, and I'm afraid I might get caught up in his war. Yeah, we were good friends, but friends are the ones who most often become sacrificial lambs."

Slowly, Ethan nodded. "Okay," he said. "I see what you're saying. But even if you are investigated and then eventually indicted for your role in his homeless schemes, I'd be able to work with the feds on that."

"Really?"

"Yeah. It was shady and so wrong, but compared to what Simon has done, you're a small fish. The government has limited resources, and so they go after the sharks. And there are too many sharks out there for them to come after you. You weren't falsifying or forging records, and you weren't causing individual homeowners any kind of loss or pain."

I swallowed at those last words, but I pushed my thoughts aside. What was important was that Ethan was telling me I would probably be in the clear.

He said, "Now, if the feds do come for you, it won't be easy. You'll definitely have some fines to pay."

I waved my hand as if that didn't matter. "I can handle any fines."

"And," Ethan continued, "you'll probably lose your license. As far as prison time, I don't like to make promises, but this is as close to a promise as I can give. You probably won't do any time."

"I just can't believe this." I sighed with relief. But then Ethan added, "But what I'm telling you is contingent on one thing." He paused. "You've told me everything, right? Simon doesn't have anything else on you?"

He peered at me as if he didn't trust me, and I was so grateful he couldn't see the lump in my throat. I knew I should probably tell Ethan all of it, but at this moment, I couldn't bring myself to share the worst of what I'd done.

And really, there was no need to do that. From what Ethan had just told me, what I'd done with Simon had ended long before this investigation began, so it wouldn't have any effect on Ethan's ability to defend me.

I lifted my chin, squared my shoulders, and said, "That's all Simon has on me," as if that were the truth.

That lie was worth it when Ethan's lips spread into a smile. "Okay, Journee, I got you."

"Really?" I said, my grin much wider than his.

"Yeah. I don't think you're going to need representation, but I'll stay close, see what I hear, and if you do need me, I'll be here."

"What about the texts?"

He squinted. "I'm thinking the texts may have nothing to do with what's going on with Simon. You probably just pissed someone off." He chuckled, but when he noticed that I didn't, he continued, "But even if someone knows about the homeless schemes, again, I don't think the feds will come after you for that." He paused. "You're gonna have to work that out with God, but as far as the feds . . ." He shrugged. "You're good."

I was just so grateful, and before I even thought about it, I leaned over and wrapped my arms and half of my body around Ethan. It was a bit awkward with the console in between us, but we'd made out inside this car so many times, I knew exactly what body parts fit where. I closed my eyes, nuzzled against him, and inhaled his scent. The fragrance of his cologne took me back. I'd purchased his first bottle of *Obsession* for him, more for the name than its citrus notes and musky undertones. I whispered, "Thank you, thank you," over and over.

Just touching him set my flesh on fire. That familiar stirring was back. Last night, it had confused me; today, I welcomed it. If we weren't in this car, if we'd been in my condo, I would have had my way with this man.

I cupped his face in my hands, and his eyes seemed filled

with confusion. I understood; I didn't quite understand how we were back in this place either. I guessed it just meant we should never have been apart. Slowly, I moved my lips toward his, but before we touched, Ethan laid his hands against my shoulders and pushed me back.

Shaking his head, he said, "No, Journee."

When he pressed harder, I bounced back in my seat. "Why are you saying no? We both know what is happening between us. You didn't even want to go to my apartment because you didn't trust yourself with me."

He frowned. "Where did you . . . That's not the reason," he said, sounding like he was offended by those words.

"Then why are you doing all of this?"

"All of what?" He leaned back against the door as if he was trying to get far away from me. "Helping you?"

"Yes."

"I'm helping you because you're a friend and—" Before he could finish, a tap on the window startled me so much I bounced in the seat and bumped my head on the car's roof. I wasn't sure what to focus on first—the blazing headache I would have in the next few minutes or the person who'd interrupted the most important conversation I'd have this year.

Before I could make sense of this, Ethan hopped out. I watched him rush to the curb and pull a woman into his arms; then their embrace turned into the kiss that Ethan was supposed to be giving to me.

I pushed the car door open, jumped out, and Ethan stepped back, glancing at me as if he'd forgotten my very existence.

"Oh . . . Journee," he said as the woman clung to him like an appendage he'd just grown.

"Yeah," I said, folding my arms and turning all my attention to the woman, who looked like she'd just stepped off a runway in her tie-dyed halter maxi dress and chunky platform mules that helped her almost match Ethan's six-foot height. With her smooth chocolate skin, natural coils that framed her face and skimmed her shoulders, and makeup so light, I wasn't sure she really had any on—I hated her.

"Journee?" She called my name with a smile that made her look even more beautiful. "Oh my God." She pressed her hand against her chest. "It's me. Ivy." And then she pulled me into a hug.

My arms stayed at my sides, since I didn't embrace strangers. I was as confused as Ethan, who stood behind Ivy staring like—what is going on? It wasn't like I could help him. I didn't know this woman. She said her name was Ivy, and the only Ivy I'd ever known was . . .

She leaned away. "I can't believe this is you. How many years has it been?" Her curls bounced with every word she spoke.

I squinted, and then I saw it. It couldn't be . . . but it was. Ivy Franklin. Or as I had always referred to her, Poison Ivy.

"So, wait," Ethan said. "You two know each other?" His tone was as incredulous as I felt.

"Yes!" Ivy said, as if she was delighted. "We grew up together. Well, in Sunday school, because you know I went to Imani and Journee was on scholarship at the Moreland Gifted and Talented School."

My eyes narrowed at "scholarship." Poison Ivy hadn't changed.

Ivy continued, "But, yes, Journee used to be a member of Wheeler Village."

This definitely was Ivy Franklin. The daughter of Jamal Franklin. The pastor of the megachurch Wheeler Village Baptist, one of the preeminent houses of worship in the city. And the man who found me a home after my mother left me on the church's doorstep.

"Wow!" Ethan said.

"It is so good to see you," Ivy said.

She sounded sincere, which I didn't get. Because the way I remembered our relationship, we never liked each other. Or maybe it was just that I didn't like her. Maybe it was the taunts of *"poor little homeless girl"* that Ivy and her friends used to sing on the playground behind the church whenever I passed by their little circle. Or how she embarrassed me every chance she got, like she did when we were twelve, and all the kids stood waiting to perform in the church's Christmas play. *"Is that a new dress, Journee? Oh, wait, it looks like one my mother made me donate to the less fortunate last Christmas."* From the time I was seven through my teenage years, Ivy's teasing and taunting was relentless, as if it were her job.

But then I remembered, this scorn I had for her didn't go one way. Ivy *definitely* didn't like me. Because of the one time when I got the best of her. We were sixteen, and there was a guy in the teen church choir whose name I couldn't recall now. But once I figured out that while Ivy loved him, he was sniffing after me, I finally had my chance to get back at her for all the hateful things she'd done to me, and I took it. I didn't even like that guy, but for about eight weeks or so, I made sure Ivy thought that I did. My most triumphant moment came when I found her in the church bathroom bawling after I'd made sure she saw me kissing the boy at the church picnic.

"This is amazing," Ethan said through my memories, though he didn't sound like he was excited by this reunion.

"Yeah, it really is," I added, wondering if Ivy realized she was the only one among us smiling. "So I guess you know each other," I said, glancing between the two.

"Yes!" Ivy wrapped her arm around Ethan again like he was the branch to her vine. "We know each other for sure." She laughed. "Ethan is my fiancé."

The heat I'd felt moments ago in the car with Ethan had melted everything inside me. Now, I stood as stiff as an iceberg.

Ethan explained, "I told Ivy to Uber over here; we're on our way out of town for the weekend."

"We're just going to our place in Galveston," she offered as if I'd asked or cared. Her words made me wish, though, that I'd taken Windsor up on her offer, so that I could tell these two I had somewhere to go, too.

"And," Ethan continued, "I wanted Ivy to meet you, not having any idea that—"

"We already knew each other." Ivy finished his sentence the way Ethan and I used to do for each other.

There was no way I could continue to stand there and breathe at the same time. "Well," I said, "I guess you'd better get on the road."

"Yeah." Ethan grabbed the small suitcase I just noticed next to Ivy, right as his cell phone rang. He said to Ivy, "I'll put your bag in the trunk, but I gotta take this call."

"Okay, baby," she said, her saccharine sweetness wrapping itself around all of us. As he answered the call, Ivy turned back to me.

"It really is good to see you again," Ivy said, sounding as if she meant it.

I studied her, wondered what her game was. "I'm surprised. I mean, growing up, we didn't share a single day of friendship."

"Oh, I remember." Her smile dimmed just a little. "Especially after that little thing in church with Jason."

Jason. Was that the choirboy's name?

She said, "But we're all grown up. And"—her smile was all the way gone when she added—"I have the man I want. So nothing in the past matters."

I couldn't tell if this chick was throwing shade or sending me a message.

"I hope we can be friends, since Ethan will be working with you. He told me you contacted him."

I frowned. "He told you about me?"

"Oh, yeah," she said in a casual tone, as if their discussion had been a small matter. "He said something about an ex who needed some help." She paused and looked me straight in the eye when she added, "And that her name was Journee."

I crossed my arms. "So you knew?"

"Knew what? That you"—she pointed her French-tip manicure in my direction—"were the Journee?" She waved her hand and almost blinded me with the diamond on her finger that looked like it weighed a thousand tons. "My goodness. Still a little self-centered, I see. You're not the only Journee in this world. I mean, look at that actress, Journee . . . what's her last name?" She shook her head. "Nope, I didn't know you were Ethan's ex."

She was lying—this I knew for sure. But why?

"But like I said"—she kept on talking as if I cared about what she had to say—"I'm glad to know it's you, and I'm hoping we can all be friends."

"For what purpose?" I spat those words at her.

"Because it seems like Ethan wants to help you," she said, smiling as if she wasn't getting my message. But then the ends of her lips turned down and she lowered her voice. "Now, I'm sure if I asked him to stay away from you, he would. But there's no need for me to *eliminate* anyone in Ethan's past, just like I wouldn't want him to do that to me."

I guessed she *had* gotten my message. "Eliminate me?" I said. "Do you think I'm a threat to you, or are you threatening me?"

Before she could answer, Ethan returned and opened the

passenger door. He reached in and handed me my purse. His eyes were steady when he asked, "So you're good?"

Now he was the one sending a message, asking me if I understood what he'd been trying to tell me in the car. There was no chance of us getting back together. I'd read every single word he'd spoken, every action he'd taken, wrong. "Yeah." I glanced between him and his fiancée. "I'm great."

He nodded. "I don't want you to worry about this thing with Simon; enjoy your weekend. Nothing much will happen over the next few days. Even the government shuts down for this weekend. I'll be back on Tuesday and I'll text then."

"Okay." I kept my eyes on Ethan and still wondered, how could I have been so wrong?

He said, "Until Tuesday, just lie low."

When I faced Ivy, she was wearing that saccharine smile again. "I'm sure we'll see each other soon, Journee." Then she slipped into the place in Ethan's car that used to belong to me.

Ethan nodded his good-bye and jumped into the driver's seat. I wanted to walk away, but I couldn't. My feet were planted as if my body were punishing me by forcing me to watch the man I still loved drive away with the woman who'd made my difficult childhood harder, flaunting everything I lacked with every chance she had. It was amazing that here we were as adults, and her taunting continued. Because with me having nearly everything that I could want in this world, Ivy had the one thing that it seemed I'd never have again—Ethan.

I watched as the BMW weaved into the traffic, and I stayed there until I couldn't see that car, that man, or his fiancée anymore.

4

This Labor Day weekend, I had truly labored, trying not to think about Ethan. Or Poison Ivy. But my efforts had failed. I'd been consumed with thoughts of the two of them every moment of the almost seventy hours that had passed since I'd watched them drive off toward the Galveston sunset.

On Saturday, after I'd tossed through the night, I called my sister hoping that by talking it out, I could make sense of what had happened. She and Norma had arrived in San Antonio and were already settled in, so of course she could step away from our mother and talk. Windsor gave me her supportive shoulder as I paced through my apartment and vented with flailing arms about my encounter with Ethan from Thursday night until he'd driven away with Ivy on Friday.

"Wow," Windsor said when I finished. She was quiet for a moment before she added, "Why were you in Ethan's office in the first place?"

I'd left out my reason for contacting Ethan; I hadn't told Windsor about the texts or my concerns about Simon, keeping all my business close, the way I always did. Plus, with Windsor always worried about Norma and her bronchitis, I didn't want my sister worried about me.

So I told her, "Ethan called me . . . He had a real estate question."

"Oh, that's surprising." She paused, and I wondered if she believed me. But then she said, "Well then, I guess I can see how you thought he might have, perhaps, maybe would have been in-terested in the two of you reconnecting. Because he called you."

"Why all the sarcasm?" I asked, plopping onto my sofa.

"Because a man calling me about business wouldn't be enough for me to think he wanted to reconnect romantically. I mean, Ethan was always very direct with you, right? Why would he come at you under some business pretense when he wanted a personal connection?"

"Maybe he wanted to feel me out," I snapped. "Maybe he didn't want to get hurt if he found out I wasn't interested in get-ting back together with him."

"Okay," Windsor said, not reacting to my tone, "that's pos-sible, but were there any other signs?"

My sister asked the question I'd been asking myself, but this was difficult to explain. There was nothing I saw, nothing I heard—not really. It was all in the way I felt when I was with Ethan. And I was sure he'd felt the same way. But I said, "Yes, there were signals all over the place."

"Oh."

That word made me frown and sit up straight on the sofa. Her *oh* didn't sound as if she believed me. It sounded more like, *Oh, okay, whatever you say.* "What does that mean, Windsor?" When she hesitated, I added, "Just tell me. You don't usually have a problem saying what you have to say."

"Well," she began, sounding a little too eager to speak her mind, "I just don't see how wanting to have a discussion about business led you all the way to reconciliation."

Why did I make this call? I thought. But I said, "You had to have been there."

"Either that . . . or I need to be looking at the world through Journee-colored lenses."

Ouch! "What?"

"Sometimes, instead of seeing what's in front of you, you see what you want to see."

Damn! "I don't do that."

"You do. I tell you that all the time. You do it with Mama, and now it feels like you're doing it with Ethan. You have a hard time seeing anyone else's side to a story. All that counts is what you see, what you believe. It's your pride, Journee. You know everything, even how people are feeling and thinking. You never take anyone else's perspective into consideration because you're always right, no matter what anyone else says or feels."

I stood as the ire began to rise inside me. But I wasn't going there; I wasn't getting into an argument with Windsor, because this wasn't about what had happened with Ethan. She'd taken us to a whole 'nother place—my mother. She never missed an opportunity to attack me about that. Well, it wasn't happening today.

"Oh, girl," I sang, sounding like her words hadn't touched me, "I have another call coming in. I've got to take it; I'll talk to you later."

I hung up the phone, wondering if Windsor believed that ploy I'd used on her so many times. Talking to her left me worse than before the call. Now she had me wondering, had I made it all up?

Sunday had been better only because I didn't call Windsor. Instead, I'd sulked alone, pondering how I could have been so wrong.

Today, though, I was determined to salvage some part of my weekend. That was the only reason why I was here at the gym, just as the sun was peeking over the horizon. I steered my car into the parking lot; it wasn't packed, but I'd expected to be the only one getting up before sunrise on a holiday just to work out.

Moving quickly, I passed the check-in desk, then made my way to the locker room, and within minutes, I was on the elliptical machine, with Drake blasting through my earbuds. But after five minutes, the thoughts were still there. After ten minutes, I began to see images of Ethan and Ivy holding hands, skipping across the sand, laughing and frolicking on some beach. By the time twenty minutes had passed, I turned off the music and just let my thoughts run wild.

My mind settled on one memory: how my desire to do what I thought was right collided with one moment of incredibly bad timing.

I didn't usually walk the people I introduced to Simon to the elevator, but Mrs. Lyman had touched me so. When I met her several weeks before, as I was canvassing the streets around the Toyota Center, she'd been rolling a shopping cart with a few plastic bags stuffed inside, but what I noticed first were the little twin girls, dressed in dingy white T-shirts that fit more like dresses than tops and faded jeans. They were so small, they couldn't have been more than two, maybe three. My heart constricted; in that moment I saw me and my sister.

When I introduced myself, Mrs. Lyman told me she'd heard about me from one of the men who used to stay at the shelter, and she begged for my help. "That kind of money would go a long way for me and my girls."

Mrs. Lyman didn't have to say much more. I moved her to the top of the list, made sure Simon saw her within a few days, and convinced him to add two hundred dollars to his normal fee for the woman.

"You have no idea what you and Mr. Simon have done for me and my girls," she said as we stopped before the elevator bank. "I was thinking that maybe it was time for me"—her voice cracked as she continued—"to find a home where I can place them. Maybe put them in foster care until something happens, because I hate having them on the streets."

I shook my head. "No, Mrs. Lyman." I took her hands into mine. "Please don't do that. Even with all that you're going through, your girls would rather be with you than without you." She glanced down at her hands, and I realized I was squeezing them too tightly. "I'm so sorry," I said, moving back just as the elevator doors opened.

Ethan stepped off, holding a bouquet of flowers. His grin was wide when he saw me, but his eyes moved to Mrs. Lyman, and his smile faded away. I watched Ethan take in the sight of the woman, who had dressed as decently as she could, I supposed, in a pink sweater that was stretched and frayed at the collar and black pants that hung on her thin frame. But it didn't take any kind of special intelligence to know she was out of place in this office.

As Ethan's eyes narrowed, I tried to push Mrs. Lyman into the elevator, hoping that if she didn't speak, I'd be able to convince Ethan not to believe his eyes.

But I didn't get my wish. "Oh, those are pretty flowers," she said to Ethan; then, to me, she added, "Ms. Alexander, again, thank you. We'll be off the streets for at least a few weeks because of that check from you and Mr. Simon."

Short of putting my hand over this woman's mouth and dragging her onto the elevator, I didn't know what to do. Finally, she stepped on, and when the doors closed, I pasted on a smile, held my breath, and faced Ethan.

Before I could begin an explanation that hadn't yet fully formed in my mind, he shoved the flowers into my chest and turned back to the elevator, punching the button as if it were an emergency.

"Ethan," I began.

He whipped around. "You promised."

"I didn't promise a thing." The words slipped out before I could stop myself; I had just confessed, which hadn't been my plan.

"So you continued with this the whole time?" He spoke through

clenched teeth, but I could still hear his astonishment. "You've been scamming people for the past year?"

"Let me explain."

"There's nothing to explain," *he said just as the elevators opened. He rushed inside, and the only reason I didn't say anything more was because there were others on the elevator.*

GLANCING AT MY watch, I couldn't believe that only fifteen more minutes had passed. I felt like I'd been striding on that elliptical for a lifetime. I hopped off and glanced at the weight machines but then walked in the opposite direction and into the locker room. The gym hadn't been the escape that I'd hoped for.

I opened my locker but then sank down onto the bench. I wanted to get away from my thoughts, but the memories were holding me hostage. Closing my eyes, I returned to that day when our life of perfect harmony crashed:

Ethan was gone, but his expression, the way he glared at me before the elevator doors closed, stayed. He was upset, but he was wrong, he didn't understand. And so, after an hour, I decided to go home. I had to prepare for the talk Ethan and I needed to have. I'd be able to calm this situation; of that, I was sure.

But when I entered my condo, I paused at the threshold. I hadn't expected Ethan to be home; it was only two in the afternoon. But he sat in the living room, leaning back on the sofa, with his feet resting on the ottoman and his eyes on the television, though the sound was muted.

Stepping inside, I waited for Ethan to turn toward me. He did not. So I tossed my purse onto the sofa and moved to the kitchen. I pulled a bottle from the wine refrigerator and filled two glasses, but when I faced the living room once again, Ethan still wouldn't look at me. My eyes were on him as I strolled across the room. I offered him a glass, but still he did not move. I placed both glasses on the table before I lowered myself onto the sofa next to him, kicked off my shoes, and tucked my feet beneath me. "Let's talk," I said.

He nodded but kept his eyes on the television. "Do you know why I came by your office today?" His question was only rhetorical because he continued, "Do you know why I wanted to bring you flowers?" Now he turned to me. "I was approached by a few members of the Harris County Democratic Party. We had a meeting this morning, and they want me to consider running for city council."

"Oh my God, Ethan," I said, forgetting for a moment why we were sitting here. "Why didn't you tell me about the meeting? This is what we've wanted." I reached for him, but he stiffened, and I pulled my hand back.

"Yeah, I was excited, and all I wanted to do was celebrate with you. And bring you flowers for standing alongside me with this dream. But now . . ." He shook his head. "But now, what you're doing will cost me something I've really wanted."

"What?" I squinted, not understanding.

"I can't run for office." The sadness in his tone weighed heavy in the air. "Not with your real estate scams."

I swung my legs onto the floor and sat up straight. "What does my career have to do with you?"

He grunted, or maybe that was a chuckle, I couldn't tell. "It amazes me that as smart as you are, your self-centeredness blinds you to the world around you."

My eyes narrowed.

"I can't run for office because what you're doing is a crime," he explained. "I can't run for office because there is no doubt in my mind that just a bit of opposition research will lead to the discovery of what you've been doing."

With my hand, I swatted his words away. "I told you before that even if what Simon is doing is a crime, it's a victimless one. And no one will ever be coming after me."

This time I was sure he chuckled, but there was only bitterness in the sound.

"I'm serious," I said. "I truly don't get why you think my career will impact you. That's ridiculous."

"Is it? Let me paint the picture for you. I'm running for office and the other person wants to win. So they hire the best opposition research firms, who search for everything they can on me, but they'll find nothing. Because I've lived my life, since I was ten, so that I could run for political office one day. When they can't find anything on me, do you think they'll stop? No, they'll go to the woman I've been living with, the woman I want to marry."

I inhaled. Even though we hadn't spoken specifically about getting engaged, we'd often talked about being married. From the beginning, both of us saw our future together.

He continued, "So they'll investigate you, and because they're good, they'll find what they're looking for. And when they find that, do you think they'll stop with you? No, they'll come right back to me because you were committing a crime while living with me. And I knew and did nothing."

"Okay." I held up my hand and moved to the edge of the couch. "You're doing too much right now, Ethan. This sounds more like a script for a B movie than real life. But let's just say what you're telling me is true. If someone were to find out about what Simon and I are doing, all we have to say is you didn't know."

His eyebrows rose and he stared at me for so long. "I never noticed this about you before." I frowned before he added, "Lying comes so naturally to you."

My frown deepened. "There's no reason for you to call me a liar," I snapped.

"Well, would it be better," he said, his voice still steady, "if I called you a cheat? Or are you fine with me just calling you a criminal?"

His words surprised me because this was not the way Ethan and I operated. We were always calm and collected when we spoke to each other, always with respect.

This was so new to me, and my first instinct was to jump up, fight back, and call him every name I could think of. But that would do nothing except separate us. So I would be the grown one here.

I swallowed my rising anger. "Let's say what you're telling me is true—"

"It is."

"Then if anyone ever comes for me—and that's not going to happen—I'll just get on television and show Houston how Simon and I have helped the poor. How we've done what the city should have been doing. Can you imagine?" I said. This was something I just thought of, but as I talked it out, I could imagine what a news conference would look like and what it would do. "I can have some of the people we've helped standing up there with me. People like Mrs. Lyman and her little girls. By the time I finish, Ethan, forget about the city council. They'll be asking you to run for mayor."

Again his eyes stayed on me, and the way he stared, it was as if he was seeing me anew. "You believe what you're saying, don't you?" He sounded surprised and sad.

"I believe in what I'm saying and what I'm doing."

"So even though I'm an attorney, an officer of the court, you think you know how this will play out better than me?"

I pressed my lips together so that I wouldn't tell him the truth. Of course I knew better, because I was looking at the big picture, and he only saw this situation one way.

"So what do we do now, Journee?" he asked, but didn't let me respond. "Because I love you and I can't sit back and watch you go down this road."

A minute ago, Ethan had me ready to fight, but now I softened. What I had to remember was that behind all of this, Ethan loved me.

That was his motivation; he thought what he was doing was right when he was so wrong. I said, "Can you just trust me on this?"

The corners of his lips drooped, and he shook his head. "I can't. Because you're wrong, and if you don't stop, all of this is going to come tumbling down. But there is something I can do—I can help you." He scooted closer to me on the sofa and took my hands into his. "I can help you find another position with another firm and make it easy for you to walk away from Simon. I have connections to make anything happen for you."

"And what kind of connections do you have that are better than mine?"

He squeezed my hands. "Then we'll do it together. But no matter what, you have to quit. You have to leave Simon's firm now."

Leave Simon's firm? Walk away from all the money I was making? And for no reason beyond Ethan's not liking what I was doing? That wasn't going to happen. I said nothing, just gave my answer in my silence.

"I'm trying to help you, Journee."

I resisted the urge to snatch my hands away from his. "And how many times do I have to tell you that I don't need your help, Ethan?"

"Why do you always have to say that? Why can't you for once listen and accept my help?"

"Because I don't need you to help me or save me. I know what I'm doing. I was doing this before I met you, so I don't need you." Because his eyes dimmed and the ends of his lips dipped, I added, "Not in that way."

Ethan's chin dropped to his chest. And after a few moments, he lifted my clasped hands and kissed my fingers. His lips lingered for a second longer, then he stood and crossed the living room to our bedroom.

I sighed and bounced back onto the couch. I guessed he just needed some time to cool off and accept what I'd said. And I needed these few minutes to figure out how I was going to convince him to chill. It didn't take me long to know what I had to do. Picking up the glass of wine, I decided to give Ethan about half an hour, then I'd strip and saunter into the bedroom. The sight of me would solve every problem we'd ever had.

The thought of that made me chuckle, and then I heard Ethan behind me. I turned, and my eyes widened. Ethan stood with a small suitcase and duffel bag. He couldn't have packed that quickly. Was that why he was home when I arrived? Maybe he had a business trip scheduled and he'd forgotten to tell me.

Slowly, I stood and faced him. "You didn't say anything about having to take a trip." My voice quivered because I wasn't quite convinced that my assumption was correct.

He blinked over and over. "I've done all I can, Journee."

"What does that mean?" I asked, although I already knew.

"I can't do this."

I closed the space between us. There was no way he'd be able to leave if I was right in front of him. Standing close enough to kiss him, I said, "You're walking out because you don't agree with me? What about love? You said you loved me."

"I do. I love you with everything in me. But I can't love you more than I love myself."

"I'm not asking you to do that."

"Yes . . . you are." His voice quivered as he continued, "And now, my prayer is that one day you will come to recognize the help you need from those who love you."

WITH THOSE WORDS, Ethan Thomas kissed my forehead, and then he rolled that suitcase out of my condo and walked out of my life. That was the end. It was amazing that after being together for three years, we were able to end our relationship with just a few email exchanges and with Ethan making a couple of trips back to the apartment when I wasn't home. We had very little contact, giving each other no room for a second chance.

The sound of laughter made me pop up from the bench. Behind me, two women entered the locker room, laughing and chatting, probably not even noticing that I stood there.

When they walked to the other side, I swiped the tears that had fallen from my eyes, grabbed my bag, and walked out of the gym.

scooped up the last spoonful of my açai bowl, then tossed the container into the trash bin behind me. Leaning back in the plastic chair, I figured I'd sit in the smoothie shop a little longer. Normally, there were long lines and no vacant tables in this shop; today, I sat alone.

Glancing out the window into the strip mall shopping lot, I watched people rush from the gym next door to their cars, their calendars probably filled today with friends and family gatherings. I sighed; my only objectives had been to go to the gym and have breakfast. Missions accomplished; now what?

This was an unfamiliar feeling; I couldn't recall the last time I felt lonely. I didn't have many whom I called friends, but I had acquaintances and business associates and my sister. My days were filled with lunches with Windsor and coworkers and clients, and business dinners, with an occasional date sprinkled in. The weekends were just as busy; there was always some industry event to attend. I loved my single life, but over the past few days, it felt like my heart had shifted, making me want more.

Ethan.

I shook my head! No! I wasn't going back down that rabbit hole. I wasn't going to give a single thought to him and Poison Ivy. Grabbing my phone, I swiped through my emails—nothing but spam. Clicking over to my texts—no new messages. But then, scrolling up, I paused on the text I'd received three days ago:

The prayers of the righteous may availeth much, but no amount of prayer will save you now. Vengeance is mine.

Like I'd done every time I read this text, I squinted, trying to make sense of this and the two dozen or so others I'd received. Ethan didn't think this had anything to do with Simon, but again, he was wrong. The timing of Simon's arrest and the first text was too perfect to be a coincidence.

So who was sending these messages? Every time I asked myself that question, there was only one answer: Simon. No one else knew anything about me—not really. He was the only person who was aware of everything I'd done, and again, the timing of that first text . . . it had to be him.

The more I thought about it, the more certain I became. And if I was right about Simon, that meant I was right about his reason, too. He was going to use me to find some way to get free.

My fingers tapped a rhythm on the tin table. I needed to be proactive and stop this before it began. Make a deal with Simon, tell him I'd help him somehow. No doubt I could convince him to keep my name out of any legal discussions.

Bouncing up, I grabbed my gym bag, then marched to my car with purpose. Sliding inside, I dumped my bag into the passenger seat, pulled out my cell, and scrolled to Favorites, where Simon's number was still listed. For a moment, I paused. It was just a little after eight; was it too early?

No! Usually, by this time, Simon had been in his office for a couple of hours.

As the phone rang, I thought about how I would handle this: I'd play on our friendship, tell him I'd been thinking about him, and let him know how much I cared. And then I'd say—

"Journee?"

My planning had taken my mind so far away, I'd almost forgotten I'd made this call. "Simon!" I exclaimed, inserting a little relief into my tone. I wanted him to know how happy I was to hear his voice. "How are you?"

"I'm surprised to hear from you," he said without answering my question.

"Really? Well, I should have called you sooner, but I've been—"

"Why are you calling?" I frowned as he cut me off. "Why are you really calling?" His question sounded like a demand. His tone didn't sound like he was glad to hear from me.

"I . . . just wanted to know how you were doing." I paused; this call didn't feel like the good idea it had seemed just a moment ago. "And I wanted to let you know that—"

Again he interrupted me. "Are you wired?"

"What?"

"Are you taping me?" Paranoia was thick in his tone.

"No. Why in the world would you—"

"Are you working with the feds?" His questions came at me like rapid-fire.

"What? No! Simon, you know me. I would never do anything like that. Why would you even think—"

"I'm really shocked, Journee," Simon said, going off as if I were his enemy. "I can't believe you would do this to me."

I shook my head. "I don't understand."

But he didn't hear those last words. Simon ended the call, leaving me staring at my cell.

What. Just. Happened?

I couldn't wrap my brain around that conversation. I tapped his name on my cell again. He needed to listen to me, to hear everything I had to say so that I wouldn't be caught up in his mess. But then, just as quickly, I ended the call. There was no way I could talk to him, not when he sounded so paranoid.

What was going on? Why did he think I was working with the feds? Why did he think I'd go against him? Was it because he would go against me? There was no way I could leave the conversation this way. I needed a new plan for Simon. No, actually, what I needed was to restart my day and rethink everything. That's what I was going to do. Go back to bed and maybe take a bottle of wine with me.

As I moved to press the ignition button, I frowned. My tire pressure light was on. A tire needed air? How was that even possible? I'd just had my car serviced, and the Bentley service center checked everything.

Hopping out, I checked my front tire, then circled to the back and moaned. "Are you freaking kidding me?" I muttered as I leaned down to examine the wheel—the tire was completely flat, which made no sense. Why hadn't the tire pressure light come on to show the air was low when I was on my way to the gym?

I sighed in exasperation. It was barely eight o'clock, and everything that could go wrong had done so. Moving back to the front seat, I reached for my cell just as it vibrated with an incoming text:

> I wouldn't turn my back on anyone if I were you. You better start worrying because you're about to go down. Vengeance is mine.

"What the—"

"Hello." A voice floated over my shoulder, shocking me, making me jump high in the air.

"Oh my God," I said, pressing my hand against my chest as I turned and faced a guy, one of the gym regulars I recognized.

His eyes narrowed. "Are you all right?"

I took the moment to catch my breath and study him at the same time. He was attractive enough, with broad shoulders and toned biceps. It was the concern in his light brown eyes that I liked best. He carried a little spare tire around his middle, though, and I tried to remember when I'd first seen him here. I'd been coming to this gym for about three years now, but judging from the extra weight around his waist, he'd started about two and a half years after me.

"I'm sorry if I startled you," he said. "I saw you over here and thought, since I'd seen you in the gym a few times, I should say hello. It looks like you're busy, so . . ." He began to back away.

"No, wait." He paused. "I'm sorry. I was just distracted."

"Yeah, I know," he said. "Looks like you were about to make a call."

"Yeah." I glanced down at the text again. "I was . . . because I have a flat tire."

"Whoa!" he said.

I nodded and pointed, and then he followed me to the back of my car. He squatted and checked out the wheel. "Dang, your tire is shot. It's literally resting on its rim, like it doesn't have one drop of air left." He stood, reached toward me, and gave me a lopsided grin. "I'm sorry. I should have done this right off the bat. I'm Quincy."

"I'm . . ."

"Journee," he said before I could finish. "I know." When I tilted my head, he added, "I heard one of the guys at the front desk yell out to you when you were leaving. And I thought, what a great name." I gave him a small smile. He continued, "But I bet you don't want to tell me the origin of your name right now. Did you call roadside service?"

"Not yet." I sighed as I grabbed my wallet for my AAA

card. "And with today being Labor Day, I know I'll be waiting a couple of hours. I'm telling you, this is not my day."

"Well"—he dropped his gym bag at his feet—"I'm not sure about that. I mean, I'm here and I know how to change a tire."

I froze, glanced up at him. "Are you serious?"

"Uh, yeah. And let me tell you a secret. If you ever meet a guy who doesn't know how to change a tire, run the other way."

That made me smile—a little.

"Listen," Quincy said. "I don't normally fool with luxury vehicles, but if you've changed one tire, you should be able to change them all, right?"

Tossing my wallet aside, I pressed my hands together like I was about to pray. "If you can do this for me, I'll pay you whatever you want. Whatever the going rate is for changing a tire on a holiday so early in the morning."

He laughed as if that were a joke. I didn't because I meant it. "It's cool," he said. "How do you pop the trunk on this machine?" Within minutes, he had my skinny spare and the jack on the ground. "Now, the only other thing I'll need is the owner's manual. I just wanna make sure everything is in the same place on a Bentley as it is on the cars us regular folks drive."

This time I did laugh, and I gave him the manual. As he squatted again and got to work, I asked, "Is there anything I can do?"

He paused, and his glance traveled up, then down, my frame, and I was glad I'd worn my matching Actively Black mesh sports bra and leggings. "Nah," he said. "Just stand there and stay beautiful."

I glanced down and away from him, surprised at how his words made me feel—a little bashful, an unfamiliar emotion. I leaned back on the Mustang parked next to me and pretended to be studying my phone. With my eyes lowered, I checked out the man through my lashes. He was what those old women in the church used to say all those years ago—a tall drink of lemonade on a hot summer day. Everything about him was refreshing. His smile. His eyes that sparkled. His high cheekbones. He moved as if he knew what he was doing with that tire, and soon I didn't even pretend to be looking at my cell. I lowered my phone and just stared at the man. The day's heat was rising, and beads of sweat peppered his forehead.

As if he felt my stare, he glanced up, wiped his perspiration with his hand, and grinned. "What?"

"Nothing." And then I gave him back what he'd given to me. "I'm just . . . enjoying the view."

He did exactly what I'd done. He grinned and looked away—bashful. That made me smile. By the time he finished, about thirty minutes later, his tank top was soaked, pasted to his chest.

He reached into his gym bag and grabbed a towel. "You're good now," he said, wiping his hands. "But remember, this is one of those temporary spares. I wouldn't go farther than forty miles, fifty tops, no high speed, and no highways." He wiped his forehead once again. "Really, the best thing for you to do is to go home and park this baby until someone can take care of it tomorrow."

"Okay," I whined. "What a way to spend the holiday, right?"

As he packed the tire and jack back into the trunk, he asked, "You had big plans for today?"

"Not really."

"Well, maybe I can change that. I mean, you said you wanted to pay me, and"—he held up his hands—"I don't want payment, not in that way. But I was thinking, I don't have any plans either. Maybe we can have breakfast together. We can go someplace close so you won't have to drive far. I mean, if you're not too busy."

As I studied him again, he shifted from one foot to the other, and I thought, this guy is shy. That was what did it for me. That and the fact that I welcomed this distraction from Ethan and Poison Ivy. "I'm not busy, but instead of breakfast, maybe we can meet for lunch," I said. "This will give us both a chance to go home and change into something more—"

"Presentable," he finished for me. "Thank you for that, 'cause I'm sure I look a mess."

A mess wouldn't have been the words I would have chosen. He looked rather sexy standing there sweating, with his biceps glistening. But I told him, "Yeah, you probably do want to go home first." I laughed, then got serious. "I really appreciate you, Quincy. You saved my whole day."

"And I appreciate the chance to take you to lunch."

"It's going to be my treat, but I want you to choose. I don't live far from here, so if you can think of something in this general area, I'll be able to drive over."

He grinned. "That'll work. I guess we should exchange numbers."

We chatted for a little while longer before he gave me his number, and I texted him mine. "I wanna lock you in," I said. "Quincy . . ." I paused, waiting for him to give me his last name, but he just stood there. I laughed. "Have you forgotten your last name?"

He blinked as if the question surprised him. "Uh . . . no, no. It's . . ." He glanced down and hesitated for another moment before he added, "Carothers. I'm sorry; I was just distracted because you're so beautiful."

Then, with the key in his hand, he opened the Mustang that I'd been leaning against. "Oh, that's your car."

"Yeah. I was walking over here. That's how I saw you."

I nodded. "Well, it was a good thing for me that you were parked right here, or you might have missed me."

He shook his head. "Nah, Journee. I would never have missed you."

Again his words made me glance away. "Okay." I slipped into my car. "I'll talk to you in a little while."

"You can count on it," he said, and once more, gave me that lopsided grin.

When I slid into my car and locked my door, this time my sigh came with a smile. Something good just might come out of this weekend after all.

6

This was just lunch. With a guy I'd just met. In a parking lot. At the gym.

Yet here I stood in the middle of my closet, with seven different sundresses lined up. Why was I making this much effort for a practical stranger whose only purpose was to take my mind away from Ethan and Ivy? After today, I'd never see him again, except for maybe at the gym.

Tightening my robe, I turned off the light. I had about two hours before I had to make a decision. But right as I had that thought, my cell vibrated with a text: **Really looking forward to lunch. Just wanted to let you know. I'll get back to you with a place. See you around noon.**

For a guy who was meant to be a one-lunch stand, Quincy was certainly making all the right moves. But then my smile dissolved, because right above his text was the one that had shaken me earlier: **I wouldn't turn my back on anyone if I were you. You better start worrying because you're about to go down. Vengeance is mine.**

This text had come in right after that strange call with Simon. Could he really be the one sending me those messages? No, with the way Simon reacted on the phone, he wasn't the culprit. If he was about to use me as a get-out-of-jail-free card, he wouldn't have acted as if he thought I was the one who was the enemy.

Strolling into the living room, I plopped onto the sofa, laid my head back, and considered, if not Simon, then who? Once again, I scrolled through all the strange texts. All threats, all scriptures. Not a single mention of money. So it wasn't black-mail.

"Then what?" I whispered as I walked onto the balcony. I wasn't a very good Nancy Drew, because if it wasn't Simon, I didn't have a single idea of who could be doing this. If it wasn't professional, then I was really at a loss.

But I shook my head. This had to be professional. My business was the only reason why someone would come after me. Focusing on real estate at least narrowed down the group of who this could be. There were the fifteen brokers who worked with Simon while I was there, and now I had six brokers working with me. There was Tasha, my assistant, and then the network of real estate agents, other brokers, along with the agents and officers at the banks and finance companies who funded my clients.

That was a very long list, but the fact remained that no one knew what Simon and I had been doing. I certainly hadn't discussed our last scheme with anyone. And Simon wouldn't have either. Like me, there were few whom he trusted . . . except . . .

My thoughts stopped and I stood straight up. "Oh my God," I whispered, stumbling over to the chair. Suddenly, it was obvious. "Vivian."

Could it be? Could my childhood best friend, former college roommate, the woman who I really owed the start of my real estate career to, be behind all of this? It has to be her, I thought as better times between us came to my mind. None of this would be happening—the good or the bad—if it weren't for Vivian:

I stood in front of the coffee machine listening to the percolating, grateful that I worked for one of the country's largest grocery retailers. Because if anyone charged me for each cup I had every day, I'd have to pay half of my meager midlevel-accountant wages for my hourly caffeine fix. At least this would be my last cup of the day.

"Hey, girl." Vivian bounced into the break room. She paused, frowning. "Isn't it a little late for coffee?"

I glanced at my best friend, dressed in a tailored money-green pantsuit that looked new. "You look nice."

"Thanks," she said as she grabbed a bottle of water from the refrigerator, then bounced into a chair at one of the small tables. "So, what's going on with you today?" she asked, sounding like she'd had caffeine shot straight into her arm just moments before.

I moaned before I took a sip of coffee, then slumped into the chair beside her. "Today is like yesterday, which was like the day before and the month before and the year before." With a sigh, I slid lower in my chair. "Remember how eager I was to join this company?"

"My goodness, you sound like you want to lay your head down on this table and cry."

There was a chuckle in her tone; so much for my best friend sympathizing with me.

She said, "Oh, come on, Journee. You weren't alone in your ex-citement. I was excited, too, although I didn't go around quoting the accounting department's slogan like you did." And then she raised her voice an octave, which I guessed was meant to mimic me: "'The grocery business is all about pennies, and we need a few brilliant accountants to make our pennies count.'" She laughed. "You were cute, though."

I rolled my eyes, and that set her off even more. She doubled over with laughter.

I ignored her chuckles. "When they recruited me, I didn't know they literally meant I'd be counting pennies. I'm telling you, Viv, if I have to look at another ledger, I'm going to beat myself over the head with a bag of nickels."

Vivian laughed so hard, she had to wipe the tears from her eyes.

"I hate to say it, girl, but I've been telling you since high school that you didn't want to be an accountant."

If I had one of those pennies for every time Vivian had given me that advice, I'd have homes in Paris, Dubai, and the Maldives. But I'd been absolutely sure, when I'd chosen accounting as my major at the University of Texas at Austin's McCombs School of Business, that I was the smarter one. First, I was a wiz with numbers. I had a photographic memory when it came to anything numeric, and so accounting seemed the best way to utilize my skills. And second, every company, no matter their size or profitability, needed an accountant. I'd be forever employed.

Vivian disagreed, though, and told me time and again that I was making the mistake of my life.

"We only get one shot at this college degree, and we need to be majoring in money," she said. "Do you know how much marketing majors earn after four years at this place? It's not even a consideration for me. I'm all about the Benjamins."

Vivian was so wrong. Getting a college degree wasn't just about the money; it was about being employable. Well, it turned out Vivian was wrong until she proved just how right she was. We'd started here, both in entry-level positions, but while I was still pushing pencils and paper and earning just enough not to qualify for food stamps, Vivian had already risen to a junior executive position who went on photo shoots, attended community meetings, and escorted celebrity spokespeople around the city. She was pivotal in designing the customer cash-back loyalty program, which earned her special recognition and a $1,000 bonus. She was making moves while I was still eating ramen noodles like I had when we were starving college students. It was fine then; struggling through college was a rite of passage. But now? All I had to show for my time here was that I was overworked, underwhelmed, and unfulfilled.

Finally, I told Vivian, "You're right; I should have listened to you."

Vivian nodded. "You're hardheaded; you don't listen to anyone. Well, maybe you'll listen to me now." Lowering her voice, she said, "I got something I wanna show you." She glanced over her shoulder as if she was on some kind of clandestine mission, then reached into her pocket. "Take a look at this."

I frowned when she handed the paper to me. "A check? What is—" Before I finished, my eyes zoomed in on the four zeros that followed the number nine. Scanning as fast as I could, I took in all the information: pay to the order of Vivian Wallace, dated today. In the top corner was the name ClearWater Mortgage, and at the bottom, a signature was scribbled that I couldn't decipher. "Ninety thousand dollars?" I squeaked out, and glanced up at Vivian. "Is this real?"

She tossed her blond weave over her shoulders. "Girl, please," she said. "It's as real as your hatred of your job."

"Where did you get that kind of money?" I asked. "Another bonus?"

She leaned back as if she couldn't believe I'd just asked that. "Hell no! If you think I got that kinda money here, you need to lay off that caffeine," she said, and then flashed a smile. "This is a commission check."

I gave her a long side-eye as all kinds of thoughts of what "commission" really meant rolled through my mind.

Before I could ask, she told me, "A commission for a major real estate deal closing."

"Real estate?" I asked, as if I didn't understand the meaning of those words.

"Yeah, I've got a little gig on the side with my uncle Simon. You remember him? My uncle who used to take us roller-skating." She didn't pause to see whether I remembered him; she just kept on, telling me about having been a mortgage broker at her uncle's firm for the past six months.

"And you didn't tell me?"

"Journee, who can tell you anything? You're always so laser-focused on doing your thing your way. To hell with what anyone else has to say." She shrugged. "So, instead of talking to you about it, I figured you'd only hear if you could see it with your own eyes. And you know what? This wasn't even my first check."

"This is unbelievable." I stared at the check until Vivian took it away from me. "So is this why you haven't been hanging out on the weekends."

"Yeah, girl. I've been making this money. I had to get my license, but that's done now. I'm officially a junior broker with Uncle Simon, and this was my first check now that I'm licensed."

"That's junior money?" I shook my head, still grappling with everything Vivian had told me. "So what the hell is senior money?"

She laughed. "I'll let you know, because I plan to be making it soon." The way her eyes danced, I had no doubt about that.

I sat there just staring and thinking. Vivian had always been a hustler. All throughout college she'd had some kind of gig. She'd sold diet teas and gourmet coffee. And I could never forget when she'd been a representative for that shapewear company and had all the Black girls on campus walking around looking snatched.

"I can't believe you're making that kind of money, and only part-time."

"And that's exactly why I'm resigning today."

"Resigning? I thought you liked it here. They've treated you so well."

"Girl, please." She crossed her arms. "I never got it twisted; this is just a job. And I'm as loyal to these people as they would be to me if one of their daughters came in here and wanted my position. Well, if any of their daughters wants a job, she can have mine, 'cause starting Monday . . ." She stopped, patted her pocket, and sang, "It's all about the Benjamins, baby . . ." She stood and strutted out as she hummed Puff Daddy's song.

For a moment, I sat there frozen in my shock, but then I jumped up, ran after Vivian, and dragged her back into the break room. "Ask your uncle if he needs another junior broker."

"So you're finally going to listen to me?"

"I want in, Vivian," I said, hoping that was enough to answer her question. "What do I need to do?"

Vivian laughed. "You've been my girl from the eighth grade. You know I've got you! We'll always have each other's back."

OVER THE NEXT months, I kept my day job as my best friend kept her word and got me in with her uncle. She helped me register for my classes for the broker's test, and once I passed, Vivian became my cheerleader, encouraging me to leave my job.

It had taken longer than I would have liked before I followed her lead; I wanted to have a few broker's checks in my bank account before resigning from the job I hated. From my first deal, I received six referrals and built out from there. I had clients waiting in line, and once I banked a $50,000 check, that was it. Eleven months after Vivian showed me that check, I gave deuces to the corporate world and embraced entrepreneurship as if it were my new lover.

Vivian and I had a good start together at ClearWater Mortgage. When I worked the business part-time, I often brought Vivian in to work with me on my cases. She handled the things I couldn't while I was on my nine-to-five: gathering all the paperwork, meeting with clients and people at the banks and finance companies. She was a blessing, and I blessed her with 25 percent of my commissions. Between her own clients and mine, Vivian was making quite a bit of money.

I didn't mind sharing; I wouldn't have been in my position without my best friend. And even with what I gave her, I was building up a clientele and my bank account.

But when I came on full-time, I didn't need Vivian's assistance. Being free to work my business full-time, I went all in, working my own referrals, attending as many networking events as I could, and building an impressive list of clients and resources.

Within seven months of joining ClearWater full-time, not only had I surpassed Vivian in terms of number of clients and earnings, but I'd impressed Simon so much that he began to bring me in on some of what he called his VIP projects, something he hadn't done too often with his niece.

Her uncle's obvious professional affinity for me had been enough to strain our relationship, but our friendship really hit the fan when Simon fired Vivian for complaining to her boyfriend about the homeless idea she had. She'd told me more than once that Simon wasn't compensating her sufficiently for helping him bring hundreds of thousands of dollars into his firm.

I sympathized but told her to be patient; I was sure Simon would recognize her in some way. Vivian's boyfriend, however, had a different approach after hearing her grievances—without conferring with Vivian, he'd confronted Simon at a company Christmas party. That hadn't gone well. The boyfriend was out with Vivian, and Vivian was out at ClearWater.

Those two weren't the only relationships severed at that time. Vivian stopped speaking to me because I wouldn't quit when Simon fired her. Like I said, I was sympathetic, but not stupid. I was earning serious money; why would I give it up because she'd had a lapse in judgment?

Although I saw Vivian at industry events, we hadn't said anything beyond hello to each other in six years. But even with this history, I couldn't imagine Vivian sending me those texts.

Grabbing my phone, I scrolled to the last message: **I wouldn't** turn my back on anyone if I were you. You better start worrying because you're about to go down. Vengeance is mine.

When Vivian had been fired, she'd been enraged . . . angry enough to want . . . vengeance?

Why was I sitting here asking myself these questions when I could go to the source? Jumping up, I rushed to the balcony door, but just before I stepped back into the living room, my cell vibrated in my hand: **Hey beautiful. What about meeting at the breakfast klub at about 12:30?**

I smiled. While I really wanted to know who'd been sending me those texts, that would have to wait.

t was like a parade that started at the front door and snaked along the side of the restaurant, down the block, and around the back. Was I supposed to stand in that line?

Slowly, I rolled my car around the corner and spotted Quincy standing under a tree, exactly where he'd texted and told me he'd be waiting. I eased my car to a stop and rolled down my window. "Really?"

He bent over, leaned his arms against my car. His face was only inches from mine when he said, "What?"

I inhaled and was pleased. His cologne was Creed—Aventus, if I had to bet on it. This man cleaned up well. I said, "I know you don't expect me to get out of this air-conditioned car and wait in that line." Once again, I took in the scores of people leaning against the George Floyd mural painted on the side of the building. "This is exactly why I've never eaten here."

He pressed his hand against his chest, then staggered backward like that guy in those reruns of that old show *Sanford and Son*. I rolled my eyes but chuckled as Quincy gasped. After his pretend heart attack was over, he held out his palm. "Come on, give it to me."

"What?"

"Your Black card, because it is against the Black law to be a Black Houstonian and have never eaten at the breakfast klub."

"Nope, you cannot have my card, and nope, I'm not standing in that line no matter what I've heard about all that good food inside there."

He laughed. "No, come on. Park right here," he said, point-ing to the spot under the tree that I was sure wasn't really a park-ing space. "Trust me."

I smirked. There were few in this world I trusted, and I cer-tainly wouldn't normally trust a man I'd known for three hours. But for a one-and-done lunch date, I'd do what he asked.

Once I stepped out of my car, Quincy placed his hand on the small of my back and led me through the lot, but as I turned left to go to the end of the line, he took my hand.

"This way," he said as he moved us toward the front door.

"Uh . . . Quincy," I began, having to double-step to keep up with his pace. "I'm not about to jump a line and get in between Black people and their chicken and waffles on Labor Day."

He laughed but still gently pulled me along. At the front door, a young Black man who looked to be in his thirties or for-ties (which meant he was probably in his fifties) stood greeting guests as, two by two or three by three, parties were led into the restaurant. When the guy spotted Quincy, he held out his arms. "Q, my man," he said.

"What's up, Marcus?" Quincy said as the two bumped fists.

"Just you," the bearded man said. He glanced inside. "Looks like you got here right on time. Your usual table is just being cleared off now."

"Great," Quincy said. "Looking forward to introducing my lovely date to your award-winning food."

"Ah, welcome." Marcus grinned at me, bowed a little, then held the door open for us. I didn't look back. I wasn't trying to see the side glances and the rolling eyes I was sure were on full display in that long line.

The moment we stepped inside, a hostess greeted us, her voice raised just a little over the din that filled up this space. "Hey, Quincy." She grabbed two menus from the hostess stand, then led us to a wooden table near the corner by the floor-to-ceiling windows.

"Your waitress will be right with you." She handed us the menus. "Can I take your drink orders?"

"I'll have my usual orange juice," Quincy said, then motioned to me.

"Just coffee," I replied. "No cream, no sugar."

When she walked away, I turned to a grinning Quincy. "You like your coffee straight, with no chaser. Impressive."

"All black," I said. "Just like me."

He nodded. "You left out the beauty part. Black and beautiful."

Now I was the one grinning, and I turned away for a moment, taking in the sight of the packed restaurant. "So," I began, "you got it like that where you can just walk in while seven thousand people wait outside?" I laughed, but then stopped when Quincy's wide smile faded.

A shadow crossed his face. "Nah, actually, it's not that big a deal. I met Marcus a few years back when . . . I came into a little bit of money and wanted to do some investing. He's the owner and was looking to expand the restaurant, and it was a perfect partnership."

"Investing?" I said.

Quincy let that word hang in the air for few seconds, then said, "You wanna check out the menu?"

I nodded and scanned it as if I were really studying the choices. But how was I going to come here for the first time and not order the chicken and waffles? As the people at the table behind us broke out into laughter, I kept the menu up to my face and pretended my eyes were lowered.

What a difference a shower—and some nice clothes—made. Nothing was more attractive to me than a man who was well put together, and everything from his gray linen pants and matching short-sleeved shirt to his cologne gave me a measure of this man. To this point, I'd seen him only in passing, wearing tanks and gym shorts, and always sweaty. That gave me one impression. But now that I'd had a sniff of that $300 fragrance and watched him waltz into one of the busiest restaurants in Houston without having to wait, my sense of him had altered. Quincy was a man of means.

Even though Quincy raised his head and set aside his menu, I kept my eyes lowered until the waitress approached our table. Then I ordered the chicken and waffles, while Quincy chose the fish and grits.

When she stepped away, Quincy's smile still hadn't returned. So once again, I surveyed the restaurant. It had such a homey feel with the lush plants all around and the paintings by Black artists lining the walls. "This is nice," I said when the waitress returned, setting my coffee and Quincy's juice on the table.

"It is," he said. "What makes this place so great is beyond the food. Marcus has made this feel like home. He loves his customers, and every chance he gets, you'll find him laughing and chatting it up with them. And don't let him have a little time, because he'll break out the dominoes."

"That's so cool."

"I love coming here; there were times when this place was my refuge." I tilted my head, waiting for Quincy to explain, but then he said, "So, should we get all the awkward stuff out of the way?"

"What do you mean?"

"You know, the standard questions, like where do you live, what do you do for a living." He chuckled, and I was glad to see that smile back. "I call them the first-date interview questions."

First date. I laughed. "Well, I don't think that's awkward. I mean, without interviewing, how would you get to know anyone?"

"True." He nodded. "And I'd love to know about you. So . . ."

"I guess that means I go first." I shrugged, even though I was curious about that darkness that had crossed his face moments ago. "What do you want to know?"

"Anything. Everything." His smile was gone, and his stare was intense. Made me glance away. He said, "But let's start with the basics. I'm curious about what you do, 'cause I gotta say, your car—that's a statement."

I waved my hand. "Come on, now. This is Texas, and you know how we do. People front all the time."

"True, but I have a feeling that's not you. So, what are you? An actor, a model . . ."

I laughed. "Oh, the charm, Quincy."

"What?" He held up his hands like he was saying he was innocent. "I'm not lying. You could be either, and those are the only people I know who ride around in two-hundred-thousand-dollar cars."

"Well, I'm about to blow up everything you think you've ever known about Bentley owners, because"—I paused, letting him think something huge was coming—"I'm a mortgage broker. I have my own company."

He smiled as if he wasn't disappointed at all. "Impressive. Have you always worked for yourself?"

Whoa. That question made me shift in my seat. This was the first time since Simon's arrest that his company had the potential to come up in my conversation. I hedged. "I used to work for one of the bigger firms, but," I added quickly, "I've been on my own for three years."

"Three years? I heard that when an entrepreneur makes it past their second anniversary, that's considered success."

"I'm working hard, climbing to the top, and doing it while trying to help people get the right funding for their homes."

"So, where did you work before you started your business?"

I shook my head, waved my hand. "I doubt if you've ever heard of the company."

He shrugged. "Try me. I may just be a teacher, but——"

I leaned toward Quincy. "You're a teacher? Oh my God. I love teachers."

He laughed. "What a way to change the subject."

"No, I mean it." I reached across the table and squeezed his arm. "A teacher is why I've achieved so much. He literally saved my life when I didn't have a lot of confidence because I'd been homeless!"

His eyes widened at my words and my seriousness. But at first he didn't say anything as I pulled my hand away from him.

Quincy waited a few beats before he lowered his voice and said, "It feels like there's a story there. And I'm here to listen to however much or little you want to share."

I swallowed, but before I could say a word, his cell phone vibrated. He glanced at the screen and shook his head. "I hate to do this, Journee, but I have to take this call."

He had no idea how much relief his words gave me. I waved my hand. "Of course," I said. He pushed back his chair and had his phone pressed to his ear before he strolled out of the restaurant. I watched until I couldn't see him anymore.

Whew! My words had just tumbled out. My background wasn't a secret, but was this where I wanted to start with a man who was little more than a stranger? Did I really want to tell Quincy how my mom, my sister, and I became homeless after my father died and that began a horrible downward spiral?

That was a time in my life that I tried so hard to forget, but the memories were always there. Maybe it was because some of those days I wanted to remember. Because in the midst of our homelessness, sometimes there was joy . . .

"Come on, baby girl. Put that bag on your shoulder; it will be easier for you to carry."

Mama thought I was struggling because the bag with our clothes was too heavy. But that wasn't it. I wanted to figure out the name on this building. "La . . . La . . ." No matter how hard I tried to sound it out, I couldn't.

"La Quinta," Mama said as she carried a wiggling Windsor in her arms. "That's a Spanish word."

"Say it again, Mama."

"La Quin-ta."

The syllables rolled off her tongue, sounding like a song. I learned a lot in school, but I learned so much more from my mama. She always said I was so smart, but Mama was the one. She was the smartest woman on earth!

"La Quin-ta," I repeated.

Mama stopped walking. Her eyes were filled with surprise; she always looked at me that way. "My goodness, Journee. You said that perfectly."

I grinned; all I ever wanted to do was please Mama.

"Okay, baby girl. Let's get in there."

From the outside, this two-story building already looked great, but inside, it was even better. This was nothing like the homeless shelter where we'd been for the past three days. There, we had to share a big room with hundreds and hundreds and hundreds of people. And the whole time, my stomach growled because they never had enough food.

But now we were staying in our own room in a hotel because Pastor Franklin had given Mama something—she said it was a voucher—and we would be here a whole month.

*When Mama opened the door and we rushed in, the first thing
I did was run to the bed. But then I stopped and looked at Mama.*

She laughed. "Yes, you can jump on it."

*I hopped right on up there and squealed as I jumped, trying to go
high so that I could touch the sky.*

THE ENDS OF my lips twitched into a smile as I remembered
that time. That had been the best month. We had one warm
bed, which I liked 'cause it was more comfortable than sleeping on the cracked plastic seats in Mama's car and the lumpy
mattresses in the shelter. Then, in the morning, I took showers
with lots of water, and for the whole month I went to school
every day (which was the best) and none of the kids taunted
me with their stupid songs: *Smelly little poor girl, the stinkiest one in
the whole world . . .*

*When I returned to the hotel after school, we had plenty to eat, and
afterward, Mama sat down at the desk in the room with me. While
she bounced Windsor on her lap, we did my homework together.*

*"I'm so proud of you, Journee," she told me when I finished doing
my math timetables.*

*"You are the smartest little girl," she kept saying after I read her
the paragraph I'd written with the school's librarian about Mary
McLeod Bethune.*

*And when I came back to the motel one day and named all the
planets, Mama exclaimed, "I can't wait to see what you're going to
be when you grow up."*

"I'm going to be like you, Mama."

*"Oh, no," she said, shaking her head. "You're going to be much
better than me. And do you know how I know?" I shook my head
and she continued, "You got skipped a grade. Remember what I told
you that meant?"*

"That I knew all the second-grade work already because I was special."

"Yes!" Mama's smile was always so bright whenever we talked about this. "Your teachers say you're special and you're gifted."

I didn't really know what "special" and "gifted" meant, but if it made Mama smile and laugh like this (because she was hardly ever happy), I wanted to be special and gifted for a long time so that Mama would laugh for the rest of her life.

"And that's why you went straight to the third grade." Mama pulled me into her arms and hugged me and Windsor. "My two princesses are going to be something special when they grow up."

IT WAS THE best time ever, except for one thing—as the days passed, Mama didn't seem to have any happy times; she got sadder and sadder, and soon all she did was cry. I couldn't figure out why when we had everything we wanted.

"Why are you crying, Mama?" I kept asking her.

"I'm not really crying," she said. "I'm as happy as you are. And, Journee, I want you to know that Mama wants you to always be happy. No matter where you are, no matter what is going on in your life, I will do whatever I have to do to make sure you're safe and happy."

AT THE TIME, I didn't understand what her words meant. Because I was happy when I was with her, whether we were in her car, at the shelter, or in the motel. But even though I tried to tell her that, Mama just cried and cried.

What didn't make sense then soon became clear. Because at the end of the best month, my mother blew up my entire life.

"So, where were we?"

I glanced up in shock. Quincy was sitting across from me.

How deep in my thoughts had I been that I hadn't even heard him come back?

He said, "I'm really sorry I had to take that call, but now"—he tapped his phone, and even from across the table I could see the screen fade to black—"all my attention is on you. So . . ." He leaned toward me. There was so much kindness in his eyes, in his manner and his words. "You were saying you love teachers."

Those weren't my last words; I was sure he remembered that I'd mentioned I'd been homeless. But he was too much of a gentleman to ask me about that situation. He was giving me a way to return to this conversation wherever I wanted to begin. I said, "I really do love teachers. Every teacher I've ever had believed in me. But it was in high school when Mr. Murphy not only encouraged but challenged me. No excuses, ever, was what I learned from him. He said I was the smartest in the class and he wouldn't allow me to use anything as justification for not being at the top all the time." I paused and added, "Not even the days I'd been homeless when I was a child."

Quincy nodded slowly. "Homeless," he repeated, but there was no judgment in his tone, just a little surprise. He said, "I'm trying to reconcile that car out there with you being homeless."

"It's true. We lived in the streets for only about a year, but when I look back on my childhood, that time is what I remember most." I paused. "But even though I wouldn't mind telling you about it, would it be okay if we didn't talk about this today? I mean, there are parts of my life that make me sad, but in the end it was decent. I was taken off the streets by an older woman who really gave me a chance. And look at me . . ." I paused. "Mrs. Hunter, God rest her soul, would be pleased; I had a happy ending," I said, though even I heard the sorrow in my tone. "And not everyone can say that."

As if on cue, the waitress appeared, setting our plates in front of us. Neither Quincy nor I made a move to pick up our forks. Instead, he reached for my hand. "Would you mind if I blessed the food?"

Now, I'd been on plenty of dates since my breakup with Ethan all those years ago, but Ethan had been the only man who always said grace. And now there was Quincy. I answered his question by taking his hand into mine, and we bowed our heads. When he thanked God for our food and new friendships, the sadness I'd been feeling lifted.

"Amen," I said, then squeezed his hand. "Thank you."

"For what?"

"For listening to the part I could handle today and not being upset that I didn't want to talk about it too much."

Quincy tightened his grip on my hand as if he didn't plan to let me go. "I get it, but I want you to know that even though we just met, you can trust me. You'll always be able to trust me," he said, as if he had high expectations that our time together would go beyond this lunch. "So whenever you want to talk, I'm here. Because I want to know everything about you."

I nodded; his sincerity was in his countenance. It was palpable.

Finally, he released me, and when he picked up his fork, he said, "So . . . do you want to know *anything* about me?"

I laughed. "Of course. I want to know everything."

"I'm just asking because my life . . . well, nothing propelled me to end up in a Bentley."

"Would you stop?" I playfully punched his arm. "I may have a Bentley, but you're an investor," I said, motioning around the restaurant. "I didn't know HISD was paying like that."

"Oh, I'm not part of Houston's school district. I teach at KIPP Sharpstown, which is a charter school."

"But still . . ." I shook my head, then paused as I savored my first bite of that waffle.

"Well, the money I have . . . it came to me through a situation that was out of my control. I inherited it and invested wisely," he said.

"Clearly," I said, now cutting into some of the best chicken I'd ever tasted. "So, do you invest in stocks, bonds, crypto?"

"Stocks, mutual funds, or EFTs," he said, shaking his head. "A little real estate and then small businesses like this. But my financial adviser handles most of it. I stick with what I know: I teach." He went on to tell me that a teacher had inspired him, too: his fifth-grade teacher, who came to school every day in a shirt and tie. "He told me that if I looked good, I'd feel good, and if I felt good, I'd do good."

"I love that," I said. "My fifth-grade teacher inspired me as well. Mrs. Watson said, 'Good, better, best, never let them rest. Until your good is better and your better is best.' She wrote that on the chalkboard every morning as if each day it were a new idea." I shook my head. "Teachers have always made a difference in my life."

He nodded. "Sometimes, though, I think, teachers may have too great an impact on their students."

"That's impossible."

"Oh, yeah?" He put down his fork, and a twinkle brightened his eyes. "You know the story of Jack and the Beanstalk?"

"Of course."

"Well, I read that story in class one year, and about a week later, when I took the kids out for recess, I was missing a student. I hurried back to the classroom and found Myles pouring beans down the sink in the back of the room 'cause he was trying to grow a beanstalk to escape from class."

"No!" I exclaimed. "You're kidding."

"I'm not," he said, and then he kept on entertaining me with what he called Stories from the Hood. I laughed so hard, my thoughts far away from where we'd started this conversation.

"And then there's Danny," he said, beginning his fourth story. "I couldn't get him to buckle down, so one day I told him he had to stay in the classroom through lunch and recess until he finished his work.

"That little seven-year-old stood up, grabbed his backpack, and said, 'I didn't sign up for this. School is my parents' idea. I'm not taking it anymore.' And he marched right out of the classroom."

"Oh my goodness." This time, I had to hold my belly, I laughed so hard, imagining a little boy with a backpack bigger than he was, stomping away.

"Danny was serious. But just as he stepped out of the classroom, he ran straight into the principal, who was doing his morning walk through the halls."

Then Quincy shifted and told me about the gifts he'd received over the years: a key chain made out of a seashell that a little boy found on a trip to Galveston, the little girl who picked flowers from her parents' garden and gave him a new bundle every Monday so that he'd have a beautiful week. "Working with kids is amazing," Quincy said. "And knowing that I'm impacting our country's future is the greatest blessing to me."

The waitress had long ago cleared our table when Marcus came over. "Q, you know you're my boy, but—"

Quincy raised his hands. "My bad. I didn't mean to hold the table so long; I just got caught up."

"I understand." Marcus glanced at me with a smile. "I hope you enjoyed the breakfast klub."

"I did," I said to Marcus, but then my glance turned to Quincy. "I really did."

Quincy and Marcus did one of those brother-to-brother embraces, and then Quincy led me from the restaurant. As we walked toward my car without saying a word, my mind churned. What could I say to extend this *first date*, because I didn't want my time with Quincy to end?

Yes, he was a man who rescued damsels in distress, and yes, he had captured my heart being a teacher. But the best thing— I just enjoyed being with him. He made me laugh (which was number one on my Bae Credentials list). He had a great career that he loved. (Also on my list.) He seemed grounded and normal . . . and reminded me a lot of Ethan.

Once we got to my car, Quincy and I leaned against it and, standing side by side, we laughed as he continued his stories about the kids he loved. We were there for more than thirty minutes before I said, "I have to get out of here because I have used every muscle in my body. I have never laughed so much."

"You want to know the best part for me?" He didn't give me room to answer. "I loved seeing you laugh."

Inside, I sighed. "I really enjoyed myself, Quincy."

"So"—he leaned a little closer to me—"does this mean I passed your test?"

I frowned. "What test?"

"Oh, I'm sure after I changed your tire, you went home and did that thing that women do. You went on the internet, checked my social media, checked all my photos, sent my picture to the FBI, checked my credit score and my tax returns . . ."

I laughed again. "Well, I didn't do any of that because my plan was to have lunch with you as a thank-you for being such a great tire-changer and that's it. There was no need for me to know any more."

"Ah. One and done."

I leaned back and away from him. "What you know about that?"

He held up his hands. "I plead the Fifth." He paused. "So one and done was your plan of action before," he said. "What's your game plan now?"

I kept my eyes on Quincy as I opened my door, slid in, and then locked myself inside. His eyes filled with surprise, and then he frowned as I turned on the ignition. But his expression changed to one of expectation as I rolled down my window. "My plan now is to go home, and while I don't have time for social media, I'll start with your credit score," I kidded.

He grinned, and I stepped on the gas, screeching the tires a little, then pulled back. Once I slowed down, I watched Quincy watch me through my rearview mirror. Just looking at him made me smile, and I thought, I didn't need to check out anything. I already liked this guy. And then a second thought came to me: Ethan and Poison Ivy who?

8

The moment I stepped into my condo, my cell phone vibrated. I glanced at the screen and then answered. "Hey," I said, surprise in my tone. "I didn't expect to hear from you so soon."

"Really? I would've called sooner, but I wanted to give you time to get home."

"Well, your timing is perfect. I just stepped inside. So what's up?"

"I wanted to hear your voice."

I was so glad this wasn't a video call, because I certainly didn't want Quincy to see me grinning and giddy like a tween. "So"—I kicked off my shoes, then settled onto my sofa—"now that you've heard my voice . . ."

"I know," he said with a sigh. "I want more. I need more. I certainly hope there's no limit to how often I can call you, because I plan on blowing up your phone."

This guy . . . his lines . . . this was a difference between Quincy and Ethan. My ex wasn't into all the things that made women swoon. He stated his case—just the facts, just like a lawyer. But Quincy—I'd met this guy three minutes ago, and he was talking like he was all in. I realized this was just his thing; obviously, words were his love language. So while I wasn't taking him seriously, there was no reason why I couldn't enjoy the flattery and the attention for what it was and for the moment. "But this time"—Quincy broke through my thoughts—"I am calling for a reason besides just hearing you. I wanted to make sure you got home safely because, you know, you and tires . . ."

I laughed. "Well, I'm safe. Thank you for calling and caring."

"Always," he said. "So what are your plans for the rest of the day?"

Leaning back, I snuggled into the sofa's pillows. "I have a big week coming up. A huge contract at work, so today, I'm just gonna chill."

"If I'd known that, I would have monopolized more of your time."

"We were kicked out of the restaurant, remember?"

Together we laughed and kept on talking and laughing. We covered the gamut of important world issues, like the Academy Awards slap that was heard (and seen) around the world. Our conversation was easy, just like it had been at the restaurant. By the time I hung up an hour later, my cheeks ached from smiling.

Tucking my legs underneath me, I set my phone in my lap and settled into the lotus position. I closed my eyes and rested my head against the back of the sofa, feeling so satisfied, so complete, as if I'd just lived through a few hours of the most perfect day. I breathed deeply and after just minutes, the exhaustion from the past few sleepless nights pulled me in, and I drifted away on the memories. Quincy's face, with that lopsided grin, filled my dreams.

But then I felt myself falling, falling, falling deeper into sleep, until I crashed into the darkness. I knew where this was taking me, and I fought hard to open my eyes. But the darkness dragged me in, and I floated back in time to a different day, one that I tried to keep buried but had been conjured up by our conversation today . . .

As I stood in the shower, Mama sat on the toilet and washed Windsor with the water in the sink. Even though I couldn't see her from behind the shower curtain, I heard Mama's cries. Today, though, I didn't ask what was wrong. I was sad, too. This was leaving day; we wouldn't be sleeping in this bed another night.

I wished we could stay forever, but the first night we were here, Mama told me it was only for a month. Now I didn't know if we were going to another shelter or if we were going to sleep in the car. Not that it mattered. No matter where we were, Mama made everything all right.

After I dried myself off, I went back into the room and got dressed, staying real quiet so Mama wouldn't get any more upset. She put on Windsor's clothes, then her own, before she grabbed her purse and lifted Windsor. I hoisted the bag with all our clothes onto my shoulder and followed Mama out of the room. The walk to Mama's car felt so different from the day when we arrived. When she opened the back door to strap Windsor inside, I walked around to the other side to get in the back with my baby sister like I always did, but Mama stopped me.

"Baby girl," she said, "why don't you ride in the front with me."

My eyes got big. Even though we had to leave the hotel, today was gonna be a good day if I could ride up front with Mama. She never let me do that; she said that was for big girls and I had to wait until I was ten. Even though I had three more years, I'd been counting the days, but I didn't have to count anymore.

As we backed out of the parking lot, I asked Mama, "Am I going to school today?"

She shook her head, and now, even though I was sitting in the front seat, I wanted to cry. It wasn't because of school; it was because it felt like I could almost touch Mama's sadness. "You're not going to school today, baby. Maybe . . . maybe tomorrow."

"It's okay." I wanted to reassure her. I hadn't missed any days

the whole time we were here in the hotel. And whenever I did, the teachers always said that I was really smart and could always catch up. I asked, "Where are we going now?"

She paused for a moment. "I have to . . . I need to . . . I want to give Pastor Franklin a letter. He's waiting for it, so we have to . . . go to the church."

Well, if I couldn't go to school, I'd take church. Wheeler Village Baptist Church was my second-favorite place, and Mama took us every Sunday, even when we were sleeping in the car. It was a huge church, and at the end of every service, Mama walked down that long aisle to the altar, got on her knees, and cried. The first time Mama did that, I was so scared. But Pastor Franklin explained to me that my mother was just crying out to the Lord.

Pastor Franklin and his wife and many other ladies, like Mrs. Hunter, who gave me peppermints every Sunday, would go down to the altar with Mama and sit with her until she was all cried out. Then, after the service, the Franklins took us to his office and gave us a shopping bag full of food.

But what I liked best about Pastor Franklin was that whenever we got ready to leave the church, he hugged me, and that always reminded me of my daddy.

As we drove, Mama began to sob like she did on Sundays, and now I was beginning to get scared 'cause it was only Thursday. At every stoplight, Mama leaned over and hugged me, but by the time we got to the church, her tears were all gone.

When we pulled in, the church's parking lot was empty except for Pastor Franklin's Escalade, and Mama parked her Honda right next to it. She turned off the ignition and then just sat there looking out the window.

Mama didn't move for so long, I called out to her.

She didn't say a word, didn't look at me. Just reached for her purse and pulled out an envelope. She stared at the front of it for a moment before she finally turned to me. There was still water in her eyes, but the tears stayed inside. "Journee." She said my name so softly, and she stayed quiet for a few seconds more. Then, "I want you to go inside and give this letter to Pastor Franklin."

I took the letter from her but I didn't move. It was like my legs didn't want to go. Mama leaned over and kissed my cheek a dozen times. Her voice cracked when she said, "Okay, go on, now."

Something was wrong—it felt like she was saying good-bye.

"Mama?"

She blinked real fast. "Yeah, baby."

"Can you go inside with me?"

"I . . . can't." Her words were getting stuck in her throat. "Your little sister" was all she added.

I looked into the back seat. Windsor was sleeping the way she always did whenever we got in the car and drove around. I wanted to wake her up, but Mama had explained that little girls needed lots of sleep. When I turned back to Mama, she nodded. "Go on," she whispered. "What's in that envelope is really important."

Oh! I thought, feeling new hope. Maybe this was something that would give us another voucher for another hotel. But still, I couldn't move.

Mama's tears were back. "Go on, Journee. Pastor Franklin is waiting."

I jumped out of the car and ran as fast as I could. The side door was really heavy, but I got it open and dashed inside, going straight to Pastor Franklin's office. His door was open, but I knocked the way Mama had taught me.

"Pastor Franklin?"

He glanced up and at first there was surprise in his eyes, but then his head lowered a little. It seemed as if he was expecting me. "Come in, Journee," he said softly.

Even though I wanted to hurry up and get back to Mama, it

wouldn't be polite to rush in and rush out of Pastor Franklin's office. "Mama said to give this to you." I handed him the letter, then swung around, but he stopped me before I could take two steps to the door.

"Wait, Journee." He pointed to the couch against the wall. "Can you sit over there while I read this?"

No! I wanted to shout. I have to get back to Mama. But I was in God's house. Mama told me this was sacred ground, and although I didn't know what that meant, I knew I couldn't shout at Pastor Franklin. So I did as he asked. My heart pounded as I waited, watching him read the letter. It took him a long time because it wasn't just one page. I counted as he read each—four pages. At the end, he tsked, and it looked like he went back to the beginning. Please hurry up, I cried inside.

Pastor Franklin sighed, then walked over and sat next to me. "Journee," he began. "The first thing I want you to know is how much your mother loves you."

I nodded, but now it felt like my heart was trying to break out of my chest.

He continued, "And right now, she's having a very hard time."

"I know. And I'm trying to help her." I felt like I really needed to add that.

He nodded. "You've done a good job. She told me how well you're doing in school."

"Yes, Pastor Franklin. Because every time I do good, Mama's happy."

He smiled, but his eyes were sad. The way Mama's eyes had been. "Well, the most important thing to your mother right now is that you continue to do well because the teachers have told your mother you're a gifted student."

Mama seemed to have told everybody about that.

"Your mother wants you to keep doing well. She wants you to

be able to go to school every day, and she wants to make sure you're taken care of."

"Mama takes care of me."

"She tries," he said. "But right now, even though she wants to with all her heart, she can't take care of two babies. It's hard for her, and she doesn't want it to be hard for you. So . . . she gave me some papers here"——he glanced down at the envelope I'd given to him—— "and for just a little while, you're going to stay with Mrs. Hunter. Do you remember her?"

MY PHONE VIBRATED, and I sat up straight, startled. My eyes darted around and for a few seconds, I expected to see Pastor Franklin behind his desk, surrounded by all of those book-shelves that were stuffed with a million Bibles.

But I wasn't there. I was here, twenty-seven years later.

Grabbing the phone, I answered, "Hey, Sissy, where are you?" I was still a bit discombobulated and couldn't remember if Windsor and Norma were still in San Antonio.

My sister said, "We're on our way back. I wasn't going to leave until tonight, but Mama's sick; she needs to see Dr. Patter-son." I scooted to the edge of the sofa, but Windsor answered my question before I asked. "It's her bronchitis again," she explained. "Flared up something fierce this morning. This was the first time she ever had a fever, and I'm worried because the last time Mama saw Dr. Patterson, she said Mama was getting worse."

"Okay, I'll call Dr. Patterson." I paused. "How is . . . Norma?" I asked, more to be polite than to show concern.

"She's stretched out in the back seat. Having a hard time breathing." Now it was her turn to pause. "I can pass her the phone." Then she lowered her voice. "Right now, with the way she's feeling, she'd love to hear your voice."

This dance between my sister and me was never-ending. I

said, "I'll call Dr. Patterson, then call you back." I hung up to save Windsor the effort of her incessant begging.

This day had been a cacophony of emotions, but no matter where any emotional road began, somehow it always crashed at the feet of my mother. Here I was once again, reliving all of that despair. It still hurt to think of that year because 1995 was the last time I loved my mother.

It was Windsor who'd found me a decade ago, seventeen years after Norma had given me away. There were no words to describe the thrill I felt when the little girl I'd named and last seen asleep in the back seat of Norma's car knocked on the door of my one-bedroom Southwest-side apartment. I was one year out of college, and she had just turned eighteen. But following a vow she'd made to herself when she was old enough to understand that she had a big sister, she'd saved money from the part-time jobs she'd held through high school. And when she graduated, she moved our mother back to Houston from Dallas, where they'd been living from the day after Norma abandoned me.

Windsor finding me was like having a large piece of the puzzle of my life snapped into place; I felt a completeness with her that had been missing since I was seven.

But my mother? All the love I'd had for her had been scraped away by the yearning that, for a year, sent me to bed crying and waking in the morning with those same tears. I was going to die from that pain, and the only way to survive was to smother the memory of my mother. I couldn't forget her altogether, but the love I had for her, I strangled it until there was no love left— although the longing and the yearning somehow remained.

I did have a decency toward Norma, though, giving her exactly what she thought she'd given to me. All of these years later, after she and Windsor had returned to Houston, she continued to struggle financially, though now it was because of the severe bronchitis that had attacked her ten years before. I didn't want my mother, and especially not my sister, to once again find themselves on the streets. So as soon as I was able, I made sure Norma had a home, even put the deed in her and Windsor's names. The two-bedroom house I'd purchased in Third Ward was just a few blocks from where Mrs. Hunter had raised me and was almost the exact same floor plan. Then I made sure Norma didn't have to work, supplying her basic needs and paying for stellar medical insurance so she'd have solid care. She was comfortable and cared for—that was the least I could do because she'd at least done that much for me.

And then, I gave Norma something else she'd given to me—silence. For all that time, I'd never heard her voice or seen her face. It was as if she had died—or, as I used to think, it was as if she wanted me to be dead.

Windsor knew all of this, which was why I never understood her unrelenting quest to forge a reconciliation between Norma and me. Would my sister ever come to truly realize that I had no desire to bridge the divide that Norma had created between us? Would she come to understand that my "never" was real and meant to last an eternity?

With a sigh, I released all those memories and turned my attention to the call I had to make. Dr. Patterson wasn't in her office, but I left a detailed message with her service, then tapped on my sister's contact to call her back. Just as I did that, though, my phone vibrated in my hand. A new text:

Your present cannot fix your past. Vengeance is mine.

9

I yawned, leaned back in my chair, and closed my eyes. Maybe if I had just five minutes of rest, which would be far more than I had last night, I'd find the gusto to face this day. But between Norma finally being released from the hospital under strict medical instructions and her doctor's care and that last text, my mind hadn't allowed me to rest.

Your present cannot fix your past. Vengeance is mine.

Opening my eyes, I wondered if moving instead of sitting would help. Slowly, I crossed the room, then paused in front of my window. Today, I hardly noticed the view of the Houston skyline miles away. My mind was on the text and the only conclusion I could draw after reading it dozens of times.

If this was about my past and my present, then these texts, these threats, had to be coming from Vivian. She was the only person in my life who straddled both of my worlds. She'd introduced me to her uncle, but we'd had an almost fifteen-year friendship before we became competitors at ClearWater.

Before that final falling-out, Vivian and I hadn't had a single disagreement. That was because even when we met at the age of thirteen, we both understood the power dynamics between us—Vivian was part of the haves, and I was completely a have-not. Standing next to me, Vivian was superior in every way: fresh hair, cute clothes, her mom took her to the nail shop for regular mani-pedis, and her dad made sure she had a flip phone, her own computer, and a television and a VCR in her bedroom.

The sweet woman who raised me, Mrs. Hunter, did the best she could, but she couldn't compete with that. Mrs. Hunter was already in her late forties when she welcomed me into her home. An unmarried woman who'd never had children, she'd been thrilled when Pastor Franklin had put out a call to his congregation for help right after my sister was born. Mrs. Hunter had been the first one to step up, reassuring my mother that if she ever needed assistance, she was prepared to take one or both of her girls until my mother could get herself together.

From the moment I entered her home, even as a despondent child, Mrs. Hunter treated me as if I was a blessing. But there was no way she could or wanted to compete with Vivian's parents. I was always clean and fed . . . and except for the longing I had for my mother, I had the stability I hadn't had since my dad passed away. My bedroom wasn't furnished with designer pieces, but it was certainly functional, with a double bed and a thirteen-inch TV. The greatest extravagance Mrs. Hunter could afford was the three or four new outfits she bought for me at the beginning of every school year.

Things between Vivian and me evened out a little when I attended UT on scholarship and received $75,000 from an insurance policy when Mrs. Hunter passed away the summer before I entered college. But it wasn't until I joined Vivian at Clear-Water that I became her equal and then, after several months, surpassed her in gaining clients, income, and, finally, her uncle's attention.

"Uh, what are these?" My assistant's voice floated over my shoulder.

Facing her, I tilted my head in surprise at the bundle of yellow roses she held, which was so huge, her face was hidden.

"Oh my." I moved toward her, grabbed the vase, then placed them on the corner of my desk.

She stood back, pressed one hand into her tiny size 4 hip, and then demanded with the authority of someone three times her size, "'Oh my' is not an appropriate answer. So I'll ask again . . . Boss, what are these?"

I laughed; it had been hours since I'd laughed like that with Quincy. "They look like flowers." I inhaled their fragrance, then read the attached card: *Yellow roses represent joy, but there aren't enough yellow roses in the world to represent all the joy you gave to me yesterday. Thank you for the best Labor Day.*

It felt like so much had happened between our last call and this moment. But the memory of him and his words came back to me. Again, I was sure that this was not the man, these were just his moves. But how could I not love this?

"Journee!"

Now I laughed as I faced Tasha. "What?"

Tasha stood with her arms folded. "You get a gazillion roses, read the card, float away into the ether, and you think I'm just gonna stand here? Come on, 'fess up, Fester."

"I hardly floated into the ether," I said with a chuckle.

But there was no humor in Tasha's tone as she continued, "It looked that way to me. So who sent these?"

Her persistence only matched mine. So I said, "A friend."

"What friend?"

"A new friend."

"How long have you known said friend?"

"Uh, Tasha," I began, feigning annoyance, although I wasn't irritated at all. Over these few years, Tasha and I had become close enough to be concerned about each other's welfare. Still, I asked, "What's up with the twenty questions?"

She shrugged and settled into the chair across from me. "I've never seen you smiling the way you smiled when you read the card that came with those flowers."

I glanced at the bouquet once again, and was pleased with Quincy's timing. He'd given me quite a reprieve. "I met a guy yesterday."

"Yesterday?" She turned up her nose as if she didn't approve.

I nodded. "Yeah. At the gym. We had a great chat that continued through a wonderful brunch, and we had a really good conversation afterward."

She nodded, and her tone softened when she continued, "Do you like him?"

I shrugged. "He seems like a nice guy, but you know how I am."

"So hard to please."

Exactly! But what Tasha didn't know was "hard to please" was another way of saying he wasn't Ethan. And in this case, it was true. Quincy wasn't Ethan . . . Quincy was a better version.

"Well, I hope it works out."

"It was a single date; there's nothing to work out."

"He sent flowers," she said, now sounding hopeful for me.

The only comeback I had was "He sent flowers and changed my tire at the gym. Speaking of that, can you call the dealer, tell them I need a new tire and installation? And have them send someone; I won't have time today to take it in myself."

"I'll call them right now." She moved toward the door, then paused. "Do you think we'll hear from Mr. Yung this week?" The smile on her face belied the anxiety in her eyes.

I smiled to reassure her. "When I had dinner with him on Thursday, he gave me the impression they would make the announcement this week. Don't worry; we got this."

"You really think so?"

"I'm as close to sure as I can be. So . . ." I held up crossed fingers.

In return, Tasha pressed her hands together, then bowed her

head as if she was in prayer, and quickly, I did the same. What was I thinking, holding up my fingers like that? I wasn't lucky. God had blessed me. The life I had now was His promise fulfilled. His answer to all my childhood cries.

Clearly, though, I wasn't the only one who would be blessed with the WestPark revitalization contract. Once I won this bid, Tasha would get that raise she needed. When I'd interviewed her for this job, she had confided that her brother was serving seven years on a drug charge. The only reason she'd left her former employer was because she'd needed to earn more in order to support her brother financially.

Every chance I had, I gave Tasha a little bonus: when the team exceeded sales objectives, when Tasha beat a deadline—it didn't matter what: if I could help, I did. But what I'd be able to give her with this contract would take a lot of pressure off her. No worries, I thought. It was coming.

And because it was coming, I had to get back to work. There would be time to think about Vivian and figure out what she was doing—after I took care of my business. As I reached for the top file on the stack piled on my desk, the sweet smell of the roses tickled my nostrils. I paused and took another moment to inhale. Even with all that was going on in my life, I didn't want to let this moment pass and not appreciate how special Quincy's gesture was.

Setting aside my work, I picked up my cell:

The flowers, my goodness, Q. They're beautiful! I texted.

Quincy wouldn't see my message for a couple of hours, since at this moment he was probably standing in the middle of his fifth-grade class, explaining that an evangelist wasn't someone who played an evangelo. I chuckled now, remembering the story he'd told me yesterday. But before I could even put my phone down, it vibrated:

No flowers are as beautiful as you. Thank you for
making my Labor Day weekend so complete.

I was surprised to hear from him so quickly, though I was
more focused on his text than his timing. *This dude.* But as much
as I wanted to wallow in Quincy's words and sit back and smell
these roses, I returned my focus to the file in front of me.

And then . . . Tasha busted into my office.

"Oh my God, Journee. I can't believe this." She rushed to
my desk. Her voice shook as she added, "Look!" She shoved
a newspaper in front of my face. An article was circled with a
black marker.

The headline screamed: *Major City Contract Awarded.* And then
the subhead: *Quality Mortgage to Provide Funding.*

"What?" I snatched the newspaper from her; the entire time,
my gaze was stuck on the headline. Finally, I turned to Tasha.
This had to be some kind of joke. But Tasha's expression—
her eyes still wide with shock—let me know there was nothing
funny about this. "Quality Mortgage? That's Vivian's company,"
I whispered in disbelief.

Tasha nodded. "I can't believe this."

I glanced back at the article, still not able to read beyond the
headline. This was impossible. My eyes narrowed as I remembered Mr. Yung's final words to me:

"Ms. Alexander"—he shook my hand—*"I am truly looking forward to
working with you. You'll be hearing from us very soon."*

So how had we gone from that to this? And this decision
had to have been made not too long after our dinner for this to
appear in this morning's newspaper.

Tasha plopped down in the chair. "What went wrong?"
When I faced her, she straightened up and did her best to
blink away her disappointment. Of course, we both knew we

wouldn't win every contract; we'd won a lot but also lost quite a few. This was different—because of the promises Mr. Yung seemed to have made and because of the greater financial impact this would have had on my company, and thereby everyone who worked for me.

Tasha said, "I'm so sorry, Journee. Do you think there's anything we can do?"

I shook my head, my eyes still on the article. After a few seconds, I felt Tasha stand and move out of the office, closing the door behind her. Now I forced myself to read the first paragraph: *Vivian Wallace, the owner of Quality Mortgage, has won the coveted WestPark revitalization bid, which will have her overseeing the funding of a multimillion-dollar, five-year contract to establish low-income housing along Houston's WestPark corridor.*

Pausing, I tried to recall every single conversation I'd had over the past months. Every city official had led me to believe that not only was I in the running, but I was at the top. And then there was Mr. Yung, the city director, and his assurances. Something wasn't right . . . and what was wrong was Vivian. But how had my ex–best friend bested me? Did this have anything to do with the texts she'd been sending?

I forced myself to read the entire article. There were no clues inside the three-paragraph announcement. Most of it was about how the city was pleased to be working with its first Black female contractor at this high level and how impressive Vivian Wallace and her company were.

Setting the paper aside, I held my head in my hands. There was really only one thing for me to do if I wanted to understand what had happened. I had to make this call or I wouldn't sleep for weeks. It still took me a couple of seconds to pick up the phone, scroll through my contacts, and then inhale before I tapped on the number.

I had been a yoga enthusiast for years, and so I breathed, balancing my body and my mind. Inhaling, then exhaling, then . . .

"Mr. Yung's office, how may I help you?"

"Yes, uh . . . hello," I stammered. "This is Journee Alexander. May I speak with Mr. Yung, please?"

"Let me see if Mr. Yung is available."

As soon as she put me on hold, I knew this was a bad idea. He wasn't going to take my call; this was unprofessional. To Mr. Yung, this was just business, and I needed to disconnect this call so that I'd be considered for any future opportunity.

But before I could press END, I heard, "Ms. Alexander."

I froze in shock, then stammered, "Uh, yes, Mr. Yung. Thank you for taking my call."

"I can't say I'm surprised," he said, his tone stiff with his professionalism. "I thought I might hear from you."

Another shocker. So he *knew* I'd call because there was something wrong with this decision. I said, "Well, I do know calling you is a bit unorthodox, but, Mr. Yung, I read the announcement in this morning's newspaper, and I was more than surprised, especially after our last conversation on Thursday."

"I never said you had the contract."

"No," I quickly agreed. "No, you didn't, but . . ."

"I think, in fact, I said the final decision had not been made."

"You did say that. But I'm calling because I thought I was one of the top contenders and was looking forward to working with you. So I'm hoping you can give me some insight into what happened . . . so the next time I can put myself in the best position for a win." I paused, and when he was silent, I added, "I just want to know what happened."

He had to hear my frustration mixed with my confusion and disappointment. He said, "May I be frank with you, Ms. Alexander?"

"Yes." I scooted to the edge of my seat as if that would help me hear—or understand—better. "Of course. Please."

"J. Alexander and Associates was our first choice, but things changed." I held my breath. "As you know, we had to take our final recommendation to the mayor's office, and on Friday your application was immediately rejected."

"But why?" In the split second that passed between my question and Mr. Yung's answer, I tried to imagine what Vivian could have done with the mayor's office—bribe them?

Mr. Yung said, "There is a concern that you're under a federal investigation."

Was that a statement or a question? Either way, those words were a sledgehammer to my gut. *Breathe, breathe.* "Investigation? I'm . . . I'm not aware . . . of any investigation."

"I'm not at liberty to say any more than that. But I'm very sorry, Ms. Alexander, the decision is final. Truly, I wish you the best."

I didn't have enough breath in me to thank him and say good-bye, too. I just ended the call because it would have been unprofessional to sob in that man's ear. *You're under a federal investigation . . . investigation . . . investigation.*

That word reverberated in my mind like a boomerang app.

"Oh my God." I sat frozen in disbelief. How could the pendulum have swung so far in the past thirty minutes? With all that was going on, the one thing I'd been confident of this morning was that I was about to add a couple of million dollars to my company's bottom line. But all of that money had vanished—poof!—in the time it took me to read a newspaper headline. And now I didn't even care about losing that contract, because being investigated by the feds was bigger than anything else that could happen in my life.

Even though I'd gone to Ethan, I didn't really believe this

was going to happen. My purpose in meeting with him was to get his help: I needed to know who was sending the text messages, find out if and how I was being connected to Simon, and then get reassurance from Ethan that if somehow I was being coupled with Simon, he would be able to untether me.

Now, not only was I being investigated, but I knew who was setting me up. The texts, losing the contract, the investigation—this was all Vivian. But why? Was this about her being fired from Simon's company six years ago?

And how? What could she have said to the mayor? She couldn't have used the homeless scheme to wipe me out as her competition, since that scheme had been her idea. And she wasn't aware of the one scheme that I feared could really be my undoing. I didn't know if Simon and Vivian had ever reconciled, but I did know that he wouldn't have shared with her what we'd done. Simon and I were the only ones who knew about that.

So what had Vivian told the mayor's office, or . . . had she talked to the feds? And now that she'd given me up, how far was this going to go?

I wasn't going to live in a world of so many unanswered questions. Vivian wasn't the only one who could fight, and she wasn't the only one who could outmaneuver the competition.

Grabbing my cell once again, I scrolled through my favorites and pressed Ethan's number. When he answered, I greeted him with "Ethan, thank God you're back."

"I'm not. I'm about five minutes away."

"Great, you're not going to believe what happened. I don't know if you want to talk now or if you want me to wait until you get in your office."

"Well, Journee, I'm not sure I want to talk to you at all." His tone was filled with annoyance.

"What?" I said, falling back into my chair.

"When I agreed to work with you, I told you it couldn't be like before. This time, you had to follow my advice."

"I have," I said, wondering what he could be talking about. "I haven't done a single thing."

"You called Simon."

His tone and his volume let me know I'd been wrong. Ethan wasn't annoyed; he was pissed. But what was wrong with calling Simon? "I called Simon just to find out—"

"That was the biggest mistake you could have made."

"Why?"

"Because his attorney called me this morning. Apparently, Simon told him you were probably working with me and he thinks we're both working with the feds."

What kind of twilight zone had I entered?

"I'm not trying to do this, Journee. It would be best if you found someone else to help you."

"No, Ethan, please, no." I panicked. In the past, I would've let Ethan walk away, but with daggers coming at me from every direction, I needed him to help me navigate this mess. "I didn't know it was a problem to talk to Simon. You never told me not to call him."

"I told you to lie low while I was away."

"And what does that mean?" I continued to plead my case. "I had no idea I couldn't make a phone call. I was just trying . . . trying . . . trying . . ." My voice trembled, and I paused before I broke. Now I was the one who was pissed—at myself. After all the pain I'd endured as a child, I'd grown up to be an adult who never cried. I never allowed myself that vulnerability.

But it was the weight of all that had fallen on me from last night to this moment. Gathering myself, I finally said, "Please, Ethan. I will do as you say because . . . I need you," once again pushing aside my pride. "I found out this morning I *am* being investigated."

"What?" I wasn't sure if it was my words or my tone that softened him.

"Can we meet, please?"

He hesitated, then said, "All right," his anger seemingly gone. "Give me an hour to get settled in my office."

"Can we meet at my place?"

"Your office?"

"No, my condo. I'm trying to hold it together, but—"

"No." He said that with such force, I could almost see him shaking his head. "I'm not comfortable there, Journee."

"Why? Because of Ivy?" I asked. "What happened in the car . . . I didn't know you were engaged. But I know it now. And I respect that. I promise you I do. I just need . . ." I couldn't finish because I needed every ounce of my energy to hold back under all the pressure that was building.

"All right," he said, though he sounded more like he was giving in rather than this being what he wanted to do. "I'll see you in an hour."

"Thank you."

He hung up without acknowledging my gratitude; he was still upset. That call to Simon hadn't been about ignoring Ethan's advice, but he wouldn't have to worry about me anymore. Because now that I was under investigation, there was no amount of pride in me that would keep me from doing what Ethan told me to do.

I slipped my purse over my shoulder and glanced at the roses and then the newspaper. Like last night, this morning had been a roller coaster. But that contract was far from my mind. All I wanted to focus on was not being set up by the woman who said she'd always have my back. I was going to fight, and if I went down, Vivian Wallace was going with me.

10

D riving home, visions rolled through my mind like an old film reel—me in an orange jumpsuit; me carrying a tray with a bowl of some concoction that looked like oatmeal but smelled like fish; me standing in a seventy-square-foot space with a bed, a metal commode, and my only connection to the outside world being through a barred window.

This was unbelievable because of all I'd done to overcome my childhood and then make my life right after working with Simon. To me, my work at J. Alexander and Associates had achieved two goals: first, it was the manifestation of all the dreams I'd had as a child. Not that I had ever thought I'd grow up to be a mortgage broker, but I did have visions of earning money and living with the accoutrements that I was blessed to surround myself with. I'd prevailed over my abandonment, and now I was making amends for the dirt I'd done and the pain I'd caused. That had been my commitment: to give back all that had been taken away because of me.

Now Vivian was trying to destroy all that I was trying to do; she was trying to destroy me.

I stopped in front of my building's valet and told the young man that someone from Bentley would be by to service my car. Then I asked the concierge to send Ethan right up when he arrived. Inside my apartment, I stripped and jumped into a cold shower, needing the water to shock me out of my distress. It worked; less than ten minutes later, I was back in the game.

When the doorbell rang, I was in battle mode, ready to

stand with Ethan as he defended me. But when I opened the door and he blew by me like the wind, I realized I had to win this fight with Ethan first.

The moment I closed the door, he spun around. "I need you to hear me. I cannot protect or defend you if you're throwing obstacles in my way."

"I didn't know that's what I was doing. I was just—"

He held up his hand to cut me off. "I get it. You didn't think it was a big deal, so let me be clear. From this point forward, you talk to no one. You don't make a call, you don't write a letter, you don't send an email or a text, you don't go to anyone's home—you do nothing. Not unless you first review it with me."

"Okay. And I'm sorry."

My quick apology made Ethan's shoulders relax, and he exhaled all his frustration. There wasn't much he could say after my apology, especially since he'd never seen me this way. I wasn't exactly groveling, but before this moment, he didn't think I had a contrite bone in my body.

Ethan nodded, then followed me into the living room. He paused before he entered and glanced around. I tried to imagine his point of view. Did he notice the changes I'd made since the last time he was here—the paintings I'd commissioned, the ceramics I'd had imported from Pompeii? Or as he stared at the sofa, was he overcome by memories?

When he didn't move, I asked, "How was your weekend?"

He blinked as if my question had dragged him from the past. "It was good," he said as he sat down. "But I want to get to the situation at hand." His words sounded like a reminder to both of us that he was only here because of business. "You said you were being investigated? How do you know that?"

Sitting across from Ethan, I filled him in on the WestPark revitalization deal. I told him how I'd thought I'd won the contract, and about the surprising newspaper article, and about the call I'd made to Mr. Yung.

"So all he said was that someone from the mayor's office told him you were under investigation?" he asked, as if he found that hard to believe.

"He said I was under a federal investigation," I said, using Mr. Yung's exact words. "Now I wish I'd recorded the call."

"No!" He held up his hand like a stop sign. "Although Texas is a one-party consent state, I don't want any more complications with you. I'm just curious, that's all. And maybe a little confused. Why would the mayor's office be involved in a federal case?"

"I don't know, but I think I know who's behind it." I showed him the text I'd received the night before, and then I repeated how Vivian had been the one who won the contract. "I think these texts are from her and may not have anything to do with Simon. This could be all about her trying to take my business, and that's why she's helping the feds."

He shook his head. "I mean, I know you two had a falling-out, but would she go through all of this?"

"You must've forgotten how livid she was when her uncle fired her."

He began to nod slowly. "Yeah, something about how she was giving away the company secrets—or company scams, I should say."

In the past, those would have been fighting words, and I hated that Ethan was able to throw that at me. But I had nothing to gain by defending Simon or myself. So I ignored his words and said, "Whatever happened, she was really upset when she was fired. And remember how much of a mess it became when she asked me to quit?"

"Yeah, I remember some of it. So you're saying after all these years, this is payback for being fired?"

"Yeah. She's definitely the type to carry that kind of grudge."

"Against you and not against Simon?"

"I'm still trying to connect the dots, but I'm telling you, all lines lead to Vivian. It wasn't a coincidence that I got the text last night and lost the contract this morning."

"It doesn't make sense, because if Vivian told the feds about that homeless scam, she'd be giving herself up as well."

"I know; I told you I don't have it totally figured out."

"Hmmm," he hummed. "This isn't Vivian. Besides her not having anything on you that she can use, the feds hardly ever move on the word of one civilian. But instead of us sitting here trying to figure this out, let me get to work. My first focus, though, is to find out if there is even an investigation, because who's behind it isn't important. In the end, who gave the FBI what they needed won't matter. It'll be what the FBI has on you."

All this time, Ethan and I had been using the term "the feds." But hearing those letters—*FBI*—was chilling. I took a deep breath and willed that thought away. Ethan was here. And whatever was about to go down, I *was* going to get out of this. All I had to do was remember that I always began far behind the starting line, yet I was always the victor.

He said, "Okay, I'll put out some feelers. See what I can find."

"Any chance you can just call the FBI"—I had to swallow the lump that lodged in my throat after saying that—"and find out?"

He was shaking his head before I finished asking the question. "Not a good idea, especially if there isn't an investigation; that is certainly a way to get one started. And anyway, the Department of Justice would never confirm or deny an investigation. So I'll find out the way everyone else does—through connections and leaks." Ethan stood, and I followed.

"Thank you for coming over. Is there anything I should be doing?"

He spun around. "No. Do nothing, and this time, I mean nothing. And if in a few hours you're not sure of what nothing means, call me and I'll give you the definition." He turned toward the door, but after just a few steps, he stopped and faced me. "You've told me everything, right?"

I swallowed. "What . . . what do you mean?"

"I don't know," he said, peering at me. "It's my gut. And something is telling me . . ." He paused. "Have you told me everything? Everything about your business with J. Alexander and Associates?"

"Yes," I said, and nodded. "There is nothing that anyone can say about my firm."

"Okay." His eyes narrowed a little more when he asked, "And you've told me everything about Simon, right? When you worked with him?"

This time I only nodded. Because if Ethan was working from his gut and I spoke, he'd know for sure I was lying.

He paused as if he noticed that I hadn't said anything. So I nodded again, and he still studied me like I was an amoeba beneath a microscope. I willed my feet to stay still and my arms to remain by my sides. Truly, I wanted to profess nothing but the truth, but I couldn't. Because Ethan and I were still standing on shaky ground. If he found out what Simon and I had really done, he might walk out my door and not look back. And now, after knowing for sure that I was under investigation, I needed my ex.

Finally, I gathered myself enough to say, "I don't know what can be in your gut, but I told you everything I can think of regarding Vivian and why this is happening," I said, trying to speak some semblance of truth. "And I told you everything about

Mr. Yung." My honesty ended when I added, "There's nothing else to tell."

"Okay," he said. "Maybe it's just because there are so many moving pieces to this situation and it's happening so fast. I'll be in touch."

As he moved to the door, I said, "Ethan . . . when we talked on Friday, you were pretty sure this wasn't too big a thing. That I probably wasn't looking at anything too serious, even if I was under investigation."

"If what you've told me is true, nothing's changed since Friday on my end."

I nodded and smiled as if I were relieved. But when he walked out the door, it took everything to quiet the rumble of impending trouble inside me.

hadn't received a call from the concierge, so when my bell rang at just a little before seven in the morning, I knew who was on the other side of the door. But when I opened it, the fireball that always blew into my condo whenever Windsor dropped by instead limped inside. My sister hobbled as if her fire had been extinguished and she hadn't seen a sunrise yoga in the past year.

"It's Mama" was all she said as she staggered past me.

I took a deep breath to calm my heart and thoughts. No need to get ahead of Windsor's words. Tightening my bathrobe, I followed my sister into the living room. My voice was steady when I asked, "What's wrong with Norma?"

Windsor plopped down on the sofa and sighed as if exhaustion had overtaken her. "Do you know what it's like growing up without your father?"

I was surprised that this was her answer to my question, but I sat next to my sister and stayed quiet, ready to listen. It had been months since she'd mentioned our father. And every time she did, my heart broke. Windsor had never known the man who loved her before she was born and died before she could love him.

When my sister didn't add anything more, I said, "I'm so sorry about that, Sissy. I wish you'd known Daddy, if only for a little while. You would have never forgotten him."

Those were words I'd said to her so many times before. In the past, she'd simply nodded, but now she said, "Do you know what I do remember? I remember that he left us penni-less."

"That's not what happened." I shook my head. In all the times we'd discussed our dad, she'd never uttered a single nega-tive word about him, so where was this coming from? "Daddy worked hard, at two jobs, so that Mama . . ." I paused; I hadn't called Norma that in years, but that was who she was to me two decades ago. Continuing, I said, "He wanted her to be a full-time mother because he wanted the focus of our family to be on us. Everything he did was in order to make our lives better."

"Until he died," she said, as if she were accusing him of committing some kind of offense when he took his last breath, "and left us penniless."

I wanted to snap back at my sister. How could she say any-thing bad about our father, the only parent we had who'd taken their parental responsibilities seriously? I was only six when my father passed away, but I knew for certain there wasn't a single circumstance in which my father would have given me or Wind-sor away. I didn't want to get into a battle with my sister, though. Something was going on with her, and I needed to understand what it was. So instead of attacking, I kept my tone even. "Is that what Norma told you?"

"No, she has the same fairy-tale memories of him that you do. But what I know is that twenty-eight years ago, this man died and left us with nothing," she said, sounding like a judge who'd just found a defendant guilty.

"Do you think Daddy wanted to die so young and leave us behind like this? Of course not," I answered for her. "Daddy didn't expect that to happen to him."

She shrugged as if she was insinuating that our father had had a choice in his demise. "He smoked cigarettes, he got lung cancer, he died and left a pregnant wife, a young child, and only a couple of hundred dollars in the bank. Mama's life hasn't been the same since. And now . . ."

My eyes narrowed. "Now what?"

She sat up, and when she faced me, her whole countenance had changed. She was on the brink of tears, her eyes wide with fear. And now her voice and her tone were softer. "Dr. Patterson said that Mama may need to have a lung transplant."

I sucked in air.

"And do you know how Mama got this?" She kept talking. "She got it from Daddy."

"What?" I leaned back and squinted, trying to understand what Windsor was saying. "Bronchitis isn't contagious."

"No, but his smoking and her being around that every day for all of those years damaged her lungs."

"Norma is blaming Daddy for being sick?"

"No, it's Dr. Patterson. I kept asking her how Mama got this, and she gave me the list of causes for chronic bronchitis. Did you know that smoking was number one . . ." A tear dripped from her eye. "There's a chance that before I'm even thirty, I'll be an orphan, having lost both of my parents to almost the same thing." Gone was the arrogance she'd had when we'd started talking, and in its place was a child's anguish and fear.

I pulled my trembling sister into a hug. "No, Sissy, no." I held her as tight as I could. "That's not going to happen. We're not going to lose her. We'll do everything we can to save Norma." Pulling back, I held her shoulders and looked into her watery eyes. "You hear me? We're going to fight this. Just tell me what we have to do."

With her fingertips, she swiped at her tears and tilted her head. "How do you do that?"

"What?"

"You're willing to do everything you can to save our mother. Everything except talk to her."

I held up my hand. "Windsor, I'm not getting into this with you today." I stood, hoping the space between us would let Windsor know this part of the discussion needed to end right here. "Just tell me what Dr. Patterson said and what we have to do."

"No, we're going to talk about this," she demanded. "Because you want to take care of Mama, but you haven't said two words to our mother since you were seven years old. Do you know how crazy that is?"

I was tired of going through this with my sister, and now my tone matched hers. "It's only crazy to you because you can't understand me or my decisions. But how could you? Norma kept you but threw me away."

Windsor pounded her fists on the sofa. "Would you stop saying that? You know Mama asked that lady to take care of you because she wanted to give you a future you wouldn't have with her."

"And so what?" I shrugged. "She kept you because she didn't want you to have a future?"

Windsor jumped up. "Is that what's bothering you? That I stayed with Mama, living in a car, while you slept in a bed and went to school every day? I thought you got over that a long time ago, Journee, but if you haven't, all you have to do is look around. Look at where you live, what you drive, the clothes you wear—hell, you even have your own designer. And then look at your education, your business, and your achievements. And when you finish with all of that, take a single look at me, because that's all you'll need. Then ask yourself which of us got the best end of this deal. Because at this point, all I have to show for Norma's decision is that I'm twenty-eight years old and still living with my mother because I never got the education you received. I didn't get any of the blessings that came from her decision to do right by you. So if either one of us has the right to be mad, it's me."

I crossed my arms and glared at my sister. "It's not a blessing when your mother abandons you, and it's not doing right when you give your child away and make no contact for years. And even then, she wasn't the one who reached out to me. You did. So just leave this alone and let me do what I have to do, the way I have to do it."

She returned my glare, then finally shook her head. "Fine." Grabbing her messenger bag, she strapped it across her body, then stomped across the room.

I watched her for a moment as she marched toward the door. Then I called out, "Where are you going? What about what we're going to do with Norma?"

Her hand was on the doorknob when she whipped around to me. "You know what, Journee? I'm so tired of you, and I don't have time to be in the middle of this mess anymore. If you want to know what's going on with your mother, you call her doctor. But let me tell you something. For the one who is older and educated and so sophisticated, you aren't very bright. Because I see something you can't even see.

"I just pray that you won't live to rue this day and these decisions you've made and these grudges you've held. I'm praying so hard that you won't one day be staring down into a casket, filled with remorse and regrets, and asking yourself, what if?" Without another word, she stepped out and slammed the door behind her.

I stood there, astonished, then rolled my eyes. A casket? Really? When had my sister become a drama queen? But as I stared at the door, which seemed like it was still vibrating from the way she'd slammed it, I thought, Windsor was not prone to histrionics, especially not when it came to Norma.

Maybe this wasn't Windsor being extra. Maybe this was her trying to tell me the truth. Those were still my thoughts as I sipped my first cup of espresso. I was ready to start my day, but I couldn't get Windsor's words out of my mind. Finally, the only conclusion I could come to was: there was really a chance my mother could die.

MY CUP OVERFLOWED, but not in the biblical sense. On my drive to work, my mind was filled with thoughts of Windsor and Norma, but I didn't allow myself to drift to thoughts of death. I couldn't, because if anything happened to Norma, Windsor wouldn't be the only orphan.

But then, just as quickly, my thoughts switched—to the federal investigation. Did the Department of Justice, one of the most powerful agencies in the country, really have my name on one of their files?

My mind vacillated from one spine-chilling scenario to the other as I maneuvered my car into the parking lot of the River Oaks Tower. My only hope for today was that business could take my thoughts away from my personal life.

The moment I turned off the ignition, my cell phone rang, and the screen flashed, *Quincy Carothers*. For the first time since the last time I spoke to him, I smiled and pressed the Bluetooth to answer. "Good morning."

"Good morning to you." His baritone resonated through my car. "I was just checking to make sure you hadn't forgotten about me. I left you a message yesterday."

"I'm so sorry. Yesterday was—"

"Busy," he finished for me with a chuckle. "I figured that; you're a busy and important lady. But I wasn't going to let another day go by, because, like I said, I won't let you forget me."

"And how could I do that when I have those beautiful flowers sitting right on my desk to remind me of you?"

"Okay, that's what I like to hear, but I was thinking of something more personal to keep me at the top of your mind. Have dinner with me tonight."

I hesitated.

He said, "Look, I know you're busy with that contract coming up, and I would never do anything to interfere with your work. But you have to eat, and I can promise not to keep you out all night."

His words took my smile away. That wasn't his fault, though. There was no way for Quincy to know I'd lost the contract and because of that, I'd be much more available than I expected. Still, I had a lot going on.

But in the middle of all of this, Quincy was like an oasis. "You know what?" I said. "I'd love to do a quick dinner."

"Great," he said. "I'll call you after I make the reservation."

There was more bounce in my step as I made my way to my office. And I was smiling, something that hadn't come easy in the past days. Thinking about seeing Quincy for dinner gave me something to look forward to.

Then . . . I sat at my desk and opened my email. And clicked on the first one:

Journee:

I hope this finds you already having an amazing day. I wanted to tell you I've asked two associates to join me on your case. This is not something that I usually need to discuss with my clients, but in this case I wanted to make you aware—one of the associates is Ivy.

I wasn't sure if you knew that Ivy worked with me or even knew that she was an attorney. But she is, and she's amazing.

I paused, rolled my eyes, and sighed.

There is no doubt she will be a major asset to this case. Because of who she is, as you can imagine, she has contacts in this city and beyond. In this instance, we'll be able to use her contacts in the Department of Justice. Just wanted to bring this to your attention because this is an unusual situation.

If you have any questions, we can discuss. I'll be out of the office today . . .

I shut my laptop. What the hell? How was this supposed to work? I'd gone to Ethan because I trusted him, but *trust* was not a word I'd ever associate with Ivy Franklin. Oh, I'd trusted her once, but I was young, beyond dumb, and so vulnerable. All I wanted at the time was a friend. And Ivy pretended to be mine for five minutes.

I was only nine, still yearning and longing for my mother, not able to find my place in Mrs. Hunter's home or in the church that I used to love. Even though I went to school every day and slept in a bed each night, I still felt homeless. Or maybe what I was feeling was motherless, and I didn't know the difference.

But then Ivy invited me to her tenth-birthday party. And I thought I finally had a friend.

"You must come," she'd said. "Everyone from church will be there, and several of my friends from school."

If I'd been older, I would have been suspicious. Because just the Sunday before, Ivy had been singing some little jingle about my being poor. But I wanted a friend so badly that I made myself believe she (and her friends) had changed in just seven days.

When Ivy had told me it was going to be a costume party, that was even better, because now I wouldn't have to worry about what to wear and how I'd look next to those girls.

Ivy had said, "The party is going to be so much fun, but there's just one rule. No one can talk about what they're going to wear. Not until that day."

The secrecy had made it even more special, and after much thought, I dressed up as Wonder Woman, wearing red leotards, a short blue skirt, and red tights. What made it perfect was the red cape and gold headband that Mrs. Hunter made. When Mrs. Hunter drove me to the Franklins' home, I insisted she leave me at the curb. She couldn't escort me to the door as if I were a baby. That wouldn't make a good impression among my new friends.

So, by myself, I had rung the bell, and when Pastor Franklin opened the door, at first he smiled, but then he frowned, and finally his eyes opened wide. He didn't react fast enough, though, to stop me. I stood there, looking like a poor superhero, while all the girls were dressed in the latest fashions: some in baggy pants and cropped tops, and others more dressed up in colorful minidresses.

The laughter was instant and resounding, the sound bouncing off the walls. Even when Pastor Franklin shouted, "Enough!" in his booming Sunday voice, the giggles didn't stop.

I'd gotten out of the house fast that day. Mrs. Hunter had returned within five minutes of my telephone call to her. After that, I became even more of a pariah because Ivy's parents had sent all the girls home after her stunt. And, of course, every one of those ten-year-olds blamed me.

Her parents' punishment hadn't stopped Ivy, though. Her teasing and taunting were relentless, enough to stay imprinted in my memory forever.

If Ivy's goal had been to belittle me, she had been a master at her craft. But what had worked then, wouldn't work now. If she had joined this case to find a way to take me down, she would soon discover I was no longer that little girl. She was no match for the woman I'd become.

Although . . . it would be quite a gift to Ivy if she were to stumble upon the secret I kept. At all costs, I could never let that happen. Ethan kept telling me what I'd done with the homeless people wouldn't land me in prison. But I wasn't so sure he'd feel the same about the scheme Simon had brought to me that had truly elevated my financial status. Could I find myself in prison because of this?

I leaned back in my chair, closed my eyes, and remembered it all . . .

"So, you know what to do, right?" Simon said.

I rolled my eyes. "Simon!" I slapped my hands in my lap. "How many times are you going to ask me?"

"I just want to be sure, 'cause if we do this first one right, this will lead to big money."

"I know. And no matter how many times you say this, I promise you, I got this. This is the next level, so let's level up."

He grinned, then brushed down his cashmere blazer, glanced in the rearview mirror, and straightened his tie. Together, we walked up to the ranch-style house in Independence Heights. Simon rang the doorbell, then gave me a once-over as if he hadn't picked out the *floral knee-length dress and navy kitten heels that I wouldn't have ever worn, not even on Halloween. But he said we needed church-girl vibes—though, in a way, I was a bit insulted. I'd been a church girl once.*

"Mrs. Bailey!" Simon exclaimed when the seventyish-year-old woman opened her door. "You didn't tell me you were going to a photo shoot today!"

Mrs. Bailey's eyes narrowed until Simon motioned to the white turtleneck and black slacks she was wearing. "Surely you're not hanging around the house looking model-fabulous."

Mrs. Bailey shook her head, but her smile revealed that she appreciated the compliment. "Forever the charmer." She turned to me. "And you are . . ."

"Wilhelmina," I said. "Wilhelmina Jones."

Without looking at him, I knew Simon's eyes were bugging out of their sockets. I hadn't told him that I wasn't going to use my name. It seemed nonsensical to me that while Simon was operating this program under a different company, he was still using his own name. That wasn't how I was gonna roll. I wanted to keep my legitimate identity away from what I was doing here.

"Wilhelmina . . ." She turned to Simon. "Is that what you told me her name was?"

"I . . . I don't think I mentioned it." He was lying, but he'd get out of this. "I think I just told you I wanted to introduce you to a client." He turned to me and added, "And Wilhelmina is one of my favorites."

"It's so nice to meet you. Come on in." She moved aside to allow Simon and me to step over the threshold. "I've made tea and blackberry cobbler."

Following behind her, I took in the space of the dark living room. Maybe it was because just about everything in the place was brown—from the well-worn velvet sofa and two mismatched chairs to the carpet that was just as worn and matted at the entryway. When we stepped into the dining room, the brown color scheme continued with the dining set and the huge hutch overstuffed with a collection of teacups and mugs.

"Have a seat," she said. "I'll get the tea."

When she stepped out of the room, Simon turned to me and mouthed, Wilhelmina?

I shrugged, then nodded, and we both grinned as, for the next several minutes, Mrs. Bailey moved in and out of the kitchen with first the tea and then saucers covered with blackberry cobbler. I wasn't sure why my heart pounded as I watched her. This was just an acting gig. And in the end, Simon and I were here to do what was best for Mrs. Bailey.

After she had served us, she sat at the head of the table, took a sip of tea, and sighed deeply.

"Thank you so much for agreeing to see me." Her eyes were on me. "When Simon told me he had a client he wanted me to meet, it was a huge relief because"—she reached over and patted his hand—"it's not that I don't trust him, but this house"—she paused and glanced around the room—"is special to me. I raised my daughter as a single mom, and from the time she was ten, she promised she would buy me a house. And when she graduated from college, that was the first thing she did. She bought this house and wouldn't even let me help her with the mortgage. And do you know, about six or seven years ago, she paid it off?"

"That's wonderful," I said, even though Simon had already filled me in on Mrs. Bailey's situation.

Mrs. Bailey kept on. "It was, and she turned over the deed to me. But once I got that deed, I kept getting all this mail and all these calls about how I could take out a home equity loan and use the money to go on vacation. That didn't interest me. I wasn't going to spend money on frivolous things, but when the prices in the grocery store kept going up and my social security check was buying less, I thought it would be a good idea to take out one of those equity loans to give myself a little wiggle room.

"The first time I did it, I paid off my loan easily. But this last time . . ." She tsked. "My property taxes went up so high that between paying that and being on new medication that I can't afford, I just couldn't keep up with the payments anymore, and that's when the bank decided to foreclose, since I used this house as collateral." She sighed.

All the questions I would've asked Mrs. Bailey, Simon had already answered. The only family Mrs. Bailey had was her daughter, who would have, of course, helped, but she was in the middle of a battle of her own—a divorce and a fierce fight for custody of her two sons. Knowing that all of her daughter's money was being sucked up by legal fees, Mrs. Bailey hadn't even told her what she was going through.

Simon said, "I told Mrs. Bailey there was no way I would let anyone foreclose on her home. I'd help her, just the way I helped you." He turned back to Mrs. Bailey. "It's a blessing to be in the business of helping people save their homes."

"That's such noble work you do," Mrs. Bailey said. Turning to me, "So he saved your home, too?" she asked.

"Yes, ma'am," I said, beginning the spiel I had practiced since Simon had come to me with this idea. "My father left our home to me when he passed a few years ago. I was doing fine until I lost my job. I didn't know what to do until I met Simon at church. When he told me he could help, I was afraid it was too good to be true."

"Yeah. That's what I kept saying," Mrs. Bailey said. "And when I told my girlfriend Lorraine, she said that same thing. Told me to be careful. That's why I was so glad when Simon suggested I talk to someone he's helped. And I appreciate you taking your time and coming over here so I could look you straight in the eye. I didn't want *to talk to anyone over the phone. I believe in eye-to-eye contact." She paused. "So you've been happy with what Simon did for you?"*

"Very," I said, surprising myself at how easily I slipped into this lie. "It was really a simple and easy process. I signed my house deed over to Simon"—I glanced at him with a grateful smile—"and for that, he paid all my past-due payments. Then, for six months, I didn't have to make a single payment while Simon negotiated with my lender to give me another mortgage. By that point, my credit was better, and finally my lender was willing to work with me. Because of Simon, the house is back in my name. Simon saved more than my house; he saved my life."

"Glory be to Jesus." Mrs. Bailey held her hands up in the air and closed her eyes. "I'm going to save my home. Glory!"

I glanced at Simon; his eyes were closed, and his hands were raised, too. I kept my hands in my lap and only lowered my head just in case Simon or Mrs. Bailey peeked. But there was no way I was going to play with God. The only stability I'd had in my life as a child was the Lord and Wheeler Village Baptist Church—first with my parents, then with Norma after my father passed away, and lastly with Mrs. Hunter, who kept me in the pews, where she prayed for me every Wednesday night at midweek prayer and twice on Sundays at the early and late services.

Even now, I had a relationship with God. I didn't go to church, but that was because while I loved Him, I didn't care for too many of His people. Still, God had blessed me tremendously financially, and I wasn't going to mess up all He'd done for me by mocking Him . . .

I MOANED AS I opened my eyes. It was painful to think about that now, though at that time, it had been so easy. Simon had convinced me that he was helping people who were so deep into the foreclosure process they were going to lose their homes anyway. Distressed homeowners, Simon told me, didn't have the money to catch up on past-due payments. In just months, the banks were going to sweep in and take possession of their houses, leaving all of these people (who just happened to be single, elderly women with an emotional attachment to homes that contained a decent amount of equity) with nothing.

At least after they had signed their deeds to Simon, the homeowners did receive something in return. While he never had any intention of negotiating with the banks on their behalf, or giving these women any chance to get their homes back, Simon did give each of them $20,000—and some huge lie about how he'd done all he could, but they'd lost their homes.

At the time, this had made sense to me. Yes, Simon and I were lying, but these homeowners were already victims when we met them, victimized by the banks and other mortgage lenders. We didn't make them victims; we saved them.

That is . . . until one of the homeowners became a victim *because* of the two of us. And that was when the hundreds of thousands of dollars I'd made over the years from this scheme became nothing to me.

After that, I'd done all that I could to turn my professional life around, but now that Ivy was working this case . . . I had to admit that I was afraid. Very afraid.

Grabbing my phone, I texted Quincy: **I'm so sorry, I can't make dinner. Rain check, please?**

A few seconds later, when the phone rang, I didn't answer. I turned off my cell, leaned back in my chair, and wondered what I was going to do.

12

H ey, girl." Terez greeted me at the entry of her upscale boutique. She locked the door behind us, then led me past the one-of-a-kind dresses and suits and evening gowns displayed on mannequins and hanging from racks.

In the back of the fourteen-hundred-square-foot retail space, we pushed aside the purple curtains and entered her studio, where all the designer magic happened. But for her after-hours meetings with clients for their seasonal consultations, this was more like a meditation room. It was as if Terez had created a cloud for her VIPs, a respite to sink into and rest in perfect peace.

I stepped inside the world where everything was a soft beige or warm tan and the light was subdued. Walking across the carpet felt like moving on air, and when I sat, the softness of the vegan leather embraced me. I exhaled.

To think I'd almost canceled this appointment. I'd questioned how I could spend time choosing colors and fabrics for winter dresses and suits when there were so many more pressing issues in my life right now. But this was what I needed; Terez's studio rivaled the lounges of any of the best spas in the city.

Terez said, "Okay, don't sit there too long, because you'll never get up." She chuckled. "Everything is in the changing room, ready for you."

"Okay." I forced myself to stand and make my way to the back of this lounge.

"And while you're changing," Terez said over her shoulder, "I'll fix you some coffee. A new blend I picked up in Turkey."

It didn't matter what kind of coffee—I was down for whatever. Because every time I came for my consultation with Terez, she had something new beyond fabrics: Greek coffee that was dark, rich, and smooth, or a Turkish blend that at first sip I was sure would keep me awake for two days, or silky Italian coffee that was so good, I returned the next day for another cup. Terez considered herself a coffee connoisseur now, importing beans and coffee from around the world.

Terez spent as much time in Europe and the Middle East as she did here in Houston, searching for leather in Turkey, or silk in Greece for her Grecian-inspired designs, or organza in Italy. Her discoveries were a windfall for my wardrobe.

Minutes later, I was wrapped in an oversize plush bathrobe, and settled back in the chair. I was ready, though, to be measured for the new season and to try on prototypes that Terez had set aside for me.

Terez handed me the coffee cup, and after the first taste I wanted to forget about clothes. All I wanted to do was sit in this chair and put my life on pause. As I brought the cup to my lips once again, Terez said, "I thought your sister was coming with you."

I froze, the cup in midair. "Why would you think that?"

A ringtone from the song "Weightless," which Terez once told me was the most calming music in the world, echoed through the space. Someone was at the front door of her store. "Excuse me for just a second," she said.

I took another sip, and wondered why she would think Windsor would be with me. My sister and Terez had never met, although they knew of each other. But then I shook my head and leaned back. This was not the place for my mind to be cluttered with thoughts that would never matter. The only thing I needed to focus on was—

"Journee."

I shot straight up, and my eyes locked on the woman in front of me. Twenty-seven years. It had been twenty-seven years since I'd last seen Norma Alexander, and for each day of those passing years, I'd wondered what this moment would be like.

"Journee."

It always sounded like a hug, the way she spoke my name. And even now, after three decades, it sounded the same. And that longing, that yearning that I had for her that overwhelmed me at seven, returned. I wanted her to call my name again.

But while her voice was the same, that was all that was familiar. In my mind, my mother had stayed the same age, with skin a couple of shades darker than my favorite teddy bear, and just as soft. And her dark hair was long and silky, so much better to play with than any of my dolls.

This woman before me with hollow eyes and dark, stringy, shoulder-length hair didn't look anything like the woman who had loved me till I was seven. She seemed a couple of inches shorter, but then I realized it was just the way she stood, slumped forward, her shoulders sagging. And why was she almost totally gray? How old was she now? Fifty-four? The years had not been kind to Norma; she looked like she was in her seventies.

"Journee."

This time, she took a step toward me, and I held up my hand. "What . . . what . . . what are you . . . doing here?" I stumbled over my words.

"I wanted to see you." Her voice was so soft. "I wanted to talk to you."

Glancing over her shoulder, Terez and Windsor entered the room. While Terez was the personification of what I imagined a deer caught in headlights would look like, Windsor stood stoic, almost smug. Opposite demeanors—and in an instant,

I knew what had happened. Windsor had somehow found out about this appointment, tricked Terez into giving her information, and then brought Norma here . . . all because she was mad at me.

I glared at my sister. "How could you do this?"

Windsor stepped to Norma's side. "The way you talked about Mama yesterday, I couldn't let this go on. I can't, Journee. I know where this is going, and you'll hate yourself. And if I didn't do anything to fix the situation, *I'd* hate myself. You have to talk to her."

"You don't have any right to tell me what to do!" I growled.

"Uh . . ." Terez began, looking between the three of us. "I'm going to step out of the store for a moment. When you're ready"—she glanced at me—"just text."

"No!" I exclaimed, feeling embarrassed that my sister had brought our dysfunction into the light this way.

"Yes," Windsor countered. She gave me a harsh stare, then turned to Terez. "I'm sorry to have to do this, but if you're up for a cup of coffee at that shop across the street, I can explain why I misled you."

Terez's eyes were filled with sorrow when she glanced at me, but her nod to my sister let me know she'd rather be anyplace but here, even at a diner drinking American coffee. She scurried out of the room. Windsor rested her hand on Norma's shoulder and led her to the chair next to mine. I wanted to jump up and run out of there, but the fact that I wasn't dressed kept me in place— part of Windsor's plan, I was sure. Plus, I knew it wouldn't do any good. Windsor would probably follow me home, bringing Norma with her.

When Norma was settled, Windsor whispered words to her that I couldn't hear. Norma nodded, then Windsor left without saying another word to me.

I still heard their footsteps in the front of the store when Norma said, "It is so good to see you, baby girl."

Are we really going to do this?

Then Norma added, "My sweet, sweet baby girl."

I couldn't help it; I laughed in Norma's face, although my laughter sounded more like a groan. "Your sweet baby girl? You didn't treat me that way, Norma. You discarded me like I was a worn-out shoe."

Her head reared back at my use of her government name, and I guessed Windsor didn't tell her that part. But she needed to understand that because she didn't feel like being my mother back then, she would never get the benefit of that role now. She was just Norma to me.

Norma nodded as if she understood. But before she said another word, she bowed her head and coughed and coughed, her chest rattling. I pressed my butt into the chair, held my hands together, and willed myself to stay in place. She didn't deserve my concern.

"Excuse me. I'm sorry," she said once the bout ended. Looking up, she added, "I've dreamed of seeing you for so long."

This was not the way I planned to spend my evening of peace, and since I wasn't willing to waste any more time, I cut away from the small talk and asked her the only thing I needed to know. "Why didn't you want me?"

"No," she said, shaking her head before I could even finish. "It wasn't like that." She coughed again, sounding as if she wasn't going to stop. Again I willed myself not to go to her side. Finally, when she was able, she said, "Windsor told me about your conversation, and that's why I asked her to bring me to you. You know how much I've wanted to see you over these years, but after trying all those times, I thought it was best to respect your decision. I know how much I hurt you. That was never my intention, but what I intended doesn't matter. Only how you felt. So I just prayed one day you would see me."

"That doesn't answer my question."

She nodded. "There was so much going on in my life at that time, sweetheart, and I wasn't able to take care of you."

"But you were able to take care of Windsor. You loved her enough to make whatever sacrifices you had to so you could be her mother."

"I did. But in my mind, I was making the same sacrifice for you."

I rolled my eyes just like I did every time Mrs. Hunter had said something similar to me. *"Your mama did what was best. That's how much she loved you."*

Mrs. Hunter was a sweet woman, but I didn't believe her, just like I didn't believe Norma. Still, my heart ached with questions. "What was the difference between me and Windsor?" I asked her the question that had bothered me the most. "Why was it best for me to be abandoned, Norma?"

She flinched again at the way I addressed her. "The first thing you must know," she began, the words spilling from her so fast, as if she was feeling like there was a time limit to how long I would sit with her, "is that I loved you then, I loved you all the years you were away, and I love you now. That love never changed."

I crossed my arms. "The years that I was away?" I seethed as I repeated her words. "I wasn't away—you *gave* me away."

She gasped. "Mrs. Hunter was supposed to explain it to you. She called me every day while we were at that motel, and I kept praying I wouldn't have to make a choice that I didn't want to make. Praying that something would change for me, but I couldn't find a job because I was homeless, and I was homeless because I couldn't find a job. Everyone told me I couldn't allow you to live like that anymore."

"But you haven't answered my question. Why me?"

"Because you were this bright, brilliant ball of sunshine who brought nothing but light into Reye's and my life."

Reye. My dad.

"When I say you were brilliant, Journee, you really were. You were reading when you were barely three. When you were four, your dad taught you how to write your name and numbers. At five, you could multiply numbers and recite the alphabet backward. I couldn't even do that. As you got older, you were getting smarter—I could see that.

"Then the teachers told me how gifted you were." She paused, pulled a tissue from her purse, and dabbed at the corner of her eye. I stared at her, not moved. "After your dad died, after I lost our apartment, after I realized I was going to be living on the streets with two children, I couldn't get in the way of the future I imagined for you. I had to give you the best chance. And that chance wasn't with me."

I shook my head, not accepting a single word. "There had to be something else you could have done besides throwing me away and forgetting about me."

"No!" Her response was so loud and so emphatic, she startled me. "Is that what you think? If I could have stayed in your life, I would have, but Mrs. Hunter was concerned about confusing you, and I thought she was right. I didn't want you to see me and Windsor and then beg to come with us. It was the most painful thing I've ever done in my life, but I left Houston because I didn't want to take the chance of seeing you anywhere . . . or, worse, you seeing me. I trusted Pastor Franklin and especially Mrs. Hunter; she promised me she would give you a good home so you could thrive. It was because of her that you were able to attend that special school. She did bless me by keeping in touch.

Over the years, I spoke to Mrs. Hunter so many times and she told me you were getting along just fine."

My eyes widened at that news.

Norma said, "You must know I was always in your life. I never left you. Not in the truest sense."

I sat stone-still, just staring, saying nothing.

"Please, Journee. I understand how difficult this is for you, but after speaking to Windsor, I knew this time was right. I'm sure she's told you . . . my bronchitis . . . is chronic. It's getting worse, and I want to do everything I can to help you understand . . . before." She stopped as if she'd spoken a complete sentence. Then she added, "Pastor Franklin has been praying with me all these years that our relationship would be healed. He said we all would benefit from counseling and he's willing to do it. I'd love that. I'm hoping you'll agree."

Agree to counseling? With Pastor Franklin? Ivy's father? At Wheeler Village, the scene of Norma's crime against me and where too many of those ten thousand members could end up in my business?

The only reason I continued at that church after Norma abandoned me was because Mrs. Hunter dragged me there. But every time I was there, it was as if I was sitting in the center of my pain, reminded of that day when I wished I'd never gotten out of that car. It was agony, which finally ended when Mrs. Hunter died. The last time I set foot in that church was to attend her funeral right before I left for college.

No, I wasn't going back there. And even if Pastor Franklin agreed to meet us elsewhere, I wouldn't do it. First, I didn't need to be counseled, and second, I wasn't going to give another Franklin information to use against me.

"If that's your solution . . ." I jumped up from my chair and dashed into the changing room. I expected Norma to follow, but she didn't. Maybe she wasn't able. Dressing so quickly, I put my top on backward (and left it that way), then returned to the lounge, where Norma still sat. She looked up as I grabbed my purse.

Her eyes were filled with tears. "There isn't anything that I can say?"

I stared at her.

"I have dreamed of this moment," Norma cried, and then she coughed. She struggled to speak but somehow continued, "Please."

Still, I gave her nothing but my glare.

"Baby girl, please forgive me."

Now I moved toward the door, then rushed through the retail store; the whole time, Norma's cries followed me. Right as I reached for the front door, I heard Norma cry out, "Please, I love you, Journee."

I stepped outside and closed the door on anything else that woman may have wanted to say.

13

The only good thing about this week was that it had come to an end. Because another day would have meant another disaster. I couldn't imagine anything happening to me today that could rival all the setbacks of this week, but then this morning it seemed as if this payback karma wasn't through with me yet.

Joseph Brown, a real estate investor who'd been working with my firm since I opened it, called. At first, I'd been happy to hear from him. He'd been a steady client, which meant a steady source of income, and for the past month we'd been working on financing for a new six-unit building he was buying.

But after all the greetings and small talk, Mr. Brown informed me he had to back out of the deal.

"I'm sorry for all the work you've put in, Ms. Alexander," he'd said, "but you, of all people, know that life happens, and now I'm faced with a few financial challenges that suddenly came up."

Now, of course circumstances and situations arose all the time—people buying homes couldn't get their down payments together or unexpected expenses derailed the best of their intentions. But a move like this, which two weeks ago would have only been unfortunate, was now suspicious. Had Mr. Brown heard that I was under investigation? Did he know something I didn't?

And my day didn't get any better when Ethan called to tell me he'd spoken with the person in the mayor's office who'd given Mr. Yung the information about the federal investigation.

"I'm not sure what to think about this source," he said. "Apparently he overheard something at a cocktail party last Friday."

"Really?" I was indignant. "So because of some gossip at a party, I lost a major contract?"

"There's obviously more to it than that, Journee, but that was all the information I could glean. Now that Ivy is on this, she's working her sources. But in the meantime, you're going to have to sit tight. Because there's nothing we can do until the feds make their move."

This was so frustrating. I felt like I was sitting in the middle of a football field, a target with nowhere to hide. The reason I'd gone to Ethan was because I wanted to develop an offense. But as Ethan explained, go on the attack against what? I didn't need to bring trouble to my door. I guessed that meant I had to sit and wait for trouble to come to me.

It was difficult to follow Ethan's advice, since I wasn't convinced his legal strategy of waiting was better than what had always been successful for me—being proactive. But, keeping Ethan's words in mind, I got back to my business of brokering and kept only one eye open for trouble. With the other, I turned my attention to the junior brokers, meeting with each of them, reviewing their client applications, discussing marketing plans, and setting goals for this fall. Then Tasha and I discussed upcoming municipal, state, and even federal projects on which we could place bids. In other words, I tried to be normal when my life was anything but.

When the clock struck five, I was out of there. I was never one to leave the office before six or seven, but with the way this week had unfolded, my office wasn't a safe space.

Now, as I crept along in the Friday traffic on 610, all I really wanted to do was grab a case of wine, climb into bed, and drink and drink and drink until I was oblivious or it was Monday, whichever came first.

But Quincy wasn't having that. After I had canceled on him on Wednesday and then told him I couldn't have dinner with him last night, when he called this morning he told me he'd been worried.

"I don't like the way you sound, and if you give me another excuse not to see me, I'm going to take drastic measures."

"I can't imagine you having any kind of measures to take."

"Oh, really?" he said with a smile in his voice. "Well, let me tell you, I have sources. And if you don't meet me tonight, I'm going to use every one of them, find out where you live, and then sit outside your door until you let me in."

He laughed when he said that, but I had images of Quincy actually finding a way to get past my concierge, then waiting outside my apartment until one of the neighbors called the police because there was a man committing a crime: sitting in the hallway while Black.

So I agreed to meet Quincy, for an early and very short dinner. I still had weekend plans with my bed and a case of wine.

I was only about seven minutes late when I pulled into the parking lot of Davis Street, an upscale Midtown restaurant, and I could imagine Quincy already pacing in front of the door, wondering if I was going to send a last-minute text. Moving fast, I turned off the ignition and grabbed my purse just as my phone vibrated. That was Quincy; I was sure of it.

I tapped the screen to read the text message:

If you feel the walls closing in, it's because in moments of pain, we seek revenge. Vengeance is mine.

I tossed the phone into my purse, leaned back against my seat, and closed my eyes. Damn! Honestly, after all the tribulations I'd been through this week, I'd forgotten about my text stalker. But why shouldn't she join in? Vivian had just put an exclamation point on what had been the week from hell.

And now the threat of this text was even more pronounced. About revenge and vengeance.

Revenge? What had I done to her? If this was about her uncle firing her, then her stealing my multimillion-dollar contract should have made us equal.

All I wanted to do was confront Vivian and end this madness. I wasn't sure what she thought she could accomplish with these messages, but whatever, she needed to know she didn't really want me as an enemy.

But I couldn't do that. Because Ethan wanted me to stand down and stay low. With a sigh, I shook my head. I would follow Ethan's instructions for as long as I could. But at some point, Ethan was going to have to understand that his was not a winning strategy. Offense always won the games. Taking action was always more critical than being reactive.

Then . . . a tap on my car window startled me. I pressed my hands against my chest and peered through the glass and into the eyes of Quincy.

It took a moment for my heartbeat to stabilize and then I opened the door.

Quincy said, "Are you trying to decide whether or not you're coming in?"

He chuckled, but I didn't, because after that text, what I wanted to do was back out of this lot and drive straight home. But I didn't tell Quincy that. "Of course not. I was just . . . thinking about . . . something that happened in the office today."

"Is everything okay?"

"Yeah. Definitely," I said with cheer that I didn't feel. I shut my car door, then added, "I should start all over. It's good to see you, Quincy."

His grin was wide and bright. "And it's good to be seen by you. The way you ducked and dodged me this week, I wasn't sure this date was ever going to happen." He pulled me into an embrace, and I savored the feeling of resting in his arms. But I allowed that to last for only a moment before I pulled back. "Wanna go inside?"

He held out his arm the way a gentleman would, and I laughed. I hooked my arm through his, and he led me into the restaurant. There was a mass of people hovering at the hostess stand, which is exactly what I expected at Davis Street. This Southern soul food restaurant was one of the most popular eateries for the upper-echelon crowd.

But even with all the people waiting, Quincy just nodded at the hostess and we were led to a white-clothed table with three pillar candles in the center. I slid into the chair with my back to the window while Quincy sat across from me.

The moment we settled in, he said, "I've been really concerned about you."

Resting my arms on the table, I leaned toward him. "You said that when you called, but I'm not sure why. I mean, I'm sure you've had someone cancel a date before."

He shrugged. "Maybe once or a dozen times."

I laughed. "A dozen times? I doubt that. But seriously, there is nothing to be concerned about. It's just been one of those weeks."

"Ah," he said, then nodded. "That major contract."

"Yeah." I sighed. "But I don't want to talk about that." I glanced around at the restaurant. The air was festive. Every table seemed filled with people celebrating some occasion. Beside us, a man and a woman sat with a heart balloon floating over their table, while behind them was a long table with half a dozen HAPPY BIRTHDAY balloons hanging in the air. Laughter rose be-

hind us, where a group of men—executives, I assumed—in expensive tailored suits were raising their glasses in a toast.

"We certainly don't have to talk about work," Quincy said,
bringing my attention back. "That's not my favorite subject. You
are." Even though his stare was intense, as if he might never look
away, I kept my eyes on him. Even when he added, "You look
lovely." He gave me and my short-sleeved denim coatdress a long
glance.

"You look good yourself," I said, feeling more comfortable
now, giving compliments to Quincy and receiving them from
him. And I really did like the long denim jacket he wore over a
white T-shirt. It was casual yet still chic. "We match."

"Indeed."

The waitress came for our drink orders—a bourbon and
Coke for him and a Lemon Drop martini for me, although I
almost asked her to bring me two.

"So," he began when the waitress walked away, "I know
we both want to push work aside, but always know I'm a good
listener. And if you're having any problems at the office, who
knows? I'm a problem solver. Maybe there's a way for me to
help."

Even in the best of times, there was nothing Quincy could
do with my business. I knew that, and I was sure he was aware
of that, too. But his eyes were filled with such sincerity, and that
touched me. "You're sweet," I said. "But you know what I want?
I want to do what you said. Let's both focus on our new favorite
subjects."

My words turned on his high-wattage grin again, just as
the waitress returned with our drinks. Then she took our orders
with a swiftness. As she walked away, we held up our glasses and
toasted each other, saying nothing, but it felt as if we were toast-
ing everything.

To new beginnings, I said inside.

I set my glass on the table. "You know, with all the conversations we've had, I'm not even sure if I know whether you're from Houston. Did you grow up here?"

And in an instant . . . there was that shadow like last time, crossing Quincy's face—a darkness that made his eyes turn black and his nostrils flare. But it lasted for such a short moment that I wondered if I'd really seen it. Quincy half smiled. "I did grow up here. I like to say I was born, bred, and built right here in this city," he said, as if that dark moment hadn't passed between us. "I even stayed here for college."

That surprised me. For some reason—the way he spoke, the way he dressed, even the way he talked about money—Quincy seemed more exposed to the world to me.

He continued, "I attended Rice, majored in English, and though I did live on campus, that was as far away as I got. Even when I graduated, I lived within a few miles of my mom's house."

"So that must mean you and your mom are close." My words were meant to be a compliment, a personal acknowledgment of the way I wished it were for me and Norma.

But Quincy turned away and stared into his drink. "We *were* close. Until she died," he said, with his head still down. "She died while I was away. The only time I left the country."

Ah, so he *had* traveled.

He said, "I'd taken what my mother and I thought was the gig of a lifetime. I accepted a three-year assignment to teach English as a second language in Greece."

"Oh my goodness," I said. I wanted to add how wonderful that sounded to me, but I couldn't. He was talking about his mother dying.

"I only completed a year of the program. Came right home when I got the call about her and never went back." This time, when a shadow crossed his face, I understood. He was probably remembering the exact words he'd been told that day.

"Quincy"—I reached for his hand—"I'm so sorry."

He shrugged, though his pain was etched in the lines that creased his forehead. "Death happens, you know?"

"I do." I nodded. "I still miss my dad."

"Oh!" There was surprise in his voice. "I didn't know."

"I was much younger than you, just a child. But it's hard to lose a parent at any age."

"Yeah, and here I am, bringing us down about my mom, and now your dad."

"I'm glad you told me." I grasped his hand once again. "We're friends, and I want to be here for you, like you've already been for me. I mean, I can't change a tire, but I'm a good listener, too."

My hope had been to bring a smile to his face; he grinned. "Well, if you like to listen, I love talking about my mom. I don't know what it is, but I'd really like you to know what kind of woman she was."

The waitress interrupted, and as she placed Quincy's lamb chops and my blackened catfish and truffle rice on the table, I placed my hand over my heart, so touched by Quincy's words. How sweet was this man? His mother had passed away, yet he wanted to share her with me.

"Journee." Quincy called my name. He held his hand toward me, and I grasped it. This time, he didn't ask—Quincy just blessed the food. Then, as jazz from the pianist rose into the air and mixed with the chatter and laughter around us, Quincy entertained me with stories of his mom. Just like he'd done with the children in his school, he kept me laughing about his mom and six of her church friends who'd convene at her home for Sunday dinners.

"It was a whole mess, though, because not one of those ladies would remove her hat. No, sir." He laughed. "Those hats were their badges of honor, so even through dinner, they had to wear them. It was a sight at that dining room table—six women, repping every color of the rainbow, all reaching for the corn bread at once, their hats colliding in the middle like bumper cars."

His description was so vivid, I could see the women in their red, blue, orange, and yellow hats crashing into each other before they tried to get out of the way.

Then he shared stories about his mother's Saturday bingo nights, and how he went with her at least once a month.

By the time we pushed our empty plates aside, Quincy had switched up the conversation a bit. "And there was always talk of a grandchild. At first, she wanted me to get married, and I can't count the number of times she tried to set me up."

Like Ethan, his mom, and me.

"But," Quincy continued, "when she realized that wasn't working, she gave me permission to have a child out of wedlock!"

I pressed my hand against my mouth but couldn't stifle my laughter.

Quincy chuckled along with me, but then he became serious. "My birth was an interesting situation. My mother never married, but she wanted a child. She was in her forties when she made a deal with a guy she was dating. He was just a good friend, not husband material, she told me, but they made an agreement. She said God had blessed her with the only thing she ever really wanted in this world—me."

"Oh, Quincy. What a wonderful story."

He nodded. "I never missed having a dad because I didn't feel like he was absent. My mom made me feel like my biological father wanted me as much as she did, but in a different way." He shrugged. "It made sense to me when I was five, and I grew up believing that."

"So cool. You've told me just a few stories about her, and I feel like I've come to know your mom."

"It would've been nice if you could've met her. She would've liked you."

"I wish I had been able to meet her, too," I said.

He was silent for a moment. "Who knows?" he said. "Houston is the smallest big city in the country. You may have run into her one day."

I squinted, thinking about his words. As spread out as this city was, it was like a small town with too many people connected in too many ways. Like me and Ethan and Ivy. But I loved the thought that I may have passed Quincy's mother one day at a gas station or a restaurant, or even walking in a park.

"Even though I lost my mother way too soon, I'm so grateful. Because I did receive the greatest gift. I experienced the unconditional love of a mother, and there's nothing like it."

I grabbed my glass and turned it up, finishing off my martini. I wanted to raise my glass in the air and shout over all the music and conversation around me, *Bring me another one . . . or three.*

"Journee?" When I gazed at Quincy, he said, "It feels like I lost you for a moment. Was it something I said?"

I rested my glass on the table and exhaled a short breath. "No, I was just touched by what you said about a mother's love . . . that's so true. There's nothing like it . . . and I wish I'd had it."

As if Quincy knew that I'd need some time, he let several beats pass before he said, "So, I know you didn't want to talk about this the other day, but like I told you, I'm here for as much or as little as you want to share."

I massaged my temples, the entire conversation with my mother yesterday flashing through my mind in just seconds.

"You don't have to talk about it," he said quickly, "because I'm not trying to stress you out."

Facing him, I said, "And you're not. It is just such a long, complicated story."

He shrugged and glanced at his watch. "I've got time and two degrees from Rice. I can comprehend complicated."

I laughed. "Okay, that just broke the ice."

He held up his hands. "Just trying to make it easy for you."

"And you are. It's just that this isn't something I talk about too often, but to keep it short and uncomplicated, after my dad died, things went south for my mother. We were homeless for a while, and then my mom decided to just give me to another woman to raise."

His eyes were filled with the same disbelief that was in his tone. "She gave you to a stranger?"

I shook my head. "It wasn't that bad. She worked it out with a woman from our church and the pastor, I guess. Even after all of those years, I can't really tell you the whole story. All I know is that from the time I was seven until I was sixteen, Mrs. Hunter took me into her home and gave me nothing but love."

He tilted his head. "All of those years."

I nodded.

"And you still called her Mrs. Hunter?"

Now I was the one to lower my head for a moment. "What else could I call her?" I inhaled my emotions. "She wasn't my mother; I called her Mrs. Hunter until the day she died."

He covered my hands with his.

I swallowed hard so that I'd be able to get more words to come out. "All I ever wanted was my mother. And I never saw her again, until . . . recently."

"Wow. So you've seen her?"

I nodded and thought about how different my answer would have been the day before yesterday. "My sister and I reunited about ten years ago, but"—I shook my head—"not my mother and I." I paused before I added, "I don't want to have anything to do with her." Now I sat up straighter, squared my shoulders, and, with defiance in my eyes, prepared myself for his attack.

This was the reason why I didn't discuss Norma with too many people. Only Ethan and Windsor in recent years, and both of them had far more sympathy for Norma than for me.

So I waited for Quincy's judgment and wondered if this would be the end of our friendship. Because if Quincy went too far to the left, I was going to get up and walk out of this place. It was hard enough to take it from Windsor, but anyone else . . . there was no need for me to live with their opinion. Anyone beyond my sister wasn't necessary to my life.

I sat frozen until Quincy squeezed my hand. "I understand."

I blinked, trying to make sense of words I'd never heard from anyone in any discussion of my mother.

As the joviality continued around us, Quincy leaned closer to me. "I can't imagine what you went through. By the time we are seven, we know the depth of our mother's love. We've lived with it, accepted it, grown with it. And for that to be snatched from you . . ." He shook his head. Were those tears in his eyes? "I just cannot imagine," he finished.

I sighed with relief and gratitude. Quincy understood when no one ever had before.

"Oh my God." Then before I could think about it, I added, "I could kiss you right now."

"I wouldn't mind that," he whispered, without cracking a smile.

Heat rose beneath my skin. "I didn't mean that. I mean, I wouldn't mind, I mean . . . oh, God." He laughed. "Let me start over."

"You don't have to," he said through his chuckles, and sat back. "I know what you meant."

"But you can't understand how much your words mean to me. For all of these years, everyone has judged me for the way I feel, and you . . . not only didn't you do that, but you understand."

"If anyone were trying to see this from your perspective, they would understand, too." He shook his head. "I don't know, Journee. If I were in your shoes, I couldn't say that my reaction would've been much different. I think I'd be pissed for life, too."

"Are you finished?"

Both of us glanced up, shocked at those words, as if neither one of us recalled where we were. At the same time, we nodded to the waitress and were silent as she cleared our table.

That gave me time to reflect on Quincy's words. How wonderful was this man? All this week, as I listened to him speak and as I read his texts and notes, I thought his words were just that—just words, with little meaning or substance. But this . . . what he said tonight. This was honest and sincere, and this supported me. This man . . . maybe Quincy Carothers was exactly who he was presenting himself to be.

When the waitress walked away, Quincy asked, "Should we order dessert? Or perhaps another drink?"

"Yes to both," I said. "Because I don't want to end this evening on that subject."

"You don't have to worry about that. Even if it ended now, it would still have been wonderful for me." Then he raised his finger to get the waitress's attention again.

Within minutes, I had a new martini in front of me, and Quincy asked, "So, when you're not busy doing the grand work of helping people get homes or at the gym working out and getting flat tires, what else does the fabulous Journee Alexander like to do?" He was giving us both a reprieve from the serious turn the conversation had taken.

I took a sip of my martini. "That was a smooth transition."

He popped the collar of his jacket. "I know. I'm good, right? Or Michael Jackson might have said that I'm bad."

I leaned back in my seat as if I wanted to get a better focus on this man. "What you know about Michael Jackson?"

"Listen," he began, as if he was about to school me, "I am officially the number two MJ fan in the whole world, second only to my mom. She taught me everything I know about the king of pop. And . . ." With a smile, he added, "I'm sure she's rocking with him in heaven right now."

After that, our discussion veered everywhere: from the lyrics of our favorite Michael Jackson songs to our favorite movies— I loved Christmas movies, while we laughed at how *Love Jones* was his favorite and he made me promise never to repeat that— to our favorite foods, although we both agreed we just loved to eat.

When we finally gave up our table three hours later, I was almost sorry I'd told Quincy I wanted this to be an early evening. Because once again, I didn't want to leave him.

Like at the breakfast klub, once outside, we leaned against my car and continued chatting as the evening breeze chilled the air from the eighty-five degrees that had suffocated the city earlier. I shivered, and Quincy took off his jacket and wrapped it around my shoulders.

"Thanks," I said.

He nodded. "I hoped hanging out with me gave you the escape you needed."

"This was exactly what I needed . . . and wanted. You helped me so much tonight. In ways you cannot even imagine." Although I didn't mention Norma, I was sure he knew I was talking about my mother.

"All I know about life is that whatever you put out in this world always comes back to you. It's true what the Bible says— you can tell much about a person by their fruit."

The Bible. I liked this. He did more than just bless his food. He read the Word of God . . . just like Ethan.

"And with what you do, Journee, helping people find the homes they want, that has to be God's work."

I cringed. Even though that was the way I handled myself today, my past haunted me. "The real estate agents who find the homes are the ones who do the glamorous part, while I'm in the back room crunching the numbers and making sure the money works for everyone."

"Well, the money is the main thing. People only get homes or lose homes because of money. So don't belittle what you do. Be proud."

"I am." *Now*, I wanted to add.

"Well," he said after we'd been standing outside for another hour. "I have to apologize. You said you wanted a short dinner and an early night."

"I did, so I guess I should be going."

"Yeah," he said, though neither one of us made a move. Until Quincy leaned forward, his lips aimed toward mine. And just before our lips touched, he paused. "You said you wanted to kiss me." His voice was so soft, the words were almost lost in the breeze.

But I heard him, and I nodded, then pressed against him, welcoming his lips.

It was sweet, it was sensual, it was a kiss the way the French meant it to be. When I shivered again, it wasn't because I was cold; it was time to pull away. Quincy leaned back, but only a little. He moaned and, with the tip of his finger, traced my lips.

"I have been dreaming about that for this whole week." His voice was thick. "And that was way better than my dreams."

I had only one response. I kissed him again. We only stopped when we heard laughter coming from the front of the restaurant. I said, "I think we better stop acting like teenagers."

He laughed. "All right. So when can we act like teenagers again?"

You wanna follow me home? I said, "I have some things to do this weekend, but let's work it out."

"Bet," he said as he opened my door.

I slid in, then remembered that I had his jacket and rolled down the window. But when I slipped it from my shoulders, he shook his head.

"Nah. Keep it. That jacket is my insurance policy that we'll see each other sometime this weekend."

And just like that, my weekend plan to stay in bed with a case of wine was forgotten. "Let's talk, but maybe I can cook dinner for you."

"Are you teasing me?"

I shifted the car into drive, gave him a finger wave, then rolled my car from the parking lot. *Was* I teasing him? He'd just have to figure that out.

14

The warmth of the rising sun heated the jogging trail as I strolled past Kinder Lake, where a couple was already out kayaking. But the tree-lined path provided plenty of shade, and being outside, just steps from my front door, was invigorating. It wasn't even eight o'clock, yet I was already up and out.

I had new energy, and it was all because of Quincy. From our dinner conversation to the two hours we'd spent on the phone when he called me just a half hour or so after I left him in the parking lot, Quincy had uplifted me.

Last night, he'd told me over and over that I was right about Norma, closing with: "Don't let anyone invalidate your feelings, Journee. You feel what you feel, and you don't have to explain your feelings to anyone."

His words made me feel seen and understood. Quincy got me. The only thing that challenged me a little—from what I'd told him, Quincy wasn't feeling Windsor:

"I'm surprised you have a relationship with your sister, especially with the way you say she badgers you. Sometimes you have to get toxic people out of your life."

While he was in tune with me, he was wrong about Windsor. She wasn't badgering me; she was just doing what she thought was right. And there was definitely no way I wanted her out of my life.

I wasn't worried about that, though. He'd come to understand that and come to love Windsor, too, I was sure. Aside from his erroneous assessment of my sister, Quincy was the heaven to the hell that loomed all around me.

We were just a week and two dates in, and already I wanted to spend more time with him, especially after that talk, especially after that kiss. We'd agreed to have dinner on Sunday—at my place. And I was looking forward to seeing where our time together would take us.

The phone rang the moment I had that thought, and I smiled. Because I was sure it was Quincy. But then I glanced at the screen. Windsor. I let the phone ring and ring until it went to voice mail. Seconds later, it rang again, and I sighed before I sat on a bench. Although this conversation had to happen, it wasn't one I wanted to have now. I hadn't had many mornings recently when I awakened with a smile, and I was sure my sister was about to strip all my happy away.

But I knew my sister, and when she called back a third time (which was something I would have done), I knew she wouldn't stop until I picked up, so . . .

"Windsor." I pushed her name through my lips, trying to sound rushed, as if I were a bit under pressure and just by my tone she'd know I was too busy to speak. "Can I call you back?"

"Why?"

I frowned; she'd never questioned me like that before. "Because I have so much to do. I'm . . . not home. I'm . . . preparing for a meeting." I leaned back on the bench and crossed my legs.

"On a Saturday morning?"

"Yes," I said, hoping I sounded frazzled. "I have an important presentation coming up this week." Then I muted the call as a motorcycle barreled by. After a second passed, I added, "I asked everyone to come in for a meeting this morning."

"It must be really special if you're up and out this early on a Saturday. So you're in your office?"

"Yes. I was running into the meeting right when you called; that's why I can't talk right now."

"Well, actually, I think you can take a little time for your sister."

I pulled my cell from my ear and stared at it. Really? I answered, "So you have no problem taking me away from my work?" And then I felt a jab on my shoulder. Before I turned around, I knew. There was my sister right behind me.

Windsor clicked off her phone, then rounded the bench and sat next to me.

Both of us stared ahead, our eyes on the lake, and I wondered how long Windsor had been watching me. Finally, she said, "So I guess you'll be meeting with all those geese out there."

"There aren't any geese in the lake."

"Exactly." She faced me, but I kept my eyes ahead. "Then your important meeting can be with me."

"Okay, what I just did to you was janky."

"Yeah, it was. Kinda like how when we're on the phone and you don't wanna hear what I'm saying, you pretend you have another call coming in."

Damn. "It's just that I'm in a great place right now, and I really don't want to break it by revisiting that stunt you pulled bringing Norma to one of my fittings, of all things. How embarrassing was that?"

"For you, maybe, but not for me. And embarrassing you was exactly what I was going for. Nothing else had shocked you into doing what's right."

How different her words were from Quincy's. Maybe I did need to put a little space between us.

"Like I said, I don't want to talk about this." I hoped the fact that I still wouldn't look at her would put a period on this whole conversation.

But it didn't. "Well, if you don't want to talk about that, maybe you'll want to talk about this . . ." A beat. "I got the job."

I whipped my head to the side. "Get out!" I said, jumping off the bench with excitement. "You got the job?"

Now she grinned as she nodded. "That's what I came here to tell you."

"Congratulations, Sissy," I said, easily pushing aside what was going on with us and Norma. "But you know what? I'm not even surprised." I waved my hand in the air. "I knew the job was yours."

"Yeah, because of you. Not only did you make that call so I had the first interview, but that dress." She was laughing when she added, "I'm telling you, Sissy, I waltzed into that office wearing that Terez original, and what else could they say besides *You're fine and you're hired*?"

Even though the mention of Terez's name brought back the memory of Thursday, I laughed with Windsor. "I know for a fact that it was more than that waltz in that dress. Windsor, you're going to be a phenomenal ad exec. You're personable, and you're like a whole whirlwind, a force all by yourself. By the time this is over, you'll be running that company. I'm so glad you have this opportunity. I can't wait to see what you're going to do with this."

My sister was silent for a moment before she said softly, "That's some compliment coming from you."

"You sound surprised."

"I am. I didn't know that's how you felt about me. I mean, it's not like I've set this world on fire in any way."

"Not yet, but you're on your way." I took her hand into mine. "You never had the chance to prove what you can do, but this new opportunity is going to be perfect."

She squeezed my hand and lowered her eyes. "Thank you

for saying that." Her voice was still soft. "I mean, I wasn't even sure you would ever speak to me again."

Just like that, I was taken back to Thursday. But I was far more sad than mad. How could I be mad when she was doing what she believed was right? I respected that. "I wish you hadn't ambushed me. I wish you'd talked to me."

"Talk to you?" Her tone let me know she was astonished. "That's all I do is talk to you about Mama."

"But ambushing me like that while I was in my bathrobe? You knew I couldn't get away."

"And that was the point." For a few seconds, she pressed her lips together as if she were trying to stop them from trembling. "Sissy, Mama is really sick, and she needs both of her daughters now."

Her words didn't move me. "There is so much I can say to that, but how could she possibly need me? She doesn't even know me. We only spent seven years out of the thirty-four that I've been alive together. There are dozens of people in her life who she knows better than me."

"And that's so sad, but wouldn't it be great if you two could get to know each other now?"

"If Norma weren't sick, we wouldn't even be having this conversation."

"Yes we would." The quickness with which she answered surprised me. "I love you and Mama too much to not want the best for both of you. And what is best is living a life of love and reconciliation, no matter how much time Mama has left."

That feeling that had come over me two days ago when I saw Norma for the first time returned. The yearning, the longing.

"Mama is hurting, Journee. And you can take a great deal of that pain away, especially since you're the cause of so much of it."

"No"—I shook my head—"don't put her pain on me."

"Everyone knows what she did to you, but now you're the one rejecting her."

So . . . Windsor didn't realize that was my objective? To reject Norma the way she'd rejected me? Norma had laid down the rules, and all I was doing was following them.

Windsor asked, "Seeing her . . . did that do anything for you? Did you soften toward our mother, just a little?"

My cell vibrated, saving me from having to respond, and my smile was instant when I read the text: **Good morning, beautiful. Is it too early to tell you I'm counting down the hours to our time together tomorrow?**

If there was one thing I'd learned in my years on this planet, it was that everyone sent their representative to the first weeks of dating. That wasn't my thing. When I met a man, he got what he got. I was Journee Alexander from the first moment.

But with the men I'd dated, they worked hard to put forward their best until they couldn't hide their true selves anymore. But through our conversations, I was beginning to believe that Quincy was very close to the man he was showing himself to be.

Never too early, I texted back. **Did we set a time? What's good for you?**

The texting bubble appeared and then: **Anytime after church. I can't wait to see you.**

And he even goes to church. I guessed I had a type when it came to men.

I texted: **So, what should we do? Three or four?**

And in seconds, he responded: **Let's say three; I don't want to waste even that one hour.**

"Awww, this dude."

"Uh . . ."

Okay . . . this was awkward, and weird. How had I forgotten that I was sitting right next to my sister?

"Another meeting?" She smirked.

I wanted to give that snicker right back to her, but I couldn't. I had to stop myself from giggling. "Kinda." When she rolled her eyes, I said, "Okay, I met a guy."

"And . . ."

"I kinda like him. I haven't known him very long. So I can't say where this will go. We'll see."

"Well, you know the rules—when you've dated him for a month, then I get to meet him."

"Yup."

We laughed together because in the years after Ethan, following Windsor's rules, I'd introduced my sister to one guy I was dating. That was it; no one had lasted beyond a month. That had been cool with me. I didn't want anything that would take my focus away from my business.

But maybe now . . . with Quincy . . . I'd definitely know where this was going after tomorrow.

"Well, let me get back home. I have to go to Austin on Wednesday for training, and I have a huge binder of information to study before then," Windsor said, standing from the bench.

"That's so exciting."

"It is. Thanks again for this, Journee. And thank you for taking my call"—she rolled her eyes—"and talking to me."

I chuckled. "Thanks for coming by to tell me your good news. I'm so proud."

"And I'm proud of you."

"Why? Because I'm seeing a guy I might like?"

"Because even though you don't know it or won't admit it yet, seeing Mama the other day, that was just the beginning."

The ends of my lips curved downward.

She held up her hands. "No more ambushes. I can promise

you that. Not only will I not do that to you, but I won't ever do it to Mama, because she walked out of that place so hurt."

I shook my head, not accepting that guilt.

"But"—Windsor nodded—"I think there will be more meetings to come."

My first thought? Over my dead body, but then I shoved those words in my mind aside. Death. Too close. And truly, that was not what I wanted for Norma.

So I said nothing and hugged my sister when she embraced me. Then I watched her sweep across the park to McKinney Street until she disappeared around the Hilton Hotel. Today, though, I didn't feel as bad as I usually did when Windsor lectured me about Norma. I wasn't sure of the reason why, but I hoped it wasn't those feelings being stirred up inside me—that yearning, that longing. Norma didn't deserve any of my emotions.

When my phone vibrated again, I was grateful that Quincy was texting, taking me back to my happy place. In the seconds between reaching for the phone and reading the message, I wondered what Quincy would say that would, like always, send me swooning. My smile was wide until I read: In due time, your foot will slip . . . your day of disaster is near. Doom is about to rush upon you! Vengeance is mine.

In the past, the texts had unnerved me, even frightened me a little, although I didn't like to admit (or accept) that. But this time I was smoking mad. Because now Vivian was infringing upon my fleeting moments of euphoria.

Standing, I speed-walked toward my condo. This was going to stop now.

was taking a chance on so many levels. If Ethan found out about this, he'd walk away for sure. But from the beginning, I'd always known his way wouldn't get me out of this situation; Ethan wasn't proactive. What we needed was information, and I was about to connect a major dot for my attorney.

Before I reached the front of the house, I glanced over my shoulder, taking in the lavish homes in the Memorial area, then I banged on the door like I was one of those federal agents. As if she had been standing there waiting for me, Vivian swung the door open. Her eyes widened just a little, but she didn't seem particularly surprised.

My ex–best friend stood silent for a couple of seconds before she glanced over my shoulder. "Nice car." That was it; that was her greeting as she stepped aside so I could enter her five-thousand-square-foot home, which was way too much house for one person.

The foyer was the same as I remembered, with the winding staircase, but what was new were the paintings by Kehinde Wiley. I'd known Vivian was doing well, but I hadn't realized she was doing buy-paintings-by-a-famous-artist-who-painted-President-Obama well. Of course, she'd be doing better now that she'd stolen the WestPark contract from me. But was her success connected to the texts? To her uncle? And what did all of this have to do with me?

Standing in the middle of her foyer, I said, "I wasn't sure if you still lived here."

"Why not? You still live in your condo."

My eyebrows rose almost to my hairline. How did she know that? Did her stalking go beyond her texts? But then I shook that thought away. Vivian had talked me into purchasing the two units, and she knew how much I loved living downtown. Of course she'd assume I'd still be there.

But her words lingered in my mind.

"So." She leaned against her staircase and folded her arms. "I really appreciate your coming down here to congratulate little ole me."

My eyes narrowed, even though I'd expected Vivian to gloat. "I don't know how you did it. I don't know how you won the WestPark contract."

"Easily." She shrugged. "They wanted the best woman, and when they compared the two of us . . ." She left her insult there before she said, "So just go ahead and congratulate me, and then you can be on your way."

I crossed my arms, my stance letting her know that I wasn't amused and I wasn't leaving. "Congratulations aren't in order for one who cheats. I came here to talk about those texts you've been sending me."

She didn't flinch when she asked, "Texts? You think I've been sending you texts?"

"I know you have," I snapped back.

"And these alleged texts that I've supposedly been sending, they're coming from my number? Or is my name attached in any way?"

If I were a violent person, I would have smacked that smug sarcasm right out of her tone. "Oh, please, Vivian," I said, waving her words away. "You're much too bright for that."

She paused for a moment, then burst out laughing. "I take it, then, that these texts are anonymous, so why would I admit to sending them?" She was still chuckling when she added, "Okay, I'll bite. What are these texts about?"

I hesitated, then decided to play along. I wanted to keep Vivian talking because one thing about this woman: she usually talked until she gave herself away. "They're threats. Telling me that I'm going down. Oh"—I paused—"and scriptures. I've been getting plenty of scriptures."

The moment I said that, I wondered . . . Maybe these texts weren't coming from Vivian. Because the extent of her spirituality was being able to spell the word. I doubted if she could find Genesis in the Bible.

Her arms fell to her sides as if she was now interested. "Scriptures? Like 'May the Lord judge between me and you, may the Lord avenge me against you, but my hand shall not be against you'?" She smirked.

There was no way for me to hide my shock.

May the Lord avenge me against you.

I recalled the last text: . . . *in moments of pain, we seek revenge.*

Avenge. Revenge. Weren't they the same? Clearly, I'd been fooled. Somewhere Vivian had picked up a little spirituality. Or maybe she just used Google. Either way, I'd been right—the texts were coming from her.

I took a step toward her. "Why are you texting me?" I asked, trying to put as much of a threat as I could into my tone.

She chuckled. "Come on, Journee. If I were threatening you, I would make sure you knew. I'd want you to know I was torturing you." She paused. "Because you would deserve it." She spun around and moved toward her kitchen.

She hadn't given me an invitation, but I followed her anyway, thinking what she'd just said was probably the truest thing she'd said to me in years. She would want me to know the texts were coming from her.

But still, my gut told me Vivian was somehow involved in all of this. If she wasn't the one, did she know who was sending those messages? And did she know why?

Inside the kitchen, I sat at the glass dining table I'd helped her pick out when she moved here almost five years ago as she snapped a K-cup into her Keurig. As it brewed, she leaned against the counter and folded her arms once again. "So since you're still here, all up in my house, I guess you have more questions."

"Have you spoken to your uncle?" I decided to begin the next phase of my interrogation there.

"Nope, not since he fired me and made it perfectly clear that you were the Chosen One."

"I had nothing to do with you being fired."

"We both know that Uncle Simon firing me for talking to my boyfriend was just a pretense. The truth is, helping the homeless was my idea, but you turned out to be a much better grifter than I could ever be." She grabbed her mug from the coffee machine, and I was surprised when she came to the table and sat across from me. For just a flicker of a moment, the years of competing for projects and Simon's attention melted away, and this was just like the first night in her house when the two of us had sat here for hours, dreaming about all that we wanted to be.

I said, "I was never a grifter. I never cheated anyone out of money."

With the lift of an eyebrow, she called me a liar, and just like that, all of those good old feelings went away.

"I worked hard for every dime of my money, but I'm not going to defend myself to you. I will tell you it was never my intention to get in between you and your uncle."

"Of course, Journee," she said, and took a sip of her coffee. "It's never your intention to do anything because you're just poor little homeless Journee Alexander, who is always trying to do right but is always in the dead center of wrong."

Now this meeting was nothing more than Vivian trying to figure out all the ways she could insult me, and I wasn't going to sit here anymore. This visit was a bust. I was convinced of the opposite of what I'd walked in here believing—Vivian wasn't the one sending the texts, and she didn't have any information about Simon.

But at the risk of being the target of another one of her insults, I asked Vivian, "Are you concerned at all that Simon will turn on you? That he will use you as currency to get a lighter sentence?"

"Nope, he's not going to turn on his own flesh and blood. Now, you . . ." She sipped and glanced at me over the rim of her mug. "If Simon was going to use someone to get less time, it wouldn't be me." She pushed her cup aside and leaned across the table. "Because I wasn't the one with him when that woman died. *That* is the kind of leverage he'd use."

Those words drained every bit of blood from me, and if it'd been able, my skin would have turned the color of the satin sheets on my bed.

Vivian chuckled. "Oh. You didn't realize I knew about that?"

No! I screamed inside, but I forced my trembling lips to remain pressed together. There was no way I was going to incriminate myself and give her any leverage over me. Her voice was even as my heart crashed against my chest.

"Well, I know all about it." She shrugged. "So you just wasted a whole morning talking to me when this is between you and my uncle. And if I were a betting woman, I'd tell you to find yourself a really good attorney." She held up a finger. "Wait! You should give your ex a call. Maybe Ethan is available."

As she laughed, I stood slowly, and with my chin up and my

shoulders back, I sauntered out of her house with a confidence that was just a façade. Her laughter followed me into the foyer, echoing in my ears. Still, I kept my head high even as I closed her front door behind me. I moved to my car, slid in, then backed out and away from Vivian's house. At the first corner, I made a right . . . then a left and another right, before I pulled over to the curb. I didn't know where I was, but I needed a moment to digest all that I'd just heard.

Vivian knew? Vivian knew! And if she knew, I'd bet every dollar in my bank account that she wasn't the only one. Now the list of suspects who could be sending me those texts was infinite.

16

T he heat on my face forced me to open one eye, and I groaned. Why hadn't I closed the blinds last night? My glance settled on the empty wine bottle on the night-stand. That was why. There was one empty bottle here, and I hoped there was *just* one in the living room.

Moaning, I rolled onto my back and stared at the ceiling. This was not the way I usually faced challenges, but wine was the great elixir. It was the only thing that had settled me yesterday when I stumbled back home with Vivian's words playing on repeat in my mind. But wine couldn't be my permanent fixer. Imagine staying in bed and drinking for the rest of my life.

Maybe I was being overly dramatic, but then I shook that thought away. Drama wasn't my thing; this was real. I'd only had one concern about the feds possibly investigating me; the only way I'd be in their line of fire was if anyone found out about the situation that was supposed to stay between Simon and me. But somehow Vivian knew, and if she did, a long list of others knew, too. How many? That was the question. And it could be that it didn't matter if the feds already had information about the day that changed so much in my life:

"Hey, Journee." Liz, Simon's assistant, tapped on my door. "Simon wants to see you in his office."

"Okay"—I glanced up from my computer—"give me a sec."

She shook her head. "He said he wants to see you now."

"Got it," I said, standing up. I chuckled. Simon was always in *such a rush when he wanted to introduce me to a new client. Rounding my desk, I stepped into the hallway, and the moment I did, I felt like I was on the floor of the New York Stock Exchange. Energy surged through the space, chatter filled the air as brokers pursued new clients, discussed new deals, negotiated with banks. This was why ClearWater Mortgage was one of the top brokerage firms in the nation and Simon Wallace was one of the most powerful men in the industry.*

I'd changed professions at the right time. The real estate industry was booming. Interest rates were low, inventory was high, and that equaled a constant flow of clients. And Simon's company provided whatever a client needed—legit and not so legit. And what Clear-Water provided for me . . . I was making so much money with my own clients—and then with the "cases" I worked with Simon on the side—it was unbelievable what I, at the age of thirty-one, had been able to bank in my five years at ClearWater.

The door to Simon's massive corner office was ajar, and I tapped on it. "Hey, Liz said you wanted to see me." I grinned, expecting him to jump up, his arms flailing with excitement about whatever he had going on.

But my smile flipped upside down when Simon glanced up. His eyes were dark, his jaw clenched, and the ends of his lips drooped.

"What's wrong?"

"Close the door." Then he motioned for me to sit. This wasn't about a client—of that, I was sure—and in the seconds that passed between moving from the door to the chair, every scenario scrolled through my mind. My stomach was somersaulting. Had something happened to Vivian?

Oh my God! I hadn't spoken to her since we had that falling-out and I refused to quit to support her. But it wasn't until this moment that I realized how much I'd missed her. Everything that had happened between us seemed so unimportant, and now I wished we'd reconciled.

Tears already burned behind my eyes as I braced myself for Simon to speak horrible words. He whispered, "Remember our last gig?"

I blinked. What? So this wasn't about Vivian? I said, "Yeah, Mrs. Landers, right?"

He nodded but stayed silent, and now I was really confused. Mrs. Landers was a sweet woman, but why would she have Simon so distressed? Her case was closed.

"What about her?" I asked, still very perplexed.

He parted his lips, paused, then said, "She died." Then he clarified, "Mrs. Landers died," although I wasn't sure if the clarification was for me or was just Simon speaking aloud the unbelievable.

"Oh my God." I pressed my hand against my chest. "That's so sad," I said, thinking of the lovely lady who was so full of life the last time we'd met.

Simon said, "It really is. She committed suicide."

I gasped, hardly able to catch my breath. "What?"

I couldn't reconcile what Simon was telling me with the silver-haired seventy-eight-year-old woman I'd come to know. She'd reminded me of that actress Diahann Carroll, who was big back in the day. Mrs. Landers had that kind of class, that kind of style, that kind of fire. The retired school librarian had gotten behind on her mortgage after she had refinanced it a few years back for a lower payment. That had been a smart decision for seven years, but then about a year ago, Mrs. Landers's adjustable-rate payment increased at the same time as her home insurance and property taxes went up. Even with her pension and social security, there was no way Mrs. Landers could afford the extra thousand dollars each month.

Finally, I asked Simon, "When did this happen?"

Simon looked away. "I just found out. I called her because she didn't cash the check I gave her last week. That much money . . . in all the years I've been doing this, I've never had someone not cash the check. Wanted to make sure she hadn't lost it. Or worse . . . was thinking about not cashing it."

I understood that. Simon told me he held his breath until each check was cashed. That was the client's final acceptance of what happened. Their house was gone, but that little money was a payoff; it kept them silent. It was better than nothing.

"A guy answered her phone and told me she was dead." Simon paused. "When I asked what happened, he said she'd killed herself. Wanted to know who I was, but I just told him I was sorry and hung up." He shook his head.

I sat there for a moment, remembering the times I'd visited Mrs. Landers. She was the only gig whose home I had visited twice. She'd asked me to come back, the second time without Simon, because she said she trusted me and she just wanted to be sure Simon was honest and upright.

Over tea cakes, she had looked me straight in the eye. "Tell me the truth, Wilhelmina. Is Simon trustworthy? Because this house means everything to me. My grandfather purchased it back in the 1920s, when Black folks knew the importance of saving everything they had so they could own property. This house has been passed through the generations to me, and it would be beyond devastating to lose it."

Her sincerity and her story had almost broken me. Almost made me tell her to run the other way, ask someone in her family, or work hard to find a legitimate source of funding.

I would have told her that if there were any other source. But Mrs. Landers was out of options; she was going to lose her home even if Simon and I walked away. She was so far behind on her payments that, unless her family had upward of $35,000 to spare (with the accumulation of interest and penalties that were rising every day),

I doubted if even they could help. The bank wanted this property back, and there was really nothing that Simon or I could do to save her—except talk her into signing the deed to her house over to us, and eventually we'd tell her that the bank refused to work with her. Then we'd give her $20,000, telling her we wanted to make sure she had a fresh start. Within weeks, Simon would sell her house, making five times more than what he'd given her.

For the first time, though, I was overwhelmed with feelings for Mrs. Landers and had to suck up my emotions. I had assured Mrs. Landers she could trust Simon because he would do everything he could to save her home, but when I returned to the office, I demanded that Simon give Mrs. Landers extra money. "Give her five thousand more," I insisted. "Take it out of my fee."

Now, as I sat in front of Simon, my stomach began to spin again, and soon my head followed. "Simon." He glanced up, and in his eyes, I could see he had the same question I was about to ask. "Do you think this has anything to do with us?"

I watched his Adam's apple crawl up his throat. "No, Journee," he lied. "And don't you ever say that again. In fact, this is the last time we'll ever talk about Louise Landers. Never mention her or this situation to anyone."

"I won't."

"I'm not kidding, Journee, don't even tell Ethan."

"We're not together—you know that. We're not even friends."

He released a long breath. "Good. Your boyfriend—ex-boyfriend—doesn't need to know about this. At all." He held up his hands. "This is between the two of us," he said in a tone that sounded like a warning. "We both have to promise to take this to our graves."

When I nodded, he swiveled his chair around to face the window. I had been dismissed.

I stood and as soon as I balanced myself, I walked toward my *office. This time, though, I didn't feel any of the energy; I didn't hear any of the shouts and yelps that came from excited people making money. Closing my office door, I lumbered to my desk.*

I sat there and stared. Sat there and thought. Sat there until I grabbed my purse and walked out of my office. I took nothing with me, but I never returned to ClearWater Mortgage again.

THAT AFTERNOON, I climbed into bed and didn't leave my condo for a week. But when I finally did, I made a commitment that I would open a new firm and use my business only for good. I was never going to be on the questionable side of mortgage financing again. That was when J. Alexander and Associates was born.

But leaving Simon, making that vow, starting my firm— none of it had been good enough. Because karma always hovered around, waiting for the right moment to strike. It looked like my moment had come.

Pushing myself up, I leaned against the headboard. I always knew my situation was serious, but now I could see there was real trouble in my future.

I thought this wouldn't go beyond negotiating with Simon so he would keep my name out of any bargains he had with the feds. But if someone other than Simon was willing to talk to the feds, then an indictment could very well be in my future.

For the first time, I was really scared. But fear didn't take away my fight, and now I had no choice but to tell Ethan everything. Because now anyone could tell him about Mrs. Landers, including Ivy. And telling Ethan would be her perfect way to finally bring me down.

It was the thought of Ivy that made me make the final decision. I'd be the one to tell Ethan, to explain, and then he'd have everything he needed to defend me—if Ethan stayed . . .

I grabbed my cell phone and held it against my chest. Closing my eyes, I spoke to God and pleaded with Him to touch Ethan's heart. Then I tapped Ethan's name on my cell phone screen.

As the phone rang, I prayed again until I heard: "What's up, Journee?"

"Good morning. Listen, I hate to bother you on a Sunday," I said, feeling no need for niceties. "But there is something important I need to discuss with you."

"Did you get another text?"

"I did, but that's not what this is about." I paused. "I found out something yesterday that's big. Something you should know."

"What is it?"

"No. Not on the phone. It's too long; it's too much. I have to see you. Do you have about thirty minutes this afternoon?"

"Uh, Journee, I don't work on Sunday. We're just leaving church and heading to Ivy's parents'."

Then, "Baby . . ." Ivy's voice came through my phone, and I realized that, one, Ethan and Poison Ivy were together, and two, he had me on speaker. Ivy continued, "I think we can spare an hour if Journee needs your help." Then she sang, "Hey, Journee," like we were friends.

"Ivy," I said. I wanted to add that I didn't want to interfere with their time together. Not because I cared about that, but I didn't want Ivy to insinuate herself into this meeting. It was going to be difficult enough to tell Ethan; I didn't need his smiling fiancée beside him.

Ivy's voice came through my phone again. "Go on, baby, I'll meet you at my parents' house." I sighed with relief until she added, "We're only choosing the wedding invitations, so it's not a big deal. I can spare you for a little while."

When she giggled, I pressed the tips of my fingers against

my head. The headache I'd awakened with had just been made worse. Did I really have to listen to these engaged people? "You know what?" I piped in. "Forget it. I'll see you tomorrow, Ethan."

"No," Ivy said. "It sounds important, and with the trouble you're in, you need to meet him now."

The trouble I'm in?

"All right," Ethan said. "Give me about an hour, Journee."

"Thank you," I said. And then, because Mrs. Hunter had done her best to raise me right, I added, "Thank you, Ivy," though there was no gratitude in my tone.

"No problem," she chirped. "See you soon, and I hope we can work everything out for you. I really do."

I ended the call and stared at my cell. That was just too odd—talking to my ex's fiancée like we were all friends. But it wasn't like I could walk away. While I didn't like her, I needed him.

I tossed back the duvet, swung my legs over the bed, and waited for the room to steady. All I needed was a cold shower, and then I'd be ready to face Ethan with the truth.

moaned when I read the text: **Counting down the hours until I see you.**

The past twenty-four hours had been so tough that I'd forgotten about Quincy. Reading the text again, my first instinct was to cancel. But this man was the only light in my life. I'd need to see him after meeting with Ethan, no matter what my ex decided to do.

So I texted back: **See you at three. I'll tell the concierge to send you right up,** then checked myself in the mirror. Cold showers were a miracle cure; I didn't look hungover. The knock on my door made me take a deep breath. I grabbed my phone and then greeted Ethan at the door.

When Ethan stepped inside and gave me a hug, I felt immediate relief. At least for a moment.

"So," he said, moving toward the sofa. "You said this was important." He paused and glanced at the blanket I'd left on the couch, and then his eyes moved to the empty bottle of wine on the table.

I'd cleaned myself up but forgotten to do the same to my condo. Moving the wine bottle to the kitchen island and tossing the blanket aside, I offered Ethan a seat. "Yeah, this is important."

"Well, I was going to call you tomorrow, because I also have some news."

I stood as he sat and unbuttoned his jacket. "I have a feeling if you had good news, you would have called me right away."

He shrugged, not committing. "So who should go first—you or me?"

"I think I should because what I have to say may affect what you'll say to me." I sank down onto the sofa.

"Ohhh-kaaay." He dragged the word out and rested his arms on his knees. "Talk to me."

His stare was intense, reminding me of better times. Telling the truth and looking at Ethan at the same time wouldn't work. So I stood and went to the window. And as Discovery Green came into my view, I began, "The homeless scam wasn't the only thing I did with Simon. There was more."

With my back to Ethan, I told him everything: about how Simon and I had started, about how I became Wilhelmina Jones, and how Simon had taken the homes away from hundreds of homeowners, then made an indecent amount of profit when he sold those houses. His profit was well into the millions, I knew . . . because, as a fee, I'd received a percentage, and I had well over a million dollars in investments I'd made with just that money.

Finally, I faced Ethan. "It was horrible, getting those people to sign the deeds to their homes to us, but, Ethan, these people were going to lose their homes anyway. There was no saving them; their credit was shot, so they couldn't get new loans," I continued, feeling as if I had to justify it all so that Ethan would agree to continue to work with me, "and their current institutions wouldn't work out new payment plans. We only worked with people who had no options, who were so desperate that they signed over their deeds on just a promise."

Ethan leaned back, shook his head, then nodded for a few moments before he said, "What made you decide to finally tell me?"

"I wish I could say I just wanted to come clean, but . . ." I paused. Did I want to add that I had seen Vivian on top of this news? No. He'd already warned me not to contact anyone. He'd stop working with me for sure. I said, "Because there's more to this story, and this has been eating at me for years." This time I sat across from Ethan. This time I looked straight into his eyes. "The reason why I finally left Simon is because there was a woman, Mrs. Landers, who . . . who . . ." I glanced down at my hands and swallowed back emotions I still felt about her. Looking up again, I said, "She killed herself."

Ethan gasped. "Whoa."

"It happened three years ago. She signed her deed over to Simon, and then weeks later he told her the bank wouldn't work with her, and he gave her a check for twenty-five thousand dollars. Days later, she killed herself."

He sat up straight. "Oh my God, Journee."

"I know." I shook my head. "I never found out if her suicide was directly related to her losing her house, but the timing . . . she never even cashed Simon's check." I sighed. "I have worked hard every day since I left Simon, trying to make up for that woman's death, but nothing will bring her back." I let a few silent moments pass, almost in honor of Mrs. Landers. Finally, I said, "I had to tell you because Simon isn't the only person who knows about this. I'm sure he's talked about it with Vivian, maybe others."

Ethan was silent. So silent that after a while, I expected him to get up and walk out the door. But then he said, "Journee, I'm going to say this only once . . ." I looked up at him. "I wish to God you had listened to me. I wish to God you understood the discernment I had about Simon. I knew it from that first handshake, and if you'd listened"—his voice was softer now—"our lives would have been so different."

I nodded, even though I was confused a bit by his words.

Of course he was talking about the situation that I was now in, but was he also talking about this situation with us? If not for Simon, I'd be the one wearing Ethan's ring; we both knew that.

"If I could find a way to turn back time . . ." I said.

"But we can't," he said softly. "We all have to live with the consequences of our decisions and move forward. And that's what we'll do. Together, we'll move forward on this." He reached across the sofa and squeezed my hand.

"I am so grateful that you're not walking out the door," I said, then paused again to hold back all that I felt inside: the relief, but also the ache I felt, realizing how much I lost when I let Ethan go.

"I'm not leaving you. We're going to fight this, but I have to be honest, Journee. If the feds have this, it could be bad." He paused. "The news I have for you—we found out you are under federal investigation." I sucked in a draft of air. "One of Ivy's connections at the FBI gave us the heads-up."

I squeezed my hands together to stop the trembling. "So, what does this mean?" I said, surprising myself with my calmness.

"Well, the good news is that now that we know, we can really get to work. It's difficult because we don't have an indictment, but with what you just told me, I'm wondering if this is what the feds are working with."

"Do you think they found out from Simon?"

He shrugged. "I don't know, but it won't matter where they received the information. All that's important is that they have it."

"Would it help to know that all I did was meet with the clients? I never did any paperwork. I never took their deeds or sold their homes."

"But you did receive proceeds from the sales, correct?" When all I did was nod, he added, "That's enough, Journee. To just lay it all out, you were still very much a part of the scam. You went into people's homes, you lied to them, and those lies coerced them into giving legal ownership to Simon. You were an accessory."

It must have been the way I sat there, still as stone, not able to move, hardly able to think, that made Ethan add, "But I promise you, we're going to fight."

I pressed down the fear that rose within me. "Thank you," I said, just as my phone vibrated.

"Excuse me," I said to Ethan as I grabbed my cell, then read the message:

You can try to run, you can try to hide, you can even try to get help. And no one will save you. You're going to prison. Vengeance is mine.

For the first time, I believed the text. There was a chance that I was going to prison, and I finally broke. Dropping the phone, I covered my face with my hands and just sobbed.

In one motion, Ethan snatched my cell from the floor, read the text, and sighed. Then he pulled me into his arms, and I did something I had never done in the years we were together—I cried as he held me.

Crying was something I just didn't do. I was about thirteen when I stopped crying over Norma, and then I vowed I'd never release tears again. But this day had changed things. The pressure—from Vivian to the federal investigation—it had borne down and squeezed these emotions out of me. "I'm sorry," I said after taking minutes to gather myself.

"I get it," he said, still holding me. "But listen." He shifted so that I had to sit up and face him. With his fingertips, he lifted my chin. We were so close as he searched my eyes. "These texts don't matter anymore, Journee. It doesn't matter who's sending them. It won't affect your case one way or the other."

My cheeks were wet with my tears. "Don't you think they're connected?"

"It doesn't matter. The texts are only meant to torment you. And you cannot let whoever is sending these messages win. Is there a way for you to change your number?"

Sitting back a little, I sniffed. "Oh, God, how I wish. But so many clients, my whole business—"

"I know. That's what I thought. But I had to ask. So if changing your number is not an option, you're going to have to ignore the texts. You're not being threatened physically, and I need your head in this fight. So are you with me? Are we in this together?"

When I nodded, he pulled me into his arms again, and I could have rested in that familiar place for hours. But a knock on the door interrupted my moment of peace. I sat up, and he asked, "Do you want me to get that?"

"Yeah. People are always confused, coming to the wrong condo, since I connected these two."

His arm was still around me as he chuckled. "I remember."

And then his eyes held mine for a moment . . . and he softened . . . and he moved toward me. Time slowed . . . and now I felt my heartbeat. Our lips were so close . . . until there was another knock on the door and Ethan jumped up.

I grabbed a tissue from a box on the end table and dabbed at my eyes.

When Ethan opened the door, I heard, "Uh . . . I'm looking for—"

I shot straight up and sprinted over to the two men. "Quincy!

You're early," I said, instead of telling him that I'd forgotten he was coming.

"Uh, no, I'm actually a few minutes late." His glance volleyed between Ethan and me as he handed me the bouquet of flowers he carried.

"Thank you. I was just finishing a meeting with . . ." I decided to leave *that* alone. I said, "Ethan, meet Quincy, a new friend of mine, and Quincy, Ethan is . . . an old friend."

The men shook hands, but their expressions were the same: hard, no smiles. Way too awkward.

Ethan said, "Well, I think we're finished." He placed his arms on my shoulders, and I gave a quick glance to Quincy, who took a few steps away from us. "You good?"

"I will be."

"Okay. We'll talk tomorrow."

Again I nodded and then watched Ethan walk out of the door with only a wordless nod to Quincy. I waited until Ethan was gone before I turned and pasted a smile on my face. "I'm so glad to see you."

"Are you?" His tone was as hard as his expression. "It seems I interrupted something."

"No." I waved my hand. "We were just having a deep discussion." I averted my eyes and moved toward the kitchen to find a vase for the flowers.

"A deep discussion with your ex?"

I slowly spun to face Quincy. "How . . . how did you know Ethan was my ex?"

"I didn't until this moment," he said. "I just felt that vibe. So . . . if he's your ex, what was he doing here?"

I placed the flowers on the counter. The vase would have to wait. "First of all, I don't think it's a good idea for you to come to my home for the first time and question me about my guests."

He held up his hands. "You're right. Let's start over." He took a breath, but his tone didn't change. "It's good to see you're still friends with an ex."

"*Friends* is a strong word," I said, folding my arms. "But we're adults."

"So," he began, sounding more like an attorney than a teacher, "what kind of business are you doing with him?"

"Quincy!" I said his name like I was scolding him. "This questioning is out of line. It sounds like you're jealous when you don't have a reason to be, for two reasons." I held up my fingers. "One, Ethan is my ex, and two, you and I are not in any kind of relationship."

He backed away from me. "I thought we were building something."

"I thought that, too, but . . ."

His frown was so deep, his eyes narrowed to slits. "So, what are you saying?"

I heard Vivian's voice: *I wasn't the one with him when that woman died.* I heard Ivy's words: *With the trouble you're in . . .* I felt Ethan's lips . . . *almost.* Finally, I said, "I'm saying . . . this is a difficult day. So maybe it would be best for us to get together later in the week."

He stared at me as if he couldn't believe this was happening. Pressed his lips together. Gave me a single nod. And then, without another word, just a minute after Ethan had left, Quincy followed him out the door.

ooking out at the heavy clouds from my office window, I thought about how appropriate the weather was—a storm was looming. Just like the past seventy-two hours of my life. Everything had changed. From the almost-kiss with Ethan, which left me reeling, confused, and unable to stop thinking about my ex, to what felt like a lovers' quarrel with a man I didn't know well enough to love or to fight with.

Most of all was the investigation. Someone was cooperating with the feds against me, and so now I couldn't move through the day without giving everyone the longest side-eye. Every person who got on an elevator with me was a suspect. Every car that rolled up next to me at a red light was suspicious. I was wary of everyone and everything.

Today, though, I couldn't spend the time focusing on all that was going wrong. That was what I'd done for the past three days, and now I had to get my head back into the game. I still had a successful business to run.

My cell phone rang, and I grabbed it from my desk. "This is Journee Alexander."

"Journee, this is Clementine Charles. I'm Windsor and Norma's next-door neighbor."

I frowned, wondering if my sister had referred this woman to me for a new home. Windsor had done that before, but usually she told me beforehand. "Yes, Mrs. Charles. How may I help you?"

"I'm calling to let you know your mother has been rushed to the hospital."

Those words took my breath away; I collapsed into the chair. "What's . . . what's wrong with Norma?"

"Your mother and I were having coffee this morning, and all of a sudden, she had an attack. She couldn't talk; she could hardly breathe. It was like she was choking. I know she has that bronchitis, so I called the ambulance right away."

I felt a bit of relief, because this was the kind of call that could have gone left. "Have you called Windsor?"

"I did, but I don't think she's landed yet. She just left for Austin this morning, you know."

Dang, I'd forgotten about her training. "Your mother needs you," Mrs. Charles said in a tone that made me wonder what she'd been told about me.

"All right," I said, slipping on my sweater. "Where is my . . . where is Norma?"

"Ben Taub," she said, as if she thought I should have known.

Ben Taub? I popped up out of my chair. Why in the world would she have been taken to the public hospital?

"I'm on my way."

After promising Mrs. Charles that I would call her back when I had news, I rushed from my office, telling Tasha I'd be available by phone. Inside my car, I took a deep breath and thought for a moment. I was on my way to the hospital to take care of Norma. Because she would have done at least this for me.

Inside the car, I called Windsor, but I kept getting her voice mail. I didn't know if she was still flying or was already in her training. Focusing on Windsor kept my thoughts away from Norma. I didn't want to let my mind wander too far as I drove the ten minutes to the hospital. Just kept thinking that I wanted Norma to be well. Just kept asking God to do that.

Pulling into the parking lot, I glanced around for a valet, and when I didn't see an attendant, I whipped into one of the handicapped spots in the front of the building. I'd just have to pay for the ticket. I rushed into the emergency room but paused at the door. Why were all of these people in here? There were so many that for a moment I wondered if they were shooting a movie . . . some kind of mass-casualty scene. Navigating through the crowd, I pushed past men moaning, women groaning, all begging for help.

Stepping over a whimpering man crouched on the floor with a blood-soaked towel wrapped around his arm, I finally made my way to the nurses' station.

"I'm looking for Norma Alexander," I said to the woman there, raising my voice a bit to speak over the din of the ER.

The fortyish-year-old woman, who was much too old to be smacking on gum like it was her source of fuel, didn't bother looking up from her computer. "Who are you?"

"Journee Alexander . . . her daughter." It was easier for me to say that than to claim her as my mother.

The woman didn't reply; she just kept tapping on that computer for so long that I wondered if she'd even heard me. Finally, she said, "Yeah, she's here. She's in processing."

"Processing? What does that mean?"

"It means she's in processing," she repeated slowly as if she thought that would help my comprehension.

I took a deep breath, telling myself that getting angry wouldn't get results. "Okay, I don't understand what 'processing' means," I said, just as slowly. "Is she in a room? Has she been seen by a doctor?"

The woman finally glanced up. I braced myself for her

attitude, but that wasn't what I saw in the woman's eyes. I recognized her exhaustion. "It means that we don't have a bed for her because, as you can see, we're pretty busy right now. So have a seat like everyone else, and I'll do my best to locate her for you."

"Locate her?" *What the heck?* "Is she lost?"

"Ma'am," the woman said, with what little patience she had with me waning, "please, I'll let you know when we find her." She turned back to her keyboard, dismissing me.

I glanced around the room, with space to fit about one hundred. But now there was standing room only. Every seat was taken except for two: one next to a woman coughing profusely and another next to the man on the floor with the blood-soaked towel.

I sat next to the man, but it didn't take me even a minute to decide Norma wasn't staying here. I went into Journee Alexander mode, calling first Dr. Patterson and then Harold Michaels, a hospital administrator at Houston Methodist whom I'd dated for about three weeks. We had no personal chemistry, but our professional partnership was off the chain. It was because I'd helped him get funding for four investment properties that within forty-five minutes Harold called me back to tell me that Norma had been located and had already been moved to Houston Methodist, just a mile away.

After thanking him a thousand times, I made my way through the maze of people, then ran to my car. Fifteen minutes later, I was in Norma's semiprivate room, watching the attendants getting her set up and settled in. The entire time, though, Norma hadn't moved, and it seemed as if she was hardly breathing. I kept asking the attendants if she was asleep or unconscious—there was a difference to me.

"The doctor will talk to you" was all the two young men told me.

Finally, the doctor, who'd been sent by Dr. Patterson, came in, and she introduced herself and then examined Norma, and assured me that she was doing as well as could be expected.

"She's been given drugs to relax her lungs so she can rest."

When I was left alone with Norma, I sat in the chair in the corner, watching her, trying to understand all that I was feeling. I was confused and afraid and prayerful.

Then Norma moaned. I sat up straight. And when her eyes fluttered, I jumped from the chair. By the time I made it to the side of the bed, her eyes were open but she struggled to focus.

"Norma," I whispered.

Her eyes widened at the sound of my voice. "Baby girl." Her voice was low and raspy as she turned toward me.

"Shhh . . ." I said. "Don't talk."

"Journee," she squeaked, her breathing sounding strained.

"Please, Norma," I said, "you have to rest."

"Thank you for coming to see me."

She grasped my hand, and her touch shocked me. Returned me to the past for a moment. Gently, I pulled away.

"Baby girl"—she struggled to sit up—"you have to forgive me."

"We don't have to talk about this now. You're in the hospital; you have to get well."

She swallowed and nodded. "We have to talk because I might not get better." She coughed, and the rattling in her chest sounded like a loose cage; it frightened me. I wanted to call the nurse, but Norma grabbed my arm this time. Her grip was surprisingly strong for someone so weak. "Please. Forgive me," she begged.

I wanted to tell her that I forgave her, so that she would sleep. But I couldn't. Because I didn't.

"I was young," she continued. "And I believed everything that Mrs. Hunter told me."

Now I frowned.

"She said it would be better for you because she taught at that special school." Another cough. "She kept saying we were a village and everyone had to do what was best for you."

When Norma closed her eyes, I almost shouted, *No!* I wanted to shake her awake. What was Norma talking about?

After a moment, Norma licked her lips, and I glanced at the pitcher of water on the stand. I filled a plastic cup with water, then raised the bed a bit before I held the cup to her lips. Norma sipped slowly; then, when she sighed, I pulled the cup away.

"Journee." Her voice was stronger now. "I didn't want to, but Mrs. Hunter knew more than I did. When she said I'd be hurting you by keeping you, I still tried. But I was struggling and I didn't know what to do. I regret listening to her. Oh . . . how I regret that. Especially when you and Windsor connected again and you wouldn't talk to me. But my regret was never greater than when I saw you again. When I saw the hate in your eyes."

"I don't hate you." I whispered that truth.

She shook her head as if she didn't believe me. "You have every right to hate me. I should never have listened to her. I should have trusted myself. I should have kept you with me. I should have . . ." Tears filled her eyes before she closed them and leaned back. When she stayed that way, I lowered the bed so she was flat on her back again.

I stood there staring at Norma as she slept again, trying to make sense of her words. Pulling the chair from the corner to the edge of the bed, I finally sat, with all the words that Norma had spoken crashing together in my mind.

Norma hadn't given me away.

At least, not in the way I'd always believed. She was a young, struggling widow who'd been coerced. By Mrs. Hunter. This was what Norma had been trying to tell me all of these years. And I'd never given her a chance.

I sat with that thought—Norma hadn't given me away. And I stared at this woman, reliving all the years and all the varying emotions that I'd wasted on her. Tears filled my eyes as I took her hand. I held her for a moment, then whispered, "I forgive you. I forgive you . . . Mama."

19

"A re you sure, Dr. Patterson?" I was on the phone with the doctor, who'd kept her promise and called with a morning update on my mother. "I really wanted to come by and see her."

"I understand, but like I just told your sister, we have to keep your mother sedated, and any stimuli could agitate her. And the hospital still has its visiting protocols with Covid. Of course, if she weren't sleeping, it would be fine, but just let her rest today and we'll reassess tomorrow."

Although I wanted to see her, I wanted to do what was best for my mother. So I agreed.

"Go on with your day and I'll keep you posted."

"Thank you, Dr. Patterson, for taking care of my mother." When I hung up, I leaned back and thought about those words: *my mother*.

There was such joy inside me, but also an equal portion of sorrow. Joy because I'd been wrong . . . and sorrow for the same reason. So much time had passed, but last night I'd prayed for God to take that guilt away. There would be time for me to wallow, but not now. My focus had to be my mother. That was what Windsor and I agreed upon last night when she rushed home and we cried together in our mother's hospital room.

Just as I picked up my cell to call my sister, Tasha tapped on my door. "Excuse me, Journee?" I glanced up. "You have a visitor?" she said, as if she were asking a question.

I frowned. "Uh, Tasha, I don't take walk-ins." My assistant knew that.

She stepped closer and whispered, "You may want to see this guy."

I felt relief, and my lips were already tugging up into a smile. Quincy!

I hadn't spoken to him since he'd stomped out of my condo on Sunday. With all that happened this week, I hadn't had a chance to think too much about him—and when I did, I figured I'd never hear from him again. I was fine with that . . . until this moment. I had missed him, especially with what was going on. "Okay," I said to Tasha.

But then a thirtyish-year-old gentleman in a classic black suit, a crisp white shirt, and a thin black tie entered. "Good morning, Ms. Alexander. I have a special message for you." He handed me an envelope.

Giving him a long side-eye, I opened and read the handwritten note on ivory-colored paper:

> *I am so sorry. I've had lots of time to think about it, but I still have no excuse. I let my heart override my good sense. Will you forgive me?*

When I glanced up, the gentleman said, "Mr. Carothers would like you to join him for lunch. He's hoping you're free."

I glanced at the pile of work on my desk and thought about my staff meeting this afternoon and, most important, my mother in the hospital. Still, I said, "I'm free." The work would all be here, I would be back in time for the meeting, and I had my phone to check in with Dr. Patterson.

"Well, my name is Edward, and I'm going to take you to him."

I snatched my purse and then rushed past Tasha, who wore a grin the size of Texas.

"Have a good time," she shouted as I followed Edward through the doors and down the elevator to a gleaming black town car parked right in front of the building.

I settled into the soft red leather seat. As Edward eased the car onto Interstate 45, I texted Windsor to check on her and then leaned back. The exhaustion I'd felt from my insomnia over the past few nights overcame me. I just wanted to close my eyes for a second . . . and then I heard:

"Ms. Alexander?"

My eyelids fluttered open, and I sat up with a start. Had I fallen asleep? No! I would never have done that. Would never have gotten into a car with a stranger to a destination unknown and closed my eyes.

I glanced at my watch. It was just approaching noon; about thirty minutes had passed. Before I could get a good look at my surroundings, the door opened and Quincy peeked into the car.

"Hey, beautiful." He held out his hand and helped me out. For a moment, I was surprised—he was dressed so casually, in a light blue button-down shirt and khaki slacks. He didn't look at all like he was coming from school; I guessed he'd taken the day off . . . for me?

He took my hands into his and as I searched his eyes, I saw his apology. Then, when he pulled me into his arms, I felt it. "I hope you know how sorry I am," he whispered. When he stepped back, he added, "But I think the best way is to show you."

For the first time, I glanced around. Kemah! My parents brought me here when I was about five so that I could see the lake. But then I returned with Simon and Vivian for a networking real estate event at Landry's when I first joined ClearWater Mortgage.

In the years since, so much had changed. The boardwalk, which had been pretty empty before, now pulsed with life, with a towering Ferris wheel at the center. I felt like I was in the middle of a carnival, even on this fall Tuesday afternoon.

When I turned back to him, Quincy said, "We're going to have lunch on the lake."

This was just the break I needed. I was almost giddy when he took my hand and led me over the boardwalk, which was crammed with people, but I paused as we passed the carousel.

"What's wrong?" Quincy's brows furrowed.

"Nothing." I smiled to assure him. "I just had a wonderful memory."

His glance followed mine, and he nodded. "I love carousels."

"I only remember riding once, when I was five, almost six. My dad took me to AstroWorld." And then I added, "It was a few weeks before he died."

Quincy put his arm around my shoulders and pulled me close. "Well, it may be time for another one of those rides. With a new man in your life."

Every time Quincy spoke, my knees weakened. He took my hand and we moved past the myriad of boutique shops and restaurants and vendors. At the top of the pier, we passed a young Black guy with locs hanging past his shoulders who was playing "Crazy in Love" on a flute. I would have never imagined a song with so much energy and so many beats on a flute. But it sounded amazing, and I could almost see Jay-Z and Beyoncé dancing right next to him, enjoying this rendition, too.

Just wandering around this boardwalk would have been the recipe for a wonderful afternoon. But at the end of the pier, Quincy stopped in front of a two-deck blue-and-white yacht with *Boardwalk FantaSea* scripted on the side. A gray-bearded gentleman in a blue-striped T-shirt, white shorts, and a sailor's cap helped me step onto the luxury boat, which could have held one hundred guests. Yet he seemed to be the only one aboard.

"I'm Godfrey," the man said. "I'm gonna take you up to the top."

Quincy motioned for me to follow Godfrey, so I did. I stepped onto a narrow, winding staircase and climbed to the top.

"I'll be taking you out for a short sail this afternoon," Godfrey said. "But imagine that I'm not even here. Just relax and have a good time."

He led me to cushioned seats along the side, and I thanked him before he disappeared into an enclosed area that I imagined was the cockpit. Before I had too much time to wonder about Quincy, he turned around the corner, rolling a table covered in a white cloth.

"This is nothing fancy," Quincy said, stopping in front of me. "I couldn't bring too much out on a boat, but I think you'll enjoy this."

I felt like a kid unwrapping a gift as I slid the cloth from the top. And I squealed at all the dishes: kale slaw, buffalo chicken pasta salad, and several tea sandwiches. There was even the pimento cheese dip that I loved, with my favorite tortilla chips. And, of course, a pitcher that was filled with sweet tea, I was sure.

"Oh my goodness. You went to the Sandwich Bar and got all my favorites. How did you even know I loved that place?"

"Tasha helped a little, but you told me the other night when we talked about our favorite foods."

I tried to recall what I'd said, but with all that had been going on, it seemed like a month had passed since then. And every time I'd been with Quincy, we'd had such full conversations. There weren't too many silent moments between us.

"I listen to you, Journee. Because even though we haven't known each other long, you mean a lot to me."

Like always . . . I swooned. The boat rocked as Godfrey lifted the anchor, and then it began its slow drift toward the middle of the lake.

I asked, "So we have this whole boat to ourselves?"

"Yup!" he said. "This place is packed on the weekends, making it almost impossible to get a private charter then. But I thought you could use a break in the middle of your workday anyway."

"You were right. This is more special."

As we sailed up the Galveston coast, we sat shoulder to shoulder and enjoyed the meal and each other in silence. When I finished, I sat back and sighed with appreciation. This was such a beautiful sight: seagulls fluttering above us, singing *ha-ha-ha-ha* as they swooped above the water, which was now the richest blue, so different from the murky brown color that hugged the Galveston shore.

My thoughts took on the motion of the boat, just drifting, and for the first time in weeks, I felt peace.

"You good?" he asked.

I blinked myself back to the moment. "I'm more than good. What a lovely way to spend a few hours after a rough week."

"I hope I didn't contribute to your anxiety. I don't know what happened on Sunday. All I know is I saw you with this guy and it looked like I'd walked into something. He obviously still cares for you—"

"Wait"—I stopped him—"no. He doesn't. Ethan and I broke up a long time ago, and now he's engaged."

His glance told me he didn't believe me. "Well . . ."

"Seriously." I reached for his hand. "He was just at my place to help me with . . . something at work. He's an attorney, and he and his fiancée are working on a project with me."

"Wow. Both of them?" He chuckled. "That's very twenty-first-century."

"I know. It's weird. But I want to assure you, I'm not interested in Ethan. I'm not interested in anyone."

That wasn't exactly how I meant to phrase my words, but before I could correct myself, he said, "Not anyone?" He leaned toward me, and his breath heated my lips. "Is there any way I can change your mind?" Then his lips met mine, and I welcomed him. We rocked with the boat and the kiss went on for seconds and seconds and seconds. I pushed myself away only because if I didn't, we were never going to stop, and when Mr. Godfrey returned, oh, what a sight he'd see.

"Whew," I said.

"So"—he gave me that lopsided grin—"mind changed?"

"Mind blown," I told him, and we laughed. "I appreciate everything about today, Quincy, especially your apology. But I want to make sure we leave with you understanding there's nothing going on with Ethan and me."

An image flashed in my mind: Ethan's lips, so close.

"Thank you for telling me. But it wasn't just Ethan that had me so unnerved on Sunday." He pushed away from me, and his eyes settled on the ripples in the water. "The last three years have been the most difficult of my life. I've been feeling like this boat—out in the middle of a lake without an anchor. It's been tough trying to find this new normal without my mother. And not having too many people to talk to about my feelings has been another challenge. I mean, how many folks want to hear a mama's boy still talking about his mother's death after all these years?"

I wanted to reach out and hug him and tell him he could talk to me anytime. But I stayed silent, feeling like Quincy just needed to talk.

He continued, "But I made it through, and I finally began to feel like I could breathe. That was when I met you." He turned to me now and took my hand into his. "You're the first woman I've approached in three years, and after what I did on Sunday, it seems I still have some healing to do."

I squeezed his hand. "I understand the need for healing. I have so many issues with my mother that I really have to work through." I paused, wondering how much I wanted to share. "She's in the hospital right now."

"Really?"

I told him about the call from Mrs. Charles and then being with my mother in the hospital, although I didn't share all that she'd told me.

"I can't imagine what that was like for you. Going from not having seen her in such a long time to caring for her like that."

"I know. It's complicated," I said.

"It sounds that way, but you've done enough for her."

I bit my lip as I wondered if I should tell him how wrong he was. But I said nothing because I hadn't had time to process all of this myself. I needed time to reverse the thinking I'd had for twenty-seven years. Needed time to understand that I hadn't been abandoned. "You know what?" I said. "Talking about this isn't the way I wanted to spend this lovely day."

"You're right. I'd rather be doing this." Again he kissed me, and then I twisted around, resting against his chest. He wrapped his arms around me, and like before, silence was our companion as the yacht coasted along the shore.

When Godfrey stepped up from the cockpit and said, "It's time for us to go back," Quincy and I moaned our discontent together.

As the boat made its slow turn, I sighed. "Back to work, I guess." When Quincy didn't respond, I asked, "Did you take off today?"

"Huh?"

He must have still been deep in thought.

"From school?" I said. "Did you take off from work?"

"Uh . . . yeah," he said. "Because I wanted to take the time to plan this lunch for you."

"I know your kids missed you, but I'm so glad you did."

We turned our attention to the approaching boardwalk and waved as a group of tourists took pictures of the yacht as we approached. Once Godfrey anchored it, he helped us disembark, and after thanking him, Quincy took my hand. This time, I wasn't going to just walk by the vendors; I had to at least stop at the handcrafted earrings and wooden bangles, which I knew Windsor would love. For a moment, I paused . . . should I get something for my mother? But as I studied the crafts, I realized I had no idea what she liked. With a sigh, I purchased gifts for Windsor and nothing for my mother.

Afterward, Quincy and I strolled arm in arm to the end of the boardwalk, where Edward waited with the limousine.

Once again, I didn't want to be apart from this man, and that both surprised and intrigued me.

Edward nodded to Quincy as we approached the car; then he got inside while Quincy opened the door for me. But we stood there holding hands, and he said what I'd been thinking: "I wish this day didn't have to end."

He kissed me, and it didn't matter how many times he did: I wanted to melt into his kisses forever. Finally stepping back, I whispered, "So, what are you going to do now?"

"Well"—his voice sounded as thick as mine—"after I make sure you're safely in this car, I'm going home to think about how wonderful this afternoon has been."

"So you have no other plans?"

He shook his head, then frowned as I slipped my phone

from my purse. With two taps, I found the number; then I put the call on speaker.

"Hey, Tasha," I said to my assistant when she answered. "I'm not going to make the staff meeting this afternoon. Can you just gather everyone's status reports and I'll go over them tomorrow?"

"Sure."

"And secure my car in the garage. I'll Uber to the office in the morning."

"Got it. Is everything okay?"

"Better than okay," I said as Quincy's lips spread into that smile of his. "I'll see you tomorrow." And before Tasha could ask any more questions, I ended the call.

He leaned in close, his lips almost touching mine. "So, what were you thinking?" he whispered, as if we were sharing a secret.

"Well"—I lowered my eyes and glanced up at him through my lashes—"I invited you to my home for dinner on Sunday, but . . . you never ate."

His light brown eyes shined. "I am a bit hungry now." Then he took off as if he were running the one-hundred-yard dash. I laughed as Quincy sprinted around the car, said a few words to Edward, and was back at my side in seconds. "Come on," he said, taking my hand. Let's go to your place . . . to eat."

I couldn't wait. Because I was hungry, too.

t had taken far too long. First the drive back from Kemah on 45 was almost like sitting in a parking lot and took us fifty-five minutes to get to my place downtown. But it wasn't just the traffic. Even as we waited for the elevator in my building, I had no patience. The one-minute wait dragged on so long it felt like an hour. But once the elevator doors parted and we stepped inside, it was worth the wait.

We were all over each other, lips and limbs intertwined as if we were trying to become one. We were still connected when the elevator stopped and we stumbled into the hallway. How we got to my apartment, I will never know.

I hated the moment when, at my front door, I had to break away from Quincy so that we could get inside. His breath was heavy and hot behind me, and once I opened the door, I pulled him inside. Kissing him, I walked backward, leading him into my bedroom. Once in there, Quincy pulled away and cupped my face in the palms of his hands.

"Are you sure?" He was breathless.

If he knew all that I'd been through this week, he wouldn't have asked that question. But instead of telling him that, I pressed into him. This time, our kiss was softer, gentler. As if our bodies knew that now we had time. Quincy moaned as we melded together, and his desire was so apparent. Slowly, we moved toward the bed, and Quincy laid me down as if I were a precious possession. And then he unwrapped me like I was a gift, moving slowly, as if he wanted to savor each moment, removing my sundress, then taking off my red lace bra, and finally, rolling my matching panties from my hips. Quincy rose over me, his gaze drinking in my nakedness. With his fingertips, he traced my cleavage; then he kissed me.

God, this man was sexy, and I had waited long enough. Rising up, I unbuttoned his shirt as he loosened the buckle on his pants. In less than a minute, his bare body was pressed against mine, and already, I was gasping.

Quincy smothered me—with his tongue, with his hands, with his legs. His hands traveled the terrain of my body, setting every bit of me on fire. There was not an inch of my body that he didn't caress. I'd invited him to dinner, and he feasted on me like I could possibly be his last meal. And I leaned into every bit of this pleasure.

I was so hot, I could hardly breathe. I couldn't kiss him enough; he couldn't caress me enough. There was only one thing that would extinguish the flames within me.

I rolled him over, rocked onto my knees, and straddled him. He grinned, but I couldn't even smile. Not until . . . he began to fill me, a little at first, and then more and more and more until I exhaled. I closed my eyes and we began to dance. A slow waltz, and as we twirled together, we began to sing. The sounds of our pleasure echoed through the room. Now we danced and we sang, faster and faster, until we had no more notes left.

I collapsed onto Quincy, then after a few seconds rolled onto my back. Months of hunger, weeks of pressure, had left me wanting, but now I was satiated. Together, we tried to get our breathing into rhythm once again. It took a few minutes before I could speak.

"Thank you for dinner," he finally said as he wrapped his arms around me and pulled me into his chest.

I said, "And can I say that I'm hungry no more?"

He chuckled and kissed the top of my head. "I'm glad." After a few moments, he rose up on his elbow and smiled down at me. As I caressed his chest, he asked, "Can I tell you that I thank God for flat tires?"

I laughed as he kissed my nose. "Yeah," I said, still giggling. "I will never see a flat tire the same way again."

His smile faded, and I tilted my head in question. He said, "I think we have something pretty wonderful here." With his fingertips, he traced the side of my face, but then he lowered his eyes when he added, "So if you're up for it, I'd like to give this, to give us, a try."

Awww! I lifted his chin and made him look at me. "Are you asking me to be your girlfriend?"

He leaned over and kissed me before he said, "I'm asking you to be my woman."

My response: I wiggled until I was beneath him; then, this time with our eyes fully open, we made love again.

MY BEDROOM HAD finally descended into darkness as my head rested on Quincy's chest. He slept, his breathing deep, but my eyes were still wide open. I lifted my head to glance at the clock on the nightstand. It was just a bit after eight. We had been in this bed for five hours, and I wanted five hours more, and then another five hours after that.

I smiled. I was glad that I enjoyed Quincy as much in the bed as I enjoyed him on a boat. *I'm asking you to be my woman.*

That was still a wow for me. Now, I was no prude: over the past three years, I'd shared my bed with a couple of men. But I didn't allow anyone to fall asleep or to stay overnight. No one had slept in this bed since Ethan.

That flash again: Ethan's lips so close to mine.

I squeezed my eyes shut, trying to rid myself of that image. Quincy was the man I wanted. When Quincy stirred, I froze. I didn't want to wake him. I was sure this was just a nap and that he'd wake up soon, because I really did need to feed him real food. I wanted to take care of my man.

My man.

That thought should have brought a smile to my lips, but how could I really be happy about this with all that loomed over me? Maybe I needed to tell Quincy what was going on before we got too deep. Maybe he had enough grace inside him to understand. Maybe he'd listen to me and not judge me but stand by me.

So many maybes. Too many for me to take the chance right now. I didn't want to mess up this very good thing that lay next to me. Not yet.

I eased away from Quincy, then slipped from the bed and grabbed my phone and bathrobe before I stepped from the bedroom.

I really did want to make sure Quincy had a nutritious dinner before he left . . . or stayed. It didn't matter to me. But first I had to check on my mother.

The call was quick to Dr. Patterson. My mother was resting and would sleep through the night. Next, I texted Windsor, who texted back that she was going to Austin in the morning, but just for the day.

Sighing, I settled onto the sofa. That part of my life was at least steady for the moment. Now Quincy. Opening my food delivery app, I scrolled through the selections. What would Quincy want? After the evening we'd had, I was sure he was famished.

Before I could choose, my cell rang and Ethan's name flashed on the screen. I glanced at the bedroom door, then accepted the call. "Hey," I whispered.

"How's it going, Journee?"

"I'm good." This time, I pushed back the image of our lips before it came to my mind. Too many moments of awkward silence filled the air, and I wondered if Ethan was remembering our almost-kiss, too.

Finally, he said, "I have something I want to discuss with you."

I glanced at my bedroom door, then stood and crossed the room to the balcony. Tightening my robe against the cool air, I asked, "What's going on?"

"Do you have time this evening? Ivy and I wanted to come by and discuss something."

My eyebrows rose high up on my forehead. "Ivy?" He wanted to bring her here? Where Ethan and I had declared our love for each other?

"Yeah. Ivy found out some interesting news, so she should be the one to tell you. And I'd rather we do this face-to-face so we can discuss it thoroughly."

Leaning against the balcony's railing, I said, "Is this good news or bad news, Ethan? Should I be expecting the feds to come knocking on my door?"

"It's interesting news. We can swing by in about ten minutes."

"Uh," I began. "Tonight's not good."

"Ohhh-kaaay," Ethan said.

"But I can come to your office tomorrow," I added quickly. "Just tell me the time."

"I'll check our schedules and then text you"—a beat—"so I won't disturb your evening again."

Was that a tinge of jealousy I heard?

"Okay, I'll see you tomorrow."

All kinds of emotions: happiness, sadness, fear . . . and even some jealousy rolled through me as I ended the call. But then I spun around and into the arms of Quincy, who stood wearing only his pants. "Oh my goodness. I thought you were still asleep."

"I rolled over, and when you weren't right there in my arms, I had to find you. So . . . everything okay?"

"Yeah, yeah," I said, averting my eyes and stepping into my condo. "Just some work stuff, but I'll handle it tomorrow." Now facing him, I planted a smile on my face. "So, I still owe you a dinner, and I was going to order in something. What would you like?"

He stepped to me and took my hands into his. "There's something going on with you."

It felt like my breath was stuck inside me. I tried to remember all that I'd said on the phone. What had Quincy overheard?

He continued, "But I can tell you're not ready to talk to me about it. And that's okay. I mean, I might be your man, but you don't know me like that."

I laughed.

"At least not yet. Seriously, though," he said as he pulled me closer, "I just want you to know you have a man who will be here when you need him. And you have a man who not only has your back but who can pray for you, too. Got it?"

"I got it," I said, and exhaled. "And thank you for understanding. I just need some time because everything between us is so good right now, I don't want to mess it up. I don't want you to look at me differently."

"Whoa," he said. "What did you do, kill somebody?" He laughed like that was the greatest joke he'd ever heard. I didn't part my lips. When he finished cracking up, he said, "Just know that I got you, okay?" He kissed my forehead and pulled me into his bare chest. "Now that I'm here, baby, I'm going to make sure you have everything in your life that you deserve."

When he held me tighter, I couldn't remember another time when I'd needed assurance so much. I had a lot to thank God for, but in this moment, my gratitude was for Quincy.

21

The last hours had been a roller coaster of emotions. Last night, I basked in the blush of new love as Quincy and I sat on the balcony and fed each other Chinese food and shared more stories about our lives. Then we'd made love for what felt like another five hours before we finally collapsed and slept.

Before the moon had completely bowed to a new day, Quincy had awakened, showered, and dressed, and then given me what felt like a thousand kisses before he left me panting at the front door.

A couple of hours later, I'd gone to the hospital to see my mother. She was still resting, being fed intravenously. But when I stepped into her room, her eyes opened, as if she felt me there. I only stayed long enough to see her smile and to give her one of mine, then talk to Dr. Patterson and get her assurance that my mother was progressing fine. "We just want to continue to observe her," the doctor told me.

But now, as I returned to Williams Towers to see Ethan and Ivy, I felt like I was living in three worlds: my mother's, Quincy's, and this one . . . which could change my life completely.

When I stepped off the elevator this time, there was someone sitting behind the large reception desk, beneath the gold letters that read: THOMAS & HOFFMAN LAW.

"I'm here to see Ethan Thomas," I said to the red-haired, middle-aged woman.

"Oh, yes," she greeted me as if I were a VIP. "They're expecting you. I'll let Ms. Franklin know you're here. You can have a seat."

I nodded but was too nervous to sit, and so instead I strolled past the dozens of photos of the partners and associates of this law firm that hung on the lobby wall. In front of one photo, I paused. There she was: Ivy Franklin.

"Hey, Journee."

I spun toward the singsong voice and faced Ivy. Today, she didn't look like a model for *Weekend Today*. In her winter-green St. John's sheath and four-inch heels that matched, she looked more like the face of chic corporate America.

"It's good to see you," she said, pulling me into a hug, doing that friend thing again that I just didn't understand. "Come on back. We're going to meet in one of the conference rooms."

Following her, for the thousandth time I wondered in what universe this was a good idea. We stepped into a room with three mahogany bookshelf–covered walls, each filled with leather-bound volumes.

"Ethan will be joining us in a few minutes," she said as she pulled out the chair at the head of the conference table. "He's finishing up a call."

I took a chair a couple of seats away from Ivy, then pulled out my phone. There wasn't anything in particular that I had to do, but I would rather watch TikTok videos than chat with Ethan's fiancée.

But it seemed Poison Ivy wanted to talk to me. "Isn't it amazing that we're working together?"

Holding my phone up, as if she'd interrupted me from something important, I said, " 'Amazing' is one way to describe this."

I glanced back down at my phone, but she kept talking. "I told my father that we reconnected and he was thrilled," she said.

"He really hopes you'll come by the church; he'd love to see you again."

I said nothing, still holding up my phone.

She kept on as if she didn't need me in the conversation. "Who would have thought all of those years ago that one day you'd get in trouble and I'd be the one to rescue you?" Then, after a pause, her smile faded just a little. "At least, I hope I'll be able to help, because, Journee, whew"—she shook her head—"you've gotten yourself into quite a situation."

Staring at her for a moment, I finally placed my phone on the table. "Ivy, why are you here?"

Her wide eyes filled with what seemed to me to be fake innocence. "What do you mean?"

"I mean, why are you here pretending to want to help me? Because the last time I saw you, I think it was at the church party for all the college-bound kids, and you made it clear then how much you loved humiliating me."

She leaned back in the chair and swiveled. "Hmmm, I can't seem to recall that."

"Let me help you out—the annual church celebration recognizing all the college-bound students. We were all supposed to walk across the stage, and as each name was announced, our picture and a photo of our college were supposed to appear on the screen. It worked for everyone, except for me. Do you remember what happened?"

She shook her head.

"Somehow, my UT picture didn't appear. Instead, someone flashed one of me and my mom at a food pantry when I was seven years old."

"Oh, yeah"—she nodded—"I think I remember that now. It was so sad. Especially the way everyone laughed."

"Wasn't the laughter your objective? Just like at your birthday party or the millions of other times you tried to humiliate me?"

"Are you holding on to all of that?" She waved her hand as if none of that mattered. "We were just kids."

"I have no doubt that your objective, as far as I'm concerned, is the same."

"Oh, come on, Journee. Why would I want to humiliate you now?"

I shrugged. "I always knew your mean-girl antics weren't about me. It was always about you and your insecurities. So what . . . or who . . . are you insecure about now, Ivy?"

Her smile faded, and she leaned forward as if she was ready to attack. But before she could say a word, the conference room door swung open and Ethan rushed in. "Sorry I'm late. Busy morning already. So"—he sat next to Ivy, on the other side of the conference table from me—"have you two started?"

The first thing I noticed was that the tie he wore with his dark suit matched Ivy's dress. Really? Were they *that* couple?

"No, Mr. Thomas," Ivy said, her countenance changed. The saccharine was back as she glanced at me. "We thought it best to wait for you."

I wasn't sure what to do. Should I pick up with Ivy where we left off to find out what her deal was? Or should I just get to the reason why we were having this meeting? Or was getting up and walking out an option, since I was sure Ivy wasn't on my side?

Before I could make a decision, Ethan began, "I know I told you that it really didn't matter how the feds got the information on you, but Ivy pointed out that it did matter."

He glanced at Ivy, and she picked up. "We've always moved on the assumption that this was about your real estate dealings because of the recent Simon Wallace indictment. But I've never been convinced of that. The feds could be after you for any reason."

"When Ivy pointed that out," Ethan continued now, "we decided to start with the obvious. Did Simon make a deal with the feds using his relationship with you? And the answer is . . . no. Even though he's facing decades in prison, Simon hasn't made a deal; he hasn't mentioned your name to anyone."

I blew out a long breath.

Ethan said, "So he's out. And since he's the most obvious person to be speaking with the feds, we're thinking this may not have anything to do with your business dealings."

"Well, as I told you, it could be Vivian or any number of people."

Ethan nodded. "I would have still bet on it being Simon, and so that's a big possibility crossed off our list. But what we wanted to speak with you about is, could this be about anything besides your real estate dealings?"

I shook my head. "No, there's nothing else going on in my life that would interest the feds."

"Are you sure?" Ivy smirked. "Because if the texts you've been receiving have anything to do with the investigation, it seems much more personal than professional."

My eyes narrowed. But all I said was "Not only is nothing happening in my life that would interest the feds, but all you have to do is look at the timing. This investigation started after Simon's, right?"

"We don't know that," Ethan said. "But probably."

"This is professional, not personal," I assured them both.

"Okay. We wanted to have this discussion because, right now, we're working in the dark. But we'll keep checking with our sources, and in the meantime, I wanted you to know that any defense will probably center on the fact that you never touched any paperwork."

"Yes," Ivy piped in, "you were an innocent mentee who was just following one of the most successful brokers in Houston." When Ivy turned to me, she added, "Because what else were you supposed to do?"

Ethan seemed to miss all the shade when he said, "I'll come up with some key points today, and we'll begin a draft so if anything happens, we're ready."

A knock on the door made all three of us glance up. "Ivy, your ten o'clock is here."

"Okay"—she pushed her chair back—"I have to go. Good to see you again, Journee," she sang. "Talk soon."

I half expected her to kiss Ethan, but I guessed they maintained some semblance of professionalism in the office, even if they did dress like Barbie and Ken, the Black version. After Ivy left, I stood to push back my chair, but Ethan held up his hand.

"Do you have a few minutes?"

I nodded and settled back into my seat.

He got right to it. "I owe you an apology for what happened on Sunday."

I stopped him from saying anything more. "I don't need an apology or an explanation," I said. "We were just caught up. I was upset; you wanted to comfort me. I know it was no big deal."

He exhaled as if my words had given him great relief. "Thank you. Because it's important for you to know that I'm very much committed to Ivy."

My jaw clenched. So this was all about Ivy? This wasn't about me? He didn't care about how I'd be feeling or what signals I'd taken from him? "Oh, I know you're committed to her. Just like I'm committed to Quincy."

His head reared back. "Quincy, the guy I met on Sunday?"

I lifted my chin. "Yes. He and I are in a relationship, and I'm really very happy," I said, sounding like a talking head for one of those online dating commercials.

His eyes narrowed as if he was studying me. "How long have you known him?"

I frowned. "Why does that matter to you?"

"It's just that . . ." He paused as if he didn't want to continue, but then he did. Looking straight at me, he said, "I don't trust him, Journee."

I didn't mean to, but I laughed out loud. For almost a minute, Ethan just sat there, staring at me, waiting for me to recover. "Are you kidding me? You don't even know him. You were in a room with him for ten seconds, tops, and—"

"I got the same feeling from Quentin—"

"His name is Quincy."

He continued, "The same feeling that I got when I met Simon. He's shady; he's a liar. I don't like him. And you know I have insight when it comes to—"

"And you know what? I don't like Ivy. She's so shady that she's lying straight to your face."

"What? That's crazy."

"She and I were never friends. Yet she lies over and over about that. So it seems you should take your insight and use it in your own relationship."

"Okay, this has gotten out of control," he said, in a tone that I knew was meant to de-escalate the situation. "I'm really coming from a good place, Journee. I know I don't get a vote in this—"

"Damn straight."

"But that doesn't mean I don't care about you. Look at the situation you're in now. God knows, I wish I'd fought harder to convince you to get away from Simon. And that's why I'm fighting now. Yes, I just met Quincy, but it doesn't take me more than a few seconds to measure a man. I don't have a good feeling about him."

"Well, you know what?" I said, pushing my chair back so hard it fell over, but I didn't even bother to look over my shoulder. "It's a good thing it doesn't matter what kind of feelings you have for him. Because in our relationship, the only feelings that matter are mine and Quincy's."

What I wanted to say was he and Ivy could take their law office and stuff it all the way up their perfectly toned behinds. But although that's what I would have said a few years ago, I was in too much trouble to let my pride end the best defense I was going to receive.

I was steaming mad, though, and I wanted Ethan to know it. So I didn't glance at him as I stomped by, and I certainly didn't part my lips to say good-bye. When I got to the elevator bank, I pressed the button over and over, willing it to come faster, because if Ethan or Ivy came out to me right now, I'd end up with zero lawyers and lots more trouble.

I paced in front of the elevators and then heard the *ping* that one was arriving—thank God!—just as my phone vibrated. I stepped into the elevator, checked my messages:

> You can run from a lie, but you can't hide from the truth. And the truth is finally catching up to you. Vengeance is mine.

And then the elevator doors closed.

was in front of my mother's home, standing at the door, still stunned that I was here. Even though I'd been with Windsor when we brought our mother home two weeks ago, and I'd been coming by every morning since then, this still didn't feel natural to me.

Trying to navigate through twenty-seven years was difficult. First, because I never thought I'd be in this place—wanting to spend time with my mother. And second, I still had to accept that everything I thought I knew for sure, I wasn't sure about at all.

Just as I raised my hand to ring the doorbell, the door swung open, and my sister stood there with a cup of coffee in one hand and a newspaper tucked beneath her arm.

"Perfect timing," Windsor said. "I really need to get you a key. Okay, here"—she shoved the coffee and newspaper into my hand—"I was just getting ready to give Mama her coffee and the paper. She said she wasn't hungry, but can you tell Mrs. Walker to make her eat?" she asked, referring to our mother's day aide. "And Dr. Patterson said she wanted to meet with us sometime later this week; she has new medication for Mama, so can you look at your schedule?" My sister spoke without taking a breath. She grabbed her briefcase, kissed my cheek, and swept out the door.

I watched her trot to the driveway, then closed the door. Like I'd done outside, I stood in the middle of the living room, taking this all in. I was in my mother's home.

My steps were silent as I moved across the carpet, and I

wondered if my mother would like to have hardwood floors installed. Maybe redecorating her place was a project we could do together. Something to help us connect.

My mother was sitting up in the hospital bed we'd moved into her bedroom, her eyes closed, until I stepped over the threshold. She smiled before her eyes were completely open.

"Baby girl, it's so good to see you. My day has already been made." Her greeting was the same every morning.

When I reached her bedside, she leaned forward as if she were offering her cheek for a kiss. I hesitated, then only handed her the coffee. "Windsor said you're not eating."

Her smile stayed when she said, "I'll eat later." I gave her the newspaper and she laid it aside. "Sit for a while. Let's talk."

Windsor had rearranged our mom's room so the chairs were close to the bed. When I sat, my mother reached for my hand. "How are you, baby girl?"

"The same as yesterday, but I'm not the one who just got out of the hospital."

She waved my words away. "It's been two weeks. I'm good."

"You'll be good when Dr. Patterson says you are."

She rolled her eyes and took another sip of her coffee, and then the awkward silence set in. For a few minutes, both of us focused on the television, tuned to one of the morning shows. But I heard none of the news of the day. And I was sure my mother didn't either. We both used this time to search for something we could talk about. Finally, she asked, "Do you still like tacos?"

This was how our conversations began. We didn't know each other. So my mother asked all kinds of questions, from how my business was going (I didn't tell her too much) to if I was dating (I didn't tell her anything). But some of these innocent I-want-to-get-to-know-you questions were tough—and this was one. I lowered my eyes and shook my head. Without saying anything else, my mother understood.

"I'm so sorry, baby girl."

"You don't have to apologize anymore. Yeah, I stopped eating tacos when . . . I was with Mrs. Hunter; seafood became my favorite. That's not a bad thing, right?" I tried to lighten the moment.

She smiled, but the joy didn't reach her eyes. I was sure another apology was on the tip of her tongue, but then her phone rang, saving both of us from one more moment of regret. I answered the landline, said hello to Mrs. Charles, then passed my mother the phone.

"I won't be long," she whispered as she covered the mouthpiece. "Clementine is just doing her regular check-in."

I waved and nodded, letting my mother know this was fine. I was always grateful for any reprieve that took me away from the silent seconds that often lingered between us. I wanted to get my mother and me to the place where there would be no sadness in our discussions. But we were far from there.

As my mother talked, I lifted the newspaper from her bed and studied the *Houston Defender* headline: *Feds Move in on Multilayered Real Estate Fraud Schemes in Houston.*

"Oh my God," I whispered as I pressed my hand against my heart. Keep breathing, I told myself as I struggled to read: *According to anonymous sources, the Department of Justice is getting close to issuing indictments for several individuals involved in one of the country's largest mortgage fraud schemes. This comes just weeks after the arrest of Simon Wallace of ClearWater Mortgage. It was not confirmed whether this latest investigation is connected to the Wallace indictment . . .*

A tidal wave of emotions made tears burn behind my eyes.

The reporter didn't include my name, but no one needed to tell me—this article was about me.

I glanced at my mother just as she was ending her call. She clicked off the phone and frowned. "What is it, sweetheart?"

I guessed twenty-seven years wasn't a divide she had to cross in this instance. This was a mother's intuition.

"Journee?"

"Uh . . . nothing." I stuffed the newspaper into my bag. "I just remembered something I have to do in my office."

"Oh, well, go on. I'll see you tomorrow."

I nodded and glanced at my watch. "I'm not leaving until Mrs. Walker gets here . . ." And then I heard the key in the front door.

"Well, that's her now," my mother said, though her eyes were searching mine as if she knew my concern was far more than a work task.

I waved good-bye, then rushed into the front, greeting Mrs. Walker and telling her the same lie I'd just told my mother.

Inside my car, I read the article again, slowing down this time, ingesting every word. Finally, I closed my eyes and leaned back. There was little I could do to keep this information from my family now. I was going to have to say something to my mother and Windsor, but what? I didn't want to cause my mother any stress. Then there was Quincy. I more than liked this guy. Why was this happening at our beginning? With this article in the *Defender*, Quincy was going to hear about this.

I needed to tell him something. Maybe not everything. Just enough so he wouldn't have any questions. And then whether he chose to stay or leave . . . there was nothing I could do about that. All I knew was that I needed to remove what felt like a boulder of deception from my shoulders.

It was barely nine, but Quincy would be in class already. I tapped his name, then pressed my cell against my ear, thinking about what message I would leave.

Then "What's up, beautiful?" came through my phone.

His voice shocked me. "Quincy, I thought you'd be in class."

"Nah," he said. "On a break. What's up?"

"Oh, well, I was going to leave you a message to see if you could come by tonight."

He chuckled. "Haven't I been there with you every night? I'd be a stranger in my own bed if I were to stay at my place."

I felt his smile through the phone, but I couldn't do the same. "I wanted to make sure you were planning on coming over tonight because . . . I need to talk to you."

"Okay, I got time, so talk."

I shook my head. Not only was Quincy at work, but I wasn't prepared to talk to him right now. I needed time to get my words together and pray for God's mercy. "No, I don't want to interrupt your day. It'll be fine tonight."

"Baby, how many times do I have to tell you that I'm here for you?"

"I know, and I'm so grateful. We'll talk tonight," I insisted.

"Are you at work?"

"I'm just leaving my mother's house."

He hesitated, and I knew the reason. Quincy didn't understand what he called my new devotion to my mother. "After all she did to you," he kept saying. He didn't accept my understanding that my mother hadn't given me away; it felt so much more like I'd been taken.

When he asked, "Are you heading to the office now?" I was grateful he didn't take us into another disagreement about my mother.

"Yes."

"Well, I have the solution. Just work from home today, and I'll meet you there in an hour."

"What? No, Quincy, it's not that serious," I said, although it was. "You can't just leave your students to teach themselves."

"You should meet my students; they could do it." He chuckled. "But I can get another teacher to cover me with no problem. And I'm not going to take no from you. I can hear it in your voice, and now you have me concerned."

"Quincy—"

"Journee, don't you know that I love you?"

I stopped . . . stopped everything. Stopped blinking, stopped breathing.

"Yeah"—he sounded as if his words had shocked him, too—"maybe it's too soon, and I certainly shouldn't have said this over the phone. But it's the truth. I love you, and you have to understand that what's important to you is important to me. So I'll see you in a little while, okay?"

My voice sounded small when I said, "Okay," and hung up. Still I sat in my car in front of my mother's home, unable to move. Quincy loved me? Did he mean what he said? I'd never known a man to throw those words around. Especially not a man like Quincy. One thing I'd learned about him: if he said it, he meant it.

Finally, I smiled and raised my eyes to the heavens, thanking God. I hadn't been looking for love, but God had sent this man right when I needed someone in my life, someone on my side. My plan had been to tell Quincy what I thought he needed to know.

But his words had just changed my world. Quincy wasn't just another person in my life. We were going to live this life together. So I couldn't treat him like everyone else. I had to tell him everything.

And he deserved that truth from me . . . because he loved me.

THE GOOD NEWS was that I paced for less than ten minutes before Quincy stepped into my condo and pulled me into his arms like he had just returned from war. When he kissed me, my wish was to take him straight into the bedroom. But that would only delay what I had to do. So I took his hand and led him to the sofa.

I sat, but he didn't. He shrugged off his blazer and tossed it onto the sofa before he moved behind me. The moment he touched my shoulders, I moaned. And then when he began kneading, I closed my eyes and sank into the sofa. He massaged my shoulders, then rolled up slowly along my neckline. Pressing ever so slowly, like time had no meaning and all that was important right now was me. His fingers rolled from my shoulders to my neck and back down again. He kept going as if he could press all my troubles away.

I was half-asleep when he stopped, rounded the sofa, and joined me. I opened my eyes, my head still resting on the back of the sofa. "I want to say thank you, but how am I supposed to talk after that?"

He kissed my forehead. "You just sounded so tense." With his fingertips, he traced the side of my face. "So, what did you want to talk about?" Then, suddenly, he held up his hands. "Wait? You're not breaking up with me, are you? Just because I told you I loved you?"

There . . . he said it again. I was sure he meant it when he said it earlier, even if something in my mind said it was too soon. But now there was no doubt. This was said on purpose.

Now I sat up straight. "I will never break up with you," I said, and truly meant it. For only the second time in my life, I saw my forever with a man. First, though, I had to have this conversation. "You've been asking what's going on with me, and"— I took a deep breath—"I'm ready to tell you."

He sat back. "Okay." But before I could say another word, he said, "Hold on a sec. I want to text the teacher who's covering me." He tapped a few times on his cell, then placed it on top of his blazer. "Okay, you now have my full attention." He took my hand into both of his. "Talk to me."

But sitting here, so close, while he held me . . . I wasn't sure I could do this. "Whew," I breathed, "this is harder than I thought."

"Take your time."

"Maybe I need to get up. Not sure I can look at you as I tell you everything."

But as I moved, he held me tighter. "No," he said, not allowing any space between us. "Whatever you have to tell me, it's okay. Don't you get this? You're not alone anymore. Nothing's going to change with us."

You're not alone anymore. I wasn't. Quincy was my second chance, just like the second chance I was being given with my mother.

His promise made it easier for me to say, "I'm under investigation by the feds." He didn't recoil; his eyes stayed steady on me, so I continued, "When I first began my career, I did it with a guy—Simon Wallace. And he had very . . . different ways of making money." I went on to tell Quincy a little about the homeless schemes. "I used the excuse of having been homeless and thinking how my mother could have used the money. But honestly, the whole time, I really did know it was wrong."

Quincy shrugged. "That seems like a victimless crime. And you seem kind of innocent in this, since he was training you."

I wanted to hug my man but kept on: "That's a generous way to look at it. And maybe that would work if I had stopped there." Now I told Quincy about my role as Wilhelmina Jones.

When I finished describing that, Quincy asked, "So the homeowners thought you were really going to help them?" Again, there was not a bit of judgment in Quincy's tone. It sounded as if he just wanted to know.

"They did, and while Simon presented his plan to them, I was the one who came in at the end and really convinced them."

"Wow." He shook his head.

"I know. But again, I found a way to justify it. Simon convinced me that these people were going to lose their homes anyway, and he gave them checks, some as high as twenty-five thousand dollars. That was more than they would ever get from any bank," I said. But then, after hearing my own words, I added, "See? I'm still saying that, and what I should be saying is that I was wrong."

"So these people that you scammed"—I flinched at that word—"they didn't have family or anyone to help them?"

I shook my head. "I never knew; I never asked . . . except . . ." I lowered my eyes. Did I want to share this with Quincy? No, what I'd shared was already too much. That was all he needed to know.

"Except?" he said, wanting me to finish the sentence I'd started.

Looking up, I told him, "Except I wish I had asked about their families. I wish I'd done so many things differently."

"Whew," he exhaled, almost sounding like this may have been too much. "So you started this whole story by saying the feds are coming for you. What does that mean?"

Again I told him everything about Simon's arrest, my going to Ethan and Ivy, and even the article this morning. "But though we've been told the feds are investigating me, we've heard nothing. Not a phone call, not a visit, nothing."

"Maybe they don't have enough on you. Maybe they're waiting on more information," he said, nodding as if he was deep in thought.

"I'm not sure. Oh, and there's one other thing." I grabbed my phone, scrolled through my messages, then showed Quincy the texts from my stalker.

He read the first one, then asked me to scroll through, showing him each of the texts I'd received. At the end, he asked, "Who's sending these to you?"

"I have no idea, but I'm convinced this is about what's going on with Simon and my possible investigation."

"This is deep." He gave me a long glance. "So you've been going through this alone?"

I nodded. "I had no plans of telling anyone, thinking I could handle it myself. But I told Ethan because I wanted a good attorney if anything jumped off. But it's gone beyond what I ever imagined." I lowered my head.

With his fingertips, Quincy lifted my chin, and the way he looked at me uplifted my soul. "I'm not going to say what you did was good, but that doesn't stop the way I feel about you. Nothing's changed; I'm going to be by your side until the end, okay?"

I nodded, and then he gently pulled me into him and held me so tight. I couldn't remember a time when I'd felt so safe. And that security made me feel safe enough to cry. I cried because I was relieved and because of this man who held me. In Quincy, I'd found an acceptance that I'd never really had.

But I had it now. Finally!

held my head high as I stood in the entryway of the Aventine Ballroom on the second floor of one of the most luxurious hotels in Houston—Hotel ICON. The grand neoclassical architecture that greeted every guest in the luxurious lobby continued through this massive room with its towering ceilings and chandeliers gleaming with thousands of shimmering crystals. Heavy burgundy and gray drapes that matched the carpet swathed huge windows where the fading light of the day filtered through.

"You ready to do this?"

My smile was instant when I glanced up at Quincy, so striking in his Armani. I had to admit I was surprised he already owned this tuxedo. He'd restyled the classic look with a silver bow tie that matched my strapless fitted gown. Now *we* were *that* couple.

"I'm ready," I said.

He nodded his approval as he held out his arm. I wouldn't have been here if it weren't for Quincy. Although I'd attended the Bayou City 100 in the past, this year I had decided to sit out this exclusive annual event hosted by the Mayor's Council. Between the newspaper article and the rumors I was sure went beyond Mr. Yung, I was certain I'd be the subject of long glances and hushed whispers. And on the flip side, I didn't want to spend the entire evening giving a side-eye to everyone, thinking anyone could be my text stalker or the FBI source against me.

But Quincy had convinced me to attend. "I can think of

a couple of reasons why you need to be there. First of all, you have to show Mr. Yung and his gang that you're still a player in this game."

"And the second reason?"

"Don't you want to be seen with me? I certainly want everyone to see me with the most beautiful woman in Houston."

"Just Houston?" I teased.

"My bad," he said, and just like that, I sent in my RSVP for me and my plus one.

Now, as I glanced up at my man, I couldn't believe how blessed I was. How could I have imagined this a month ago when I first went to Ethan's office? I'd felt so alone that night. But because of Quincy, I'd never be alone again.

This was such a wonderful whirlwind. I'd done more than open my heart to Quincy—I'd opened my home, too. He'd practically moved in, not that cohabitating was anything we'd discussed. It was happening organically—I didn't want him to leave, and he never wanted to go. We were our best together.

Being with Quincy had brought my stress level way down. He had all kinds of ways to make me forget what I was facing. But what was most interesting was that since I'd told Quincy everything, it had been quiet. It was as if he were some kind of charm. That article in the *Defender* had made it seem as if indictments were imminent. But nothing happened. Even Ethan was surprised. In regular email updates, all he kept telling me was: *This is good, lie low, we're just waiting.*

The only thing that wouldn't go away? Those texts. Someone had a desire to torment me, but with Quincy there, it was so much easier to ignore even those.

"So, m'lady," Quincy said in his best British accent as I wrapped my arm around his, "is there anyone you want to stop and chat with or shall we just amble about the perimeter?"

I laughed at his impression, which was really quite good. "You've got some acting chops, huh?"

He did a Jay-Z brush-your-shoulders-off move. "Well, you know how I do."

"Let's just walk around. If I see someone, we'll stop."

Quincy led the way through this mass of Houston's Black elite. As light jazz piped in from the speakers throughout, about two hundred people milled around, the women wearing designer gowns and the men in tuxedos from the most exclusive shops. They stood shoulder to shoulder around dozens and dozens of white-satin-clothed high-top tables, chatting in small groups of two, or three, or six. As Quincy and I passed by faces I recognized, many made eye contact but quickly glanced away, never pausing their conversations.

Before we got to the other side of the room, Quincy said, "Oh, there's the bar. Would you like a drink?"

"That would be wonderful," I said. "I'll have white wine."

He parked me at one of the empty tables, kissed my forehead, then moved toward the bar. My glance followed him, and for a moment I wanted to run behind him just so I could be close. When he stopped at the bar, Quincy glanced back at me, winked, then turned his attention to his phone. I smiled; I guessed I could handle being away from him for a minute or two.

My phone vibrated and I pulled it from my purse, looked down at the screen:

Karma is closer than you know. Vengeance is mine.

"Hey, Journee."

I stuffed my phone back into my purse and faced that annoying singsong voice. Ivy had her arms around me in a greeting before I could even say hello.

"How are you?" she asked.

"I'm great." Then I turned to Ethan. Although we'd been in touch electronically, I hadn't seen him since that meeting in their office when Ethan felt the need to reiterate his love for and commitment to his girlfriend right before he trashed my boyfriend. "Ethan," I said.

"You look great, Journee."

"Thanks. I didn't know you two would be here."

"Oh, this was my idea," Ivy said. "This isn't Ethan's kind of thing."

She spoke as if she'd forgotten that Ethan was my man first. There were things I could tell her about him that she had yet to discover.

"Here you go, baby," Quincy said, handing me a glass before he turned to Ethan and Ivy. Ivy's wide eyes filled with shock and then a little appreciation as her gaze roamed over my man. Ethan's eyes narrowed, his wariness apparent.

Quincy reached out his hand. "Ethan, right?"

"Yeah." Ethan shook his hand. "And this is my fiancée, Ivy."

As Ivy and Quincy exchanged greetings, I took a sip of my wine and glanced at Ethan over the rim of my glass. When he'd told me he didn't trust Quincy, I'd been so upset that I never considered his motivation. But now, as I watched Ethan studying Quincy, I wondered, was my ex jealous of my next? If that was it, I wasn't mad. I got it; I'd felt some kind of way about Ivy until . . . I faced Quincy as he slipped his arm around my waist and pulled me closer.

Ethan said, "Sweetheart, the mayor has just arrived."

"Oh, okay," Ivy said. "It was nice meeting you, Quincy, and Journee, I'm sure we'll be in touch."

We watched the two saunter away, and then Quincy asked, "Was it something I said?" He chuckled. "They ran off like they had a real appointment with the mayor."

We laughed together, but I added, "Who knows? They may, because Ivy's dad is Pastor Jamal Franklin."

"Oh, wow, of Wheeler Village?"

"Yup. So she's a VIP, at least in her mind."

Then another voice invaded our laughter. "Well, if it isn't my protégée."

I groaned. I'd been in this place for only about fifteen minutes, yet I'd received another text, had to face Ethan and Poison Ivy, and now this. Vivian looked great, though, like she always did. Her red sequined gown looked as if it had been painted on her tiny waist, which was in perfect proportion to her ample hips. But that wasn't the most interesting part of her dress. It was cut so low, her belly button peeked out. She'd definitely used yards of tape to keep everything in place.

"Vivian," I said before I turned back to Quincy as if she weren't there.

Without missing a beat, she circled the table, placed her Chanel clutch down, and picked up the conversation as if I hadn't just dissed her. "If I didn't know better, I'd think you were following me," she said.

Now she had my attention. "Excuse me?"

"Well"—she flung her blond weave over her shoulder—"first you show up at my house, and now you're here." She chuckled as if she'd told a joke, then turned to Quincy. She held out her hand. "And you are?"

"My man," I answered before Quincy could.

She dropped her hand to her side. "That's your name?" she asked, her eyes still on him.

Again I gave my man no room to speak. "That's all you need to know."

"My goodness," Vivian said to Quincy, "are you allowed to speak?"

Quincy chuckled. "I am, but it seems my lady has given you all the relevant information."

"Well, anyway"—she swiveled and faced me again—"I need to speak with you for a moment."

"Go ahead."

She glanced up at Quincy. "Privately."

"Anything you have to say to me, you can say in front of Quincy."

The way her eyebrows rose, I thought she was going to say something about Quincy's name. But instead, she said, "I don't think you want to talk about *this* in front of *him*."

"He's my man, Vivian. He knows everything."

She leaned back a little in surprise. "Well"—her eyes roamed up, then down Quincy before she turned back to me—"*you* may feel comfortable speaking in front of him, but I don't. I don't know him like that. And obviously, I don't know you anymore either."

Quincy looked straight at me. "You know what? I see the mayor over there." We both laughed, leaving Vivian glancing between us in confusion. "I'll give you two a little privacy."

He kissed my cheek before he strolled away, and Vivian and I watched him until he stopped at the bar. With her eyes still on him, she said, "I see a few things have changed."

Facing her, I asked, "Why did you want to speak to me?"

"First, can I give you a little bit of advice?" My stare was meant to dissuade her, but she continued, "I don't know how much you've shared with Quincy, but that's not your brightest move."

"What I tell or do with my man is none of your business, and I feel sorry for you if you've never had a relationship where you wanted to share every part of your life with your partner."

She shrugged, then leaned in. "I don't think you'll want to share this—have you been contacted by the FBI?"

It was because I was so shocked by her question that I responded without taking a moment to think of the best answer. "No! Have you?"

She shook her head. "But I saw an article a while back—"

"In the *Defender*."

She nodded. "You saw it, huh? After I read that, I expected to have someone beating down my door the next morning."

"I thought you weren't worried about getting caught up in this with your uncle."

"I'm not," she said with a shrug, "but it seems that this is far beyond my uncle Simon. That article read like everyone in real estate in Houston was being investigated."

I nodded. That was true. "At this point, your uncle definitely has more information than we do. I'm sure the feds had to disclose something when they arrested Simon. And a lot of information is always in an indictment."

"Sounds like you're an expert at being arrested." She smirked.

I could easily go back and forth with Vivian, but what would being petty accomplish right now? What I needed was information, so I said, "Actually, I'm surprised you haven't reached out to him."

"I haven't spoken to my uncle in over three years. Not since he called me, so distraught about that woman the two of you killed."

So that's how she found out.

"But you may be right. He would have to know far more about this investigation than we do."

"Are you going to call him?"

"It would be a fool's move to do that. You think I want my number to show up in his phone records as if we have a continuing relationship? No, ma'am."

Dang! That was a coldhearted way to treat a relative, but I

wished I'd thought of that. The feds probably had a record of my calling Simon. And with the timing of when I called him— not a good move.

I asked, "So what do you think is going to happen?"

"If I knew, I wouldn't be standing here talking to you." Then she held out her hand to me. "We may not like each other, but it would be in our best interests to work together and make a deal."

I eyed her hand. "What kind of deal?"

"If either of us is taken in for questioning . . . or worse, let's agree here and now that we won't go after the other. I won't mention your name. And you do the same for me, no matter what kind of deal we're offered."

This time when I glanced down at her hand, I noticed her bracelet, a striking gold piece that encircled her arm. But then I peeped the tip—the head of a snake.

This was so apropos for this moment. A snake wearing a snake . . . saying she wanted to shake on this. Still, I gripped her hand, deciding to take the small chance she would keep her word.

But when she grinned, grabbed her purse, and slithered away, I glanced down at my hand to make sure all my fingers were there. As I watched Vivian, in the brightest red gown, slip and slide through the room, my stomach twisted, turned, and tumbled. What kind of deal had I just made with that devil?

24

Every time one of my clients cried, I cried, too. I cried because I'd helped someone achieve their dream, but so many of my tears were still for Mrs. Landers. That was why I was sitting here now with Mrs. Barker and both of us were dabbing at our eyes.

"So is that it?" Mrs. Barker sniffed.

I scanned through the papers she'd just signed. "Yes. You're all set and now the owner of a brand-new home. Well, maybe not completely new, since you've lived there."

"What are you talking about?" the seventy-year-old woman said. "Now that I own it, it's a brand-new home to me!"

We laughed as we stood and I hugged her. It had been quite an effort to find a lender for Mrs. Barker. Although financial institutions were not supposed to discriminate based on age, many did. Once I found a lender, that financial institution had made me jump backward through hoops, making sure Mrs. Barker's paperwork was in order. I understood the caution—there were a lot of real estate scammers out there.

But I was no longer one of them, and Mrs. Barker's package wasn't just impeccable; it was honest. The down payment had been gifted by her son, she'd make the small monthly payments from a percentage of her social security check, and the rest would come from a grant program I'd found for people like her. It had been a lot of work, but I welcomed it.

While so many of the houses I sold were considered luxury,

I devoted a good deal of my time to helping low-income families find the answer to their prayers. This was what I hoped my legacy would be.

I handed Mrs. Barker the envelope with her papers. Her weathered hands shook before she raised them in the air. "Hallelujah," she shouted. "You just don't know my story." Then, looking to the heavens again, she added, "And thank you for sending me to Journee Alexander, Lord. She's one of your angels here on earth."

I cringed a bit, thinking I needed a few more clients like Mrs. Barker before God could consider my heavenly ledger clear enough to be counted an angel. But I was working on it.

If Mrs. Barker had gone on for even a minute longer, I would have been all caught up in her praise. But she gave me a final hug and squeeze, then marched out of my office to return to the house she'd been renting, which was now the home she owned.

Returning to my desk, I was on to my next project—a presentation I had tomorrow with Tillman Taylor, the owner of one of the largest real estate firms in Houston. His company wanted to streamline their process, and he was seeking a broker as a permanent partner.

This wouldn't be as huge as the WestPark revitalization deal, but it would be quite a substantial addition to my business. Tasha and I had worked on this PowerPoint presentation, and even though I knew it was tight, I'd reviewed it every day for the past week. I wanted to commit it to my memory so that as I spoke, I could watch Mr. Taylor and his team while they were looking at the slides.

But as soon as I turned on my computer and opened the folder, my mind wandered. All of this drama in my life just wouldn't let me be great.

Since the gala at Hotel ICON, it had been difficult to keep my thoughts away from that deal I'd made with that devil.

And then there were more texts.

In the past three days, I'd received three more, although it was the one from this morning that was the most troubling. I picked up my phone and read the message once again:

> If somehow you escape God's wrath, don't think it's over. You will never break free of mine. No matter how long it takes, the hate in my heart won't let me stop until your downfall is complete. Vengeance is mine.

These texts had moved from being annoying to being troubling, and now they were frightening. Someone out there hated me, but I wasn't sure if it was real or just part of the game. It wasn't Simon; it wasn't Vivian. Could it be Ivy? Could she be feeding the feds information while pretending to work for me? Could it be one of my brokers, or even Tasha? Or one of my competitors? Or someone I didn't know at all?

There were too many names, too many options.

I copied the text and pasted it into a message to Ethan, but then I paused. Suppose this text *did* come from Ivy. I deleted the message and then glanced up.

The sight of Tasha standing in my office, stiff and wide-eyed, stopped me cold. "What's wrong?"

"I . . . I need to turn on your television." She moved so fast, grabbing the remote and turning it toward the mounted TV across the room, that I didn't even have time to do more than stand up and say:

"What's going—"

The picture filled the screen. Vivian scampering out of the downtown FBI headquarters.

"Authorities say Vivian Wallace is a cooperating witness in the multimillion-dollar real estate fraud case that is extending throughout the city," the anchor said.

I stood with my hand covering my mouth as Vivian crossed the screen, shielding her face with her hands from the camera as a burly Black dude guided her to a waiting SUV. Cameras flashed all around her, but she never looked up, never stopped, and finally disappeared behind the SUV's tinted windows.

I sank back into my seat. The anchors continued, but even though my eyes were pinned to the screen, I could hardly hear their words for all the thoughts screaming in my mind. Vivian was cooperating with the FBI? So, had the gala been a setup? Had she been trying to get me to confess to something, or was this cooperation a new development that had happened in the past three days?

The news anchor cut to another story—an accident on the 610 Loop—and Tasha clicked off the TV.

It took me a few moments to speak, but finally I asked, "Did you see the beginning of the report?"

She nodded. "I happened to see it start when I was passing in the reception area. When I got the gist of what was happening, I came in here to tell you." She took a breath. "She was arrested this morning—"

Arrested?

"—and it seems it's in connection with her uncle. What I can't figure out is her bond was a million dollars and she's out already."

My jaw dropped. Arrested, and a million-dollar bond?

Tasha continued, "I'm just trying to figure out what she did to warrant such high bail," asking the question that was in my mind. "My God, that's the level for murderers."

Tasha had joined me two months after I opened my firm.

Because we'd been up against Vivian a few times for municipal and private contracts, I'd shared with her that Vivian and I had been childhood friends who had turned into fierce competitors.

"I . . . I don't think Vivian's a murderer," I said, and then my mind finished that thought: But would anyone ever consider me one?

My stomach rumbled like a volcano. It was only a matter of time before the feds came for me.

"Whatever she's done," Tasha said, "she must have cut some kind of good deal, because I have no idea how else she would have been released so quickly."

"Vivian is going to protect Vivian at all costs," I said more to myself than to Tasha.

"As horrible as this is, do you know what I was thinking?" It was clearly a rhetorical question, since Tasha didn't even take a breath before she added, "We may get that WestPark contract, because there's no way the city's going to fool with her now."

I was so startled when my cell rang that I knocked it off my desk. I snatched it up, glanced at the screen. "Ethan!"

"I just saw the news report, and from your tone, I guess you saw it, too."

"Have you heard anything? Are they coming for me?" I glanced up, and Tasha was standing in my doorway, staring at me. I was shocked to see her, but . . . she didn't seem . . . shocked by my words. Before I could say anything to her, she turned around and disappeared.

I jumped up and closed the door and at the same time lowered my voice. "Please tell me what's going on."

"I don't have any more information beyond what was on the news. We'd been in touch with Ivy's contacts, but suddenly they've dried up."

"Why?"

"We're trying to find out everything we can," Ethan said. "Ivy's working the phones now."

Ivy working brought me no comfort. Had her contacts really dried up? Or was that just what she told Ethan? "So what am I supposed to do? Just wait until they come for me?"

"That's all you can do. I'll let you know if I hear anything. Just stay calm and lie low." When he ended the call, I stared at my phone. Was this really his advice? The same advice that he'd been giving me for all of these weeks? And look where I was now.

I needed to do more. I needed to speak to Quincy.

25

When I'd called Quincy yesterday, he'd rushed straight to my place, then listened as I cried, telling him everything about Vivian's arrest. His advice had been the same as Ethan's—to lie low, do nothing. He was as wrong as Ethan, but when I sat back and tried to figure out what to do, I came up with nothing as well.

So I sucked it up and came to work this morning, prepared to wow Tillman Taylor, and it looked like I'd accomplished that goal. Fifteen minutes ago, I finished the PowerPoint presentation to Mr. Taylor and his staff, and since then, they'd fired questions at me. I answered every one, not fazed by any of their inquiries. J. Alexander and Associates would be able to handle the individual financing for each of Mr. Tillman's projects.

As I answered the questions, I watched the executives exchange glances, nod, and smile. All the men were engaged and impressed. But then there was one woman.

Mrs. Washington had been introduced as the PR director for Mr. Taylor's real estate firm, and while the others responded to my presentation, her expression—eyes narrowed, lips pressed together, jaw tight—never changed. I tried to draw her to my side by making eye contact, nodding in her direction. But nothing worked, so after the first thirty minutes, I shrugged and turned my focus to the men.

"Impressive, Miss Alexander," Mr. Taylor said as he reviewed the packet of information. "And the way you've explained your growth strategy, this will be quite lucrative . . . for both of our companies."

"Yes, Mr. Taylor. That was important for me to make sure this was a win-win for everyone."

"You've accomplished that," he said, then turned to his team. "Are there any other questions?"

"Ms. Alexander"—Mrs. Washington raised her finger—"I do have a question. It has come to my attention that you and your company—"

My heart flipped and flipped and flipped.

"—are under investigation. What can you tell us about this situation? Because I'm sure you'll understand why I was hesitant to even take this meeting. Will J. Alexander and Associates even be in business a week from now?" She glanced at her coworkers, and they nodded along with her.

My lips wouldn't part. All I did was stare at her as I tried to organize a single thought, some kind of appropriate response that Mrs. Washington would believe.

Mr. Taylor gave me a bit of a reprieve when he said, "As you can imagine, Ms. Alexander, I was very concerned when Mrs. Washington brought this information to me yesterday. But I insisted on this meeting because even from our preliminary meetings, I was very impressed and hoping we would be able to do business."

"Mr. Taylor, I can assure you that . . ." I stopped talking in midsentence when Tasha pushed open the conference room door.

"Tasha!" I snapped. This was the worst moment for her to bring me a message. I didn't care who it was from. I was in here fighting for my professional life.

"Ummm . . ." She stood there, almost trembling, wringing her hands. "There . . . there are some people here."

Really? "I'm in a—"

Before I could finish, two men in gray suits pushed past Tasha, and following them was a Black woman dressed more casually, but what she wore was more terrifying . . . that blue jacket that everyone had seen on TV with the huge letters—FBI—in gold.

I'd imagined this scenario in my mind a million times, yet the reality was far worse. I faced the men and pretended that I had no fear when I asked, "May I help you?" as if I had not a clue as to the reason for their presence.

The woman marched toward me and handed me a single piece of paper. "I'm Agent Donna Moran with the FBI." She interrupted my meeting with no apology. "This is a search warrant for these premises."

"What?" I said, acting shocked as I scanned the paper, but I wasn't reading any of the words. I was just blinking, just breathing, trying not to faint.

Glancing up, I looked into the horrified eyes of Mr. Taylor, then the others, all with similar expressions . . . except Mrs. Washington, whose face was filled with a smirk. I took a deep breath, then said, "There has to be some mistake," more for their benefit than mine.

"It's all there," Agent Moran said. She motioned toward where Tasha stood still, as if she was petrified, and now, two FBI-jacket-wearing agents rushed in, moving toward the bookshelves and the credenza in the back of the room. Over Tasha's shoulders, I saw other agents moving about and the other brokers standing outside their cubicles, eyes wide as agents invaded their spaces.

Then, almost in concert, Mr. Taylor and his staff stood. "Uh, we'll get out of your way," he said to the FBI agent as if he owed her the explanation and not me.

"No, Mr. Taylor, don't leave," I pleaded. "I can get this cleared up."

He moved as if I hadn't spoken, and his team followed him without a glance at me.

Rushing out behind them, I caught up with Mr. Taylor near the front door. "Sir, please," I said.

He stopped, and when he faced me, he eyed the FBI agents rummaging through the cubicles. "If you get this worked out, give me a call." Then I watched them all walk out the door.

As I stood in the middle of the floor, I glanced at everyone, all stunned, looking at me with questions in their eyes. And I had no answers.

I wasn't sure what I was supposed to do. Just let these people scour through my and my coworkers' things? That Agent Moran needed to stop all of this. I rushed to the conference room. But at the door, I paused. She was in there, at the other end, huddled in a conversation . . . with Tasha. I stood and watched the two women chat. Five seconds ago, Tasha had stood in front of me, shaking more than I was. Now she stood calm, arms folded, head bowed, as she listened intently and nodded emphatically at the agent's words.

A string of thoughts twirled through my mind: Tasha's brother in prison, her disappointment with losing the WestPark contract, her expression yesterday after Vivian had been arrested. I'd had a momentary thought here and there about Tasha sending me the texts. Was she the feds' source?

As if she felt my presence, Tasha looked up. Her hands fell to her sides, and she rushed to me. "Are you okay?"

"What were you talking to Agent Moran about?" My eyes volleyed between Tasha and the agent, who had turned the tables; now she was studying Tasha and me.

"Uh . . ." She glanced at Agent Moran. "She was asking me a few questions."

My eyes narrowed. "Questions like what?"

"Like how long I've worked here, stuff like that." And then, because she must've known that I thought she was lying, she added, "It really wasn't anything."

Liar! I wanted to scream . . . except my attention turned to Agent Moran as she said, "All right, let's move out."

Following her out of the conference room, I was stunned to see the other agents filing out of my office and the cubicles, carrying boxes. What was all of that?

"Excuse me," I said to Agent Moran. "Where are you taking my things? You have no right to do this."

"Ms. Alexander," Ms. Moran began, "that search warrant gives us every right, and you don't want to add to your situation by interfering with a federal investigation. You could be charged with—"

"It's a crime to ask a question about my personal belongings?" I said, my voice rising.

The agent nodded at the men, who proceeded to leave the office, and I turned to follow them.

"Ms. Alexander, I know you're upset," she said.

Damn straight! But I was smart enough to keep those words inside my head, since I wasn't sure if cursing out a federal agent was a crime, too.

"We're taking these documents down to our office, where everything will be cataloged." She spoke slowly, as if she were talking to a two-year-old. "And anything we don't need as evidence will be returned to you."

"Evidence!" I threw my hands up, then, with a breath, lowered my voice. "There isn't any evidence. I haven't done anything wrong."

"Well, then you don't have anything to worry about." Then, as quickly as they'd arrived, they disappeared, leaving behind my stunned coworkers, who were still waiting for an explanation.

I said nothing. Just walked toward my office. Before I stepped inside, Tasha said over my shoulder, "Is there anything I can do for you, Journee?"

Without looking back, I closed my office door in her face before I staggered to my desk. Everything that I'd feared had started. This was the beginning of my end. I'd been pretty sure this day was coming, but that hadn't deadened the shock.

I massaged my temples, then glanced up and frowned. Who had turned on my TV? It was on mute, but . . . I saw Agent Moran . . . coming out of my building. I gasped in horror as I grabbed the remote and listened to the anchor talking over video of Agent Moran and the others as they moved toward several black SUVs.

"It was an anonymous tip that we received at the station that led us here today, but there has been no official statement by the federal agents. The lead agent declined to comment as the agents just left this building. But inside are the offices of J. Alexander and Associates, owned by Journee Alexander, another native Houstonian who, like Vivian Wallace, is a longtime associate of Simon Wallace."

I pressed my hand against my mouth.

"Although Ms. Alexander was not taken into custody, our sources say that another arrest in this sweeping real estate fraud investigation is forthcoming."

I clicked off the television and wondered how many of my clients had just watched this. My clients, my associates, the financial institutions I worked with . . . and my mother and Windsor.

When Agent Moran had walked into my office, I thought that was the bottom, at least for today. But being on the news made this far, far worse.

26

Even though I had turned off the ignition minutes ago, I stayed in my car, just looking at the door of my mother's home. I wasn't sure why this felt more difficult than telling Quincy. Maybe it was because it felt like I'd just met my mother; she was a new acquaintance, and we were still in that stage of trying to make the best impression on each other.

Having to tell her that the Department of Justice had my name at the top of one of their investigations was not a great start. Plus, what would telling my mother do to her illness? Would her bronchitis flare up even more? She was on stronger medication that cleared her airways and the mucus from her chest, but the only thing Dr. Patterson would say about her condition was that my mother was holding steady. *Steady* was the operative word—not that she was getting better.

I had to be careful how I delivered this news, and I had to do it now because I was sure that by the time the evening news came on, what had happened to me would be televised across the channels.

But where would I begin? How would I explain this? Those were the questions on my mind as I opened my car door, but my cell rang. "Finally," I said, slipping back into the car. "Ethan," I exclaimed, "thank God you called me back."

"I was in a meeting, but you don't sound good."

"My office was just raided about an hour ago. It was on the news. The FBI came in there and—"

I didn't get to finish. "What?" Ethan's voice reverberated

through my car, rattling the windows. "I was supposed to get word if anything like that went down. Are you okay?"

"No," I said, hearing my own weariness. "I'm not. They left with boxes and boxes of not only my records but papers from my brokers and assistant, too."

"All right." His anger was still in his tone. "Did you get the lead agent's name?"

I told him, and then he asked, "Where are you now?"

"At my mother's house."

"Really?" His voice went up a couple of octaves.

It was then that I remembered—Ethan didn't know about my reconciliation. I hadn't spoken to him about anything besides my case . . . and my man. "Yeah, it's a long story. We'll have to talk about it sometime."

"At least that news is a bright spot in the middle of all of this," he said, and I wondered if it was. Could this reconciliation be interrupted by an indictment? "Okay, let me get on this. I'll be in touch. Just stay low, Journee," he said, ending the call the way he always did.

But I was so over this do-nothing strategy. It hadn't worked, and now I was going to do what I always did—save myself. I just didn't know how I'd do that yet.

Even after hanging up, I stayed in the car, staring at the house, before I moved toward the front door. With each step, I planned my words, and when my sister answered, she grabbed me in a hug.

"Are you okay, Sissy?" she whispered.

"I will be."

She took my hand and led me to the sofa. "Why didn't you tell me all of this was going on?" That was the same question she'd asked me when I had called her office and asked her to meet me here.

"I didn't think it would come to this," I said. "They're after Simon, not me," I told her, testing out the explanation I planned to give my mother.

She nodded. "Do you want me to go in there with you when you talk to Mama?"

I shook my head. "I'll be okay."

She sighed. "Well, she was resting when I checked on her a few minutes ago. She wanted to know what I was doing home in the middle of the day."

"I'm sure she'll have the same question for me."

As I turned from my sister, I almost hoped my mother was still asleep, wanting just a little more time before I had to tell her some semblance of the truth. But as I got closer to the bedroom, I heard the television, and I just wanted to sink to the floor.

"It was an anonymous tip that we received at the station that led us here today, but there has been no official statement by the federal agents . . ."

I was standing in the threshold when my mother glanced up, but furrowed brows were in the place of the smile that always greeted me. "Sweetheart, they just had your name on the news . . . with the FBI?"

Her question was in her tone as well as in her eyes. Picking up the remote, I muted the television, then sat beside her bed. "That's why I came here; I wanted to tell you myself." I glanced at the TV, where the story of my demise continued. I turned off the television.

My mother grabbed my hand. "Are you in trouble?"

"No, I'm not," I said, wanting only to comfort her. "It was . . . a complete misunderstanding."

She frowned, tilted her head, tried to make sense of my words in comparison with what she'd just seen on TV. "They went to the wrong office?"

"No." I needed to get as close to the truth as I could. "They meant to come to my office, but they were looking for papers for the man I used to work for before I started my own business."

She stared at me, wanting more.

"He's been arrested, and they're building a case against him. So anyone who used to work with him . . ."

Now she nodded. "They're looking for evidence against *him*." She eased back against her bed. "Okay," she said, sounding relieved. "That makes sense." But then she searched my eyes again. "They're not going to arrest you, too?"

I shook my head, and for the first time today the tears that burned behind my eyes overtook my anger. It wasn't easy to lie to her.

"Okay." She closed her eyes. "I feel a little tired. I'm going to take a nap, okay?"

Oh my God. Had this news done this to her? "Yeah, rest. I'll come back later."

Her eyes stayed closed as she nodded and coughed a little. I sat with her until she was asleep and then found Windsor in the kitchen with Mrs. Walker.

"How did it go?"

I nodded, then shrugged. "She's asleep" was the best I could say.

Windsor sighed. "Okay, so what do we do now, Sissy?" she asked as she followed me to the front door.

"I handle this, and you take care of . . ." I faced her when I said, "Mama."

The ends of my sister's lips twitched into a smile. She noticed my language. I'd stopped calling my mother Norma, but I hadn't embraced *Mama*—which felt like a term of endearment, and I wasn't there yet . . . not until now.

As I opened the front door, Windsor hugged me. " 'God

works in mysterious ways' is not a cliché. He'll use anything to fix everything between you and Mama."

I squeezed my sister's hand before I made my way to my car. There was no way I could get in trouble with the feds. Not now. Because of my mother. Because of Quincy. Because I finally had a good life, living right.

This would be the last time my mother would hear bad news about me. I was determined to make that vow a fact.

"LOOKS LIKE YOU need another glass."

A smile crossed my face before I even opened my eyes to see my man standing above me, holding two fresh glasses of wine. It was only a little after two in the afternoon, but I was grateful that Quincy understood my need for liquid reinforcement. He was still my solace in the middle of this storm, already here when I arrived after seeing my mother.

Just like Quincy had been doing since we'd met, he'd put on his cape and swooped in. I didn't know how he'd managed it, but he'd been here waiting for me when I came home, and since then, for the last two hours, my king had been doing everything he could to make me feel like a queen.

Quincy waited until I sat up, then handed me the glass. "Thank you," I said as he sat down next to me. After taking a sip, I added, "You know, your principal is going to get enough of you taking off for your damsel in distress."

He shrugged. "They can do whatever they wish. Call it a vacation day, or a sick day, or take it out of my check. I just needed to be here with you." After another sip, he took the glass from my hand, placed it on the table, and lifted my legs, pulling them onto his lap.

I tilted my head in curiosity as he removed my slippers. Then, without saying a word, he pressed his thumbs against the ball of one of my feet. My moan was instinctive as he moved slowly, kneading up, then down, then back up again. I was consumed with pleasure as I leaned back on the sofa and closed my eyes. I fell into the feeling as Quincy massaged every inch of my right foot before he turned his focus to my left.

I never wanted this to end, and as if he heard my thoughts, Quincy returned to my right foot—this time, his attention was on my ankles, then my calf. His fingers traveled leisurely, but with purpose, as if pleasing me was all he'd ever want to do.

Quincy went on and on and on and on with the longest massage. There was a chance I wouldn't be able to walk for a week.

When he pulled me up, put his arm around my shoulders, and then rested my head against his chest, like this afternoon with my mother, I was overcome with sadness. For the first time, I understood the meaning of *soul mate*. My connection with Quincy had been instant because we were meant to be. I absolutely saw my forever with this man, but now my past could cost us a future.

Inside, I cried out to God, pleading that this situation wouldn't tear us asunder. Certainly, He hadn't brought Quincy into my life just to rip us apart.

"You know," Quincy finally spoke up, "the more I think about it, the more I think you're right about your assistant."

When I came home, I'd told Quincy everything about what had happened, including Tasha's interaction with the federal agent. Lifting my head up a bit, I asked, "So you think Tasha could be behind all of this?"

"What you saw her doing today isn't sitting right in my spirit," he said. "Why was she spending so much time talking to that agent unless . . ."

I weighed his words. "There *was* something going on. I just can't figure out her motivation. What would she have to gain by working with the feds against me?"

He shrugged. "It could be anything. If the feds are paying, she might need the money. Maybe she wants to start her own business . . . and she needs money. Or maybe she wants to buy a home . . . and she needs money. Or maybe she owes a lot of people . . . and she needs money."

His words made sense . . . but so many maybes.

"Or maybe . . ." Quincy continued, "I've even heard of cases where someone was released from prison because the relative of the incarcerated cooperated with the FBI."

Slowly, I leaned away from Quincy. "What?" He repeated what he'd just said, and I told him, "Tasha's brother is in prison."

"Really?" I could see the wheels spinning in Quincy's mind.

"Yeah. The only reason she came to work for me was because she needed to earn more money. So she *could* have a motive. But . . ."

"What?"

"My business is legit. Anything the feds have on me would be from my time with Simon, and she wouldn't know about that."

"Unless someone is feeding her information, or she may not be telling them the truth. She could be lying and just hoping they'll find something."

"Wow," I said, thinking Quincy had connected the dots for me. Each time I'd wondered about Tasha and the texts, it had only been fleeting. But with what I saw today and what Quincy was telling me now, Tasha had a real motive. "I need to talk to her."

"No, you definitely can't do that." He shook his head, his tone definitive. "If she is working with the feds, she'll just tell them everything you said. And your words could always be twisted."

How was I supposed to face Tasha, and what was I supposed to do about what she was doing to me?

"I do think," Quincy continued, "that you need to get in front of this case if you want to salvage your business and your reputation."

"I've been trying to figure out how to do that. Ethan keeps telling me to lie low, and you even said that yesterday."

"After today, I've changed my mind. Because between that newspaper article a few weeks ago and now this being all over the news, even if you're never indicted, damage has been done, and it will be permanent if you don't make a move. You won't have banks or finance companies willing to work with you, you won't receive the opportunity to bid on municipal projects, and private companies won't be coming to you. Unfortunately, with all the press that's out there, nobody is gonna wanna touch you when there are other brokers to work with."

This picture Quincy painted made my heart crack. He was right, though. No matter what happened, this cloud of suspicion would live with me forever. "I want to do something; I want to be proactive. But what?"

"Maybe you should hold a press conference."

I tilted my head. "A press conference? With who? Who would come to something like that for me? I'm not a celebrity."

He paused as if contemplating my words. "Maybe not a celebrity, but you own a very successful business, and right now your name is in the news. We have to find a platform for you to give a counterargument to what played all day on television. What if you spoke to that reporter who was outside your building today, or even another one, so that your side could be heard?"

"Hmmmm . . ." I hummed.

"I think plenty of reporters would talk to you . . . one-on-one, to get your side of a story that's been headline news for weeks since Simon's arrest."

I nodded. "That might not be a bad idea. I could talk about my firm and what I've done to help the elderly and low-income families."

"Exactly. You can put a face and heart on J. Alexander and Associates, and when people see who you are and what you've done, that may put a little pressure on the FBI to back up."

My mouth opened wide with surprise. "Do you think something like this could change someone's mind at the DOJ?"

He shrugged. "I'm not sure. I was just thinking that right now, no one has heard from you. All everyone knows is that Simon has stolen millions of dollars from the system, and then his niece was arrested, too. Now, by association, you're tied to them."

It sounded as if Quincy had given this a lot of thought.

He continued, "The more I say it out loud, the more I think you have to do this. Just tell your story. And then we'll see where this all falls. One thing I can tell you . . . after the interview you won't be any worse off. And my prayer is you'll be in a better place."

Taking this kind of action would help me. Would get the FBI to see me in a different way. It was the opposite of Ethan's lie-low strategy, which made it even more appealing, since Ethan was wrong. Now I was going to make my situation right.

Quincy took my hands. "Let's do this," he said. "We won't say anything about the FBI or the investigation. We'll only talk about your firm."

"Yes." I nodded. "Let's do it."

"Great. So how do we make this happen?"

"Well, I don't have a lot of connections in the media, but I do know a reporter at Fox 26, Isaiah Wilson. Well, saying I *know* him may be overstating it . . . we worked together on a UNCF gala a few years ago, and we clicked. We stayed in touch for a couple of years, but it's been at least two years since I've talked to him."

"That may be exactly who we need. Someone who can't be accused of being a friend. Call him, tell him you have an exclusive for him. If he jumps at it, great. If not, we'll find someone else."

I cupped his face in my hands. "Thank you for this. Thank you for being here, thank you for caring about me, just thank you."

His kiss was gentle before he pulled me to his chest and held me.

Right now, this was all I wanted, all I needed. I wanted to stay just like this for the rest of this day, and tomorrow I would fight.

27

The raid on my office last Thursday had been bad enough. But then I became major news, the subject of a story that lasted far more than a day.

On Friday, my face appeared in the local newspapers alongside Simon and Vivian, with the headline: *The Feds Closer to Making Multiple Arrests.*

On Saturday the headline was: *Is Simon Wallace the Leader of a Major Real Estate Criminal Ring?*

By Sunday, Windsor had called, so distressed, letting me know she was doing all she could to keep the news from our mother. But that had been impossible because, suddenly, our mother was only interested in the news.

My sister had kept our mother calm by repeating my lie: "It's a mistake," she kept saying, even as my sister was in panic mode whenever she spoke to me. "Please tell me none of this stuff is true."

It was all lies and all ridiculous, but by yesterday, the headlines had reached their lowest lows. Some reporter was "just asking" the question of whether this real estate fraud case was linked to other crimes, like drug dealing and sex trafficking.

And today wasn't any better. That was my thought as I read the headline of the newspaper Quincy just handed to me.

MASSIVE SCAM TARGETED ELDERLY HOUSTONIANS

I tossed the paper across my desk. With my interview this morning, hopefully tomorrow's papers would be better.

Quincy said, "I know you're upset, baby."

"It's been a week," I said, pressing my fingertips against my temples.

"I know." He massaged my shoulders. "That's why what you're doing today is right."

As Quincy rounded my desk, I thought about all the two of us had done to make today happen. In the middle of the headlines and the hysterical calls from my sister, I'd reached out to my friend Isaiah Wilson. He'd been interested but hadn't been able to arrange an interview until today.

Just as Quincy sat, Tasha entered my office, escorting Ethan. It was difficult for me to keep my professional façade with Tasha when all I wanted to do was ask her why, then fire her. But Quincy had dismissed that idea, convincing me that I needed to use his personal strategy: keep enemies so close that you could smell their mouthwash.

Right now, though, my attention wasn't on my wayward assistant. My glance was on Ethan, who'd paused at the threshold. His eyes locked with Quincy's, and the way that muscle in his jaw twitched, it was clear my lawyer was not pleased to see my man.

We remained silent until Tasha closed the door, then Ethan said, "I thought you wanted to speak with me about what should be your next move."

"Yes." I jumped up from my chair. "I asked Quincy to join us," I said, though that wasn't the truth. Quincy had insisted that he be here. He didn't have to work hard to convince me, although right now I needed to lower the temperature or else we'd all combust. Motioning toward Quincy, I said, "You two know each other."

The men did one of those alpha-man stare-downs, and I prayed nothing would jump off.

"'Sup" was all Quincy said as he gave Ethan a single nod.

Ethan didn't even give Quincy that. Instead, he kept his eyes on me. "This is not how I operate."

"I didn't think you'd have an objection to Quincy being here, since Ivy is working with you."

"Oh," Ethan said, and turned back to Quincy. "You work here with Journee now? So if she's indicted, your name will be on the indictment, too?"

Quincy chuckled, and I crossed my arms. "Really, Ethan? Look, I'm just trying to do what's best for me. That raid really shook me, and so now"—I paused to steady myself—"all I want is for everyone who says they're on my side to work together. Please."

The men glanced at each other, then both nodded at me. Crisis averted. For now.

I motioned for Ethan to take the seat next to Quincy, though I wondered if the chairs being six feet apart was enough distance between the two.

Ethan said, "My schedule is jam-packed," as if he wanted it on the record that even after my little speech, he still wasn't feeling this situation. "So what's this idea you have?"

"First, I know you and Ivy have been working hard on this for me," I said. "And I'm hoping you'll take a minute to go over your strategy with Quincy."

That muscle in Ethan's jaw jumped again, but he nodded, then filled Quincy in on his potential defense, although the entire time, he spoke only to me. He explained how he and Ivy would paint a picture of an eager new hire led astray by her boss. Then Ethan explained how he would focus on my business for the last three years and would bring in statements from past and current clients as, basically, character witnesses. "So we believe we have everything covered, but we won't know until, or should I say unless, Journee is arrested. It's very interesting to me that they searched your office but didn't arrest you. With both Simon and Vivian, they were arrested first."

I hadn't thought about that. "So you think that's a good sign?"

"I don't know," Ethan said. "But it's different, and the feds operate carefully. Every move means something."

Quincy said, "Well, the defense you've laid out is a good start. But it still leaves us sitting and waiting, and I think we need to hit this with more force."

Ethan's eyes were on fire when he finally turned to him. "Journee doesn't pay you to think, Quincy. She pays me."

"Actually," I said, speaking up and jumping in, "that was the reason we wanted to talk to you, Ethan. Quincy and I have come up with an idea." Before Quincy could interject, I continued. Because Ethan would never accept this from Quincy, especially since this was his idea. I said, "I'm going to do an interview."

"A what?" he said, almost leaping from his seat.

"An interview," I repeated. "For television."

He leaned forward with wide eyes. "What?" His voice was soft at first, as if he couldn't believe my words. Then he shook his head. "No. Absolutely not."

"Ethan, let me explain." He sat back, but the way his lips were pursed, I wondered if he would really listen to me. "Right now, my name is being dragged all around the city. For a week, I've been part of the lead story on every station, every hour on the hour. Yesterday, I had to finally tell the brokers to work from home because they were being harassed by reporters in the parking lot. And now there's this." I held up this morning's newspaper. "There has been nothing but constant lies, and I want to get my side out. I'll never have another new client if I don't go on the offensive."

"I understand." His voice was firm. "But no."

My eyes narrowed, and his did the same.

Ethan said, "You can't do this, and this time, I pray you won't think you know everything and you'll listen to me."

Now I was the one with the tight jaw, because his words were an indictment of our history together.

He continued, "Right now, I can't be worried about how many clients you have or how many you may lose. My focus and my concern is only you. And as your counsel, I'm telling you you cannot do this."

"Well, I *am* worried about my clients, because this is my livelihood. And talking to a reporter just makes sense. Especially if the reporter is friendly."

"There's no such thing as a friendly reporter, Journee. Not if the reporter is doing his job and trying to make news. I promise you, this won't be good."

"So, is sitting back and doing nothing good?" I asked.

"Yes, it is. Especially in this situation. Because every question the reporter will ask will send you into a minefield, and believe me, the feds will be listening. If you give the wrong answer to any question, that could land you in prison."

I rolled my eyes. "Come on, Ethan, I'm not going to incriminate myself. That would be dumb."

"No, dumb is doing the interview."

Quincy jumped in. "She has to do something, because you haven't been there, man, when my lady is watching the news and I have to hold her in my arms to get her to stop crying. You haven't been there when she wakes up in the middle of the night so terrified that I have to rock her back to sleep."

What the hell? That never happened. What was Quincy doing?

"I'm glad you've been there to support her," Ethan said, not sounding pleased at all. "But what I'm talking about is keeping *your lady* out of prison. And if you care about her so much, that should be your goal, too."

Quincy eased to the edge of his seat. "Bruh, let me tell you something . . ."

A knock on the door interrupted the conversation, which had shifted that swiftly to a confrontation. Tasha peeked inside and said, "Isaiah Wilson just called. He said they're stuck in traffic, but they'll be here in twenty minutes."

When I nodded, Tasha closed the door, and Ethan stared at me in disbelief. "Journee, listen to me," he began, imploring me. "It's not too late to nix this."

"You've just had a few minutes to digest this idea, but I've been thinking about it for the past week. Truly, I've thought it all the way through, looking at the risks and potential rewards, while you can only see the legal ramifications. But I know what I'm doing. Let me handle this part, and you just focus on defending me."

"That's what I'm trying to do."

When I glanced at Quincy, Ethan followed my gaze. His eyes narrowed when he asked, "Was this your idea?"

He shrugged, but even that motion felt like he was mocking Ethan. "Journee's a grown woman who makes her own decisions. I'm here to support her—that's it."

I saw Ethan's fury in the way his shoulders hunched and the way he clenched his fists. But then, after glaring at me for a few moments, he released a long breath and relaxed . . . and that scared me. Ethan was a fighter; he hardly ever backed down when there was something he believed in. But was he backing down now? Was he giving up on me? I asked, "You're really concerned, aren't you?"

"I am," he said, sounding weary. "Because if this blows up . . ."

"Even if I tell you it won't?"

"You can't control that."

I stood and moved to the other side of the desk, closer to Ethan. "From the beginning, I've been so grateful for your help. But you have to trust me. I promise in a few hours you'll be telling me I was right."

His shoulders slackened, and the ends of his lips pulled downward. He nodded. "I have another appointment, so if you're going to do this, it'll have to be rescheduled for when I can be here."

"I appreciate that, Ethan," I said, my voice softening, "but I can do this. You don't have to be here."

He shook his head as if he couldn't believe what I was saying. "First you want to do the interview, and now you want to do it without me?"

"I didn't give you a heads-up, so I don't expect you to drop everything. I told you, I got this," I said.

His eyes stayed on me, and then he glanced at Quincy. He sighed. "Well"—he gathered his briefcase—"I guess we'll be in touch."

"We will. Definitely. And, Ethan, just remember: you know me. You know how I do."

That was supposed to make him smile. It didn't. He just walked out the door.

Returning to my chair, my eyes were on the door when I asked, "Why is this so hard? Why can't Ethan see?"

"He's an attorney; he's myopic. But you know what's best for you and this situation," he said. With just a few steps, Quincy was by my side. He took my hand, lifted me up, and pulled me into his arms. "Don't worry, Journee. We've got this."

I nodded as I wrapped my arms around him and prayed that he was right.

IT WAS A little before eleven when the front door to my office opened and Isaiah and a photographer entered.

Quincy gave me a reassuring nod as we headed to the lobby to greet them.

"Hey, Journee," Isaiah said, shaking my hand before he turned to Quincy.

"And you must be her attorney, Ethan Thomas," Isaiah said.

"Nah." Quincy chuckled. "Not me. I'm just here for moral support."

"Oh." Isaiah's glance went back and forth between Quincy and me. "Well, is it okay if Rodney"—he pointed to the man with the camera—"gets set up?"

"Of course. I was thinking we'd do it in my office, if that's okay." I led them back, thinking my office would be best, with my diplomas and awards behind me, all my accolades on full display.

They greeted Tasha as we passed her desk; when we entered my office, Isaiah and Rodney said together, "This is perfect."

"I thought I'd sit at my desk, since this is an interview about my business."

"Sounds good." Isaiah directed Rodney to begin setting up the equipment before he turned to me. "I'm really glad you reached out to me."

"And I'm really glad you agreed to do this. Thank you so much for helping to get my side of the story out there."

"There's been a lot of news about you. I've been working on background all week. This interview is the last element to my story." He glanced over his shoulder to check out Rodney. "It looks like we can get started."

As I settled into my seat and Isaiah smoothed out his jacket as he sat across from me, Quincy stood in the corner casually, his hands in his pockets, and when he smiled and nodded, I felt invincible.

The photographer miked us up, then Isaiah and I waited for the signal. Finally, Rodney held up three fingers, then two, then one, and nodded.

Isaiah began, "Thank you, Ms. Alexander, for agreeing to this interview. Now let's dive right in with how you got embroiled in what you yourself call a living nightmare."

Taking a deep breath, I made sure my shoulders were lowered and my jaw was slack. I had to look comfortable and confident. "Someone I once worked with has been accused of illegal activity that I knew nothing about. But in truth, I find it hard to believe that this man was part of any kind of fraud," I lied, trying to protect myself and Simon. "However, what's most important is that I haven't worked at that firm for many years. I started my own company, which I've built on honesty and integrity. I've strived to provide top-notch service to everyone. I'm so pleased to say I have a very long list of satisfied customers."

Isaiah smiled, nodded, then asked, "How did you meet Simon Wallace?"

I should have known he would bring up Simon's name anyway, but that was cool, since everyone watching this report already knew who we were talking about. I still wasn't going to say anything bad about him, and now that Isaiah asked this question, I thought about the agreement I'd made with Vivian. There was a good chance she'd see this interview, and I wanted to stay as close to the agreement we'd made at the Bayou City 100 as possible. Just in case that handshake meant something to her. "I met Simon through a friend," I said, thinking that was enough.

"Vivian Wallace?"

Inside, I groaned. Two questions in, and I felt as if I was already stepping on one of those mines Ethan had warned me about. "I . . . I . . . yes. Yes, Vivian and I were childhood friends, then college roommates," I said, spinning it as positively as I could.

"So you said you weren't aware of Wallace's illegal activities."

"I was not."

"But is there a chance that you participated in some of his scams?"

Oh my God. Another question I didn't expect. But I wasn't under oath, so I said, "No chance at all. I've always only cared about the clients, as has Simon."

My heart began to pound. I was dodging incoming fire, trying to protect myself, Simon, and Vivian. Glancing up, I caught a glimpse of Quincy, who now stood stiffly, his arms folded, his face filled with a scowl. Obviously, he didn't like Isaiah's questions either.

But then Isaiah entered safer ground with his next questions: How long had I been in business, what did I do specifically for my clients, and what did I love most about my job? About thirty minutes after we began, Isaiah said, "Great. I think we have everything we need."

The light clicked off on the camera, and as Rodney packed up, I exhaled. Ethan was going to be pleased.

"It may be a little late to ask this question," Isaiah said, "but I hope I didn't miss anything you wanted to get out there."

"No," I said as I passed my microphone pack to Rodney. "I think I covered everything."

"Yes," Quincy said, "this interview was all we could've hoped for."

"Thanks, man. All right," Isaiah said. "This will be on this evening at six."

"Wow," I said, "that soon?"

He nodded. "Like I mentioned, I did all the prework this past week."

"That's great," Quincy said. "The sooner the world sees this, the better."

Quincy and I escorted Isaiah and Rodney to the office's front door and shook hands, then we bid the two men farewell. When we were alone, I exhaled, so grateful this had worked out exactly the way I imagined. Now this city would know the whole story and Ethan would see that I was right.

28

The moment Isaiah left the office, I returned to my desk, wanting to share the good news. First was Ethan. I texted: Thank you for believing in me, for standing by me. Watch the news at six. You'll be very pleased.

Then I texted Windsor: Watch the news tonight at six. I paused for a moment, and then added, Make sure Mama watches, too.

Being able to send that text was even more important than contacting Ethan. I didn't want my mother or my sister stressing about this, and now they wouldn't worry. This news story was exactly what everyone who loved me needed. Now we'd all be able to breathe.

I said to Quincy, "I think I'm going home. There's no way I can wait this out in the office."

"Okay, I'll go with you."

"I thought you were going into work after the interview."

"If you can't focus, what makes you think I'll be able to?" He grinned, and it felt like the weight of all of these past weeks was melting from my shoulders.

We returned to my condo, and while I paced and sipped wine as if it were after five, Quincy turned his attention to the kitchen. Because on top of being a stallion in bed, my objective therapist, and the true support system I'd never had, my man could also burn. Within a couple of hours, the table was covered with a spread of barbecued red snapper, olive oil and sea salt oven-roasted potatoes, and snow peas with butter and lemon. But that was not enough, because when Quincy cooked, he followed every entrée with the best dessert. Tonight: raspberry soufflé.

We sat down to our late lunch/early dinner, and Quincy did everything he could to divert my attention from the forthcoming interview.

"What are some of your dreams, baby?" Quincy asked.

It was strange that my response wasn't instant, and then I realized that while I helped others achieve their dreams, no one had ever asked about mine. Sure, Ethan knew I wanted to be a major player in the real estate game, but that was it. I'd never noticed until now that I didn't dream. About a year after I walked into Mrs. Hunter's home, I didn't hope, I didn't wish . . . I didn't dream. I just survived. Even when I'd been with Ethan, we hadn't dreamed of a future; we'd just assumed.

As I thought about how to answer, I glanced around my custom condo, filled with furniture from the most exclusive shops, with the most expensive pieces of African art and European sculptures, and with a bedroom that had been turned into a master closet crammed with clothes that totaled in the hundreds of thousands of dollars in value. I didn't dream; I achieved. I filled my life with as many expensive items as I could to make up for . . . what? Missing my father? Missing my mother? Trying to get others to acknowledge me?

Finally, I told Quincy, "I haven't had many dreams."

At first he grinned, thinking that I was kidding. But when he recognized that was my truth, his eyes saddened, and he squeezed my hand. "That's really so hard to believe when I look around at all you've achieved. But I understand. It's all the damage done by your mother."

I inhaled. I may have taken a turn on my mother, understanding now that she had been young and talked into what she'd done by a woman who was probably close to twice her age. It hadn't been my mother's decision, it had been coercion, and there was a difference.

But Quincy hadn't been able to do what I'd done—even though he'd never met her, he hadn't forgiven my mother. That would change, though, I was sure. Once he met her. And once she loved him.

Then he said, "I dream a lot. I want to marry one day"—he took my hand—"and fill my house with dozens of children."

I snatched my hand away, and we laughed together. But then he became serious. "Really, Journee, all I want to do is love. Love my wife, my children, and when I do that, I know I'll love my life."

This dude!

"I have so many dreams about you," Quincy said.

His words, his thoughts, his dreams, made my heart swell with so much hope for the future . . . I wanted to live this dream alongside him. I prayed that after this interview, we would both be sure that I would.

Then that spell was broken when Quincy glanced at his watch. "It's time for us to catch the news."

I was surprised at the cheer in his voice, but then I realized he was trying to uplift me. I hated getting up from the table, but this was the first step in getting to the other side of this. This was how I was going to become Mrs. Quincy Carothers. Between having my mother back and planning this life with Quincy, maybe I could now dream dreams.

Quincy sat next to me and held my hand, and then, with his other hand, he aimed the remote toward the seventy-five-inch television. My heart pummeled my chest as I watched the opening credits for the six o'clock news on Fox 26.

"Okay, here it comes."

Again Quincy sounded excited, but even though I knew that I'd done well, it felt like a volcano was rumbling in my stomach.

My picture popped up over the anchor's shoulder, and Quincy turned up the volume just as the anchor tossed to Isaiah for his report.

"Melanie," Isaiah began, "we've been reporting on Simon Wallace for several weeks now, and while he is looking at twenty years in prison for his actions, police say his network was vast. One of the women who is being tied to this massive fraud scheme is Houston mortgage broker Journee Alexander."

A different photo of me appeared on the screen, this one in my cream-colored Carolina Herrera suit, which made my melanin pop. I smiled my satisfaction. Already this was going well. I couldn't say that I was thrilled with that opening, being linked to Simon that way. But I understood Isaiah's approach. What was going on with Simon was the bait to get everyone to watch— pull folks in—and then we'd get to the truth of my story.

"You may have heard of Alexander when, just a few months ago, she was featured in the *Houston Business Journal* as a Woman on the Move. We sat down with the businesswoman, who says she's determined to clear her name."

A sound bite played of me proclaiming my innocence.

"You sound convincing," Quincy said as he squeezed my hand.

I nodded because I couldn't speak through the rock that had grown in my throat. Yes, I loved what I was seeing so far, but I wouldn't breathe until it was over.

Isaiah continued, "Alexander says she has no idea how she got dragged into this because her main goal has always been to help people." As Isaiah spoke, a video played in the background of me working at a credit fair. I wasn't even aware that Isaiah had that footage. He had really done a lot of work on my story, and with each passing second, I was more pleased.

The footage continued with clips of Isaiah speaking to me in the office. He focused for a moment on my business and what I did for my clients, but then I was happy when he spent more time on the question, What did I love most about being a mortgage broker?

"I have the chance to help people achieve dreams they may have never achieved without me. I've seen people cry when they walked into their homes or even dance through the house," I said, thinking of Ethan's mother. "What I can do for others is so gratifying."

This interview could not have been going better than if Quincy had been the one questioning me. After this, no one would anyone associate me with Simon and his troubles.

But then . . .

Isaiah said, "However, while Alexander paints herself as the Good Samaritan of mortgage brokers, there are many who would beg to differ with that image."

The pounding in my heart stopped. Now I felt nothing.

"We spoke with someone who wanted to remain anonymous because of their involvement in this case. But that source says Alexander *is*, in fact, part of the elaborate real estate fraud, and they pointed us in the direction of this woman."

A picture of an elderly woman slid onto the screen, and I struggled to catch my breath. This was the face of the lady who'd appeared in too many of my nightmares.

"This is Louise Landers," Isaiah's voice continued.

Quincy's fingers slipped away from mine just as I muttered, "Oh. My. God."

"Friends and family members of the seventy-eight-year-old lifelong Houstonian say that a few years ago, Journee Alexander and Simon Wallace approached Mrs. Landers when she was going through a difficult financial time, and the pair convinced her to sign the deed of her home over to them with promises they would bring her mortgage current and then return the home to her. But that's not what happened."

Breathe in, breathe out. Breathe in, breathe out.

Isaiah kept on destroying me. "They never returned her home to her, never gave her a chance. Simon Wallace and Journee Alexander stole the home from this elderly woman."

I felt Quincy's eyes on me, and I wanted to remind him that he already knew this. He may not have known the names of any of the people I worked with, but I'd already told him about this. What I wanted to do was grab the remote, turn this off, drag Quincy to bed, and make love until he forgot that he'd even seen this.

But I sat frozen, dumbfounded, as Isaiah continued this horror. Now the screen showed him sitting with a gray-haired woman with doe eyes. Her petite, bent-over frame evoked sympathy.

"Louise was my neighbor for more than forty years," she said, with tears in her voice. "When I moved into the house next door, she fed me for a week as my husband and I unpacked. We were just heartbroken when those scumbags conned her out of her home," the woman continued. "She was so ashamed that she let herself be duped. The day before she had to move out of her house, she killed herself"—I heard Quincy's gasp—"and she was still clutching onto some hush-money check those fools had given to her." Now I gasped. "It's a low-down kinda person who would do something like that to an old woman. I hope that man, the lady who worked with him, and everybody else who helped him first rot in prison before they get on an express train to hell."

The scene faded, and the camera once again focused on Isaiah. "We asked the US Attorney's Office and the FBI for comment, but both agencies told us they don't comment on ongoing investigations. They did, however, say they would never bring charges against Wallace, Alexander, or anyone else if they didn't have a solid case. This evening, we also reached out to Ms. Alexander's attorney, Ethan Thomas, but we haven't heard back from his office. We'll be following this story as it progresses, Melanie."

It was only because there was a little bit of grace left for me inside the universe that the camera turned away from the man who had just ruined me.

One of the anchors said, "That's a sad story, Isaiah, and we'll be—"

The TV screen went black and the room silent. My eyes stayed on the television, though. I didn't move because I was waiting for Quincy. How was he going to react to the only part of the story that I hadn't told him?

"Wow" was all he said.

Facing him, I said, "Quincy, I told you all of this before."

"You didn't tell me that a woman killed herself because of what you did." He shook his head. "I just need a moment." He rushed from the living room into the bedroom. I wanted to go after him and tell him that it sounded worse because of the way Isaiah had framed it. But I stayed on the sofa because I needed a moment, too. That interview was so damning; Isaiah wasn't a great friend, but I'd had no idea that he was my enemy.

There's no such thing as a friendly reporter . . . I promise you, this won't be good . . . if you give the wrong answer . . . that could land you in prison.

All of Ethan's words rushed back to me. It took every bit of the energy that was left inside me to lift my cell. I tapped Ethan's number, but after it connected, his phone rang and rang and rang. "Pick up, Ethan," I cried, and then the call went to voice mail. I hung up and connected again. This time, it went to voice mail before it even rang.

I was shaking so much, it took me a couple of minutes to text: **CALL ME. PLEASE!**

A minute passed before he texted me back. **Can't talk. I'm with Ivy right now, and she's upset. We're both stunned.**

Ivy was upset? I was the one whose life had been blown up in front of the more than two million people who lived in Houston. I was the one who needed consoling. My fingers sped across the keyboard: **I need to talk to you. Please.**

I shook and waited as the text bubble started, then stopped. Then, after a couple of seconds, it was back and his text came through: **I wish you had listened to me. I wish to God you hadn't done that interview. I'll talk to you about this tomorrow. There's nothing I can do for you tonight.**

Placing the phone on the table, I sank into the sofa. I was too stunned to cry, so I just sat there. Until my phone vibrated with another message. Thank you, God! Ethan had changed his mind.

I snatched my cell: **Great interview. Love seeing the beginning of your downfall. I'm going to enjoy your fall all the way into hell. Vengeance is mine.**

I stared at that message, tossed the phone aside, and fell back on the sofa. The pain rose from my soul, and my shoulders shook with my tears. How had this happened? Did Isaiah already know, when he sat beside me today, that he was going to take a hatchet to my life? But how could I be mad at him when I was the one who gave him permission to do so?

It wasn't until I heard Quincy's footsteps against my hardwood floors that I pushed myself up. Thank God for my man. Glancing up, my pain-soaked eyes met his.

He nodded. "That suicide . . . that was a lot for me to take in."

"I'm sorry I didn't tell you that part. But even though I knew she'd died by suicide, I was never sure it was connected to me."

"So you didn't know about her clutching onto some check from your company?"

"No! I'd known she never cashed the check, but holding it while she died?" The thought of that made me sick. I was bone-weary now. "The truth is, I was always just trying to help these people. Everyone. Including Mrs. Landers."

"Well, now you know. She died because of you."

"I know," I whispered. "And I'm so sorry."

He nodded, but then glanced away as if he couldn't bear to look at me. "Okay, well, I'm going to get going . . ."

"You're leaving?" I had to catch my breath. How could he think of leaving right now? After all the nights we'd spent together, this was the night he chose for me to be alone? "No, Quincy," I said, finally pushing myself up. "I need you."

"No," he began, "what you need is some time to yourself." He paused, and now, when he looked at me, his eyes were filled with sorrow and . . . contempt. "And I need a little time, too."

There was so much I wanted to say, so much I wanted to explain, but my mind and my mouth wouldn't move. All I could do was stand there and watch Quincy walk out the door, and I prayed that he wasn't walking out of my life, too.

ighteen hours had passed since the story had aired, but it felt like I had lived eighteen years of terror. Throughout the night, my phone rang nonstop. Every journalist in Houston wanted an interview with me now. Why not? Who wouldn't want to sit down with Houston's biggest fool?

The calls continued well past midnight, but there were only three people I wanted to speak to: Windsor (who'd called me crying, but this time I couldn't console her 'cause I was crying, too), Ethan (whom I texted again, but who never responded), and then Quincy. I called and I texted, but I heard nothing back from him.

I tried to imagine what this looked like to Quincy. He'd known all of this, but the suicide was the center of the story. And the way it was told, I might as well have been the one to pull the trigger.

But Quincy had to know I was no longer that woman. I wanted to rush to him, make him understand, and convince him we'd be able to work all of this out.

But as much as I wanted to see Quincy, my first stop had to be Ethan. He was the only one who could get me out of this.

Ethan had texted me this morning. Told me he had some things to handle but to be at his office at noon. I'd arrived just about a minute ago, fifteen minutes early. The receptionist had led me into Ethan's office right away. I was sure he'd told her to bring me in as soon as I arrived just so he could begin tearing into me.

When I entered his office, Ethan didn't even say hello. Just stared at me for a long, uncomfortable moment. I wasn't sure if his glare was for what I'd done or how I looked. But a shabby gray sweats and white T-shirt were the best I could manage this morning.

When he still said nothing, I opened the conversation with "You can say, 'I told you so.' Let's start there."

"How many times have I been able to say that, Journee? This is déjà vu; we live it over and over because you always believe that you know more than anyone. It never occurs to you that someone may have good advice." There was no judgment in his tone, though; only weariness, as if he was just so tired of me. He rubbed his temples. "My phone has been ringing all morning. Every media outlet is trying to get a statement from me."

"I'm sorry. My phone rang all night, too." Then I quickly added, "I didn't speak to anyone," wanting Ethan to know I had learned my lesson and would do anything he said from this point forward.

"It's a little late for that."

"I know," I said, sitting straight up, prepared to take my chastisement like a woman. "I'm so sorry I didn't listen to you, but you won't have to worry about that anymore."

"You know, you've said that before," he said, still sounding so tired.

"Being humiliated on television, exactly the way you said, changes one's perspective. You're the expert; I accept that now."

"And I'm the person who is trying to do what's best for you."

I felt like a schoolgirl trying to get an A from my teacher. "I understand," I said with a nod.

"What about Quincy?"

Just the mention of his name made my heart ache. Would I ever hear from him again? I shook that doubt away. Quincy was just in shock. "Quincy . . . he's upset with the interview, too. So I know he understands the importance of listening to you now."

He nodded. "Honestly, Journee, Ivy and I talked about dropping you as a client last night."

I pressed my lips together to stop all the curse words that I wanted to shout out. Ivy wanted to drop me? That . . . she had some nerve. I wasn't her client; if I'd had my way she wouldn't have been anywhere near my case.

But I said nothing because I was teetering with Ethan.

After a long pause, he said, "We decided to keep working with you. But . . ."

I exhaled and held up my hand. "You won't have any more challenges with me."

He was silent, and in that pause, I heard his warning. I nodded, and he did, too. Then Ethan said, "Okay, so because of that interview, or maybe in spite of it, things are moving forward with your situation. I got a call from the US Attorney's Office this morning."

My heart was a sledgehammer in my chest. "Are they going to arrest me?" I managed to squeak out. When Ethan said nothing, I fell back into my chair.

"That depends on your next move."

My next move? That sounded like a way out. Slowly, I sat up, waiting for my heart to calm down.

Ethan said, "The FBI wants to interview you. They want to talk to you. About Simon."

This time, my heart stopped. "What exactly do they want to talk about?"

"Exactly what I said. They want to have a conversation with you. They're not offering a deal because you haven't been arrested"—he paused—"yet." Another beat. "But what they are offering is that in exchange for your cooperation against Simon, they will work with us."

"Oh my God! Are they really asking me to give information about Simon that they will use against him?"

"Yes," he said. "They want to know about all the scams you're aware of based on your personal experience."

"On my personal experience? Are they saying they know for sure I'm involved in this?"

"Journee"—he sighed my name—"they know. If the reporter was able to get that information, trust and believe the Department of Justice has so much more. They probably have the name of every person you scammed and for how much."

"But where are they getting their information? I thought Simon wasn't cooperating."

Ethan sighed, but said, "From what Ivy has been able to determine, that is still true. But we don't know what Vivian is saying. She's cooperating, so I would suspect she's telling them a lot about Simon and about you."

I knew she couldn't be trusted.

Ethan continued, "But it doesn't matter who's feeding them. They know, and as your attorney, all I care about is what I can do for you. Now, I told the US Attorney's Office I would call back to set a time for us to go in. I'd like to set up something for even this afternoon, or at the latest, tomorrow. What's good for you?"

How was I supposed to do this? How was I supposed to go against Simon when he'd been indicted for all of these months and he'd never said a word about me? I wasn't Vivian. I couldn't do it. "Ethan, I can't. I can't go in there and give Simon up like that."

Ethan rested his arms on his desk, leaned forward, and glared at me. "Let me explain this to you." The way he whispered scared me even more. "You don't have any choice. If you're not willing to cooperate, they will come after you, Journee, and they will come hard." He held up his hand when I got ready to protest. "I understand this loyalty you think you have to Simon, but the truth is, like I told you all those years ago, if he really cared about you, he would never have involved you in all of this from the start."

"Do you know there was never one case where Simon didn't give them money?" I said, trying to give Ethan a reason to support me on this.

"I am so tired of hearing that, Journee. Because giving someone a dollar with one hand while taking a thousand from them with the other is called thieving. He cheated everyone he did business with, including you."

"It wasn't like that." I shook my head. Folded my arms. "I can't do it. I can't turn on him when he's been protecting me all this time."

"The only reason he's not speaking, Journee, is because he knows that if he doesn't say anything about you, you will do the same for him. But he's the one the feds really want. I told you that before. He's going down, and if you live by this code, you'll go down with him."

I threw my hands in the air. "What happened to this great defense that you had planned for me? What happened to me being that naïve new employee who knew nothing?"

"That was how we wanted to do it. But this game belongs to the feds now. They set the rules, and this is what and how they want to play this game."

I shook my head. "You're a great attorney, Ethan. There *has* to be some other way."

"There's not."

"I don't believe that. You just got the call this morning, so you haven't even had time to investigate other ways to get me out of this. Find another option."

Slowly, he leaned back in his seat and pressed the tips of his fingers together. He was quiet, as if he was thinking, and I breathed. Thank God, he was going to listen to me.

Then: "I'm no longer going to be able to represent you. You're going to have to find someone else."

My mouth dropped in shock. "What? You want to drop me just because I'm asking you to find a different solution?"

He shook his head. "It's not just that." There was a weary sigh in his tone again. "It's been a struggle from the beginning. From the first day, when I told you to lie low, and you contacted Simon . . ."

"But I didn't know that's what you meant."

"I told you not to do the interview, and you did it anyway."

"Only because I was sure it would work."

Leaning forward, he said, "And now I'm giving you a way out of a very serious situation, and once again, you think you know better than me."

"I don't know anything better than you," I said, my voice rising. "I just know that Simon has protected me for so long, how can I turn on him when I'm sure there's another way?"

"You have an answer for everything and the only person you seem to be able to take advice from is *Quincy*," he said, as if it pained him to even speak that name.

I held up my hand. "So, wait. You're dropping me because you don't like my boyfriend?"

"Again you're not listening. I can't adequately represent someone who refuses to take my advice," he said.

I shook my head, as if dismissing his words would keep him from quitting. "No, you can't do this."

"I can, and I did. And just so you know, this isn't a reflexive reaction. Like I said, Ivy and I talked about this last night."

My eyes narrowed. "So you're listening to Ivy? Why would you do that when I didn't ask for her opinion? I didn't even ask for her to be on my case. But you put her there when you know she doesn't even like me. She is—"

He held up his hand, stopping my rant before I could really get in everything I wanted to say. He chuckled, although there was no joy in the sound. "You may want to keep my fiancée's name out of your mouth because you don't even know . . ."

I wondered if Ethan could see that I was steaming; smoke had to be billowing from my eyes and my ears. He wanted me to keep her name out of my mouth? Like Poison Ivy was some kind of special prize? Hell, he was settling for her, I knew that.

And I was settling, too. Because why was I even working with Ivy? I still wondered if she could be behind all my troubles. This whole meeting was probably her idea—she wanted me to turn on Simon, and then she would still make sure I served prison time. And her motivation: she saw me as much more than competition—she knew I was a threat to her little engagement.

I snatched my purse from the chair, slung it over my shoulder, and stood up. "You know what? Fine," I popped off. "Because with you as my attorney, things haven't been going all that great anyway. With a little bit of reading, I can probably represent myself and do a much better job."

He was unfazed by my outburst, although his sad eyes spoke a thousand words. Then he slid a card across his desk. "Someone once said a woman who is her own lawyer has a fool for a client. I hope you'll find an attorney who knows what they're doing. Here's one I recommend."

I glared at him before I glanced down at his card. I had never begged anyone, and I had never depended on anyone. "I'll figure it out. Just like I always have."

If he was moved by my words, I didn't know it. Because I spun around and marched out the door. If I'd known where Ivy's office was, I would have stopped by there and cursed her out. But instead, I stomped to the elevators and was so glad when one came quickly. Adrenaline rushed through my body, making my heart race and my blood pressure rise. I was shaking so hard, but I wasn't sure if I was shaking because I was angry . . . or if I was shaking because now I didn't have a lawyer. But the US Attorney's Office was still out there. And I was really, really scared.

30

There has to be another way ... there has to be another way. That thought reverberated through my mind the entire weekend as I searched the internet. The one thing Ethan had been right about—I wasn't going to be a fool; no way could I represent myself. But before I chose an attorney, I wanted to understand exactly what I could be facing. Simon had been charged with real estate, wire, and bank fraud. On Friday, I really didn't have any idea what that meant, but after this weekend, I now knew.

What I learned made me more confident that I wouldn't face the same charges. How could I? It was Simon who committed the actual crimes. Now all I had to do was find a great attorney who could see what I'd been trying to tell Ethan—there had to be another way.

I checked my makeup in the bathroom mirror, then clicked off the light. Reaching for my cell on the nightstand, I checked my texts. But I had no new messages. Not from my stalker . . . and not from Quincy.

It seemed impossible that I hadn't heard his voice since he walked out of my place on Thursday. All I wanted to do was talk to my man, but at least he had texted.

Saturday morning: **Just hold on, give me a little time.** I read that text over and over, grateful to hear from him, since he'd been silent on Friday.

Then yesterday: **I went to church this morning and prayed. Just know my feelings for you haven't changed.** That text had brought tears to my eyes. If he was praying for me, we'd navigate this together.

It was because of yesterday's text that I'd awakened this morning with vigor and determination. I'd find an attorney who would agree with me today; I didn't care how much it cost.

Grabbing my purse and keys, I marched to the front of my condo, ready to go to war . . . and win. But the moment I swung open my front door, I froze.

Agent Moran stood with her hand in the air as if she'd been ready to knock. She wore the same FBI jacket as the last time. With a team of blue-jacketed agents behind her. Without preamble, she said, "I have an order from the United States government to temporarily seize all your property." That was her greeting as she handed me several pieces of paper stapled together.

My keys fell from my hand. "What?" I exclaimed, snatching the papers and scanning through the pages as fast as I could. I understood little; it was all legal blather to me. But my mind zeroed in on the words that were clear: *civil assets seizure, criminal activity,* and *warrant.*

The papers trembled in my hand as the detective picked up my keys. "You won't be needing these." She dropped *my* keys into *her* pocket.

"I . . . I . . . don't understand."

"We're seizing your property," she repeated. "The government is taking possession of your home and your car, and everything inside those assets, as well as your financial accounts." She said all of that with no semblance of emotion, no malice, but also absent of any concern or sympathy.

"My financial accounts?" I was incredulous. "How in the world can the government do this? Just decide to take my possessions? Is this America or what?"

Agent Moran stepped into my apartment as if she'd been invited and motioned for the other agents to follow. When they fanned out across my condo, she turned to me. "It's because we live in America that we can do this, Ms. Alexander. We try to protect all citizens, and if we believe that your possessions were acquired through ill-gotten gains . . . well, then the government has the responsibility to make all parties in this situation whole."

What did that even mean?

"I can assure you this is legal. Actually, I'm surprised you weren't expecting this—surprised your attorney didn't prepare you."

Did Ethan know about this? Was this happening because I wouldn't cooperate with the feds?

The agent added, "You may want to call your attorney."

I awakened my phone, scrolled to Ethan's number . . . and hesitated. He wasn't my attorney, and I didn't want him to remind me of that in this moment. No, I could do this without him, but I had to find someone to help me. Trying my best to breathe, I called Quincy. I prayed with each ring . . . until his voice mail came on.

"Ms. Alexander." My eyes were glassy when I looked up at the agent. She said, "I can give you ten minutes to gather some clothes, but that's about it. You're really not supposed to be here at all."

"It doesn't seem possible; it doesn't seem right that people I don't know"—I glanced around at the strangers moving around my unit—"can come into my place and suddenly say that everything I own now belongs to the government."

"This is a temporary seizure. That's why I keep mentioning your attorney. He needs to know we're here, and he can tell you what to do."

"But I haven't been convicted of anything. I haven't even been arrested."

For the first time, there was a little bit of sympathy in her eyes. "Everything you need to know is in those papers. You don't have to be arrested or convicted if criminal activity is suspected."

"I'm not a criminal," I shouted. "How many times do I have to tell you this?"

The sympathy that was in her a moment ago was shoved aside by her impatience. Her tone was tight when she said, "I suggest you do two things right now. Get your attorney on the phone, but only *after* you pack a few of your personal belongings, because now you only have about eight minutes to do that."

"But what am I supposed to do?" My lips trembled. "Where am I supposed to go?"

She glanced at her watch, then looked up at me.

I took the hint and rushed into my bedroom. My mind spun with a thousand thoughts: I had to get my clothes, I had to speak to Quincy, I had to find an attorney, I had to get to my office, I had to . . . I had to . . . I had to.

Sliding one of my large suitcases from the corner of my closet, I stood in the middle of the space, wondering where I should begin. How long would I be gone? How long would the government have this temporary seizure? And then a new thought came to me—could temporary somehow become permanent?

A sob threatened to escape, but I pushed it down. There were not enough minutes left to cry. I grabbed clothing without thinking, folding a few dresses, a couple of suits, several pants and tops. Then I stuffed shoes into the suitcase. I moved to the chest that held my underwear, and then my jewelry. But when I opened the side that held my diamond earrings and necklaces, the agent was suddenly right behind me.

"You're only allowed to take clothes." I spun around to face her. "The jewelry is part of the order. We're confiscating all of it."

This time, I couldn't hold back my cries. My hands trembled so much, it was difficult to close the drawer. And for the fiftieth time, I wondered, how in the world could the feds do this?

Closing my suitcase, I ran past the agent into the bathroom, gathered as many of my toiletries as I could, and dumped them all into a travel bag. Rolling everything into the living room, I stood in the middle of this moment and watched as agents studied my furniture, then scribbled notes on pads, cataloging what belonged to me.

"Thank you, Ms. Alexander," the detective said, as if she was dismissing me. She pointed toward the door, and I shuddered as I was escorted out of my own place. Then she added, "Also, we've seized your office, so everyone who was there has been sent home."

Well, that was one thing I could take off the list of what I had to do. With a strength that I never knew I possessed, I lifted my chin, pushed back my shoulders, and walked out of my condo with dignity.

THIS IS THE most humiliating experience, I thought as I rolled my suitcase past the concierge. Of course, I'd done this dozens of times, but the way the concierge averted his eyes let me know he understood I wasn't taking a trip. He'd been the one to unlock the elevators for the FBI agents. They'd probably had to show him the warrant.

But I kept moving, and Willie, one of my favorite doormen,

greeted me with a smile. "Hey, Ms. Alexander," he said. His cheer let me know that somehow he missed the FBI invasion. "You didn't call down for your car. Want me to bring it up?"

I wondered if there were agents with my car right now. Or were all the agents in my unit, and they planned to take my car last? Could I perhaps get my car and get away? But then I shook my head. No need to make this situation worse. "No," I finally answered Willie. "I just called an Uber." Glancing at my cell, I added, "It'll be here in three minutes."

"Okay," he said, and then, because there was still some mercy left for me in the universe, Willie stepped away to assist a car that entered the carport. But just as he did, the door to the garage opened, and I realized there was no mercy at all for me.

There was my car, in all its glory, on a tow truck bed. I tried to look away, but then Willie rushed to me. "Ms. Alexander, what's up with your car?"

Mercy returned when my Uber rolled up and I didn't have to answer Willie. Inside the Toyota Camry, I sat back and wondered how things had gone so bad, so fast. It had been, what, just thirty minutes ago when I was preparing to go into my office and face this battle?

Within ten minutes, the Uber driver pulled up to the car rental place on McKinney, and as I maneuvered my luggage inside, a new panic rose inside me. What if the feds cut off my credit cards? How would I live until this all got sorted out?

I tried to remember Agent Moran's exact words—they were seizing my financial accounts. Did that include credit cards? Still, as I waited in line, I perspired like it was the middle of August and not just weeks before Halloween. When I was called to the counter, I stood in front of the car rental agent, who chatted easily about the weather and how good the Rockets would be this year. I only talked when I had to give her all my pertinent information, license, and credit card, because anything else . . . I didn't care.

"So, which size car would you like?" Chatty Cathy asked me.

"Premium," I said without thinking, then held up my hand. "Wait." I glanced down at the chart on the counter: compact, midsize, full-size, premium. In the past, when I'd rented cars on vacation, I had never given the selection a thought: *Give me the most luxurious car you have*, I always said. Of course, nothing matched what I drove at home, but I got close.

Now, though, I needed to preserve my money, not knowing how long this was going to take. So I said, "Midsize—no, full-size." Then I finally gave her a smile and apologized.

I prayed as I inserted my credit card into the payment terminal, then held my breath until APPROVED appeared on the screen. Still, my hand shook as I electronically signed the contract. I didn't exhale until she said, "All set," and handed me the rental agreement. "Enjoy your day," she chirped.

I rolled my luggage to the car before anyone could change their mind. Thank God my credit cards still worked. That meant I could use the cards to get cash, since I didn't have access to my bank accounts. Once I got a $5,000 cash advance, I felt a bit better.

Now I had to decide what to do next. Of course, I could go to my mother's home, but how would this affect her? Maybe I could just say that I wanted to hang out with her for a while. And then try to entertain her every hour so that she never saw the news.

But who I really wanted to see, who I really wanted to be with . . . was Quincy. I knew that once he found out what was going on, he'd be right there with me. I could move in with him and keep this from my mother . . . even from Windsor for a little while.

Glancing at my phone, I knew if I called him, he wouldn't answer. He said he needed time, but now . . . I needed him. I sat there thinking, thinking, thinking . . . and then my phone vibrated with an incoming text:

> Do you know how much I'm enjoying watching your downfall? The wealth of the wicked is stored up for the righteous. Guess which side you're on? Vengeance is mine.

I felt a new emotion as I read this text—I felt nothing but hurt. Someone was watching, someone was waiting, someone thought I was among the wicked. Now I wanted to see Quincy even more. I tapped my destination into the GPS and then maneuvered the car from the bank parking lot onto the street.

The blessing in Quincy's school being so close—only about twenty minutes away—was that I didn't have time to talk myself out of driving to his place of work, then marching inside the building and demanding to see him. Because that's exactly what I would have done if the drive had been one minute longer. I thought of every reason why I shouldn't do this: Quincy was at work and shouldn't be disturbed; he'd be too surprised that I'd just show up like this; he didn't want to see me yet.

But I kept going because this was best for me.

Rolling into the parking lot, I eased into one of the visitor parking spaces before I entered the blue building with the huge letters KIPP SHARPSTOWN above the front door. I went straight to the admin office, and a young woman who didn't look much older than the children in this school stood to greet me.

"May I help you?" she asked, sounding as perky as the agent

at the rental car place, and I wondered what was up with these Gen Zers.

"Yes," I said, and then I wished I'd thought this part of my script through before I'd entered. "I'm here to see Quincy Carothers. I'm sure he's in class already, but I only need to speak to him for a moment."

"Who do you want to see?" she asked.

"Quin-cy Ca-ro-thers," I said.

She raised an eyebrow as if I'd insulted her, though that was not my intent. Then she said, "I don't recall a student by that name."

"Oh, no, I'm sorry," I said. "He's a teacher."

"Oh." She shook her head. "We definitely don't have a teacher here by that name."

"Excuse me?" I said.

"No. One. By. The. Name. Of. Quincy. Carothers. Teaches. Here."

I would have accused her of being rude if I hadn't been so shocked. "That's not possi . . ." I paused. There were thirty-four KIPP academies in Houston, but I was sure he'd told me Sharpstown. But with everything going on, what I remembered was wrong.

"All right, thank you," I said.

She was much nicer when she added, "I'm sorry I couldn't help," sounding as if she meant it.

All the way back to my car, I tried to recall the conversation I'd had with Quincy when we talked about where we worked. I was sure he'd said Sharpstown.

Inside my car, I sighed. Quincy was the fuel I needed to fight this fight. So I held my cell, closed my eyes, then said a prayer. "Please, God, touch his heart."

Then I texted: I know you wanted time, but something

terrible just happened to me and I need to talk to you. Please.
I placed my cell in my lap and then just waited. It wasn't like I
had anywhere to go; I could sit in this parking lot until someone
came out and asked me to stop loitering.

But in less than a minute, my phone rang, and when I saw
Quincy's photo fill the screen, I couldn't answer the call fast
enough. "Quincy!"

He said, "What's going on?"

"Are you at work?"

"Nah. I didn't go in today."

He sounded so low, so dejected, so different from the man
who smiled with his whole soul whenever we were together. Was
this about me?

"I really wanted to see you. I wanted to see you so badly that
I even drove to your school."

"What!"

"Well, not your school. I drove to KIPP Sharpstown, and
they said you don't work here."

The phone went dead . . . or so I thought, until Quincy finally said, "I work at Northside, but why would you just show
up to my job like that?"

"I would never have done this," I said quickly because his
annoyance was apparent, "unless I really needed to."

"Okay, so, what's going on?"

His tone was so different. Had I already lost him? "I really
need to see you, baby. I don't want to talk about this over the
phone. Can I come by?"

He gave me another pause as if he had to think about every
word he spoke to me. "Okay, I'll come by. Give me an hour."

"No! That's part of what I wanted to tell you. I don't . . . I
don't . . . the feds took my condo."

"What? How can they do that?"

I had been steady the whole time, but having to say that aloud made a sob rise up in me.

"Okay," Quincy said. "Come over here."

"Thank you." But suddenly my relief turned into a frown. "Wait, Quincy. Do you realize I've never been to your place? I don't have your address."

"Yeah. Right. Okay. I'll text it to you."

"Thank you."

"And, Journee"—he paused again for a moment as if he was thinking again—"don't worry. I want to hear everything that happened, and then we'll plan. I promise you, this will all work out."

He ended the call, but his words left me with such hope.

31

As I entered Quincy's neighborhood, I was reminded of my time with Simon. There were many families here in the Fifth Ward who had been struggling—and became Simon's clients.

I sighed; I never knew Simon's true intentions. He and I never discussed why he came up with these schemes. But while I knew there was plenty of money in it for him, as evidenced by the six-thousand-square-foot home he owned in River Oaks and the Bentley he had years before I had one, I didn't believe that it was all predacious. Surely, he'd wanted to help those who were no longer in the position to help themselves—just like I did.

When I eased my car to a stop in front of Quincy's address, thoughts of the past vanished—thank God!—and I smiled. Quincy hadn't told me that he owned a newly constructed home, but I wasn't surprised. There was so much of this happening in the Fifth Ward as gentrification pushed itself into the innermost parts of Houston. Luxury homes and white people were showing up in places neither had ever been seen before.

I loved this two-story home. It could have been a piece of art with its design (the garage was on the lower level and the living space began on the second level) and steel-gray color. This house looked like something that should be in the center of the ritzy Uptown area. Parking in the driveway, I paused when I got out of the car—should I take my suitcase up with me? And then I thought, nah. It was too heavy, and Quincy would want to do that anyway.

I trotted up the stairs, thinking without even having seen the inside that this was going to be very comfortable for us until Quincy and I figured out what was happening with me.

When Quincy opened the door, he did not disappoint. His face, at first, was drawn, his exhaustion evident. But then he granted me his smile. His grin was so wide, and then when he pulled me into his arms, my heart began to sing.

"God, I've missed you," I whispered into his ear.

I was surprised when he pulled back and didn't respond in kind; he only took my hand and led me into the living room.

His home was gorgeous, as modern as mine, but that was where the similarities ended. His style was the antithesis of my condo. Whereas I used white as the foundation of my decorating, his furniture was all black, a dramatic contrast to the snow-white walls, but matching the black granite countertops and laminate flooring.

I lowered myself onto the soft leather sectional, which molded to my body as soon as I sat. Ahhh! All I wanted to do was lie back and have Quincy hold me. But when I settled on one end of the sofa, he moved to the other.

"So the feds seized your condo?"

My eyes narrowed; I was surprised those were his first words to me. He didn't ask how I was feeling. How I had made it through the last four days. He didn't ask anything about me. Only sat with his arms folded, the space and his crossed arms a barrier between us.

I began with "Yeah, and not just my condo. My car, my bank accounts. This morning, the FBI showed up and seized everything, even my business."

His arms dropped. "Journee," he said softly. "I'm so sorry to hear that. Tell me what happened."

I took a deep breath, then recounted for Quincy every ghastly moment, from when Agent Moran had stood at my front door to how she'd given me so little time to take so few things. "I couldn't take any jewelry; I couldn't take my computer. It was one of the most harrowing things I've ever experienced."

"That's unbelievable. So, what happens now? And most important, what is Ethan saying?"

"I'll start with Ethan, because that speaks to everything. He doesn't know. He's not my attorney anymore."

"What?" His head reared back. "Did he dump you because of the interview?"

Dump me? Why was that his assumption? "It was my decision. Of course, he didn't like the interview, and then we had a disagreement about how to proceed and what I should say to the feds. But"—I paused—"there was something else."

His eyes narrowed.

"That something else was you."

"What do I have to do with this?" His eyes were still squinted in confusion.

"He thinks I listen to you more than I do him." I shrugged. "That's probably true. I trust you."

"You don't trust Ethan?" He shook his head as if he didn't understand.

"I do, but it's different. With you, there are no ulterior motives. You advise me because you care for me."

For a split second, it looked like Quincy flinched. But I must have imagined that, because he nodded, and then with a small smile he eased over to sit closer to me.

"I don't know what I'm going to do," I said, wringing my hands. "I had to rent a car, and the only cash I have is what I took out from one of my credit cards."

"Wait? They didn't freeze your credit cards?"

"No, thank God. And it's a good thing, because, Quincy, I feel like they left me with nothing. My whole life has been taken away. I don't even know where I'm going to lay my head tonight," I said, dropping that clue right in front of him.

He stared straight ahead. "This is too deep. Well," he began, and when he put his arm around me, I exhaled. At least one part of my situation was about to be solved. He said, "I have a friend who's a criminal attorney. Maybe I can get him to help."

I had to blink a couple of times to understand these words I hadn't expected. I was practically crying on his shoulder about my home being taken from me and he was offering an attorney? Of course, I needed a lawyer, but . . .

"That's terrific, Quincy," I said, forcing enthusiasm into my voice. "I need someone, and so, I don't mean to push, but do you think you can call him now?"

"I would, but he's out of his office today. I'll hit him up tomorrow and definitely put him in touch with you."

That gave me a sliver of relief, but it wasn't what I was looking for. Still, I said, "Thank you," and then we sat in an awkward silence that I'd never before felt with Quincy. After a few moments, he said, "Let me get you something to drink. I was going to ask you if you wanted water or juice. But you look like you might need some juice with a little something added."

I glanced at my watch. "I wish. It's not even noon."

He said, "Well, you know what they say," and then together, we said, "It's five o'clock somewhere."

We laughed, and it almost felt like old times . . . and by *old times*, I meant five days ago. "As much as you know I love my wine, I'll be better with a cup of coffee."

"Sure. I don't have one of those fancy machines that you

have," he said. "But I have a Keurig." When he reached for my hand and squeezed it, I wondered if I was just imagining the edginess between us.

As he headed for the kitchen, I stood and strolled through his living room, taking in his art, the sculptures and the paintings. It really surprised me that I hadn't been here before. Why not? It wasn't like Quincy lived in one of those cliché bachelor pads with dirty socks strewn around and empty beer cans lined up on the counter. Quincy's home was showroom worthy. As if the designer (because he had to have one; of that I was sure) who had helped him furnish his home told him the whole place would go up in smoke if he didn't keep it looking exactly the way she'd left it.

Moving to the mantel, I took in the dozens of framed photographs, a pictorial display of Quincy's life. Not something that I'd ever seen in a guy's home before, but I enjoyed the pictures of Quincy from Little League Softball and Pop Warner football. Through these photographs, I watched him grow up from middle school to high school, and then his graduation from Rice.

But it was the picture that held the space of distinction right in the center of the others that had my attention. It was an old photo, obvious from the way it had yellowed with age, even inside the frame. I was drawn to it because of the two people posing—a striking woman, in her late forties or so, I suspected, only because of a little graying hair around the edges of her stylish '90s Halle Berry haircut, and a young boy, about nine or ten. The slender woman could have easily been a model. And the boy . . .

I glanced up as Quincy returned to the living room. Holding up the picture, I asked, "Is this you?"

Then there was that shadow that I hadn't seen in weeks. That darkness crossed his face, stayed longer than ever before, but was still gone quickly.

"Yeah," he said, placing my coffee and his glass of juice on the table. Then, moving beside me, he took the picture from my hand. "That's me and my mom." He placed the photo back in its place.

"She's beautiful," I said. I couldn't take my eyes away from her. Not only because she was gorgeous and so regal, but her face . . . "Your mom looks familiar."

"You think you two may have met?"

I stared at her for another moment, then shook my head. "I would remember her," I said. Glancing at Quincy, I said, "But can you imagine? If we had met, do you think she would have introduced us?"

I grinned until he exclaimed, "Absolutely not!" It was my horrified expression, I was sure, that made him self-correct. "She didn't think any woman was good enough for me."

Nodding, I turned away and went for my coffee. The mug warmed my hands as I sipped and Quincy drank his juice. Nothing but silence. What was going on?

Finally, Quincy said, "Listen, I don't want to rush you 'cause you got a lot going on, but I was just on my way out when you called."

"Oh," I said, putting my still-half-full mug of coffee down. "I'm sorry, I just . . ."

"Don't apologize." He shrugged as if it was no big deal. "You didn't know. And really, I hate that I have to go, with everything that's happening with you."

"Well," I said, looking around but not moving. Was he really asking me to leave, knowing my condo had been seized? Again silence settled between us, and when he said nothing more, I stood but still did not move. *How can you let me go?* I screamed inside.

Lifting my purse from the sofa, I stared at Quincy, my eyes doing what my lips would never do—I pleaded with him. But he smiled, nodded, then exited stage left, moving toward the door.

My heart contracted as I followed him. He paused at the door, didn't open it, but instead turned to face me. "I know you're going through a lot, but I promise, I'll be there until the end."

"Thank you," I said.

"And I'm going to call my friend first thing in the morning." When I frowned, he added, "The lawyer."

I nodded. "I appreciate that" was all I said as I shifted from one foot to the other, willing him to remember how much he loved me.

Then, as if he did remember, he pulled me close and gently kissed my forehead. I almost melted right there, until he stepped away and opened the front door. "Get some rest, baby," he said.

I stepped over the threshold, still not believing this was happening. Still thinking he would pull me back into his home. But once I stepped outside, the only thing Quincy did was close the door. Right in my face.

I stood there thinking Quincy would open the door again and pull me inside. But he didn't, and after waiting for too many moments, I started down the stairs.

Just as I got to my car, my phone vibrated. I glanced down: **For whatsoever a man soweth, that shall he also reap. Vengeance is mine.** I slid into the car and rested my head on the steering wheel. I'd lost everything.

snuggled into the cushions of my mother's couch but couldn't find that comfortable space. I really had to get her a new sofa. Then I remembered: I had no money.

Turning onto my back, I stared at the ceiling, willing my eyes to close so that I could get some rest. But my eyes stayed open because of a single thought that churned in my mind:

Quincy put me out!

I was sure he'd never characterize it that way, but that was what I felt after this man had said his feelings for me ran deep, after he had stayed at my place more in the past month than he'd been at his own, and after he had learned I'd lost my home . . . This man hadn't invited me to lay my head next to his.

At least he'd texted just as I got to my mother's house last night: I'm going to give my friend your number. Just wait for him to call you; he's a really good attorney, better than Ethan. No need for you to reach out to anyone. He's the guy I want you to have.

That was it—he hadn't even asked where I was. Maybe my drama was a little too much for him. But then, that couldn't be true, because he was still looking out for me, making sure I had a good attorney.

I tucked my hands beneath my head, shifted again, and just as I closed my eyes, the lamp on the table next to me came on, making me squint against the brightness.

"Windsor?" My sister came into focus, standing over me. "I

didn't even hear you come in here." I pushed myself up. "Did I wake you?"

"No, this is my normal time. I just woke up and got a little worried when I didn't see you." She plopped onto the other end of the sofa.

"I couldn't sleep. Plus, I hated taking up half your bed."

"It was fine. I know my bed isn't anything like that yacht in your bedroom, but I don't mind sharing."

I tried but couldn't smile. "Thanks, Sissy."

A few silent moments passed, and by the way my sister looked at me, I knew our hushed conversation from when I'd first arrived last night was playing in her mind. She sighed. "I can't believe you've been going through all of this—and I'm still mad that you never told me."

"Shhh." I held my finger to my lips and glanced toward the hallway leading to our mother's bedroom.

Windsor waved her hand. "Mama won't hear anything; she won't even be turning over for another thirty minutes or so."

I leaned back but kept my eyes on her room down the hall. "Do you think she believed me?"

Windsor shrugged. "She doesn't have any reason not to. I mean, we came up with a good lie, and in the process, Mrs. Walker got a couple of days off. You're just going to have to live up to this—if you're covering for her sick aide, you're gonna have to do the work." She grinned; she was teasing, but my sister meant what she said.

Sitting up, I said, "I'm ready, I'll be here; what else am I going to do?"

"Don't get too good. She may fire Mrs. Walker and hire you full-time."

Another joke that was all too serious to me. "Depending on

what's going to happen, I may need a job. I just hope Mom won't ask for references."

That was my attempt at humor, but neither of us laughed. I said, "I'll make it through; I'm sure of that." I prayed my words were true.

"I know you will. You're my hero, Sissy, and"—she took my hand—"I'm going to be with you all the way." Then she sat back. "In the old days, like a few weeks ago, this is where I'd add something like *Mom will be there for you, too.* But I think you know that now." I nodded and she added, "She would back you all the way, so I think we need to tell her."

I was shaking my head before she even finished. "She's not strong enough to deal with this. Her bronchitis . . . I'd never forget myself if it got worse."

"I get that. But how long do you think we'll be able to keep this from her? It's better if she hears it from you and not on the news or something."

"Well, there was no coverage of what happened yesterday, so I think the media has moved past me, at least for the moment."

Windsor tucked her feet beneath her, settling in as if we were having a slumber party. She asked, "What do you think the FBI is going to do next?"—reminding me this was no party at all.

I shrugged. "I don't know. That's why I really need to get an attorney, although I'll be limited financially now." I sighed. "I'll have to figure that all out."

"That's another reason we have to talk to Mom. If they took everything from you, she can help."

"No," I said in a tone that let my sister know there was no room for negotiation. "I'm not bringing her into any of this."

"You may not have a choice."

"This is going to be fine, Windsor. Once they go through my papers and then whatever they seized at my place, they'll see there's nothing there. They'll have to move past me."

She nodded, as if she'd given up that fight—for now. "Well, here's hoping you're right. And let's revisit telling Mom, but"—she glanced out the window—"as dawn breaks, it's time for me to get up. Let's go, Sissy. You'll see all the things I do with Mom before you and Mrs. Walker get here in the morning."

I swung my legs over the sofa, actually happy to have something to do besides thinking about Quincy and the FBI. Tightening my robe, I tiptoed behind my sister into our mother's room, but when we entered, she was already sitting up in bed with her arms crossed, like she'd just been waiting. "I thought I heard y'all. I was about to come out there and join in the festivities."

While I chuckled, Windsor's voice was stern when she said, "I hope you're kidding, 'cause you know you're not supposed to move around without assistance." When my mother waved her off, my sister added, "I'm not playing with you."

The two exchanged a few more lines, and I relished their early morning banter. For the next hour, I helped Windsor care for our mother. From the shower to dressing her, what might have been a stressful time for other caregivers was almost relaxing, very cathartic for me. I was taking care of my mother, and it felt like a blessing! In the middle of my storm, I paused to thank God for this calm.

Once my mother was back in her bed, I stayed with her while Windsor dressed, then my sister did the same for me.

By the time I came out of Windsor's bedroom dressed in jeans and a UT sweatshirt, I followed the aroma that filled the house straight to the kitchen. As my mother sat at the table,

Windsor stood in front of the stove, a pan of sizzling bacon before her.

"Look at this, Sissy," Windsor said when I came into the kitchen. "I can never get Mom to come out of her room and eat with me. But you did it." She motioned for me to sit next to our mother—a plate piled high with waffles and bacon was already set for me.

This wasn't how I usually started my day. Espresso was enough for me—I never wanted this many calories before noon. But what the heck—calories were amazingly medicinal. When I slid into the chair, my mom squeezed my hand.

"Do you know how wonderful it is to have both of my girls here with me?" Tears glistened in her eyes, but her smile was wide, and for a moment, I drifted back on memories to the days of my childhood when my mother's smile was my security. As she held my hand, I felt that once again.

"Don't cry," I said, lifting her hand and kissing her fingers.

"Oh, don't mind me." She dabbed a paper towel at the corner of her eye. "These are happy tears. This moment . . . this is the happiest I've been in my—" The banging on the door sounded like the thunderstrokes of a thousand storms and stopped my mother from speaking and my heart from beating at the same time.

"Who the hell is trying to break down my door?" My sister stomped across the room, her anger building with each step. She moved faster than my brain; I wanted to yell out, tell her not to open that door, explain that we had to hide. But before I could get a word out, she swung it open and three men—and Agent Moran—crashed inside.

"What the hell?" Windsor shouted while my mother screamed.

In just a few long strides, Agent Moran crossed my mother's

living room, her eyes trained on me. "Journee Alexander, we have a warrant for your arrest."

"Oh my Lord!" my mother yelled. "What is going on?"

"You can't come into my house and do this," my sister cried.

My sister and mother screamed at the agents, demanding answers, insisting that they leave. All I could eke out was "Please." What else could I say? I wasn't shocked like my mother; I couldn't be defiant like my sister. But I could beg them to do this quickly because . . . I didn't want my mother to see this.

One of the marshals yanked my hands behind my back to cuff me, and my mother cried out, "That's my daughter. You can't do that!"

But Agent Moran didn't care about me or my mother. "You have the right to remain silent," she said without emotion. "Anything you say can and will be used against you in a court of law." My hands ached already when the other marshal lifted me up from the chair as Agent Moran continued to recite the Miranda warning. Finally, she ended with, "Do you understand these rights as they've been explained to you?"

As the agents led me from the kitchen, my mother jumped up. "Where are you taking my daughter?" she demanded to know, stumbling behind us. "Please," she wheezed. Before we reached the door, she grabbed one of the agents' arms.

Agent Moran stepped in front of my mother.

"No!" I exclaimed. "Please leave her alone. She's sick. Please."

I was grateful that Windsor was at her side, holding her up as she began to cough. But Agent Moran had no concerns about my mother. She stared at her before she said, "Ma'am, if you interfere, you will be arrested," as if she were a criminal.

"If you touch my mother," Windsor threatened the officer, "you're going to have to deal with me."

Oh my God. I closed my eyes. In a moment, my mother and

sister would have handcuffs around their wrists, too. I had to get out of there.

I'd never felt as helpless as when the marshals led me outside and I heard my mother's squeals. "Please, please, Journee!" she croaked, struggling to gasp enough air to speak. "Where are you taking my baby girl?"

My heart shattered into millions of tiny pieces. All I wanted to do was turn around and hold her. But how could I comfort her? I was the cause of her pain.

If there was any mercy in my life, it was that there was no one outside; in just an hour or so, this street would be filled with young children on their way to school. But this was the quiet of the early morning.

After I was stuffed inside the unmarked car, I leaned my head back and closed my eyes, but that didn't block my mother's cries. "Journee! Journee!" echoed in my ears even when we were blocks away from her home.

I prayed Windsor would be able to calm her, convince her that all would be well, even though I knew that nothing in my life would ever be well again.

I WAS IN jail.

Sitting inside a ten-by-ten space with bare gray walls. How could this be my life?

The whole process had been surreal—from the car ride to being fingerprinted and then photographed, before I was handed one of those orange jumpsuits that was two sizes too big, socks, and a pair of slides. I had to strip in front of the officers and then change into this jail garb. When I slid my feet into the shoes, the heel was half off the left one, and I walked like I had a limp.

The guard gave me a ziplock bag with a toothbrush, toothpaste, a bar of brown soap, deodorant, and feminine products before another officer led me to a cell.

Now I sat, just waiting. For at least three hours, I'd been waiting to make my phone calls. When I had first asked about that one call I'd known about because of TV, the guard told me I could make three and she'd be back for me to do that.

I just need Quincy. I just need Quincy. That was my mantra; whispering his name calmed me.

"Alexander!" I jumped up. The woman, who didn't look anything like what I imagined correctional officers to be, with her face made up as if she were about to go on a photo shoot, unlocked the cage. "You can make your calls now."

I limped behind her as she led me down a narrow hall, where at the end, an old-fashioned black metal desk sat with a landline phone on top. I stared at the telephone, wondering how many people had used this, wondering how many germs were incubating on that receiver, wondering if they had any Covid protocols at all.

"You got a problem?" the officer asked as I just stood there.

"No." I grabbed that phone as if it was my lifeline and took a breath before I pressed the receiver to my ear. I dialed Quincy's number. It rang . . . and rang . . . and rang, and when his voice mail came on, I hung up, not wanting to waste one of my calls. "No one was there," I said, just to make sure the officer wouldn't hold that call against me. "So that one doesn't count."

"Oh, really?" She sounded amused and shook her head. "You get three calls. I don't care if you're talking to a live person or to a machine or to God. If you dial it, that's a call. So you've just used one of yours."

"Oh my God," I said. "I didn't even leave a message because I didn't want to waste my call."

She folded her arms. "Well, you just did. You got two more, and you have ten minutes."

My head throbbed. I didn't need a headache right now. Not when I had to figure out the best use of my last two calls. It wasn't as if I had a long list, so I redialed Quincy's number and prayed this time he'd answer. When he didn't, I waited for the voice mail, then spoke quickly, because if his message cut me off . . . "Quincy, you're not going to believe this, but I've been arrested and I'm at the Harris County jail on Baker Street. I have to get out of here, so can you get"—I paused, not even knowing the lawyer's name—"your friend the attorney to come down here? I'm sure he's been calling me all morning, but my cell is at my mother's house and . . ." I held back a sob. "Just get down here as soon as you can. I love you, Quincy." I did love that man, and I knew, even with the awkwardness between us over the past few days, he loved me, too. So I repeated, "I love you," and then ended the call. I pressed the receiver to my chest as if I were holding Quincy.

"You have one more call and about four minutes."

Four minutes? I hadn't been on the phone that long. But I said nothing. Even though she had on more makeup than the model on the cover of *Sports Illustrated*, she was still a correctional officer, and that title alone made me afraid.

I dialed Windsor's number and was shocked when she didn't answer. Dang! I wanted to hang up and dial again, because surely Windsor had been waiting for my call. When her voice mail came on, I said, "Windsor, I want you and Mama to know I'm fine. Quincy is on his way, and he'll get me out of here. I'll call you again when I can, but please don't worry. And please make sure Mama is calm and she doesn't worry either. I really am fine."

Because sobs began to rise within me, I hung up without saying good-bye. I couldn't let my sister hear any weakness.

Three calls . . . and I'd spoken to no one. I followed the officer back to the cell, sat on the cot, pulled my legs to my chest, and just waited. Just waited and tried not to cry.

held on to the bars of my cell as if standing by the door were going to bring some kind of miracle. I needed one, because an entire night had passed and I hadn't heard from anyone . . . not Quincy, not the lawyer, and not even Windsor. That, I couldn't believe, but I figured her hands were full with our mother. I couldn't imagine all that she had to do to keep our mother calm through this.

She would call me, or probably even come down here today. But as much as I wanted to speak to my sister, Quincy was at the top of the list.

"Hey, Alexander"—my head whipped to the right—"you have an early visitor," the guard shouted as she approached my cell.

"Thank God," I whispered. "Quincy."

I was talking to myself, but the guard shrugged. "I don't know who it is," she said. "I'm not the one who checks IDs. But you're lucky whoever it is came right at nine, 'cause you'll probably get a whole section of the room to yourself."

This time I rushed behind the guard with no concern for my shoe. The officer explained the rules as we moved through what felt like a labyrinth of halls, completely confusing me, which I guessed was the point. It would definitely be hard to break out of here.

"No touching, no sharing any food, no exchanging of gifts."

I didn't care about any of that as we rounded a corner and I followed the guard into a large, stark room filled with six-foot-long folding tables and cheap folding chairs at each one.

There were already about a dozen people sitting at the tables, but my eyes scanned, and with a laser focus, I found him. Quincy was on the far side, away from everyone else. Inside I shouted *Hallelujah* as I dashed over. When I stood in front of him, it took everything within me not to break the first rule. All I wanted to do was throw my arms around him. But all I did was smile and say, "Hey, baby."

"How are you?" he said. It surprised me that he didn't stand. This was the man who opened every door for me, who pulled out every chair for me, who massaged every part of my body just because. But now he just sat there.

I slid into the chair across from him—my focus on the rules—and I realized from his tone and his countenance, Quincy was as shocked as I was that I was locked up.

"I'm so grateful you're here. Finally. It's been horrible."

"It's jail," he said. "It's not supposed to be a four-star experience."

Again that was an unexpected response, but it was clear Quincy was traumatized. Like me, this was probably the first time he'd ever been inside a jail, and now all I wanted to do was comfort him and let him know we'd get through this.

Around us, men, women, kids, and even a couple of toddlers chatted and shared laughter. There were enough people so the guards' eyes wouldn't be on us, and the woman who'd brought me out was engaged with another officer. So I took my chances and reached for Quincy's hands. I just needed to touch him; he just needed to feel me. But before our hands could connect, he pulled away.

I got it. He'd been told the rules as well, I was sure. I said,

"After I left you the message yesterday, I thought you'd come down with the attorney."

"Nah, I couldn't do it yesterday," he said. And the frown on his face faded a bit as the corner of his lip twitched into more of a smirk than a smile. "It took a minute for you to get processed into the system. You couldn't have visitors before that."

"Oh, I didn't know. I don't understand how any of this works." I shook my head. "But I'm so glad to see you now."

"Oh, trust and believe I was gonna come see you."

I frowned. Quincy's words were fine—*trust and believe I was gonna come see you*—but his tone . . . it felt as if we were having different conversations. He continued, "I was going to be here for justice."

"I know," I said, reaching for him again. "If there is any justice in the world, your friend will be able to get me out of here. Where is he, by the way?"

His eyes bore into me. "I think the justice you want and the justice I've received are two different things."

At first, I frowned, not understanding his words. But I began to understand that this wasn't the Quincy I'd come to love.

Before I could gather my thoughts to ask him what was going on, Quincy continued, "For whatsoever a man soweth, that shall he also reap."

Those words were like a ram, thrusting me back into my chair. Those words, that scripture—that was the last text I'd received. I squinted, trying to understand.

But then, I thought, no, no, no. This wasn't about the text; he didn't even know about this last one. Quincy was trying to tell me something I didn't yet understand.

That was what I said in my mind, but my heart already knew. I pushed aside the panic bubbling inside. I said, "The attorney.

Did you contact him? Is he coming?" as if changing the subject would also change what I knew was happening.

"So, even with that scripture, you still don't get it?" He leaned toward me and chuckled. "You're a trip, sweetheart. But if there's one thing I've learned about you in the weeks I've had to suffer in your presence, it's that you're smart. And so you already know there is no attorney."

Suffer in my presence. What did that mean? That was a question I asked myself, but not Quincy. I didn't want to know. Because if he told me the truth, I'd have to admit and accept how wrong I'd been. "You told me you . . . had a friend . . . who could . . . help me."

He shrugged. "I've said a lot of things. But why would I help you when I helped the US attorney put you in here?" He motioned around the room, and every text I'd received flashed through my mind.

Vengeance is mine.

Vengeance is mine.

Vengeance is mine.

"What? Why? I don't understand. What're you talking about? What do you mean?" The questions spilled out of me as if I had no control.

He didn't respond, at least not verbally. Instead, he reached into his jacket and pulled out a folded piece of paper. With care, he opened it, then flattened and smoothed it out.

As I watched him, I truly didn't know this man sitting in front of me. Everything about Quincy looked the same: his thick eyebrows that framed his light brown eyes, his chestnut-brown complexion, his lips—oh, those full lips that had given me so many hours of so much pleasure. But this wasn't Quincy.

Finally, he slid the paper across the table. My eyes focused on . . . what was this? A funeral program? Then I homed in on the photo in the middle. Of the beautiful woman. Who, when I last saw her in person, reminded me of Diahann Carroll.

Mrs. Louise Landers.

I had so many questions, and then I had none at all. My hand felt as heavy as a slab of concrete when I lifted it to slide the program back to its owner.

"No!" Quincy shouted, startling me. He lowered his voice when the guards glanced our way. "Look at this." He opened the program and jabbed his finger on the last paragraph of the obituary. "Read this," he said through clenched teeth. "The last sentence."

It was hard to see through the tears I had not yet shed. But I was able to read what I had already figured out: "She leaves her beloved son, Quincy Landers, to mourn her passing." When I closed my eyes, a tear was set free and trickled down my cheek.

He said, "I'm sure you have a lot of questions."

I shook my head. I had nothing to ask, nothing I wanted to know. Because the part I had figured out already hurt too much. All of this time, our whole connection—it was all a lie. But . . . but that couldn't be true.

Quincy, though, had much to say. "I guess I should introduce myself." He held his hand out to me, but I left him hanging, my only weapon in this war that he had declared against me. "I'm Quincy Landers. And who are you?"

I didn't move.

He brought his face as close to mine as the table between us allowed. "Let me remind you of who you are," he said, his tone filled with venom. "You're the bitch who killed my mother."

I shook my head and found my voice. "It . . . it wasn't like that at all."

"It was exactly like that," he said. "My mother's life was destroyed because of you, and since she died, I've done everything in my power to make sure your life would be destroyed, too."

"So this has been"—the words squeaked from my throat—"an elaborate plan to destroy me?" Even as I asked, it didn't seem possible.

"From day one," he boasted. His smile returned, and he leaned back like we were just chatting. "It was easy enough to find you, although at first I was confused by Wilhelmina Jones. That's what my mother said your name was when she called and told me how you and Simon cheated her.

"But I had Simon's business address from the check my mother died holding. So I went to his office, hung around outside, befriended some of the women, who were willing to entertain a good guy who could change a flat tire . . . and I got all the information I needed to find you.

"After that, it was just about tracking you and gathering information. You're really easy to follow because you don't pay attention. Do you know how many times I stood behind you in line at the grocery store or Starbucks?" He paused. "You know, you may want to be more careful in here. 'Cause when I think about what these women are gonna do to you . . ." He laughed so loud, the guards' attention turned to us once again.

My eyes narrowed as the past weeks replayed in my mind. There had been so many wonderful moments. It couldn't have all been staged. "So none of this was real?" I wasn't really speaking to Quincy; I was trying to get what I thought I knew and what was happening to come into balance.

"None of it," he said. "I planned this for two years, taking my mother's insurance money, living on that so that I could take a leave of absence from my school just to find you."

"You went through all of that?" It seemed impossible that anyone would spend that kind of time to come after me.

"Yup!" he said with glee. "Joined the gym, got to know you, made you trust me." He shrugged. "And when I saw you were about to make a play for Ethan, I moved in. He didn't even know he was playing for my team, but he made it easier because you were so jealous of him being with Ivy that any man changing a tire would do."

"My God."

"I know," he said, "impressive, right? From driving that wedge between you and Ethan to talking you into doing the interview and then feeding information to your little reporter friend to recording your confession—which was helpful to the feds, by the way. It was all so easy." He held up his hands in victory as if he was proud of everything he'd done.

I fell back in the chair and groaned.

Quincy sighed, a sound of satisfaction. "And it was all worth it just to sit here and tell you everything."

I shook my head, defying him and his words. "I know how it was when we were together. It wasn't all a lie."

He laughed in my face. "Don't kid yourself, sweetheart. It was an epic lie. All of it. You were nothing more than a decent lay that I screwed to get what I wanted. And it didn't cost me too much. A couple of meals and you moved me into your condo."

A sob soared inside me, rising from my soul.

But Quincy wasn't done slashing my heart to shreds. "There was one thing I said that was the truth." His jaw clenched and he leaned forward. "I told you my feelings for you ran deep. That's the truth. Because the hatred I have for you gets deeper every day. You took away the most precious gift I had in my life. And I'm so grateful you will rot in prison, because if you weren't going to, I would have found justice for my mother myself." He stood suddenly, pushing his chair back, the legs scraping against the floor. He grabbed his mother's funeral program and stuffed it back inside his pocket. "Enjoy your life, because now that you're in here, I will certainly enjoy mine."

My eyes stung with tears as I watched him stroll toward the exit. How long was that visit? Ten minutes, maybe? That was all it had taken. The words he'd spoken, the way he'd humiliated me—all of that was crushing. But the image of the man I loved walking away without a second glance, leaving me deserted and trapped in jail after he'd set me up . . . this was something I would see in my mind's eye for the rest of my life.

But just before he stepped out, he turned back. My heart quickened as he moved toward me and I held my breath. Had this been a bad joke, or had he realized he couldn't do this because he did love me?

"Oh, yeah, there was something I forgot to tell you." With his thumb, he gestured toward the door. "Your sister's out there. She came into the waiting area hysterical, begging the guards to let her see you before I did. But I shut that down. I was here first. She'd just have to wait.

"I didn't even care that she said she came to tell you something important. But now that I'm leaving, she can come on back and tell you what she told me." He paused, and his face brightened with his grin. "Your mother's dead," he said, then spun around, leaving me buried in an avalanche of grief.

34

My eyes fluttered open, and a dull light shone above me. I blinked, trying to focus. Where was I? Twisting my head to the right, then to the left, I took in the two cots on either side of me. I was in the hospital . . . no, it was too sparse. A clinic, maybe?

My mouth was so dry, and as I tried to lift my hand to wipe my lips, I couldn't move it—I was shackled.

Reality rushed back to me. I was in jail . . . the infirmary, I supposed. And now I remembered why.

I didn't know whether it had happened an hour, a day, or a week ago, but I did remember how I'd sat frozen when Quincy had walked out of the visiting area. Frozen because I didn't want to move a single muscle that would take away from the energy I needed to make sense of Quincy's lie. Why would he say that my mother had died? Did he believe that lie would hurt me somehow?

But just minutes after Quincy stomped on my heart, my sister rushed in, eyes swollen, face flushed. And she told me Quincy's lie was the truth.

My mother was dead.

That was all I remembered, though. How long ago did that happen? Taking a deep breath, I called out, "Hello."

Footsteps, then a voice. "Ah, so you're awake," a nurse said as she approached the cot where I was handcuffed.

"What happened?" I asked as she checked my pulse.

"A little fainting spell." She made a note on a chart. "Probably stress-induced, since your sister told us she gave you some bad news."

Bad news? Was that what the death of a parent was called? I moaned at that thought, and for some reason that made the nurse chuckle.

"That's not gonna get you out of going back to your cell," she said, amused. "You're fine now, so don't try to pretend you're sick in order to get more time in here."

Why would anyone want to spend time in here, with mattresses that were as hard as concrete and nurses who had the bedside manner of Frankenstein? I asked, "How . . . long have I been in here?"

"Just a few hours. We brought you in here this morning. You were talking to your sister and fainted."

I closed my eyes. Oh, God. After the death of our mother, I could not imagine what the sight of my passing out had done to Windsor. I had to get to her.

"Can I call my sister?"

The nurse frowned and shook her head. "No special privileges in here," she scolded, as if she thought I should know the rules. "Talk to . . ."

As if on cue, a correctional officer entered. She addressed the nurse, then turned to me but didn't speak a word. She uncuffed me from the bed. Then "Let's go" was all she said after she signed a paper. She shackled my hands and feet before she led me down a narrow hallway.

I paid no attention to offices I passed. My thought was singular—my mother was dead. So how could anything else matter?

When the officer led me into a small room with just a

chair and a table, I had no questions. They could have taken me straight to prison without a trial; I deserved it after being responsible for the deaths of two women. After unshackling me, the guard left me alone without explanation. I sat in the chair and let Windsor's words play over in my mind: "Yes, Sissy. Our mom is gone."

Then, after too many minutes had passed, I stood and walked the length of the room, then its width. With each step, I tried to make sense out of what made no sense. And I tried not to think about how, if I hadn't been at my mother's house when the FBI came for me, she would still be alive.

By the time a different officer came into the room, I was curled up on the floor in the corner, wiping away my tears. She tossed a clear plastic bag onto the table with my jeans and sweat-shirt inside. "Change," she growled. "You're getting out of here."

Getting out? How? Didn't I have to have a bond? Or was I being freed completely? I scrambled up from the floor, tossed the orange jumpsuit aside, and was dressed in just minutes. Then I followed the officer as she led me through what she explained was out-processing.

After another thirty minutes or so, the officer led me to a door and opened it, and when I stepped into the lobby, Windsor raced to me. She wrapped me in her arms; I sobbed into her shoulder, and she sobbed into mine. The way we stood there, letting minutes pass, I expected one of the officers to come from the back and tell us to keep it moving or they would take us both into custody. But I guessed death gave everyone compassion—everyone except for Quincy.

Finally, we stepped apart, and without a word, Windsor led me from the building to her car. Still, I had no idea of the time, but since it was dark, I knew a whole day had passed.

I buckled up inside the Toyota, and Windsor squeezed my

hand. "We're going to be okay, Sissy." Then she navigated out of the parking lot of the Harris County jail.

I had so many questions, but I only had energy for one. "What . . . happened . . . to Mama?" The words had barely passed through my lips before the tears poured from my eyes. "It's my fault, isn't it?"

"No, Journee," she exclaimed. "Please don't say that. Mama would be so upset if she heard you right now."

"Then what happened?" I cried. "She was fine. She was saying how happy she was. We were eating breakfast and then . . ." I sobbed. "The shock of it all . . . it killed her."

"Sissy," Windsor said, her hands gripping the wheel, "we already knew that Mama's lungs were bad. This had nothing to do with you."

"You warned me. You told me I should have told her."

"But *you* were right. You were trying to protect her. And because you did, her last morning on earth was one of her best. She wouldn't have had that if you had told her what was going on the night before. She would have worried; she wouldn't have slept. But she was happy, thinking that you were going to be taking care of her."

I wanted to believe my sister's words so badly, but I was sure she wasn't telling me the truth. She was just trying to assuage my guilt.

Until she said, "I believe with everything in me that before she was born, God knew the day Mama was going to die. Nothing you could have said or done would have added one hour to her life. Because what you do will never be greater than what God does. So telling her about your situation would only have taken away the little bit of happiness she did have." At the stoplight, Windsor turned to me. "I'm so grateful you didn't listen to me."

The lump in my throat stopped me from saying anything, and we rode in silence the rest of the way. When Windsor edged the car over the gravel driveway of my mother's house, I fought hard to swallow my sorrow.

My sister turned off the ignition, hopped out, then rushed around to help me as if I were returning home from some kind of convalescence rather than from being locked up. She held my hand as we made our way into the house. For a moment, I stood at the threshold; images of the last time I was in this room flashed in my mind.

As if she knew what I was thinking, Windsor said, "No, Journee. Keep your focus on how much happiness you brought her when you two reconciled."

Her words nudged me inside, and I collapsed onto the sofa. "I wasted so much time, Windsor."

"It wasn't you alone," she said, trying to console me. "Mama should have told you the whole truth years ago."

"But the truth really shouldn't have mattered. She was my mother, and I treated her like a pariah for all of those years." Now, with all my hindsight, it was hard to imagine and understand what I'd done for all of these years. I'd never taken a call from her, never agreed to a visit with her. I gave her nothing . . . but silence. How could I have treated anyone that way?

"And do you know what else you did all of those years? You took care of Mama. And do you know what she said to me as the EMTs rushed her to the hospital? She could barely speak, but she said to make sure you were taken care of now. She made me promise to get you out of that place and to make sure you never went back."

Her words were meant to be comforting, but instead, my heart ached more. In her last moments, as she struggled to breathe, my mother was worried about me. I sighed, stood, and moved to the mantel.

The first time I'd walked into my mother's house after Windsor and I brought her home from the hospital, I'd been amazed at the pictures. There were dozens of me, from birth to one that someone had taken of the three of us at church, the Sunday before my mother had done what she thought was best.

Windsor had told me then that was why she'd been determined to find me when she was old enough. "The way Mama talked about you and all the pictures we had, I feel like I grew up with you," my sister said.

Now I studied all the photos but lifted the wedding photo of my mother and father. She'd stayed devoted to him through the years, just like she'd been devoted to me. Again I tried to press my sorrow down, but my tears flowed.

Windsor eased to my side. "We're going to cry a lot over the next days, weeks, months, and I bet years. And that's okay. Just remember: God made this decision, not you."

I wondered if I'd ever believe my sister. Returning the photo to its place, I asked, "So, what do we do now?"

"Well," Windsor began with a sigh, "we have to arrange for the services." She spoke as if she were the big sister. "But at the same time, we have to take care of your situation." She paused. "I met Quincy. He told me he'd told you about Mama." She gave me a side-eye. "I don't want to pile on now, but this was the guy you wanted me to meet?" She asked me that as if she couldn't believe I'd ever said more than hello to him.

I shook my head. "The story is so long, Windsor, and I promise I'll tell you the whole thing . . ."

She held up her hand. "I can't handle anything more right now. All I care about is giving Mama the homegoing celebration she deserves and getting you out of this trouble that you don't deserve. Anything else I'll handle in the next year or two or seventy. So, what are we going to do about your situation?"

I shrugged. "I'm not even sure I have the energy to fight. I mean, maybe I should be punished after all that's happened. Maybe it's just—"

"Hold up," my sister interrupted me. "So really? After everything I just said, you're going to have a pity party and then let whatever happens happen?" she asked, her volume rising. She stood and paced in front of me, her wild hair shaking with every word she spoke. "And you're thinking you should be in prison? And then what? Just leave me out here by myself?" She stopped moving and jabbed her finger in my face. "Let me tell you something, Sissy. You're not going to do that. It's just you and me now. We're all we have, and I'm not about"—her voice quivered—"to lose the only person left in this world who loves me." Her shoulders shook. "I'm twenty-eight, for God's sake. What am I supposed to do if you give up? What am I supposed to do without you?" Before I could jump up, Windsor sank to her knees, and I dropped to the floor with her, pulling her into my arms. I held her as she sobbed, and I wondered, how could I have been so selfish? All I'd been thinking about was how my mother's death affected me, when it was my sister who'd lived with her, who'd taken care of her. Windsor had put her life aside for our mother, while I'd been able to thrive in mine. She had to be so scared; she had to be so afraid of being alone.

"I am so sorry, Sissy," I said as I rocked her. "You're right. I'm going to fight. I'm going to be here. I promise you."

It took minutes for her sobs to subside, and finally, she leaned back against the sofa, and I did the same, holding her hand as her tears dried.

She said, "I don't want to be scared, Sissy, but I am. I can't lose you."

"And you won't." I squeezed her hand.

"So you're going to fight? You're going to do whatever you have to do?"

I nodded. And hugged her again. "I promise you," I said. I was not going to lose my sister, and I was going to make sure she didn't lose me.

AN HOUR LATER, Windsor and I sat at the kitchen table with meals we'd ordered through a delivery service untouched in front of us.

Windsor spread out the five pages of notes on the table. "There really isn't much for us to do," she said. "Here are Mama's instructions. She laid out all the plans."

"Wow." I picked up the first sheet. "She wrote her obituary?"

My sister nodded. "She said she didn't want us to have too much to do because we'd be grieving. Oh," my sister added, "here's how she wants the service to go." I glanced at the top of the page and, in bold letters, our mother had written: *KEEP IT SHORT.*

Taking the page from Windsor, I laughed out loud, realizing I hadn't done that since I'd sat at this table with our mother yesterday morning. "Did she write this?"

"Yup. All of this," Windsor said. "She even picked out the dress she wanted to wear. And"——my sister shuffled through the pages——"there are instructions for Pastor Franklin that I'll take over to him tomorrow. So"——Windsor gathered all the papers and returned them to the folder——"Mama had her game plan in place. Now, what's yours?"

I let out a long sigh. "I need to find a new attorney, that's where I have to begin. But that's going to run fifteen to twenty thousand dollars just for a retainer."

"You don't have to worry about that. I got you."

I leaned back. What was she talking about? She'd only been on her new job for a minute; certainly, she hadn't had time to save for a good dinner at Pappadeaux.

My expression made her laugh. That wasn't what I had been trying to do, but I'd take it, since a little while ago I'd sent her to her knees in sadness. Windsor said, "Maybe I shouldn't have said that *I* had you. It's really Mama. Between her insurance policy and this house, we'll be able to handle whatever you need."

"The house," I said, more to myself than Windsor, but then I turned to my sister. "Is that how you got my bond?"

She waved her hand. "Girl, that was a process. They weren't even going to take you before a judge until tomorrow. But Pastor Franklin was with me at the hospital when Mama passed, and of course he was worried and he asked about you.

"Mama told him you two had reconciled, and he was thrilled about that. But when I told him you'd been arrested, he got right to work. Before five o'clock, there'd been an emergency hearing and your bail was set. But I couldn't handle the house with the bondsman until this morning."

"So Mama died yesterday."

It wasn't a question, but Windsor nodded. It was hard for me to take in that my mother had been gone for hours before I even found out—because I was in jail. My sister explained, "I couldn't tell you over the phone. And I tried to get in to see you yesterday, but you had to be processed or something like that. Even Pastor Franklin tried to get an exception, but they said no. It was just a mess." She blinked back tears, and I grabbed her hand.

"Thank you, Windsor."

"Not me. It was Pastor Franklin."

Pastor Franklin. I hadn't seen him since Mrs. Hunter's funeral. Yet here he was again, so very much in my life, trying to make it right.

"Once he got your bond, I was able to get moving on the house."

It may have been small, but I had a village. Now, though, it was time for me to stop relying on others. I was in trouble, but I was a fighter—always had been. It was time for me to go to war.

"Are you tired?" I asked my sister.

"Yeah, but I won't sleep."

"I know. Neither will I. So, can I use your laptop? I need to find an attorney."

She grinned, and when she hopped up and dashed into the bedroom, I sat for a moment in the chair where I'd last been with my mother. "I'm so sorry," I whispered into the air, and prayed that somehow she could hear me. "I'm so sorry, Mama. But I promise I'm going to take care of Windsor, and in the end, I will finally make you proud."

35

The door to my mother's bedroom creaked open, and I pushed myself up, my eyes focusing on the figure in the doorway. "Windsor?" I clicked on the lamp on the nightstand, and suddenly, the room was aglow with a yellow light that radiated throughout. And in the center was a figure with golden wings. The light was too bright for me to see anything else. The figure edged toward me, her feet never touching the floor. I'd never seen anything like this before, but I had no fear.

Then the light shifted, and I saw the woman's face.

"Mama!"

She was so beautiful as she smiled and sat on the edge of the bed. Her skin was smooth and soft and her hair long and flowing—she looked like my seven-year-old memory.

"Yes, baby girl." Her voice was soft music. Her fingers caressed my cheek, wiping tears I hadn't even known were there.

"Mama, I'm so sorry."

"You have nothing to apologize for, baby girl. I'm so happy . . . it's beautiful here."

Still, I wanted her to know. "Can you forgive me?"

"There is nothing to forgive," she whisper-sang. "There is only love. That's what I wanted to tell you. Only love."

"I love you, Mama."

"Release it all, baby girl. So that you can have the love."

"What do you mean?"

"There's so much in your heart, and love needs space."

I shook my head, not understanding.

"Make room for the love."

"Okay, Mama. I will," I said, even though I didn't know what she meant. But in this moment, I wanted to please her. I wanted to say yes for all the times I'd told her no.

Now her smile widened and the room brightened even more. "I love you, baby girl. I love you then, now, and forevermore."

She leaned forward and kissed my forehead. I closed my eyes, wanting to savor this time. Then I opened my eyes . . .

"Mama," I called out into the darkness. I pushed myself up in the bed and turned on the nightstand lamp. The room became bright with the glow of a 60-watt bulb, and I was alone.

How was that possible? I'd heard her, I'd felt her; it had been such a holy moment.

"IF YOU WANT to know . . . where I'm going . . . where I'm going . . . soon . . ."

The first notes of my mother's favorite gospel song brought me back from the dream I'd had last night to the front pew of Wheeler Village. Now, hearing "Goin' up Yonder," I had another memory. Of another time, in this same place, for this exact occasion. I'd sat on this same front pew beside my mother all those years ago at my dad's services as the choir sang this song. On that day, I'd rested my head on my mother's shoulder, needing to be as close to her as I could. I remembered the way she kept glancing down. Even as tears spilled from her eyes, every time she looked at me, she smiled. And her smile wrapped itself around me, and I felt safe and loved.

I glanced to my right; Windsor's head rested on my shoulder, and I patted her hand. She looked up and I smiled, and then she laid her head back down.

I'd had a shaky start, that first night with my sister, when Windsor bailed me out of jail. But I'd steadied myself and stepped in as her big sister. It was a role I cherished and thought I'd been fulfilling for ten years. But in these past days, I realized it was a role I'd served from afar. I'd had the chance to see how Windsor had carried so much on her shoulders. Now, since our mother's passing, I'd been able to bear the burden with her. We lived together in our mother's home, planned these services together, accepted consoling visitors together . . . and we mourned together. The only time we were apart in the past four days was when Windsor went to visit Pastor Franklin to discuss these services.

That was a meeting I wasn't ready to take. The pastor was too close to Ethan and Ivy; I needed a few days to mentally separate the pastor from his daughter. If it had been my decision, I wouldn't have had the services here at Wheeler Village at all. But this was my mother's choice, and I was doing for her in death what I hadn't done for her life—I was honoring her and her wishes.

"Let the church say amen."

My eyes focused on the pulpit where Pastor Franklin stood. For the first time, I wondered if Ethan and Ivy were here among the thousands of parishioners. I was so shocked that the five-thousand-seat sanctuary was almost half-full. Surely, all of these people didn't know Norma Alexander.

"I'm not going to keep you long," Pastor Franklin said. "I have my instructions from Sister Norma to keep this short." Light laughter rose through the congregation. "I'm not kidding. She left me notes." He held up two pages, and this time the laughter was louder, and even I had to smile.

"Norma didn't want me to go on and on about her. She told me to choose my words carefully and to only speak about what was important. And in her letter to me, she asked: 'Pastor Franklin, what is my legacy?'

"That was such a thought-provoking question, asked by a

woman who wasn't known to many in the world. But she was correct to ask that question, because we all leave a legacy, something we hand down, something we leave behind for others to remember us. So, to answer that question for Sister Norma, I first started with the facts of her life. She was a mother of two young ladies who both grew into wonderful women . . ."

I shifted in the pew, praying that no one would stand and shout, *Not the older one. Have you seen the news?*

"And she had been a member of Wheeler Village for almost thirty years," the pastor continued. "She didn't come every Sunday, and for many years she lived in Dallas, although even then she remained a member.

"But there was much more to Sister Norma than that, and I wanted to capture the fullness of her as a woman. As I gave it more thought, I was drawn to the sermons I've been sharing here at church over the last weeks. We've been speaking about the seven deadly sins, and as I thought about Norma Alexander, there was one thing that stood out about her. Norma was a great example of a woman, a Christian, who never allowed pride to become a part of her life."

"Amen" rang throughout the church as if these people knew my mother.

"I'm sure many of you old-timers remember Norma. Back in the day, after her husband passed away, she struggled. And she'd come to this altar every Sunday, looking for help from her Lord. Every Sunday. She didn't care who was looking; she didn't care what people might say. This was between her and God, and we just happened to be spectators in the sanctuary."

"Yes, Lord."

"I'm telling you, Norma showed us her battles, she asked for our assistance, she knew she couldn't live this life and do right by her girls unless she accepted help. She listened to wiser voices and kept her heart open to hear from the Lord. She was not prideful; she was not boastful. There was no room for any of that in her heart because she knew pride would stop her from doing what was best for her girls. To do well by them, she could give pride no space in her heart."

Love needs space, the words my mother had spoken to me in the middle of the night, echoed through my mind.

"Norma Alexander had one of the purest hearts I've ever had the pleasure of meeting. Her heart was full of love."

Make room for the love.

"The Bible says that pride comes, and then disgrace. Because of the love she had, the equation in Norma's life was the opposite. She had humility, and then wisdom."

I swiped at the tears streaming from my eyes. Anyone watching me would think I was the weeping daughter, mourning her mother. Of course that was true. But these tears I shed were for all that I was learning about my mother. Listening to Pastor Franklin, I realized she was the opposite of me. It was the love in my mother's heart, absent of pride, that had made her accept what Mrs. Hunter had told her all those years ago.

But when my mother had returned to my life, it was the pride in my heart, absent of love, that made me lock her out. It was my pride that had kept me from listening to her, and now, because of my pride, I was truly coming to know my mother while she lay in her casket. What if I'd had just a little of my mother's love? How many more years would I have had with her?

Inside, I moaned—Windsor had tried to warn me: *I'm praying so hard that you won't one day be staring down into a casket filled with remorse and regrets . . .*

Pastor Franklin continued through my thoughts, "The reason why so many are here today is not because you knew Norma intimately. Most of you knew her in passing. Of course, in recent years, she was always on that second pew on Sunday, and she was a part of the women's ministry . . . and don't forget how she could belt out a tune in the senior choir."

My mother sang in the church choir?

"But while most of you didn't know her well enough to know her telephone number or her address . . . you knew her heart," Pastor Franklin said. "And if you knew her heart, you knew Norma Alexander."

A whimper escaped from my lips, and Windsor sat up and looked at me, and now she wrapped her arm around me, and I rested my head on her shoulder. Now I understood why there were so many people here today. These people knew my mother . . . and I did not.

"That is Norma Alexander's legacy. A life without pride, for a woman who could have easily been too proud, whose heart was pure with love.

"And now," Pastor Franklin said, sounding like he was winding down this eulogy, "another part of Norma's legacy will be this celebration of her life and anyone who wants to turn their life around because of what they've learned about this woman. If this were a normal Sunday service, I would have an altar call right now for our prideful natures. Because most people don't have the pure heart that Sister Norma prayed for the Lord to give her.

"But we can all strive for what the Lord demands from us and use Sister Norma as an example. I want everyone within the sound of my voice to bow their heads. I want to pray with you . . ."

While everyone in the sanctuary followed Pastor Franklin's instructions, for a few seconds, I sat staring at the altar where my mother's casket rested. Then I stood and stepped forward. My eyes never left the place that I remembered—where my mother had prayed every Sunday. Where she had knelt, bowed her head, and cried out to the Lord.

As I moved toward him, Pastor Franklin nodded as if he expected me, and as I bowed down at the altar next to my mother's coffin, I felt someone kneel next to me. Windsor, I was sure.

"Let us begin," Pastor Franklin said.

"Lord, you hate pride, so I'm asking you to deliver me from it." He paused as we all spoke those words, though it was difficult for me to speak as I sobbed. "Help me to put my prideful past behind me. Help me to open my heart to what pleases you: humility, wisdom, and most of all, love. In Jesus's name, amen."

"Amen," I said. I took a few seconds to settle my cries, then pushed myself up. When I stood, my sister was right there beside me. Every eye in the sanctuary was on us, and in the past, I would have rushed back to that front pew because I had too much pride to allow anyone to see me in my weakness. But today, I didn't care. I pulled my sister into my arms. "I'm sorry, Windsor." I sobbed into her shoulder. "Can you forgive me?"

Windsor gave me a few moments to cry, then she leaned back and wiped the tears from my eyes, and with a smile that for the first time I realized resembled my mother's so much, she said, "There is nothing to forgive. There is only love."

Those were the exact words my mother had said to me in the middle of the night. It was shocking to hear them spoken by Windsor. And my first thought was—what is going on? But then I just smiled and hugged my sister. The best moments were these, when we didn't understand what God had done. This was just another holy moment of the day, and I embraced it for what it was.

I DIDN'T KNOW these people, but I felt all the love. I felt more love in my mother's house following her funeral than I'd ever felt before. And I wondered, when I surrendered my pride with

Pastor Franklin's prayer, had that made room for this kind of love?

As I moved toward the kitchen to see if the women from the church needed help putting out any more food for this repast, Pastor Franklin stopped me. "Journee, do you have a moment?"

I nodded, then followed him as he led me to the front of my mother's house. We stepped outside, and he closed the door behind us. I spoke first. "Pastor Franklin, that eulogy for my mom . . . it was beautiful. Thank you."

He took my hands into his. "Your forgiveness was the ultimate gift to your mother. I had the good fortune to visit with her several times over the past few weeks, and she was complete. She had a peace I hadn't seen since the early days when she attended church with you and your dad. You gave her such happiness. Remember that."

Before I could thank him for his words of absolution, we both turned toward the sound of approaching footsetps.

Pastor Franklin said, "Hey, honey." He kissed Ivy's cheek and then shook Ethan's hand before they both turned to me.

When I faced Ethan, I saw it in his eyes—that love. The love from a friend who had known me for years, who had seen me at my best and my worst. "We didn't have a chance to speak to you at the church."

"I wondered if you were there."

"Of course. I wanted to let you know I'm so sorry, Journee. But you know how happy I was that you and your mom had reconciled."

I nodded when Ivy took my hand and gave me her condolences. "Thank you both for being here. Please go in and help us get rid of some of that food," I said with a chuckle.

Ivy and Ethan went inside, but before Pastor Franklin followed them, he turned to me. "You coming?"

"In a minute. I want to get a little air."

He nodded his understanding, and when he left me alone, I leaned against the railing. Air wasn't the reason why I needed to stay out here for a minute. I needed a moment to understand what I was feeling. Seeing Ethan and Ivy made me wonder, what if? Did I really want to talk to Ethan? Did I really want to ask him to help me when I'd already done that and look at how that had turned out? Did I want the risk of him telling me no?

No, shouted my head. But my heart spoke more softly and gave me a different message.

Turning back to the house, I stepped inside and saw Ethan sitting on the sofa while Ivy talked to her mother in the kitchen. As I moved across the living room to the kitchen, Ivy turned to me when I called her name. I asked, "Would you mind if I talked to you and Ethan privately for a moment?"

"Of course," she said. She glanced around the room. "Did you tell Ethan?"

"No, I wanted to ask you first."

Her eyebrows raised. "Oh, well . . ."

I stayed in the kitchen as she crossed over to Ethan and whispered to him, and he stood. Then, together, the two of them followed me through the dining room, past the sliding glass doors, and into the backyard.

I'd noticed earlier that no one had come out here, although Windsor and I had cleaned off the patio table and wiped down the chairs. That was where we sat now, and once we were settled, I began:

"First, I want to say I'm sorry. I know you didn't come here to talk to me; you're here for my mother."

"No." Ivy shook her head. "We're here for you. Anything you need."

I took a breath. "I hope you mean that." I paused. "It's been a lot having to say good-bye to my mother and still having . . . my situation hanging."

"I cannot imagine what this has been like for you. Especially with Quincy trying to make it worse."

I nodded. That was an unbelievable addition to an already devastating situation. Quincy seemed to want the world to know he was the one who'd worked with the US Attorney's Office. So he spoke to any reporter who'd listen, making the case even more fodder for the media. But that had been only a twenty-four-hour story.

"Thank God the feds shut that down," Ivy said.

"Oh, I didn't know that's what happened. I just thought he got bored."

"Yeah, it was the feds. One interview was enough, but he was on every station. I'm glad they ended that. You shouldn't have to deal with any of that, not right now."

I glanced at Ethan, who sat with his fingers steepled, his eyes on me but his mouth shut. Ivy was the one saying all the words I'd expected from him.

I told him, "You were right about so many things, Ethan, but you were definitely right about Quincy. And I apologize."

He frowned as if he didn't understand my words. "For what?"

"For not listening to you, never really considering your advice, because, honestly, I thought I knew better. I was wrong."

After a moment, he leaned toward me. "I didn't want to be right. I didn't want any of this."

"I know." I took a breath. "Thank you for saying that. But now"—my eyes moved between the two of them—"I need your help."

He shook his head as if he knew where this conversation was going and he didn't even want to hear my question. "I hate to say this, Journee, especially with all you're going through, but I really can't help you."

"You can," I said, not accepting his refusal to get involved, but this time for a different reason. It wasn't that I knew best; it was that Ethan was the best and I couldn't go to prison. I couldn't leave Windsor. "You helped me before."

"I tried, but this time I'm saying no to protect you. With the situation you're in, you really have to find an attorney you trust. What I can do is promise that Ivy and I will help you find someone who will be good for you."

"I don't want anyone else. I want you."

"Listen to me," he said. "You're in a lot of trouble. And I want you to have the best representation. You have to have confidence in your attorney, you have to agree on a strategy, and you have to work together. That's not you and me."

"It can be," I said, and, without taking a breath, added, "because I've learned the lesson. I don't know what's happened over the last few days. Maybe with death comes clarity"——I paused and thought of the message from my mother——"or maybe clarity comes from dreams."

Ethan and Ivy tilted their heads, curiosity in their eyes.

"It's not that I didn't have confidence in you, it was that I had an unfounded overconfidence in myself. The problem was me, not you."

He smirked, as if he wanted to say he could have told me that, but he was too kind to utter those words.

I added, "So please know this time will be different." I imagined Ethan calculating how many times I'd said that before. "I truly have changed."

He hesitated for just enough seconds for me to once again ask God to do what was best.

And then Ethan shook his head. "I can't do it. I don't want to do it. I'm so sorry."

It was not what I wanted to hear, but I nodded with a smile. Because now I had a new confidence. This confidence had nothing to do with me; it was the belief that God would handle it. "Well, thank you, not only for listening but for everything you did to this point. I will always be grateful." There was so much pain in his eyes; he hated denying me.

I turned to Ivy, smiled, and thanked her, too, before I stood. I was so calm, in such peace, knowing that if Ethan wasn't the one, then God would figure it out some other way.

I was a few steps away from the table when Ivy said, "Wait," and stood.

Ethan and I both looked at her. Her eyes were straight on me. "I believe you trust Ethan; I think I'm the problem. You don't trust me."

I wanted to protest, but why lie?

She spoke as she moved toward me. "You can trust me, Journee." She took both of my hands in hers. "I know we weren't the closest friends as kids. Wait, let me rephrase that: we weren't friends at all. But just like you're not who you used to be, neither am I. I'm a grown woman who let go of childish ways a long time ago. And right now, I'm a woman who knows when another woman needs my help." She glanced at Ethan. "So I want us to help you." Then, nodding at him, she said, "We have to."

Taking one hand away from hers, I pressed my fingers against my lips as emotions rumbled inside me. Ethan hadn't spoken, but it almost didn't matter. Because Ivy had spoken . . . with love.

But though Ethan still hadn't said anything, he must have given her some kind of signal, because Ivy said, "So if you can promise that we'll work together, but in the end you'll follow our advice, I think I can convince my fiancé to defend you."

I held my breath as I stared at Ethan. He stared back, but his look was more intense when he turned to Ivy. After the longest pause of my life, Ethan sighed, then nodded. And that sob I'd been holding back had its way. "Thank you. I know I don't deserve this, but I'm so grateful."

"Everyone deserves grace," Ivy said. "I've been given so much of it that every chance I get, I try to pass some of my grace forward, to make room so more grace can come to me."

I was in another holy moment. Those words, that sentiment. I wanted to hold on to this. Accept grace, and give grace . . . so that more grace can be given unto you.

"Journee." Ethan's voice pulled me out of the moment.

"Thank you," I said to him again. "Just know that whatever you want me to do, I'll do it."

"Well, we're about to have the first big test, because I know what the feds want from you." He paused.

"Simon."

He nodded. "That's all they want, Journee. Nothing else, just Simon. And the only way I'll represent you is if you accept the only defense you have. They've proven they're not playing. You're going to have to tell the feds everything you know."

I inhaled what felt like a gallon of air. It was Simon or my sister. "Yes," I said.

Ethan and Ivy exhaled together.

"But"—and the two stared at me in disbelief, as if they wondered how I thought I was in any kind of position to have any kind of disclaimer—"while I will tell them everything, I'm going to tell them that Simon was trying to help people."

Ethan shook his head. "They're not going to ask you that."

"I'm going to tell them anyway."

"All they want to know are the specifics of his scams. They'll never ask you his motivation because there was no way for you to know."

"I'll figure out a way to tell them."

He sighed, and when he shook his head, I wanted to take back everything I'd just said. What was I thinking? Hadn't I just told Ethan I'd learned the lessons? "I'm not saying I won't listen to you," I added as quickly as I could, "but—"

Ethan held up his hand. "I get it. Really, all I care about is you going in there and telling those attorneys everything you know. If you can figure out a way to also tell them all of that miscellaneous information that I promise you they don't care about, go for it."

I nodded.

"But," he continued, "only after they get everything they want from you."

"Of course. When we're in there, I'll follow your lead."

He gave me a long side-eye, and I smiled. "I promise." Then, with all the emotions inside me, I said, "Thank you," before I turned to Ivy.

I moved closer to her and pulled her into my arms, hugging her the way I hugged my friends. No, it was better. I hugged her like she was my sister.

t took Ethan and Ivy only twenty-four hours to review my case to see how much had changed since they'd dropped me. Twenty-four hours after that, Ethan contacted the feds, and they agreed to schedule my deposition. The only challenge: Ethan reached the feds on Friday, and they had no appointments until Wednesday.

That left the weekend and two days for me to suffer through the anxiety of not knowing what to expect. On Saturday and Sunday, every what-if played in my mind. I called Ethan so many times, I was afraid he was going to drop me just so he wouldn't have to accept another one of my calls. But it was my final question that ended all my calls to Ethan:

"What if I give them everything they want, and they still decide to throw me in prison?"

"That's a possibility," Ethan said, making my heart drop before it completely stopped. "But that's not likely to happen. I'm good at what I do, Journee. I've already talked to them about what I want in exchange for this."

"And do you think they'll hold to their deal?"

"If we hold to ours, and I'm going to make sure they do."

He made sure I was occupied for all of Monday and Tuesday. Ivy spent that time, through three meals of the day, with me, prepping for the deposition. Drilling me with questions, challenging my answers. There were moments when her actions and tone took me back to our childhood. But this time, I knew for sure her mean girl was just to ready me for federal agents who would prefer to have me *and* Simon but would settle for him.

Now, sitting in the conference room of the FBI building on Justice Park, I was ready. Or so I thought as I watched Ethan and Ivy in front of the window, whispering as Ivy shared the contents of a folder. I closed my eyes. I truly believed I was ready for this nine o'clock meeting, but the prospect of facing the feds . . .

"You're quiet."

I glanced up. I hadn't even noticed Ethan moving from the window to my side. I whispered, "We're in a federal building. I'm sure there are many cameras and recorders all around."

He chuckled as he sat next to me. "Only that one," he said, pointing to the camera set up in front of the room as if they used this often—I guessed they did.

That camera was just another thing that made me jittery. Ethan had told me this would be a videotaped deposition; the feds wanted to get every word on record, not just to use against Simon, but to come back to me. It was a crime to lie to federal agents, Ethan had told me. And the camera was a reminder of that.

I clasped my hands together to stop their trembling.

"I understand you being nervous," Ethan said. "But all you have to do is tell the truth."

"And we're both here," Ivy said from the other side. "Just do what we did in the practice sessions."

One of them on either side—I was sure flanking me was part of the strategy.

The knock on the door made me sit up straight, and Agent Moran and two men marched in as if they were on a mission. They were dressed so differently from when they had busted into my mother's home. Today, Agent Moran was dressed in just black pants and a white shirt, and the men wore pants with tailored shirts and ties, though both had their sleeves rolled up.

While the agents greeted my lawyers, I sat still. I had nothing to say to the people who'd triggered my mother's last attack. Finally, they sat across the table from us, and now every eye was on me.

"Ms. Alexander." When Agent Moran paused, I wondered if she was going to offer condolences, and then I wondered if I had enough grace to accept her sympathy. But when she only said, "You're here for a deposition today," I was glad my propensity for forgiveness wasn't being tested.

"Yes, my lawyers explained it all to me."

"Well then, we can begin. Ms. Alexander, will you please stand and raise your right hand."

I'd been prepared for this—sworn testimony. After I agreed to tell the truth and nothing but, I sat and Agent Moran began. "What is your full name?"

"Journee Alexander."

From there she asked the same question in a variety of different ways about any nicknames or maiden or married names. I had to tell the truth about my age, where I was born, the places I'd lived, and my social security number. By the time the first fifteen minutes were over, I wondered what in the world any of this had to do with Simon.

But the feds got to those questions soon enough. After I told them when I had started (and stopped) working at ClearWater, the questions became very specific:

"Ms. Alexander, there was one name you didn't mention earlier. Are you familiar with the name Wilhelmina Jones?"

From there, through their questions, I told the story of how Simon Wallace had developed a program for distressed homeowners.

"How did he find these homeowners?" Agent Moran questioned without emotion.

"Through foreclosure lists, which are public record. But Mr. Wallace truly thought he was helping these people."

"Ms. Alexander, will you please just answer the question I ask?" She scowled, and I wondered if that was a permanent expression, because I'd never seen a smile on this woman's face.

I nodded.

After Agent Moran led me through questions that got the answers she wanted, she asked, "Over the two years you worked this program, how many homeowners signed over their deeds to Simon Wallace?"

"I never counted the number of people Simon tried to help."

There was that scowl again. "Can you give us an estimate?"

"I'm really not sure. I don't think Simon was concerned about how many he could help; I think he just wanted to assist as many people as he could."

"Ms. Alexander." The way she said my name was a warning all by itself. "Would you say you went out as Wilhelmina Jones once a week, twice a week, every day?"

The way she glowered, I knew I had to give her something. "Maybe it was once a week, sometimes twice."

"And did Mr. Wallace sell all those properties?"

"I'm not sure because I wasn't involved in that part of the program. I just worked with him as he tried to help as many homeowners as he could."

"Counsel!" Agent Moran addressed Ethan. "We're going to take a ten-minute break, and you may want to advise your client about our agreement." She pushed back her chair, and the agents exited, leaving me alone with Ethan and Ivy.

Ethan did a slow turn toward me, and the way his eyes narrowed, I said, "What? I've answered all the questions."

"You have." He nodded and sighed wearily. "But they are tired of you being Simon Wallace's PR agent."

"Journee," Ivy called my name, and now I faced her. "If you wanted to help Simon, you have. You've mentioned how much he was trying to aid the homeowners"—she glanced down at her pad—"seventeen times." Now she looked at me. "But if you continue to add that exposition to every response, you will damage the agreement we reached with these agents."

"Come on, Journee," Ethan said. "You agreed to take our advice. And our advice now is to just answer the questions so we can get out of here and then we can get you cleared of all of this. That won't happen if you continue to play a game that you will never win, because you're not the one holding all the cards."

"Okay."

The second I agreed, the agents entered the room, as if they'd been standing outside listening or they had some other way to hear our private conversations.

Agent Moran asked Ethan, "Is your client ready to proceed?" like I couldn't speak for myself.

"She is."

From that point, I answered each question with as few words as possible. And it seemed that the scowl on Agent Moran's face wasn't permanent. After five hours, she stood and shook Ethan's and Ivy's hands before she turned to me with something that resembled a smile. "Thank you for your cooperation, Ms. Alexander. We'll be in touch with your attorneys after we review these tapes."

Wait! What? Be in touch? I had thought this was a done deal. I watched the agents leave and then I whipped my head toward Ethan. "What is going on?"

"Nothing," he said, as if he wasn't alarmed by their words.

"They have to go through your deposition, will probably have some follow-up questions, and then they'll offer the deal."

My heart began to do that extra pumping thing again. "I thought we already had a deal."

"We had an agreement. It's not official until this is done. And so, now we wait."

It wasn't what I wanted, but since I had no control, I waited. It would have been torture, except Windsor and I filled each day getting to know each other. Of course, she had to continue working, since she was the only one of us, right now, who was employed. But when she came home, we spent the hours talking in a way we never had. There were still times of tears as we cried over the loss of our mother, but surprisingly, the days had been filled mostly with laughter . . . and love. Windsor filled me in on the years we'd been apart, something I'd never asked her about. She told me how Norma had finally found a job in a school cafeteria but really struggled with her bronchitis. And that the only time she was free from any flare-ups was when she was in church singing.

"Mama led that choir, and you should have seen the way they'd have that church rocking," Windsor told me.

I regretted that I knew so little about my mother that I couldn't even imagine her in a church choir.

Then I shared more memories of our father, and I told her how Mama and Daddy would sing to her while I rubbed Mama's belly.

"She told me that story," Windsor said.

By the time the second week came to an end, though, my anxiety, which I'd tried to ignore, had reached a crescendo. Maybe the feds had changed their minds, or maybe it had always just been a way to trick me into turning on Simon. By Friday, I was physically sick. And then . . .

"Journee." The call finally came in from Ethan right before five. "We have an offer for a deal."

Windsor and I sat down at the kitchen table with my cell on speaker in between my sister and me. We held hands as Ethan spoke:

"In exchange for no prison time, you'll have to give up your license and agree to never operate as a mortgage broker again."

"I can do that," I said, my voice sounding so shaky.

"That means, of course, you'll have to close J. Alexander and Associates, and you won't be able to sell it. None of the assets they seized will be returned to you. Ill-gotten gains," he said, as if he needed to remind me. "So . . . that's it."

"I guess so. There's nothing else they could take from me."

"Actually, there is," Windsor spoke up. "They could have taken your freedom."

I thought about that for a moment. "Well, there's that," I said to my sister.

"Windsor, you're a smart woman." Ethan chuckled.

"She definitely is," I said. There was no reason for me to look at this news as any kind of loss; I had every reason to give praise today.

I thanked Ethan and told him to tell Ivy hello and thank you as well. We promised to get together soon, maybe after church one Sunday.

When I ended the call, Windsor said, "I meant what I said about your freedom—that's what's most important to me. We still have each other, and we still have a place to live. What else could we ask for?"

"And we still have God."

My sister grinned. "Always."

My phone vibrated, and I picked it up to read the incoming

text: **You may not be going to prison, but it's good enough for me that you have nothing!**

I'd received what felt like hundreds of these texts, but this was the first time one made me smile.

"You look happy; what's going on?" Windsor asked.

I looked back down at the text and then back up at my sister. "It's nothing."

There was no need to say anything to Windsor. I didn't want her to be concerned, and anyway, this sounded like Quincy's have-a-horrible-life farewell message. That dude was so wrong, though. Not that I was going to tell him. But I glanced at my sister again. He thought I had nothing, but as I reached for my sister's hand and squeezed it, for the first time in my life, I knew I had everything.

I did have one hope for Quincy, though. I prayed that he could find the gift that my mother had given to me, even in her death . . . the gift of peace, and only love.

About the Author

Victoria Christopher Murray is the *New York Times* and *USA Today* bestselling author of more than thirty novels, including *Wrath*; *Greed*; *Envy*; *Lust*; *The Ex Files*; *Lady Jasmine*; *The Deal, the Dance, and the Devil*; and *Stand Your Ground*, which won the NAACP Image Award for Outstanding Literature and was named a Library Journal Best Book of the Year. Winner of nine African American Literary Awards for Fiction and Author of the Year (Female), Murray is also a five-time NAACP Image Award for Outstanding Fiction nominee. She splits her time between Los Angeles and Washington, DC. Visit her at VictoriaChristopherMurray.com.

Don't miss the rest of the

SEVEN DEADLY SINS SERIES

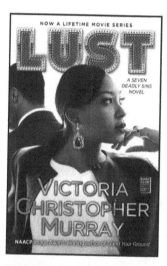

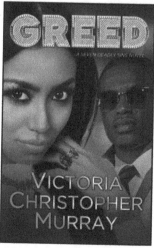

**Available wherever books are sold or
at SimonandSchuster.com**